Descent into Darkness

Darkness

Blood on the Stars XVII

Jay Allan

Books by Jay Allan

Flames of Rebellion Series
(Published by Harper Voyager)
Flames of Rebellion
Rebellion's Fury

The Crimson Worlds Series
Marines
The Cost of Victory
A Little Rebellion
The First Imperium
The Line Must Hold
To Hell's Heart
The Shadow Legions
Even Legends Die
The Fall

Crimson Worlds Refugees Series
Into the Darkness
Shadows of the Gods
Revenge of the Ancients
Winds of Vengeance
Storm of Vengeance

Crimson Worlds Successors Trilogy
MERCS
The Prisoner of Eldaron
The Black Flag

Crimson Worlds Prequels
Tombstone
Bitter Glory
The Gates of Hell

Red Team Alpha
(A New Crimson Worlds Novel)

Also by Jay Allan – The Dragon's Banner

Join my email list
at www.jayallanbooks.com

List members get publication announcements and special bonuses throughout the year (email addresses are never shared or used for any other purpose). Please feel free to email me with any questions at jayallanwrites@gmail.com. I answer all reader emails

For all things Sci-Fi,
join my interactive Reader Group here:

facebook.com/groups/JayAllanReaders

Follow me on Twitter @jayallanwrites

Follow my blog at www.jayallanwrites.com

www.jayallanbooks.com
www.crimsonworlds.com

Books by Jay Allan

Blood on the Stars Series
Duel in the Dark
Call to Arms
Ruins of Empire
Echoes of Glory
Cauldron of Fire
Dauntless
The White Fleet
Black Dawn
Invasion
Nightfall
The Grand Alliance
The Colossus
The Others
The Last Stand
Empire's Ashes
Attack Plan Alpha
Descent into Darkness

Andromeda Chronicles
(Blood on the Stars Adventure Series)
Andromeda Rising
Wings of Pegasus

The Far Stars Series
Shadow of Empire
Enemy in the Dark
Funeral Games

Far Stars Legends Series
Blackhawk
The Wolf's Claw

Portal Wars Trilogy
Gehenna Dawn
The Ten Thousand
Homefront

Chapter One

CFS Donallus
Beta Telara System
Year 329 AC (After the Cataclysm)

"Go…it is time."

Andi had sat in her place, as quiet as possible, for as long as she'd been able. But now, the moment was on her, and she knew what she had to do. She had taken command of the expedition—despite Tyler's still…tenuous…support for it—and she was completely committed to it.

Completely.

She had the go ahead from Tyler, at least for the current step of the operation, but she was going to have a real fight on her hands at some point…unless he changed his point of view. And she knew that was unlikely.

Almost as unlikely as her changing her own.

But there wasn't time then, not for second guessing…not for anything, save to do the job she'd come to do. It was time…time to launch the attack.

"Yes, Commodore…right away."

Andi listened to Ross Tarren, who was handling his duties perfectly, even his recent attachment to the navy…but still, she couldn't get one thought out of her mind.

He wasn't Vig.

Tarren had served with her as long as Vig had, or nearly so, and she valued his presence immensely. But he *wasn't* Vig. No one was, not even Tyler, at least not in the same way. She'd appreciated Vig when she'd had him—immensely, even—but she'd found his loss even tougher to take than she'd imagined.

But she pushed the thoughts out of her mind, along with the other considerations—so many she could hardly keep up with them all. There was one thought on her mind then above all others, one goal that took its place at the head of her mindset. Above the aide to her crew, even the worry for her husband, or the others she cared for.

She wanted to destroy the enemy. Not just to defeat them, not to batter them until they were crushed. No, she wanted them obliterated. Destroyed to the last survivor.

Worst of all, perhaps, she was not alone in that. Not even close. She was a leader, of perhaps one of the most prolific movements in human history, and she was utterly dedicated to her place near its head.

Even without Tyler there at her side.

She loved Tyler, of course, as much as she ever had...more even. But she disagreed with him on this, at least on the methodology for destroying the enemy. She saw only one possibility, one methodology that would work, and she was dedicated to it, with all the stoicism she could muster.

The utter destruction of the enemy.

Tyler had his share of anger at the Highborn too, of course, but he fell short of the total wrath that had taken her...and thousands of her colleagues along with her. Billions, actually, though she hadn't really connected with most of those.

Still, she knew they were there.

She had been more or less settled on her course of action before the last mission, but that had finalized it for her. Her discovery of so much of what the empire had been, and for how long it had endured, grew on her, seemingly every minute. She'd always thought of the empire as some forgotten legacy, as the source of the great finds she'd made in her earlier life, but nothing else. Until more recently, at least. She'd come to realize that the empire had been a good thing, at least in many ways, and that it had existed for ten thousand years. She knew there had been terrible things as well, evil overlords and the like…but how much worse could it have been than the miserable hell she'd come from? That was one area where she and Tyler clashed. He knew of the hellish worlds that existed, even in the Confederation, and likely more in the Union and the Alliance—not to mention the Hegemony—but he didn't *really* understand them. Not like one who'd lived there, who always had the memories…no matter how much she made and how far she got.

Still, the two had pushed aside their arguments, and Tyler had agreed to the mission she led. She knew the two of them would once again meet, likely in the center of the argument. They looked at the situation differently. Tyler believed the enemy had to be defeated, had to be reduced to an inferior force, however unlikely that seemed.

She believed they had to be destroyed. Completely destroyed.

And she knew she would win…if only because there was no alternative. The only way to prevail, the only chance at real victory, was to lunge forward with the genetic weapon. All other routes, all other methods, led only to a short protraction of the war. Defeat was the inevitable result of any other form of resistance…despite the better than expected results obtained so far. Despite the survival—such that it was—of the last defensive forces.

She had allowed the celebrations at the last victory, even as she had realized they were transitory, but she knew the enemy would strike again, long before the fleet had completed meaningful repairs. Tyler had known as well, but his mind went toward different options, pulling back from the current position, falling toward the Confederation's front line. That was all pointless, Andi knew that, but it also created other problems. Akella might have gone along with Tyler's plan, even a withdrawal to Confederation territory— with enough persuasion, at least—but the Hegemonic Council would never vote with her on it. Tyler's plan—and he hadn't come right out and said it *was* his plan...even though she knew it was there—had more than one bit of opposition. There were at least four or five plans, all fighting for attention. Many people found themselves varying between several...but Andi knew the only hope, the only way to go.

And this was the start of it, the first blow.

"Commodore...we're picking up several enemy ships. It appears to be seven...all fairly small."

Andi felt one more doubt fall before her. She couldn't be sure the enemy didn't have more ships hidden somewhere...but she was certain of her obligations. And she had forty-one ships with her. More than enough to take out seven enemy vessels...especially the small ships she saw facing her force.

"Close...we are to destroy every enemy ship." Her voice was cold, dark. No one could escape. She wanted to leave the enemy uncertain about what had happened here, relying only on the words of ground troops and residents. Actually, she'd have preferred no enemy knowledge at all, but she knew that point was hopeless.

"Yes, sir." Tarren's voice, at least, was almost as conclusive as hers. Whatever opinions had come up around the ships of the fleet, everyone who'd been aboard *Pegasus* on the last mission had come back with more or less the same opinion.

Destroy the enemy...if at all possible. The fact that her plan was limited, that even *she* knew the chances of success were fairly small, was not relevant at all. She *knew* she would not survive defeat. She could have endured that fate, save for Cassiopeia...she was reason enough to do all she could to prevail.

And if Andi failed, she'd just as soon see her daughter die rather than live as the enemy's plaything. At least sometimes. That was one area she struggled with, and she knew Tyler did, too. Neither of them wanted to survive defeat...but it was different when they were thinking of their daughter. Sometimes she was sure she'd rather see the young girl die than become a pawn of the enemy...and others she wondered if Cassiopeia didn't deserve at least a chance, even one that twisted her memories of her mother and father.

She sat back, her eyes focused on every activity around her, all the while looking like she was barely interested. She stared at every ship to the front of the fleet, watched every beam, incoming or outgoing. She knew she would lose ships, just as she realized she would prevail in the battle. And, so it happened. In the end, which came stunningly quickly, she lost five ships for seven destroyed, not bad, save for the fact that she'd put four and a half times the number of the enemy into the fight...and nearly six times the tonnage.

She wasn't surprised though, not really, and with the destruction of the last enemy vessel, she had thirty-six ships ready for the final attack. *More than enough.*

"We're closing with the planet now, Andi..."

"Very well, Ross." Her words were stiff, her tone almost nasty. For the vast majority of people, she would have left them so, but for Ross Tarren, she felt a tug of pity. Her rage wasn't directed at him, any more than any of her people. "Order the units to commence bombardment as soon as they are within range." The words were still somewhat harsh, but they were definitely softer. For a moment, at least.

"Very well…" The response was clear, and it was obvious that Tarren understood her perfectly well.

She sat and watched, as the first six ships fired almost simultaneously. The second six followed, perhaps thirty seconds behind, and the next eight another half minute behind. About a minute and a half in total from the first firing, the last ships shot their loads. *Donallus*, the flagship, launched the final volley, and thirty-one vessels, every surviving ship save the five survivors who'd lost their weapons systems in the fight, had launched.

Andi tried to imagine the amount of damage her people had done, the volume of fire her ships had managed to undertake. She didn't know how many ships it would take to cover the ground, how many it would take to ensure total coverage. With the relatively narrow focus of the population on the planet, she guessed anywhere from six ships to eighteen were necessary for a full bombardment…and she had brought almost double that highest number to bear. If the virus was truly viable, if the work the legions of hastily assembled men and women had done was good…every Highborn on the planet would be affected.

And if no unknown work had been completed in the three centuries since the empire had fallen…every Highborn on the planet would die. But first, he would carry the virus for months, taking it to different worlds, different populations…hopefully unknown.

Then, if all went according to plan, he or she would die…and every Highborn he or she came into contact with would follow.

And everyone affected by the phase two assault, the part of the plan that wasn't approved yet, but *had* to be, would follow them. There was no way to kill all the Highborn, of course, at least not without a desperate and longstanding fight…but getting enough of them before they knew what was happening, that was the road to victory.

Andi looked at the screen, at the reach of the affected

areas. There was at least a fifty-percent overlap on all habitable zones. She had enough payload to launch another attack, but no need to do so.

"Bring all ships around…we're going to hit them again." She stared straight ahead, knowing her operation was far from essential…or even wise. She didn't care if it was essential, or even if it was smart. She was heading straight back to the base, and any fight she faced on the way was not going to use the virus—the tentative virus, she reminded herself. There was no reason not to use it all.

"Forward ships ready to launch again in three minutes." Tarren, at least, seemed to agree with her. They had left with a large portion of the ready virus, but there would be more, much more, by the time they returned.

Enough for the phase two operation…or close to it…

"Very well." Andi was still, comfortable to all around her…at least externally. Inside, she was more of a mix, her own certainty mixing with the reality of the impending argument to carry out phase two. She worried about a number of potential rivals, but none more than Tyler Barron, her husband. The two had been together on most of the issues they'd faced, except perhaps her own involvement in them, but this time she was almost certain they were going to end up on different sides. She was going to be in favor of betting everything on the virus, on making it work against the enemy. And she was very afraid Tyler was going to come down on the other side, convinced against hope that he could find a way to win the fight conventionally. The fact that he'd done that on every other occasion in his life made his thinking stronger…but Andi was just as sure that this time, he'd gone too far. This time, he was going to lose…and she couldn't allow that, not if she could do anything about it.

"One minute until lead ships ready to fire again." A pause, just a short one, no more than three or four seconds, then: "No sign of any enemy activity."

Andi turned her head and just nodded. She'd known that some of her people were still worried about further enemy activity, but the truth was, the second attack added less than ten minutes to her time in system, and that was almost nothing. She would escape—or she would be caught by new arrivals—but either way, not because she had put up a second fight.

She watched, struck in some ways by the near silence on the bridge as the attack played out again. It was a replay of the first assault, six ships firing first, followed by six more, and so on. Andi watched, herself as silent as anyone onboard, until her own ship went in again and launched its second shot. Then she turned matter-of-factly, at least externally, and said calmly, "Let's go now, Ross. All ships, course A-1…out of here and back toward the jump."

"Yes, Andi…I mean Commodore." Tarren had done well enough using the proper ranks and pronouns of the navy, but he'd slipped up then, gone back to the norms on *Pegasus*, at least one time. For just a moment.

Andi smiled, keeping it to herself as much as possible. She enjoyed it, as much as she had anything on the trip out to Beta Telara. But the joy only lasted for a few seconds, and the visual representation of it even less. Then she returned to her normal, cold, emotionless view and prepared for the flight home. Which could include no enemy contact—or running into the entire fleet—or anything in between.

She looked forward, maintaining the coldness of her view. It would be what it would be…she knew that, and she was okay with it.

Mostly at least.

Chapter Two

CFS Dauntless
Vasa Denaris System
Year 329 AC (After the Cataclysm)

"She looks good, Atara...really good." Barron paused. "Better even than she *is*..." He knew enough about the ship's true condition, its *real* status, that he felt compelled to add the last remark.

"Yes..." Atara Travis was perhaps even more matter of fact even than Barron, something he forgot once in a while. "...much better, unfortunately. The main guns *look* repaired, for example, but they're not...and even if the equipment we need arrives in time, we'll still have to decide whether to take her out of action for two weeks to install it. Even three, all things considered." A pause. "That's a long time."

It wasn't a long time, not exactly, but it *was* long enough to be a problem, at least if it came at just the wrong moment. Barron knew that, but still, he found himself arguing the opposite point of view...the positive one. "We've got ten sets of primaries coming in less than a week...and one of them will definitely go into *Dauntless*. Less than three weeks, and you'll be back in the fight at close to full power." *Close* was a difficult word, of course...even with all the guns more or less operational, he

9

knew there were a hundred ways the ship would be
somewhat less than she'd be at full strength.

Full strength wasn't even a consideration then, though.
He didn't know how much time his fleet would get, but he
was sure it would be less than he needed. The enemy *would*
be back. Just when was a bit of a question, but he didn't let
himself believe, on any level, that it would be long enough.

"Well, assuming the arrival does come, and assuming we
decide we can do without the ship for two weeks, or three,
you may be right about that." A pause. "If we really go for
it, and take ten ships out of the line together, we can even
make a difference…assuming of course, we don't pick the
wrong two weeks."

Barron just nodded. In truth, he'd decided to gamble
with two weeks on *Dauntless*, but he hadn't really considered
whether he'd put all ten main gun mounts into the mix right
away. Oddly, he knew it was the same decision really, but he
found that he had two different points of view. *Dauntless
would* make it through…but when he imagined taking ten
battleship hulls out at once, his confidence slipped. It didn't
make sense, he knew…but it was true, nevertheless.

"Yeah…" He answered Travis…but he knew she picked
up on his pointless doubts. She was the one person he could
never fool. He even imagined, once in a while at least, he
could pull one over on Andi…but never Atara.

And maybe not Andi either…he just wasn't sure. As
close as he felt to her, he knew she was her own person, and
while she agreed with him most of the time, he realized they
were coming up on an area they definitely saw differently.

"I'm thinking we'll do five and then five rather than all at
once." It didn't make sense, not really, at least not with his
perception that *Dauntless* would get through. But he knew it
would make the process easier, at least. "I'm not sure we've
got the manpower to handle ten jobs at once." He knew
that was bullshit, at least in part—and he knew Atara did as
well—but he went with it.

And, so did she. "Yeah, that makes sense." Her voice suggested that she at least *thought* it might not, but she didn't say.

The two stood next to each other for a minute, perhaps even two. Then, Atara came right out and said it. "What do you really think of the current situation? Do you believe we *really* have a chance to win this fight conventionally? Or do you think we'll be forced to rely on...the other option?"

Barron heard the words, and he knew at once that Atara wasn't on the other side. She wasn't against him, not yet at least. But, she had a considerable bit of doubt, that was clear. He just couldn't tell if it was enough to pull her point of view to the other side. Tyler knew he faced that kind of a fight with Andi—and he dreaded that enough—but if Atara took the other side, too? He didn't know what that would mean. Would she even take the position against him, if that's what she decided she believed? Or would she remain by his side, even if she didn't know how she felt? She had always been one hundred percent allied to him...but he'd felt she had always agreed as well. Now he wondered.

Worse, perhaps, he wondered about himself. He was against launching a full assault against the enemy...but he was doubtful too. Was his question mark a symbol of his steely nerve, just a reasonable outlook on the complexity of the situation? Or was it serious doubt, the fact that fighting the enemy just seemed more conservative, even though it was actually hopeless?

His doubts extended, beyond just whether to undertake the mission to destroy the enemy. He had questions about that certainly, none more than the lack of assurance it would even work, but in the moments when he was being truly honest with himself, he realized there was little hope in his way either.

He also realized that part of his doubts extended from the hope that the new system *would* work. He was a fighter, and he imagined the enemy beaten and prostrate before the

Confederation...but he hadn't gotten to the point where he would risk killing *all* of the enemy. He didn't even know that all of the Highborn were as bad as the ones he'd seen, and he had to acknowledge that the enemy, as vicious as they were, clearly didn't intend to eradicate humankind. Could he inflict such a devastating punishment on them?

Of course, there were other considerations that were just as crucial, first and foremost, would it even work? He didn't know, and no one else did either, whatever their view. They were just assuming the current version, produced quickly and without any real testing, *would* be workable. There were a hundred things that could have been done wrong, a thousand. No doubt, the AI that Andi had brought back retained most of the process for creating the virus...assuming that itself was trustable...but as with so many things, she had obtained a damaged file, one that offered 95% of the formula, but left a certain amount to be calculated.

Barron knew his people would eventually get through the data...but how long would it take? Was the current version workable? Or were they months or years even, from a finished formula?

Barron realized he had gone on a long time without answering, and he turned toward Atara, and looked at her with absolute truth in his eyes. "I don't know, Atara...I just don't know. I have hesitations against increasing the level of this fight. Whatever we think of the enemy, they are *not* trying to annihilate us. But what will they do if they discern *that* is our true objective? How will they respond, whether our efforts are successful or not? Even a 100% effective formula will be difficult to apply everywhere, especially once the enemy is aware of our intention. How do they react? They withdrew from the empire, but honestly, we're not the empire, no matter what you think of our chances, and they are vastly stronger than they were then. Will they withdraw—because you know we're not going to destroy them *all*, everywhere, no matter what nonsense gets pandered about? Or will they turn the fight about on us, seek to destroy us all. That is likely to be no more of an easy success...but if they destroy our fleet and our ability to deliver canisters, even of an entirely effective formula, they will have the time, certainly."

He stopped suddenly, having gone on much farther than he'd expected. Atara was the only one in the room with him, and he'd told her just about everything...but there were doubts he hadn't shared with her, or with Andi or Clint Winters.

Atara stared at him for an instant, and then she moved toward him and pulled him close. "It will be okay, Ty...we'll decide how to proceed, and we'll do it." She hugged him for another fifteen seconds, and then she pulled back and returned the subject to a more routine level. "If *Dauntless*, and four other ships, are going into the line in less than a week, I've got some work to do reshuffling things." She smiled, more or less. "Try to focus on the matters at hand, one at a time. We don't know yet whether we've even got an effective formula...so we've got to keep pushing forward on our other agenda anyway. If it turns out the formula works...well then we'll really have something to talk about."

She stood where she was, and she held her smile for perhaps another ten seconds. Then she turned and walked away, across the room and out the door.

She was gone before Barron realized she hadn't given him a hint of her own opinion on the situation. She was normally his ally, and while she may have subverted her own intentions once or twice over the years, he was pretty sure she had actually agreed with him most of the time.

But most didn't mean all, and Atara had always been the harsher of the two of them...

* * *

"I'm telling you, it's completely dysfunctional. It was still partially operational when I pulled away from the fleet, but now it's completely dead." Jake Stockton was usually pretty good at hiding his point of view, but even as he spoke the words, he realized that they were bland, that he really had no idea what to expect from the device that still clung to his neck. He was telling the truth that it *seemed* dead, had seemed dead from shortly after he'd wrested control back, but he didn't know if it would *stay* that way.

"Yes, I know that you regained apparent total control back, but you know as well as I do that could be temporary…or partial. The thing *might* be completely dead, and it may stay that way. Or it might…" Dr. Jordan leaned backward and looked at Stockton, equal amounts of curiosity and pity in his stare. He didn't finish what he'd begun to say, though. He didn't have to.

The room was silent for a moment…and then Stockton spoke again. "What about the removal effort?" It wasn't a new topic, but it had been one Stockton hadn't been willing to consider, at least until that moment.

"No, definitely not. And certainly not with someone of your stature. Not until we…"

"I have no stature!" Stockton interrupted. "Forget what I *was*…there is nothing I can do now." Stockton's eyes narrowed, and he looked at the doctor sitting with him. "We both know that. As long as I wear this thing, I'm at best a source of information…and I've already given all of that I have." He paused, considering the situation from all angles before deciding how he truly felt. "I think it's time to consider ways to bring me back…or to let me go…"

Jordan sat for quite some time before he spoke. Then he said, simply, "We have tried five times to complete the surgery, Admiral…five times with the best teams available. And we're 0-5. And by 0-5, I mean five dead participants. We're not even sure it *can* be removed."

"But you haven't tried one for a while, have you? You've

made progress, I know you have…and my apparatus is off, or at least it seems to be. I think all of the others you operated on were fully functional. There are a lot of differences."

"Admiral Stockton, I'm not going to lie to you. We're going to try again…soon. And the status of your Collar is very tempting. But we have no idea if it would make any difference…and you're the only one with a malfunctional Collar anyway, so it's…"

"Pointless…"

"No, Admiral, not pointless. But you would be a…difficult…target. And you would be a specific one as well. All things considered, you're probably not the ideal choice for the next candidate…not when we have so many…"

"So many enemies?" Stockton knew that was the case, of course…but he was also the only one who'd overcome—at least for the moment—his Collar. "And what value do you place on my Collar being *apparently* dead? How much value does that offer? What is my desire for the surgery to be successful worth?"

"A lot," the doctor said, after a fairly long delay. "But that doesn't mean it is the smart play…and even if it is, you know the problems. The enemy targets are…well enemies. And it's still difficult to perform the surgery on them. On you, it would be…"

Stockton sighed. "So, what you're really saying is, I'm the one that makes the most sense—because you're never going to convince me otherwise—but I'm out of reach. Because of who I am." He paused for a few seconds, and then he added, "Who I was."

The doctor looked away for a few seconds before he returned Stockton's gaze. "I don't know what you want me to say, Admiral. You know you're the most important—" He thought a while, trying, Stockton thought, to come up with a word other than 'captive.' "—possible candidate. But

I don't think you can be the next, not until we successfully removed one of these, at least." The doctor halted for a moment, but then he continued. "The situation is changing, quickly...both for and against us. Just be patient and wait. Just for a while. Perhaps our next surgery will go significantly better than the earlier ones." Another pause. "It's really the best thing you can do...and it might not be that long a wait."

Stockton turned and nodded. "I know you're right, Doctor...it's just difficult. I will...wait. For a while at least."

"That's good, Admiral." The doctor stood up and looked back down at Stockton. "We'll be doing another surgery soon...and if it goes well, perhaps we will be able to work on you sooner rather than later. Just be patient."

Stockton looked up and nodded, and the doctor turned and left. Then his facial expression changed entirely.

He stared defiantly, and his hands clenched. *He* was going to be next, somehow, some way. And he knew the only likely way to achieve that goal was to get Admiral Barron onboard. It wouldn't be easy, certainly, but it was the way.

The only way.

Stockton leaned back on his bed, and he closed his eyes. He wasn't sure, not remotely, that he would survive the surgery. There were a hundred things he knew that could go wrong, and even more he didn't know about. But he was sure of one thing, as sure as he'd ever been of anything.

He wanted to get back to what he'd been...if that was even possible. And if it wasn't...well, if it wasn't, he'd just as soon die on the table.

Chapter Three

Forward Base Striker
Vasa Denaris System
Year 329 AC (After the Cataclysm)

"What do you think? What do you really think?" Akella spoke as she poured two drinks, handing one to Chronos. "I mean it...what do you *really* think?"

Chronos reached out and grabbed the drink...and he took a quick gulp before he answered. "Well, my answer to all parties would be I'm completely with Admiral Barron. I believe we have to do everything possible to fight off the enemy...conventionally."

"That's a great answer when you're asked in another setting...but I want the truth, the *whole* truth."

"That *is* the truth, at least for now." Chronos paused again, and he took another drink. "But I will be honest with you, if the formula is correct, if the first effort goes as well as those promoting it say it will, I am...uncertain."

"You might be in favor of changing your view, of pushing your support to the other side?" Normally, Akella's tone would have been accusatory, but this time, she was as neutral as could be.

Chronos just stared back for a moment, and he finished his drink. Then, he said, simply, "No...not exactly. Not yet at least." That wasn't all, however, and a few seconds later, he added, "I have come around completely to seeing our alliance with the Rim-dwellers as a core issue...but we're on the verge of a break. You know as well as I, that this fortress can't stand another assault, not one that comes within two years. And now, the Alliance has a second front, eating up a large portion of its new production. Meanwhile, we've got barely forty percent of our Hegemony worlds...and if the enemy attacks within the next year, perhaps as many as two, we're going to be faced with the question. Do we pull back? Do we fight? Do we fall back to the Confederation frontier?" Chronos didn't say anything else. Akella understood what he was saying...all of what he was saying.

An instant later, she proved just that. "You feel that if it comes to the choice of a withdrawal so far back...we'd have a better chance fighting it out up here, with the new...weaponry. Assuming, of course, the first effort shows the success we hope it does?" She looked down and then added, "At least the success we *think* we hope it shows."

"I'm not saying that, not quite. But I *am* saying we'll have to really consider what we're willing to do. The Council is difficult...and if the question comes before them to pull back, to abandon the rest of our territory, you know what they will choose. It doesn't matter what you and I decide we'll do...as far as I can tell, the Council is pretty much dedicated to holding on. They will refuse to agree to back down, and the Confederation and Alliance will have to decide whether to split off, fight alone...or stay in the battle with the Hegemony forces. No doubt, Barron has considered that reality...but he may assume that the members of the Council will vote based on reality, on the fact that the Hegemony has fallen in relative power and is no longer the major partner. I can accept that fact, if barely, but I do not believe the Council will. So that means, the Confederation and the Alliance will have to decide whether to break off from the Hegemony...or to remain tied to the current front lines."

Chronos paused for a moment, and then he continued, "Don't fool yourself, Akella…you can argue all you want, but the Council is not going to vote to abandon the rest of the Hegemony. At least probably not. You know that. You'll get your own vote, and mine…but I doubt many others. You'll lose…and if you push too hard for it, you'll end up getting ejected from the Council entirely, one way or another."

Akella had been silent for a while, but now she just nodded. Chronos was right. She had enough clout to stay in command, at least for the time being, but if she seriously suggested pulling the fleet completely out of Hegemony space she would probably lose.

"So, you're saying our choice is fighting here, more or less, one way or the other. Either with or without the—possible—germ element." She phrased it like a question, but it was, more or less, what she'd been looking at herself. "Or we stand up to the Council, despite the challenges…or even split with them, and try to issue our own edict to the fleet. Remember, that's all that really matters now…what's left of the fleet."

Chronos stared back at her. For a moment, he looked as though he had seen a light, but only for a passing instant. "That is tempting, Akella…but I'm not sure it is workable. We'd get some captains for sure, even some crews. But how many? A quarter? A third? Remember, ordering the forces to abandon the entire Hegemony is contrary to everything they've ever learned, ever been taught. We'll lose loyal ships, Akella, a lot of them. And while the split of the Confederation and Alliance forces from our own will already condemn both sides to destruction, draining away even one-fourth from our forces will only further consign the remaining Council forces to an even worse and more rapid fate."

Akella only nodded. She agreed with Chronos almost

completely, despite her occasional thoughts in one direction or another. Finally, she just said, "So we've got to remain in place—and convince our allies to do the same—or we've got to support the germ offensive…and hope it works."

Chronos looked like he wanted to argue, but he couldn't seem to find any place to disagree. Finally, he just nodded his head, looking far more discouraged than anything else. "Yes," he finally said. "I think those are the only two solutions that offer us any prospect of success…or for that matter, our allies as well. They may last longer pulling back without us, but not much longer…especially not with the enemy moving against their rear."

Akella nodded. She hadn't been much in favor of the bacteriological plan…but now she realized it might very well be the only option that offered any real chance of success. Certainly, anything that split the powers was bad, but now she realized that even together, they had a poor chance of prevailing.

A very poor chance.

The bacteriological option might be the best way to go—and possibly, it was the only one. But she had to accept the notion of truly fighting to the end.

She wasn't there, not yet. But she was closer than she'd been a few moments before.

*   *   *

Sonya Eaton stood the best she could, though the months of wear and tear had really worn down into her. She'd expected one or another of her superiors to warn her off her work level eventually, but six months later, she was still going almost around the clock. Her *subordinates* had questioned her devotion for sure, but they didn't have the authority to tell her what to do…and besides, they were almost as hard working as she was. Her effort had even proven contagious, and *Colossus* was in better shape than she'd dared to hope.

Which didn't mean it was in good shape. The main guns were still out…it was only a guess still, that they'd ever be repaired. Her ship, alone among those on her side, was an imperial construct, and that meant even the best work her people could produce was as often as not, only a guess.

There were dozens of systems still out, or only partially operational, but more were back online than she would have dared to predict just a few months ago. *Colossus* had been close to its end—*very* close—and she knew she had won the battle she'd been called on to fight by the barest of margins.

It also meant that her ship—and she thought of *Colossus* now as *her* ship—had been brought to the brink of destruction, and that for a vessel so large and still so strange, it would take years to restore it to its old status. If it could even be restored.

"What's the status of the engines, Commander?" She realized she'd come up on the officer unaware, and she was ready for his reaction. But she wasn't sure whether he had in fact seen her coming, or if his nerves were…atypical…but, he just answered her, sounding as unsurprised as he could be by her presence.

"They're bad, Commodore, really bad. But better than they were before. I'd say we've got twenty percent of maximum output…*maybe* thirty in a pinch. I honestly don't know exactly." He'd been hunched over one of the engine portals, but then he turned and looked up at Commodore Eaton. Commander Jefferson's eyes were usually dark and unreadable, but at the moment, they were brighter. Eaton noticed, at least to an extent, but she was mostly buried in her work.

"Well Commander, I appreciate the honesty, I really do. But I've got to ask what effect more time is going to have. Will a month make much difference? Or are we six months from any further improvement?" She turned her head to the side as she asked the question, and she added, "I have been slow to push for specifics, but now I've got to decide if the ship can take its place with the fleet...or if it needs to pull back before the next battle."

It was more than she'd shared with anyone to that point. She'd worked well enough with most of her crew, but she'd been fairly circumspect about the realities of the effort in progress. Unlike most of the other battered ships in the fleet, she didn't know how long it would take to fully repair *Colossus*. Three years, four? Or never? She wasn't sure how long it would take to get the ship fully operational, but she was pretty damned sure the enemy would be back before then. The question was, would she have the old bucket of bolts in good enough shape to join the fight by then. Or would it make more sense to set it aside, to hold it back for the *next* fight. She knew what she wanted to decide...but she also realized she had to consider what would actually happen in the battle.

Greg Jefferson twitched a little, and he turned his head, checking to see if anyone else present was watching. "The truth is, Commodore...we don't really know. The other ships of the fleet, even the new ones, we have at least a good idea of the work involved in restoring systems to operational capacity. Here, *we* didn't even put it back together. We could ask for help from the Hegemony, of course, but I'm not sure what they could offer us." He looked around again and then he added, "Besides, I'd just as soon keep things to our own crews...if you know what I mean..."

"I do...and I agree." Eaton had been more or less accepting of the Hegemony forces as allies, but she knew her ship—the biggest ship by far in any navy—was a point of contention. She knew the Hegemony wasn't about to press the issue with the current situation...but she was far from sure what things would look like in a universe without the Highborn. She knew the Hegemony was allied with the Confederation, and she hoped that would continue. But she realized it had only been a few years since the Hegemony had been the enemy. Things had changed radically, and she was fairly certain that some, at least, of the Hegemony leaders, had come to see things quite a bit differently than they had just a few years ago, as had many of her own population. But she knew there were people—on both sides—who could slip back to past feelings as well, and she just didn't know what the reality would be.

But she found herself coming firmly down on the side of keeping the crew on *Colossus* 100% Confederation, just in case.

She looked across the open space between her and her chief engineer, and she saw him in a different way than she had before. She'd always considered him a bit gruff, a bit *too* focused on his work. Suddenly, she realized he had a different side...and it occurred to her that she was just as focused on her work as she'd imagined him to be.

"We'll get through it, sir." Jefferson spoke softly, and clearly as well. "I can't say whether the ship will be ready the next time the enemy approaches...without knowing when that will be, it's kind of pointless to think about it." He stopped for a second, but then he decided to continue. "Let's be honest, Commodore...the truth is, if the enemy shows up with any kind of force in the next three months, possibly six, we're not going to be able to face him anyway. And I mean the whole fleet. All we can do is whatever we can, each of us, and see what happens day by day. And for you, you'll probably be approached eventually, if you haven't already, by one or more of the different groups, and asked to decide whether to support a regular defense...or..." Jefferson stopped himself for a few seconds. When he continued, he was past the point of offering any opinions of his own, focusing instead on her own point of view. "I'm guessing you are against the idea of launching any kind of desperate efforts...and I agree with you. But...well, you can't overlook that kind of possibility either, can you?"

"I guess you're right, Commander." Eaton had been exactly as Jefferson had suggested, pretty much in the camp of fighting it out conventionally...but with a little bit of doubt growing on her about whether that was truly possible.

And whether she had to consider an alternate point of view.

"Well, Commander...I'll let you get back to work." She managed an expression that wasn't quite a smile...but wasn't her normal view either. "We'll talk again...soon." She held her gaze for a few seconds, both her expression and Jefferson's looking somewhat different from their usual points of view.

Then she turned and walked away, feeling both that she wasn't alone...and much more confused than she had a few minutes before.

Chapter Four

CFS Constellation
225,000 Kilometers from Fleet Base Grimaldi
Krakus System
Year 329 AC (After the Cataclysm)

"I want every system operational in two more weeks, is that understood? It's been six months since the battle here, and that's more than enough time." Sam Taggart huffed and puffed, but she knew Isaac Johnson was aware she was only venting. It wasn't that she didn't expect the systems to be fully functional in two weeks—she *did*—or that two weeks wasn't a short time—it *was*. But she knew the work that had been done already, on *Constellation* certainly, and on every other battered hull in the fleet, had been nothing short of miraculous...especially considering the simultaneous repairs to the great hulk of Grimaldi. There was no way the station would be returned to anything close to fully functioning inside three years, and more likely four, but the work that had been done was impressive, nevertheless.

Still, Taggart was pissed, almost constantly. Her duties as second-in-command over Grimaldi and the battered fleet posted up next to the station were almost endless...and well beyond her station. She'd advanced too far and too fast, both before the battle, and even more since it, and she knew her authority was based on need and not on anything else. She speculated that others saw more in her, a heroine even to some, but she believed such thoughts were pointless...and wrong. She was just doing what she could, *all* she could...and it wasn't even close to enough.

"I believe the repairs will be completed in two weeks...or if not, it will be less than three..." Johnson didn't seem particularly up for a fight, but he was clearly trying to hold Taggart to more realistic numbers. And three weeks *was* more reasonable than two, especially for basically completing the repairs on *Constellation*...which was by far the most powerful ship in the whole contingent.

"I said 'two,' Isaac, and I meant it." Taggart was serious, but she also realized that she knew as well as her first officer, that three was probably the more realistic figure. She'd probably accept it, if necessary, but she wanted an effort made at two first.

"As you said, Commodore...two weeks." Johnson nodded, but Taggart knew he realized the work would likely take longer. She understood it as well, at least on one level. It would just take her a bit longer to truly accept. Meanwhile, there was no harm in her people working to hit the two week mark.

If she had to give in, it would be by days and not by a whole week, not at once, anyway. Two and a half weeks was far better than three...assuming she eventually gave in on the two.

For the moment, she just nodded. The work would be done as quickly as possible, she was sure of that. She had backup and even retirees returned to the colors, a group she knew shouldn't have performed well, or at least not to the standards of the line troops. But she was ready now to put a group of her returned retirees against the best in the main fleet...even when they were dealing with *Constellation*, which was one of the four most advanced ships in the navy, far beyond anything they'd ever worked on in their careers.

Not that she would ever let Barron and the main fleet know how good her people were...they might pull them away and leave her even worse than she was.

"What's the status of the rest of the fleet." She knew the answer...and she knew the word 'fleet' was a bit of a stretch, but the force was increasing in size, as new ships went to it as well as to Barron's main formation. She wasn't getting anywhere close to half the new ships, of course, but she was getting more than she'd expected, and that was good...for now.

"Well...we're stronger now than we were when the enemy attacked the first time...so that's good."

Taggart nodded slightly, knowing her aide had started with the best he had to say first.

"Still...a large percentage of the ships present for the initial fight were badly damaged. Many of them were pulled back and are still under construction. Our new arrivals have more than made up for them, of course, but the need to replace the ships that will be gone a year or longer held us back."

"Give me the real numbers, Isaac..."

There was a short break, barely noticeable—except Taggart noticed it—then he said, "We're about one hundred fifty percent of our previous strength...and that is mostly in smaller ships. We did receive two new battleships, but they're the older models, strong for sure, but no match for *Constellation*." A pause. "We've been promised at least two of the eight new *Constellation*-class ships currently under construction...but they're at least twelve months from launch."

Taggart listened, even though she knew most of the information already. And Johnson continued, though he knew most—if not all—of what he had to say was already known by Taggart. It was an almost daily routine, and it worked well enough for each of them that they continued it.

"The fleet might be twice as powerful as the force that

was here last time, but the base is going to be a fraction of its former strength...assuming the enemy attack comes within a year, even a year and a half."

"If it takes that long, we'll have a much larger fleet, too." Johnson said the words, even though Taggart knew neither one of them believed they had a year. Taggart felt lucky enough that she'd had six months...and she was worried about the next two—or three—weeks, even though she knew the enemy was far enough away that an attack within that short time was unlikely.

Unlikely...but not impossible...

"That's true...though I can only say that the enemy forces will also be stronger...likely. Their lack of a more immediate effort suggests that they've decided to wait for a larger force to come."

Isaac Johnson didn't answer, but it was clear he believed something similar. The longer they got, the larger of a force they would be able to mount...but the same thing likely applied to the enemy. And for all the fleet was larger and more powerful than it had been, her strength was probably less when the lost sections of the station were counted. Or, at best, even.

She almost followed up, but she stopped herself. There was nothing to do but the best she could...and be ready to fight it out when the enemy came again.

And they would come again...she didn't have a doubt about that.

No doubt at all.

* * *

"What do you think? I mean *really* think?" Admiral Simpson sat at the table, opposite Larson James and Antonio Graves. The two men were both captains now, both as a result of his action. Graves hadn't been a problem, but James was a surprise...no less to him than to the promotions board. He had the authority to promote anyone to a rank below his own, but he still got back a message asking if he was sure about Jaymes.

He was sure. Very sure. Whatever stuff Jaymes had done in his younger years, he had served throughout the protracted crisis, and he hadn't had as much as a drink…and Simpson was sure about that. He hadn't gone more than six or seven hours without seeing Jaymes over the past year, and he was *sure*.

And Jaymes had been more than sober. He'd been top notch, a perfect officer…during the worst fighting Simpson had ever seen.

"I think we've got a minimum of a month." Graves spoke first. "We've managed to check out the systems ahead of us—including into the Union—and we're clear for at least five or six of them. Any more than that requires some guesswork, but it seems to me, we're at the very least, two and a half weeks from an enemy attack…and more likely, as I said, a month."

Jaymes didn't say anything, but he nodded in agreement.

"Okay, so we've got the obvious answer. Now, let's dive into some conjecture. How long do you *really* think we have?"

That question stymied both of Simpson's aides for a moment. When one of them finally spoke, it was Jaymes. "Two months." A short pause. "That's just a guess, but it's based on a theory that the enemy had to report its results back home, and then wait for more ships than had been sent. I suspect it was a close call on whether to hit us again with what they had, but I probably—and this depends of course on the accuracy of our guesses on what forces they've received to date—would have come down on the side of caution as well. I mean, they've got the edge in every way, and more time benefits them better than us…almost certainly."

"But you think that time is getting close to up?" Simpson

agreed, but he tried not to let it appear so.

"Well, I just assume it's about three months each way, for a full fleet move at least...and that's half guess, of course. I might have gone sooner even, I mean two months is a fairly long period of time, but the enemy suffered badly in the fight out there too, and they had to have a fair amount of repairs. Again, it's just a guess—and if the enemy didn't have enough forces ready to send to the aide of the remnants in Confederation space, it could be even longer. But I wouldn't want to bet on more than eight months total."

Simpson looked at Jaymes, and then at Graves. Graves didn't say much, but what he said more or less agreed completely with his comrade. He said as much a few seconds later. "I have to come down completely with Captain Jaymes, sir. I don't see the enemy striking back in much less than two more months, but I don't see much more either. If they were willing to attack with what they had already, they would have struck much quicker. I might have expected that at first, but now I have to say, they've got to be waiting for a large reinforcement. But I wouldn't expect much longer."

Simpson agreed completely with his two aides, but he continued to try to hide his view, at least in part. He wasn't sure why, but he figured he would go with it, just in case it was right. And if he had to be completely honest with someone, he would make it Sam Taggart, now his second in command. He'd grown confident in her, despite her clear discomfort with her own position. She could take his place even, he'd become almost sure of that.

"So, neither of you expects a major enemy attack for at least two months?" That was what they had both said, more or less, and it was his view as well, but he wanted to get a feeling for how confident the two officers were...and how much was purely guesswork.

Again, Jaymes answered first. "Two and a half

weeks…that is all I'm willing to say for sure, or at least close to it. That's all we *know*. But that said, I'm *fairly* sure about the two months." He stopped, and he looked at Graves. "Eighty percent maybe?"

Graves nodded. "Yes, I would say eighty percent."

"Eighty percent," Simpson restated. "Okay…so eight chances in ten they won't attack for two months?"

He expected a bit of time, but Jaymes answered almost immediately. "I do expect them to take about two months to attack…but I doubt it will be much more than that. They have to allow for our own construction, and even with more of our new ships going to the other fleet, they have to imagine that some portion is coming here. I'd say we have two months, or close to it, because that is just realism, considering the distance they have between their home and the relevant area." There was a delay, a noticeable one during which Jaymes turned and looked at Graves. "I doubt we will see much more either, and almost certainly no more than three months. And I doubt very much we will get that long."

Graves nodded aggressively. "I agree, sir. No more than three months…if that."

Simpson was silent for a moment. Then he said, "Alright…thank you for your insight." He basically agreed completely with what the two had said, but he decided to keep it as much to himself as possible. "I'd say we could continue this discussion all day and all night too, but nothing would change. So, let's get back to duty. If you're right, we'll be facing off against some kind of enemy attack in two to three months. They are looking at us, too, and trying to decide what they're going to meet…and they'll be strong enough to take that out, you can be sure of that. So, we've got to be ready in two months…and by that, I mean *ready*. More than the enemy expects. Because that's the only way to win."

His words stirred up the two men. Both knew they faced

almost insurmountable odds. But both still had enough inside to allow them to enjoy occasional risings of expectation, even the varied—and occasional—thought they would win. Simpson was definitely glad for it. He would take anything he could get to keep his people moving forward.

But he didn't share the thought, not even the occasional hope that his fleet would be able to defeat the Highborn. He knew his forces faced an enemy that understood why they had lost, and they would see that it didn't happen again. He hoped for three months, even a bit more, but he was sure that was all he would have. Then he would face an enemy force much more powerful than the one he had fought before…and his only hope was to batter it sufficiently to stop it from advancing for a few more months.

Two months more, maybe three. That was all he had. He didn't intend to retreat from the coming fight. No sir. He was going to battle to the end, all of his people were, whether they knew it then or not. And the only way anything was going to retreat from the system was after the enemy force was badly damaged, and unable to pursue immediately.

He wondered who realized the true reality of the situation. Sam Taggart, at least, knew. He had never discussed it with her, but she was perhaps the only one present with a harder grip on reality than he had.

Yes, she knows…and perhaps she doesn't even believe we've got the two months…

Chapter Five

Highborn Flagship S'Argevon
Imperial System GH3-2307 (Beta Telvara System)
Year of the Firstborn 391 (329 AC)

"It took a bit more time than we imagined at first—but there is little doubt that we now have more than enough power assembled to take on the enemy. The four other vessels of the imperial class alone are probably more powerful than every enemy ship...and we have a large number of other units as well. Our decision to attack before, with only a single one of the new imperial units active, was, in retrospect, the problem...and waiting until all four of the remaining vessels have been completed, as well as the new wave of conventional ships, will prove to be the deciding factor. I see no realistic possibility that the enemy will be able to match our force...or field anything capable of putting out any significant resistance. The single enemy imperial unit survived the fight by all accounts, but it was very close to destroyed, and there is little chance that the enemy will be able to repair it meaningfully in less than a number of years. And once our new ships are received by the forces in the Union, we will be able to continue our advance there as well."

Tesserax spoke boldly, perhaps a bit too boldly for

Phazarax, who shared his basic views…but who'd also become somewhat cautious of the human enemy, and their decisive defensive efforts. He basically agreed with his— senior, or equal…it wasn't entirely clear, and the two had avoided any direct confrontations, so far at least—but he had started to allow for responses from the enemy beyond those he'd expected. This was only rationality, at least to his view, but he quickly realized that Tesserax—and most of his subordinates—failed to experience the same thing. That he didn't understand. The conquest was supposed to be completed by now, for God sake, and occupying barely half of one of the powers was far from a satisfactory level. Even if it was a big chunk of the largest power.

"I agree with your thinking, Tesserax…and yet I cannot completely disregard the enemy's actions. They have been more difficult to conquer than we expected…far so." He paused. The last two words were more than he'd been willing to say, though he *had* said them, nevertheless. "I'm not saying I am truly concerned…" This was a lie. By any measure, he was at least *concerned*. "…I'm just saying, maybe we should at least discuss the enemy's past actions…and possible future ones."

Tesserax stared at his…cohort. "I can acknowledge the enemy has been somewhat more difficult to dispatch than expected, but this is the result of poor upfront planning…and the ability of many of the powers to form an alliance more quickly than expected. I do not believe it offers any real chance the enemy will prevail…do you?"

Phazarax delayed his response for a few seconds, though not long enough to transmit that he did, in fact, at times at least, worry about the enemy. That didn't mean he thought they were likely to win the fight in the end, but he did expect more trouble than Tesserax did. "No, of course not," he said. "But still…I think we should exert more care, perhaps take the enemy more seriously that we have. We've lost far more units already than we had imagined we would...and been compelled to build a lot more of our own and put them into the fight." They'd lost a *lot* more of their own ships, as well as untold thousands of enslaved humans, too, but Phazarax didn't say anything more than he had.

"I think you are too ready to give the enemy credit for our own foul ups. Certainly, we *have* underestimated their abilities, to an extent at least—and I will accept some of the blame for that—but I do not feel they have the construction capacity to truly challenge us, nor the capability to match our science levels. Not in a realistic time frame, at least.

Phazarax nodded, but deep inside he was more concerned. He didn't think the enemy could prevail, not exactly, but he was expecting a much harder fight than Tesserax. Still, he didn't express anything further. "Of course, you are correct, Tesserax...but I am still concerned that the enemy will prove to continue to be a harder target than we expected. Perhaps we should wait longer...after all, we have ten more of the large imperial hulls under construction."

"You believe we should wait for those? They have been under construction for less than six months. It will be three years, give or take, until they are done. Would you really wait so long? And what would the enemy accomplish in three years? Again, nothing that threatens us materially, but three years will allow them to build a lot of ships, even with half of the Hegemony's space occupied by us." Tesserax paused for a moment and looked at his companion. "No, we can't allow three years to go by...the enemy will only gain in technology and learn to use what we have, and they don't yet possess. They will be harder to defeat in three years, not easier."

Phazarax listened to his comrade's words, and he realized suddenly that Tesserax was as worried as he was, at least on some level. He couldn't admit it...not even fully to himself, but Phazarax suddenly understood that his cohort was more concerned about where the enemy was going to go than where he was now.

And as he thought about that, his own perspective changed, and he wondered, was he right…or was he wrong? Did it make more sense to attack the enemy immediately, with everything they had?

He realized Tesserax, rightly or wrongly, had decided that was the case. And for himself, he just didn't know.

He didn't know at all.

* * *

Percelax sat quietly, considering his situation. He had a decent number of Highborn ships ready, as well as a surprising number of Union hulls. It had been almost enough to lead him forward.

Almost.

Two things held him back. First, the minimal information he'd been able to receive on the enemy. Their base was still mostly destroyed—though even sections of that were back in the mix—but their fleet was more powerful even than it had been for the first battle. He'd come close to winning that, he knew, and he figured his chances in a second would be better. He might have gone in, save for the second consideration, which was the size of the force advancing to meet him. With those ships, he would almost certainly prevail, and he might even do so with enough power to advance fairly far into Confederation space after the battle. He wouldn't take out the whole Confederation—at least he didn't believe he would have enough strength to do that—but he might advance far enough to cut off the flow of ships and supplies to the main fleet.

And that would be decisive.

Truly cutting the enemy forces into two pieces would set them up to be more easily destroyed. The main enemy fleet was still posted in Hegemony space, and while he threatened the heart of the Confederation, he lacked the strength to take out the enemy completely, but just maybe he could cut the line of new ships out to the main fleet. He could just sweep away the defensive forces and cut off the source of the Confederation's reproductive resources…and that would be enough. The true victory would fall on Tesserax, and on the main fleet, which would advance after the remains of the enemy forces…and join up with his own ships. He would generate praise too, he knew that, but he was also aware that the bulk of the glory would fall on the theater commander, Tesserax. He was okay with that, mostly at least. He knew that the larger forces, on both sides, would clash on the primary front…but, still, he also knew his fleet would at least imperil the main enemy production areas. And that would be enough.

He would get a large amount of the praise, if less than he deserved. His realization that Tesserax was one of the first class of the Highborn, those called the Firstborn, was substantial, and he couldn't help but look up to him, as much as he also felt petty jealousy.

The doorbell rang.

"Enter."

The door opened, and Villieneuve walked inside. The Union leader was far easier to deal with since he'd been encollared…but Percelax still remembered how much trouble the man had given him before he was given the Collar, and he still resented him, quite a bit.

"You sent for me?" Villieneuve spoke meekly.

"Yes, Villieneuve, I did. We will be hitting the enemy again in approximately two months, and I wanted to discuss the status of the Union forces. Your fleet units that fought with us were virtually obliterated, but a few have been adequately repaired to return to battle. We have also been able to commandeer a number of ships that had already been under repair—as well as a small number of newly finished units, mostly begun by your defeated enemies. I believe your forces for the coming fight will actually exceed those you possessed in the previous battle, at least by a modest amount. And that is a surprise…indeed."

"Yes, I agree with your assessment entirely. My guess is that in two months, we will have approximately 125% of the power we possessed in the last fight. As much as 140%, if we include battered but still partially functional hulls."

"No, I think 125% will suffice, especially since we will have in excess of 250% of the Highborn ships. Your percentage of the vessels involved will be a lesser portion of the total than last time, even if they are more overall, but they will still represent a sizable amount of fleet's combat readiness." It was a statement without meaning, since 'a sizable amount of the fleet's combat readiness' was far from a specific term. One percent could be considered that much, or twenty percent couldn't be. Percelax guessed that the Union forces would be about fifteen percent of the total, or perhaps twelve. He didn't consider that vital…but he was glad to have whatever he could get.

"Our forces will fight hard, Percelax…you can be sure of that."

"I know they will, Villieneuve." Percelax wasn't sure of that, not at all. He had more of the Collar deployed than he had before the last battle, and most of the Union's senior officers had been so equipped. But the bulk of the rank and file had not, not yet at least, and he wondered if they would obey their commanders no matter what they were ordered to do…or if they would stand up and refuse. Union history suggested they would do what they were ordered to do, but Percelax wasn't sure…and he calculated the odds both with and without the Union allies. Another reason he had decided to wait for the next batch of ships from home.

Still, he had to make sure Villieneuve was ready, assuming he used the Union forces. "I wanted to discuss the plan with you, Villieneuve, and make sure you are ready for…whatever we decide to do."

Chapter Six

Forward Base Striker
Vasa Denaris System
Year 329 AC (After the Cataclysm)

Andi Lafarge stepped out of the hull, walking down the long, plank to the enclosed section of Striker. The base still had massive areas that were basically a wreck, but she had to admit, there was more work done than she'd expected, just in the time that she'd been away...less than three weeks. For an instant, she told herself they could actually be ready to face the enemy when he came back, but the thought only lasted for a few seconds, before it gave way to her normal state.

As she walked down the corridor, she could see huge sections of the structure that hadn't even been touched yet. Tyler Barron had driven his people to do more than even Andi had expected, but he hadn't been able to truly escape the severe amount of construction that lay ahead of him. Despite his incredible effort, after a passing moment, it was perhaps even clearer to Andi that she was right, that there was no way to win...no way except the deadly effort she was pursuing.

Assuming it works, of course...and we're able to get it spread throughout their forces.

She realized almost immediately that even her opinion, her dedication to completely destroy the enemy, relied on several things. The effectiveness of the formula was only the start. If the first attack was successful, if the enemy was killed—and killed entirely, since nothing less would likely work—that was only the first step. The second effort, and possibly the largest one of them, would follow. She knew she didn't have to get every one of the enemy...that would likely be impossible. But she had to get enough, including on many of their ships. That was going to be difficult, very difficult...even if the weaponry she had deployed to date worked quickly.

And all the more so, since the enemy would react as soon as they knew. She was amazed that they didn't seem to expect anything of the sort yet. After all, they were defeated earlier by the same means. She knew they thought differently of the empire than they did of the remaining civilizations, but she also realized that her people had moved very far in the past ten years. Between the provision of the Hegemony's generally superior tech, to the use of *Colossus*, and the advancement that went along with it, the Confederation and its allies had come far...and fast. They still weren't the equal of the empire, of course, but they were a lot closer than they'd been only ten years earlier...and getting closer every day.

She led most of the crew off the cruiser that had been her flagship for the near-month of the total mission. She was just relieved to see that the enemy had not attacked. Yet. She knew there were a lot of questions about her chosen strategy against the enemy, but to her the biggest one was, would she have time?

That overlooked a lot of course, not the least of which was whether the operation would get its go ahead at all.

"Andi!"

She saw Tyler up ahead. She wasn't surprised to see him, not exactly, but the time away had built up some kind of question as to what to expect. She knew he had agreed to the test mission, but she was aware that his thoughts hadn't changed. But of course, he'd gone almost a month without Andi as a result. She didn't try to convince herself that they had reached any sort of agreement…but she still felt a rush of her own as she saw him.

"Tyler!" She rushed up, knowing he was one of her biggest adversaries, at least in the sense of what to do, but at the moment, wanting only to take him in her arms. She rushed up and hugged him, even as he did the same. There was something missing, perhaps, in the embrace, but there was a lot still there as well.

"I'm so glad to see you." Tyler was genuine, though again, there was a bit of hesitation in his tone. Andi knew she faced a challenge convincing him to go full in against the enemy…and she realized that he thought the same way about her. She was sure she couldn't be moved though…and she had the hope that he could. After all, he would surely do everything possible to wipe out the enemy if it was the *only* way to prevail. She already believed it was the only way—though she would have done it anyway—and she was sure his thoughts, his opinion that his forces could hold on somehow, were just the result of his military career.

"I'm glad to see you, too." She tightened her arms around him, and she knew she was only telling the truth. She *was* glad to see him, despite the fact that she expected almost no one to give her more trouble.

The two held each other for a few more seconds, but the presence of her crew members behind her cut short their reunion.

He pulled back, and he spoke to the officers and spacers behind her in the tube. "Congratulations to you all…truly." He was genuine, but Andi could hear the resistance in his tone, and the continuing disapproval of a full-scale effort to wipe out the enemy. He wasn't soft on them, not by any measure…but he wasn't ready to risk taking the battle to the very edge either. For one thing, he knew the enemy didn't want to destroy humanity…but he was unsure how they would react to a serious effort to wipe *them* out. Would they counter with their own attempt to destroy humanity…or at least the humanity that lay on the Rim, and in the systems occupied by the Hegemony?

That was a consideration, even to Andi…but she didn't want to survive anyway, not as a slave of the Hegemony. And she didn't want her child to endure in that kind of world either.

Tyler was the same as she was in that regard, she was sure of that. But he still held some hope that his fleet could find a way to win, to at least gain a brokered deal with the Highborn. She had no comparable thoughts.

She stepped up onto the pedestal, and she saw at once the half-finished nature of the work completed on Striker. She knew the massive structure had been pummeled almost to its ruin, and now she saw the cost of the miraculous work that had been completed.

"You got a lot done here in the past month," she said. It was true…but it also overlooked much work that needed to be done.

"Yes, we did. But only by focusing almost entirely on the minimum amount that needed to be done to restore each system." He gestured around, clearly expressing his awareness that the structure was a strange mix of completed…and not even started. "The longer we get, the better we'll do…" His voice descended to silence. He knew the enemy was also making good time with the break between fighting, and he was sure, on some level, that the Highborn were doing better than he was…if only because they had a smaller area to manage. He was pulling most of his new ships forward from the still far off Confederation— though he'd just gotten three Hegemony battleships from one of the shipyards his forces still controlled, too.

"You did well, Ty…really well. Better, it looks like more

than I'd dared to hope for." That, at least, was true.

"I'm glad to hear that, Andi." Tyler's voice suggested that he was as uncomfortable as she was, about the next steps, about the enemy...about the resolution between them. Neither of them had changed their view. That much, at least, was clear.

Andi knew the serum might not work, that the formula put together so quickly might deviate from the one the empire used to drive the Highborn from imperial territory. That would put her conflict with Tyler on ice, at least until her people had another formula to try.

But she didn't believe that. She was convinced the formula was right...and her mind had already gone on to phase two, to the plan to inflict as much damage on the enemy as possible. She was sure the plan would work—if only because there was no point in imagining if it didn't—and she was determined to make sure her people made the best effort possible to win.

Still, she was only human, and she had just come back from almost a month away. She could spare one evening from her efforts—and she suspected Tyler could too. She knew that wouldn't change anything that lay ahead...but it was welcome, nevertheless.

* * *

Stockton sat quietly. His covering—that's what he called it at least—had actually slipped, and the structure of the device was visible, he knew, though not to him, at least not away from a mirror. It was irritating, but he was getting tired of trying to hide it, at least when he was alone.

He knew what he had to do, and he was going to go right to the top. He wouldn't tell Stara, not until the moment had almost come. He knew she was completely against the procedure, and he understood. But the truth was, he just couldn't face life with the construction still attached to him. He knew it was possible that the implant was completely shot…but the doubts about that would last his whole life. He was far from sure he could get over all he had done anyway…but he was sure the *only way* was with the attachment removed.

Even though none had been successfully taken out yet.

That was true, of course, but it had only been attempted a few times. His situation was different, in many ways. First, he was willing and able. Second, while the doctors had definitely not perfected even a hopeful way to perform the surgery, they were much farther along than they'd been when the last effort was made. He believed all that. Even more importantly, he'd decided he'd rather die on the table than go on as he had. He was far from sure he could recover even if he was able to somehow survive the surgery…but he was sure he had to try.

He just had to convince Tyler Barron to go along with it. He wasn't sure, but he thought he had at least a reasonable chance. Barron was strange sometimes, caught between various layers of influence. But he thought he knew the supreme commander better than most people…and if he could convince him of his seriousness…

He turned and looked around, and he stared at himself in the mirror. Stara had removed all of them from the place, but he had hidden one, and now he stared at himself in it. The detritus hanging from the back of his neck was ominous, even though it appeared to be completely inoperative. He tried to go back on his recent decision, to convince himself he was being foolish, that he could survive with the attachment.

But as he looked, his opinion only hardened. He couldn't be sure the thing was dead—and no one else could either—and he couldn't live with that, even if he could tolerate the rest of it. He wasn't sure a return to his old position, or something comparable to it, would allow him to recover from all he'd been, all he'd done…but he was sure it was the only way. He'd tried to endure for Stara, and for all the others, but he couldn't do it. He had to have a real go at coming all the way back...or he had to die trying.

He was sure of that...as sure as he could be of anything...and he just had to convince Admiral Barron of it.

*   *   *

"Clint, I am glad you could make it."

Winters paused for an instant, but then he walked the rest of the way into the room. "I wanted to see what the opposition looked like," he said grimly.

"That is not necessary, Clint...you know we all want the same thing. All of us." The voice was different from the one that had first pierced the silence. The first voice had been Chronos...but the second was Andi.

"Andi...I didn't know you were going to be here." Winters was as non-committal as he could manage...which was far less than usual.

"I arranged the meeting, Clint...and I invited you. I'm afraid our Hegemony personnel are no more decided than you." Andi stopped for a moment, but then she continued before Winters could. "Please, Clint...I know you haven't decided yet...neither have Akella and Chronos. And I am *far* from comfortable speaking with you behind Tyler's back. I hope you know, I would never do anything I didn't believe was in his best interests."

Clint almost shot back a caustic response, but the desire passed almost as quickly as it had appeared. "I *do* know that...but what if you and he decide on opposite ways to go?"

Andi stared back at Clint, almost as though the others were gone for a moment. "I hope you understand me well enough to realize I would never move against Tyler." That was almost true...she hoped they would ultimately agree on the final effort, but she realized there was a chance they would come all the way to the end with different points of view. And she didn't know what she would do then. "But Tyler isn't ready to prepare for the second phase of the operation…assuming the first phase proves successful…and I believe we have to have the plan ready to proceed, at least."

"Because you want to see it carried out."

"Because I believe it is our only hope…and I feel like you at least share some of that view." She pulled her head back. "I believe all of you do…at least partially. That is why you are here."

"I thought Akella had put this meeting together." Winters had been surprised at Andi's presence, but he only just realized that Andi *had* organized the whole affair.

"No…I just came. To be honest, I am not sure how I feel about this. My loyalty to Admiral Barron is considerable, but I have responsibilities as the head of the Hegemony state as well…and they are not always in line." A pause. Then: "Particularly if we lose the next fight…or if the Confederation decides to pull back and leave the rest of the Hegemony to enemy occupation. I do not believe Admiral Barron is of this opinion, though I do believe a fair amount of those supporting his position are. And, I don't know what he will do if this proposition becomes the dominant one for a more…normal…resistance to the enemy." Another pause, then, "Or if another battle is fought at Striker…and lost."

Andi nodded. "Look, I wanted to get you together, because I wanted to discuss this with people who are at least…sympathetic…to my concerns. I admit that I feel this way, that I'm more in the direction of taking out the enemy completely…but I'd still listen to opposing views." It was the one thing she wasn't being honest about. In truth, she couldn't imagine any circumstance that would change her opinion on destroying the enemy. "But I do believe that our best attempt to destroy the Highborn, or come as close to that as possible, is the way to go. I am honest about that." A pause. "And I'm pretty sure everyone here at least partially agrees."

The room was silent for a moment. Finally, Akella spoke again. "Andi, you're definitely farther along toward launching an all-out assault on the enemy than I am…but I feel like most of the Hegemony Council will be in agreement with you." She paused, and then she continued. "I am sure they are, in fact…what I just don't know is how long I can keep them from going in with you. Or if I even want to."

Chronos was silent, but Andi could tell that Akella was the one farther from her than he was. He clearly wasn't exactly comfortable with it, but she bet to herself that without Akella, Chronos would be with her…or at least closer to it.

"Again, my purpose isn't to raise up any kind of resistance. It is simply to make sure that phase two proceeds as quickly as possible. Phase one was only a single planet. Phase two will be the actual implementation of the program…" She paused for a moment, not sure just how to proceed. Then she said, "And I'm afraid there will be much more resistance to it. I'll be honest…I don't care about the enemy, not at all. But I don't believe you need to reach that level to support me. All you have to do is believe as I do, that our efforts to defend ourselves through normal means are hopeless. You can regret that our only choice for survival is so terrifying, so desperate. As long as you believe it is our only choice. And I feel like all of you are at least halfway there…if not farther."

Chapter Seven

Forward Base Striker
Vasa Denaris System
Year 329 AC (After the Cataclysm)

"I know there has been some...discussion...about what course we are to take." Tyler Barron spoke cautiously, even with Atara. He trusted his longtime aide almost completely...but the 'almost' was poking up at him. He was fairly sure Atara would never go against him, but he wondered what she really felt.

The instant of silence before she replied only increased his apprehension.

"Admiral...I want you to know, I prefer the same option as you, the destruction of the enemy's will to fight, but..." She was silent again, at least for a brief moment. "But, I'm far from sure we can attain a victory that way." She had put forth her doubts, more or less, before...but this was the first time she'd laid out her concerns completely. "And I don't know what to do...because I feel the odds of the other plan, the effort to completely destroy the enemy, are poor as well. In truth, I don't know what to think."

Tyler wasn't entirely prepared for the level of— honesty—his aide laid on him. "I appreciate your candor, Atara...but you're going to have to make a decision at some point. And soon. Another few weeks, probably, and a couple months max. If the captured Highborn don't show symptoms, the choice will be made, of course, at least until a new formula is ready. But if they do…then we'll have to choose whether to commit a large portion of the fleet to phase two. I understand the allure of that, obviously, but I also feel it is problematical. We don't know that it will actually work, of course…and that is true, by the way, even if it is effective. Perhaps worst of all, is a definite probability that once the enemy knows what we're doing, or trying to do, they will reconsider their own efforts. I am one hundred percent opposed to the enemy's goals, but they are *not* trying to destroy us, at least not wholesale. If they move to that as an effort…they already have over half of the Hegemony. That's what, 175 billion? All of which they could destroy fairly quickly. They haven't done that…yet."

"You're right, sir…but then I'd expect you don't plan to survive a defeat. You put up the survival of the species as an argument, but it's not something you want yourself, not if you can't prevail."

Barron felt the edge of the response, and it cut at him. Mostly because it was correct. He did not intend to survive defeat…and as much as he held aloft the possibility that he would prevail, in truth, he was fully aware that the likely result *was* downfall, and the conquest of humanity by the Highborn. And that was something he was unwilling to survive.

He knew the odds were against securing a military victory, but it wasn't impossible. Not yet. At least, not certainly.

"Look, Atara…I'm not going to try to convince you we've got an edge, because we don't. I just want to be sure you consider all the possibilities. The other option…it requires the formula working…and working perfectly. Even a half-effective formula won't work. And we don't even know for a fact that the thing will have an effect at all anymore. It is over three hundred years old. If the enemy came up with a cure—not a ridiculous notion—then we're dead. Unless we fight it out...and win." Barron was sure he was right, but he also knew an argument could be worded just as well the other way.

"Admiral...I promise you I will be with you. To the end." Atara paused for a moment, and then she spoke again, "I can't tell you what I believe is the best route. I don't believe anyone knows that. It is certainly possible that the formula *will* work, and that we can present it in enough places so that it spreads adequately...but there are also a hundred things that could go wrong. And you're right as well that mankind surviving, even as the slaves of the Highborn, is probably a better result than mass death...though I, too, would choose to meet my end in that result. Perhaps in another hundred years, or a thousand, the Highborn will develop out of their current viewpoint. They may even become worthy masters, and not brutal overlords." Barron could tell she didn't really believe that, at least not the last part. "But I don't know what is best for humanity...I really don't. If I did, perhaps I would go with it, even to the extent of ending up on a different side than you. But I don't...I'm not sure there is a *right* side. So, I will go as I always have...I will assume that you know the answer."

Barron heard her words, telling him what he wanted to hear, and yet he felt only more confused. He was set in his view, determined to proceed as he had decided...and yet he was troubled. Was he right? Or was he wrong? He just didn't know.

"Thank you, Atara...I appreciate your support...and your honesty." He was correct on part of that, at least. He did respect her support.

Her honesty, he wasn't sure about.

* * *

Sonya Eaton stood stone still, watching the dozens of workers climbing along the battered hull of *Colossus*. *Dozens…just that I can see. There are thousands of people working on the ship…almost three thousand.* And that was in addition to the hundreds on the giant ship's regular maintenance crew…those that had survived the last fight at least. Eaton knew her ship had barely made it through that battle, but her opponent hadn't, and that gave her a rush that still held her up, even when she actually had plenty to be down about.

First, she still wasn't sure she could have her ship ready for the fight coming up. Actually, if the enemy came anytime within the range that she herself had projected, she knew the real answer. Worse, perhaps, she just wasn't sure she could overlook it, and tell Admiral Barron that *Colossus* was ready…not when it wasn't even close.

The ship was battered in the last fight…severely battered. And as much work as had been done in the last six months, it had only really, just begun. She had a couple years more, at least, to go, and that was before the ship was really even ready to return to battle, not when it would be fully repaired. She didn't know the time for that…or even if it was possible using Confederation technology.

"Commodore…we're going to have this work done in an hour or so. If we could schedule a test, we could scratch one more thing off our to do list."

Sonya turned. She hadn't seen Commander Horace. He was ducked behind one of the new components, hidden from her view. But he'd seen her.

"Absolutely, Commander…as soon as you are ready." She knew he only meant a small section of the ship, tiny really…and for that even, only a marginal restoration of the normal power that flowed through it. But it was better than nothing, especially for the crew members who had worked on it almost around the clock. Eaton realized that she was constantly weighed down by the sheer magnitude of the total job, but she also understood that she had to give the various crews working throughout the ship some moments of joy and satisfaction...even if the work done wasn't all that much of the remarkable total that still had to be completed.

"In an hour, perhaps...or maybe an hour and a half, just to be safe."

"And hour and a half it is, Commander. I'll be back here a little before that." She wasn't sure if Horace meant for her to be present or not, but she decided she might as well attend, at least for a few minutes. Her mind had already started to work on what she could do to reward the crew members, what kind of small benefit she could cook up in the next hour and a half. She might manage some food, though she knew there wouldn't be a lot of that...the kitchens weren't functioning much better than the rest of the ship. But she would manage something. Ideally, she'd have given her workers in the area some time off as well, but beyond an hour or two for a small party, but she just couldn't spare them. She wasn't sure when they had started, but her people were working twelve-hour shifts, and unless the current group was on hour eight or later, they'd be reassigned and working on something new after a brief party.

"Thank you, sir..."

"No, Commander...thank you. You finished this job at least a day early, perhaps even two." *And if you can do that about a thousand times more, maybe we can get this load of crap back into the line.* "I'll be back in a little over an hour...for the kickoff of the event at least." *And you'll spend most of the next hour trying to figure out where to send Horace and his crew next...*

* * *

"I'm sorry to bring this to you right now, sir. I can't imagine how much is going through your mind at this moment." Stockton spoke evenly, almost calmly. He was edgy about how Barron would respond to his request, but he'd decided absolutely how he felt. He *had* to go for it…and somehow, despite the fact that it seemed likely Barron would say 'no' or would at least try to push the operation off, part of him said the commander *would* understand.

"Jake…I understand how you feel, I really do. But you can't really expect me to restart this process right now, can you?"

"I do, sir…and I'll tell you why. Because you're ready and able to fight this to the end. And any way that happens, any way that involves any chance of victory at least, leaves you with millions of people encollared…even billions. You have to be ready for that, and I'm probably the likeliest case to survive the surgery. My device is…perhaps not completely disabled, but certainly damaged. I might have survived the early procedures, even, and we know that the research teams have come a great distance, even though they haven't been able to conduct any actual operations for almost four years." Stockton was speaking honestly, as clearly as he was able. "To be honest, sir…it's the only way I can go on much further. I can't sit here, useless, while our forces fight the most desperate battle they've ever faced…and I know you can't ever let me back in, in any real way, as long as this thing is still part of me."

Barron didn't answer, not right away. He just looked down, appearing as though this was one more thing he didn't need right then. But then, he lifted his head and he said, "Jake, I don't even know if I have the authority to order this. There would be a huge number of opinions, and not all of them would be in favor, I can tell you that. I'm still not even sure how I feel…" Barron looked over at Stockton. "…though I certainly understand your point of view."

"I'm going to kill myself, Admiral. Not today, not tomorrow…but soon. Unless you give the go ahead." Stockton hadn't been willing to say what he just had. He hadn't even known it…until a few seconds earlier. But he did now.

Barron's eyes opened a bit more, and he stared at Stockton. But he didn't look terribly surprised. "You know those words are a bit of a challenge to me, Jake." It was what he *had* to say, but his tone was missing the emphasis Stockton had…not exactly expected but feared.

"I didn't mean them that way…and it wasn't a threat…just a realistic view. I don't want to…kill myself…but I know I will, eventually. I just can't go on like I've been for very much longer. It's too difficult." He stopped for a few seconds, but before Barron could answer, he continued, "It's just too hard, Tyler. I know you can keep me under watch 24/7, though I'm not sure if you could prevent me from doing it at some point. But I don't want that. I just want to be honest…with you at least. I'm not threatening to kill myself, but I'd be lying if I told you I didn't think about it…again and again." Another few seconds of silence, followed by, "Please Tyler…I *don't want* to give up. If I thought there was no chance, I'd probably think differently. But you know as well as I do, there *is* some hope…maybe even a decent one. Let me do it…please."

Barron stood, firm and still for a moment. Part of Stockton expected him to reject the proposal outright…but part of him saw another way. In truth, he wasn't sure what to expect.

Barron looked as though he was going to respond at least three times before he finally did. "You do know, apart from the doctors—maybe—no one is going to agree with this, not now certainly. They'll know it was me that gave the go ahead, and they'll all come at me. Even if I maintain that it has to be done…there's no guarantee that it will happen. My position is weak, at least when it comes to matters such as this." Barron was silent again for a moment, and then he added, "I'm not even sure about my status as a leader, except of the Confederation forces…not with the questions that are coming up now."

"That is not true, sir..." Stockton paused for a moment, and then he continued, "I haven't gotten very involved in such matters—no one can afford to listen to me anyway—but I'd guess we are at cross purposes on this one. I'd support any measures taken against the enemy...but I'd also follow my orders. Even if they ran counter to my own personal view. And I would follow yours most of all."

"I appreciate that, Jake...I really do. But the case in point remains whether to proceed with the—very experimental—surgery. My instincts are still 'no.'"

Stockton felt a blow...but then he realized Barron wasn't finished yet.

"But I don't know what will happen going forward...I don't even know that there is much chance of our victory, whichever way we go. I just believe *you've* got to make this decision. If you're really in favor of taking the chance—and it's a *huge* chance—then we should go ahead with it."

Stockton looked back at Barron. He had expected a chance of success, but as he realized that Barron was actually giving in to his request, he understood that he hadn't *really* anticipated it. For an instant, he felt his own resolve waver...but only for the briefest moment.

"That assumes, of course, that the action team, the doctors and medical assistants, are willing to move forward on my command...solely." Barron's words continued, but Stockton was sure he could pull it off, as long as it happened soon.

Very soon...far sooner than even he'd have expected, and with as few people as possible knowing about it...

Chapter Eight

CFS Constellation
75,000 Kilometers from Fleet Base Grimaldi
Krakus System
Year 329 AC (After the Cataclysm)

"You know *Constellation*'s going to make it, at least. She won't be one hundred percent, perhaps, but she's going to be close." Isaac Johnson only spoke the truth, though in some way at least, Samantha Taggart still couldn't quite believe it. Perhaps more so, she wasn't ready to accept the fact that the work was going to be done in just two more days. She'd insisted on two weeks, but she was aware, now at least if not initially, that two weeks was longer than it would take. Hell, the more she'd thought about it, three weeks would have been good enough...but now, she saw the work being done in just ten days total.

"Yes...I know." She'd long since given in to a dozen other concerns, especially over the last few days, as it became clear *Constellation* was, in fact, going to be ready before any enemy could penetrate. Unless something seriously went wrong late in the work, she knew there would be no enemy attack, certainly not in two days. She had a minimum of two jumps from enemy space covered, and even assuming the foe had put together its attack and was about to cross the border, it would take longer than that to complete the movement to Grimaldi.

That was a good thing, definitely, but she realized it was only so good. She had her ship back, almost at least, and she had at least double the other vessels the force had possessed in the last struggle...but Grimaldi was at best at twenty percent of its previous power.

At best.

She tried to calculate the various strengths, coupling the newness of many of her ships with the oldness, but the vast size, of Grimaldi. She came up with a different answer every time, but generally, she figured the total force that would be ready was stronger than that which had stood before...perhaps even meaningfully so.

But she also knew the enemy would come with an even stronger force...and unless they got another six months—at least—there was no way they were going to hold. She tried not to think much about that...but she found herself becoming more and more likely to focus on those thoughts as time went by.

"There's more good news, Commodore. If we get another three weeks, we'll have at least thirty more ships...maybe as many as fifty."

Taggart looked at her junior. "Come on, Isaac...that's the total output from the shipyards, and while it's pretty amazing, it's also not all coming to us." She was inclined to assume that none of it would come to her aide, but she knew that, too, was unfair. Still, if her forces got a quarter of that total, they'd be doing well enough.

Unless the main fleet pulls back...

That would have been her hope for a while, but in truth, it would probably make things even worse. She resented the primary fleet's first call on reinforcements, even its continued status as the *primary fleet*, given her own position far closer to the worlds of the Confederation. She knew that was pointless, of course, and that the withdrawal of the main fleet to her position would only make things worse. The Union was battered badly, though what little intel she still had told her it was building rapidly too, and the Highborn forces attached to the enemy fleet would likely be even more of the total strength than they were last time. At least if the attack came in the next six months…which it almost certainly would.

"Yeah…fifty is probably the total output from our bases…but don't forget, the Alliance is building ships as well, as is the Hegemony. Assuming everything produced by either of them goes to the other front…it's not crazy to assume that half of our production could remain."

She felt the urge to argue that even half of fifty wasn't thirty, but she didn't. There wasn't any point. She understood what Isaac was trying to do, and she realized that she herself tended to be too negative. She *would* get a decent percent of the new production, she was sure of that…though she still wasn't convinced it would be half.

"Whatever we get, Commodore, it will be welcome…and I remind you, we've gotten a bit more than fifty percent of the last six month's production. There's no real reason to expect that to go down anytime soon."

Taggart didn't respond immediately, and when she did, at first, she just nodded. Finally, she added, "There's no point in debating this, Isaac. We'll get what we get…and no one but Gary Holsten will have anything to say about that." That wasn't entirely true, of course, but it was close. She could complain constantly, and so could her commander, Admiral Simpson. But the two seemed to agree that they would keep their focus on the system they were tasked to hold. She'd seen Gary Holsten up at Krakus…and she'd even witnessed his reluctance to go back to the home system. She wasn't the kind to trust one like him…but she'd realized, she *did* trust him. He was one of the few people who'd spent considerable time at both fronts, and she relied on him to make rational decisions.

And with the demise of the Senate, she realized he might be the strongest person in the Confederation. There was already a new body, of course, or at least part of one, but she doubted the fresh politicians had truly learned to take charge…or even that they'd be given the chance to do that.

She'd never met Holsten before she had encountered him more than six months before, but she'd been surprised by his conduct, by his willingness to step aside and allow the military people present handle the battle.

He knew better than most the situation on both fronts…and that made him the one to decide which reinforcements went where.

She found that mostly helpful…and a little bit troubling as well.

* * *

"Okay…I'm going to make this as clear as I can. I want ten percent removed from the 'to completion' dates on every ship that has three months or more to go. Is that understood?" Gary Holsten was speaking to the group present, a collection of various types sent to urge him to slow down. He found that shocking, considering that any measure of the total production was still too small to offer a real chance at victory. If he squeezed out every hull, if he got them all positioned exactly where they were most needed…maybe, he could win another battle, buy another six months, even a year. But he had to do that in two places, and it would still only gain him another half a year before more enemy ships were ready.

Before the next assault came.

He realized that the dead, most of them at least, almost all, were humans, if many were those raised for generations as Highborn slaves. There were Highborn killed as well, he realized, and probably a decent number, but ninety-eight or ninety-nine percent of those falling *were* humans.

On the enemy's side. On his own side, the figure was simpler. One hundred percent.

He tried most of the time not to think about that, but once in a while, it pushed its way through his defenses, and he couldn't help himself.

"Sir...we came to see you to reduce the production level...not to *increase* it." The response wasn't immediate, but it was close. That told Holsten who was the leader of the group that technically didn't have anyone in charge.

"Well, Mr...Wilkenson...it is time for that thought to change. Allow me to bring you up to date, though I suspect the recent Highborn-Union attack should have done that. We have the main fleet far away...far, far away, standing with our allies...and facing virtually no chance. Now, we have an assortment of ships, terribly short on battleships, lined up around what little remains of Grimaldi, ready to face a renewed enemy attack from Union space...hundreds of lightyears behind the primary front, and much closer to our relevant space." Holsten paused, but just for a couple seconds. "They are in even worse shape, I would guess. We face total conquest, Mr. Wilkenson, and all the rest of you. *Total* conquest. And not the kind you are likely to turn to your advantage. No, I can assure you, if the Confederation falls to this enemy, you will all be culled out and replaced. So, you're with us on this, all the way."

Holsten believed that, completely, but he wasn't sure the industrialists did, at least not all of them. Prior to the last attack on Grimaldi, which was a victory, at least of a sort, the Confederation hadn't even been attacked by the enemy...at least not in its home space. Those assembled knew the losses that had been suffered, of course, but Holsten knew that sort of thing was sometimes hard to truly understand. He even wondered if there weren't a few of the industrialists who actually believed he was faking the loss figures to them. He wasn't sure of that...but he didn't find it inconceivable. He just wasn't sure whether that was the result of his own foolishness…or if one or more of them truly bought that story.

Wilkenson was quiet, for a moment, but then he repeated his statement, at least that the ten percent increase was just impossible. He got about twenty percent of the way through before Holsten interrupted him. "Ten percent, Mr. Wilkenson—and all of you. Ten percent…and just be glad I've exempted ships three months or less from completion." Holsten stared out at those present, making it clear that the conversation was ended. Then he added, "Very well…I'll let you all go now, so you can get the word back up your chains…" He stood, for just a moment, and then he turned and walked away, leaving the room, and a number of shocked representatives behind.

"You think I made my point?" His words were tough, but a bit less so than they had been just a moment before.

"Yes…I think so. I'm not sure three months was quite enough time from completion to allow a ten percent reduction in work time, but I'd wager they're going to try…even as they bitch endlessly about you." Andrei Denisov stood next to Holsten, able to get around, but still fairly battered. He'd come close to being killed in the attack that took out the Senate Complex, but he'd pulled through.

"Ah…who cares? Either they'll get them done ahead of time, or at least they'll finish them on schedule. I just wanted to keep the pressure on them. Honestly, it just popped into my head." He paused. "What do you think I should do next, Andrei? Stay and watch the new Senate? Go to Grimaldi? Or get all the way out to Striker? It's been a long time since I've been out there."

Denisov understood which of the options Holsten preferred, that was clear…but he also considered it the least useful. "You can't go out to Striker, not yet. You know that. I think you might risk a quick trip out to Grimaldi, soon at least…but you'll have to get back here pretty quickly. Like it or not, this is the center of the resistance right now, at least from your perspective, and the Senate, while new and still incomplete, isn't immune from creating problems."

Striker nodded. "That's my read, too." It was, at least to an extent...though if Denisov hadn't shot down the idea of taking a quick trip out to the main front, he might have pushed a little harder. "I think I will go out to Grimaldi...and probably soon. I don't think the new Senate is ready yet to cause any real problems." He remained silent for a moment, and then he added, "Though I don't think I can go for long. As you say, they won't be calm forever."

Striker had acted almost like a dictator for the past six months, but he hadn't actually done anything to increase his power or control. It was just his position as the most senior member surviving from the old government. He'd almost tried to increase his power, permanently...but he hadn't moved on it. He'd never really considered the current moment before, and he hadn't thought about any chance he might have at gaining absolute power. Until the last six months.

He'd actually considered it...and he'd come close. No one on the capital could have stopped him, certainly not immediately after the Senate was taken out. In the end, it had been Barron, and the others out at Striker and Grimaldi that had prevented him from taking control. He'd realized he couldn't hold onto it anyway, not if Barron and the others were successful...and certainly not if they weren't. In the end, he'd realized he just didn't want it. For all the allure of having his word carried out precisely, he realized it was just something he didn't really care about. He didn't even want the power he had...that was just something that had befallen him.

He knew the government wasn't right either, that he and many others like him had struggled to hold off the various pushes and pulls of the people in power. But now, most of those who'd run the Senate were dead. Only five had been absent that day, and those who hadn't been there were from smaller worlds. The explosion had reset the situation, set back the Senate, for a while at least. What would happen after the enemy was defeated, assuming he was, remained to be seen. Holsten knew the new Senators would vie for power, and he suspected that some of the military and other types would try to assert control. In the end, he banked on the one man he was almost sure didn't want power—Tyler Barron—to take control…and ease the situation back to a reasonable level. Still, he was sure of one thing.

Tyler Barron didn't see the obligation. He saw his duty to lead the forces, to find a way to win the Confederation's survival, along with that of its allies. But he would probably fight any other level of control…and fight it with considerable strength.

Which only made it more important it was him doing it…and no one else. Holsten knew there were going to be massive changes after the enemy was defeated…assuming of course they were defeated.

He also knew there was no real point of thinking about it, not until the enemy looked like they were going to be stopped. For all the vim and vigor he felt, he knew getting there would be difficult, if not impossible. And it would take everything all the people worth anything had.

He looked at Denisov, and he made two decisions. First, the primary front was too far away, at least for him to visit anytime soon.

And second, he had to get the hell out of Troyus City, off the entire planet…even for a short while. "I am going to Grimaldi, Andrei…soon. Very soon. Do you want to come along?"

Chapter Nine

Forward Base Striker
Vasa Denaris System
Year 329 AC (After the Cataclysm)

"I want to thank you, sir." Jake Stockton stood, quietly addressing Tyler Barron. He'd had a hunch that Barron would understand his needs...but he had still expected somewhat of a fight at least. But short of one question about whether he was truly sure, Barron had more or less just given in to Stockton.

Barron turned and looked up. "I don't necessarily believe this is the right way to go, Jake. I don't know that much, and I trust that you have studied your options...but I am certain that you have earned the right to make the decision. I think most of the people around here understand that you are...potentially dangerous...but they are simultaneously blind to what you were, and what your actions over the past several years would have done to you. I may not have told you that I understand, at least as well as another could...but I do. That is why I have arranged this...and if it doesn't work out, there will be fallout, I can assure you of that." A brief pause, then: "Not that you'll care, of course. Not if it doesn't work."

"No, I don't suppose I will. And thank you again,

Admiral." He understood that Barron would face most of the scorn if he died during the treatment, and the fact that the admiral would probably survive the backlash didn't mean it wouldn't happen.

"I think this is a "Tyler' moment, Jake."

"Yes, of course…thank you, Tyler."

"Your welcome." A moment of silence, longer than the last. Then: "I have to insist that you don't tell anyone. The doctors are gathered together already, and they're getting sleep even now. But I think you do have to tell Stara. If you knew it was going to work, that would be one thing…but to be honest, you don't."

"No, I don't…and I know how she is going to react. But you're right…I have to tell her." Stockton was silent for a moment, and then he continued, "I want to prepare some notes for a few of the others. I should tell them all, but I know I can't. Perhaps I could trust you to hand them out if…"

"Anything you give me…I'll be sure it gets to the relevant parties." Barron's tone was grave. It was clear that he had assembled the best surgeons available, done everything to make success as likely as possible. It was also obvious he thought that total failure was at least as likely as success.

And possibly more likely.

It was also clear that Barron believed that the decision was Stockton's to make. Stockton wasn't surprised, at least not totally. But maybe a little.

"Thank you, Tyler." Stockton had never been one to overdue physical manifestations, but now he leaned in and gave Barron a hug. "I know this seems like a big deal…and even more out of place now than at another time. But I never thought I'd make it back…my efforts, even after I'd regained some control, were always intended as a suicidal last effort. I never expected to return to the ranks, and given the chance, I've got to try to make it all the way back. It's all

I've got, and I know there is only one way. One way to truly do it."

Barron stepped back for a moment and looked at Stockton. He was silent for a good measure, and then he said, "You can wait, too, if you want. We are better now than we were last time...and your Collar is down, or at least damaged. But we'll be even better in a couple years." Barron had intended one last effort to dissuade Stockton, but Stockton could hear the hesitancy in his tone. If Barron had any real hope for survival, Stockton wondered if he would have been so easy to convince.

Stockton had listened...but he didn't change his mind. He was out of the ranks, and he knew he had to stay that way, at least unless his surgery was completed. But he knew the situation, and the chances of outright success...and he was fairly certain he was having the surgery just out of the hope to get back before the end, to die as a warrior for his side, and not just watch everything around him be destroyed.

"You know the chances of us surviving another few years, don't you?" Stockton almost didn't reply, but at the last moment he did. "I *have* to get back into this fight, and this is the only way. If we are going to lose, then we will lose...but I have to be part of it, and not just someone watching from the side." He didn't add that he faced possibly the worst fate of all if he was captured alive by the enemy. Barron knew that.

"Okay, Jake. Go and tell Stara...that won't be easy. I'd say you should try to get to sleep early tonight too, but what's the chance of you getting any rest?" Barron knew the answer to the question well enough. "I'll see you tomorrow...we'll start early and get the operation going by noon." A few seconds went by, and then Barron added, "If we don't get this surgery going on time, or if anyone else gets wind of what we're doing, it's possible it will get delayed...or even canceled."

"I understand that…and I know how much of a chance you're taking. I wouldn't push so hard for this…if I didn't believe it was the only way."

Barron just nodded. He knew…just as much as Stockton did. He had tried, briefly to change Stockton's mind, but he had given in quickly. For better or worse, Stockton had always shared much with his commander…and he believed if the situations were reversed, the exchange would have been more or less the same.

The effort with Stara would be more difficult.

Far more difficult.

*   *   *

Reg Griffin swung her arms around, bringing her fighter more or less back on a course toward Striker. She'd sent out hundreds of patrols in the six months since the great battle, one after the other, on a never-ending quest to be somehow ready for the next fight. She knew, at least in a sense, that her fighters would not find the enemy, that the ships deployed a system or two in advance would get word back first. Perhaps it would only arrive a few days in advance, but it would definitely come before the enemy.

Still, Griffin kept people from her command in space constantly, more than she needed, usually, trying to maintain some level of readiness for the renewed fight she knew was coming. Her forces were as large as they had been, even if her carriers weren't. She had every ship overloaded with fighters, some fielding twice the number they should have been. It was a difficult operation, no doubt, but one she accepted.

It kept her busy…as busy as hell, and that kept her from Jake Stockton. She'd been thrilled to find Stockton alive, but the realization that he had some remnant of enemy control still attached to him threw her into a strange fit. She *was* still glad he was back, of course…but the device sticking out of his neck made it difficult for her to be around him. She had to spend some time with him, of course, but the more she *had* to be out flying, the less frequently that had to be.

She tried to convince herself that her assignment efforts hadn't been dominated by her desire to minimize time spent with Stockton, and she knew that she'd be leading her people out frequently anyway. But she couldn't argue that she scheduled some of the excursions to give herself something to do, some way to be apart from the nightmare surrounding Jake Stockton.

What would you do if he didn't have that alien device still attached, if he was clearly free of enemy control? She liked to think that it wouldn't be a question, that she would step aside and take the number two position. She knew that was the right thing to do, but she wasn't sure she could do it, at least not easily.

She glanced at the squadron deployed behind her. They were one of the best formations in the fleet, but she still found it rather easy to shake them up from time to time. She almost did it then, but she stopped herself at the last minute. There was no place for that kind of thing, not now. She had lost incredible numbers in the last fight, and more than half the pilots with her now were new. She realized her force, while as large as it had been in gross size, was probably considerably lower in combat effectiveness. That would have troubled her even more, but the enemy had suffered worse than her squadrons...and they had lost Jake Stockton. There was no way they hadn't suffered more, and any new forces—probably at least half—they had in their numbers would be even weaker than hers.

At least she believed that. The reality of facing the enemy had taught her not to make any blanket assumptions.

She angled her ship back toward the fleet, tightening her angle of approach. She'd come out and checked the maneuvers of three different formations, and she'd been more or less pleased. She sometimes had trouble dealing with the new fighters, but she had to acknowledge that the pilots today had performed well, despite the fact that they were mostly drawn from the new formations. She'd mixed the forces fairly well, but she had so many new pilots, she couldn't make sure all of the formations were heavy with experienced personnel.

She blasted her engines, partly out of an impulse to get back faster, and partly to see how quickly her escort managed to match. The pilots were taken by surprise, but they responded very quickly, and they closed the distance in less than thirty seconds. She was impressed.

Reg knew Stockton had practically built the modern Confederation fighter force, that it was *his* place at its head. But she had been there four years now, and that made it hers as well. She could see the logic of stepping aside, of welcoming Stockton back...and in part, she felt that way. But only in part. She didn't have anything against Stockton, not anything real at least. She knew he had been controlled, compelled to work for the enemy. But if he was able to have the device completely removed, he would be back, in every way that mattered. And Reg knew she would have to stand aside, allow him to take her place.

She understood, and she even saw the rationality of it...but she still didn't know how well she would do it. And she wasn't sure what she would do until and unless she had to. In the meanwhile, she had to lead her forces. And lead them well.

She tried to force her mind back to commanding the forces and away from concern about what to do if her old friend—and her current potential nemesis—arose to challenge her place. She didn't enjoy the thoughts she had, but she couldn't deny that she had them.

And she knew she wouldn't know what she would do to hold her position...unless it actually happened. She was sure, at least, that it wouldn't happen for a while. She was safe for the near-term future, at least.

* * *

Stockton walked into the room, alone save for Stara Sinclair. He had spent the night before talking to her, mostly arguing with her, trying to explain why he *had* to do this, why he couldn't wait, especially not for a time that might not come. Stockton told himself that Stara understood, that she herself would have made the same choice if she'd been him. And he was sure that was right. But he couldn't burn through her blizzard of resistance, at least not until just an hour or two ago. He wasn't sure if Stara had actually realized *why* he had to do it, or just if she had been worn out fighting and realized she wasn't going to convince him otherwise.

He was just as glad to have her with him—awake the whole night. Partly because he knew it might be his last evening…and partially because it didn't give her any time to try to interfere. He didn't really expect that kind of resistance from her, but he was just as glad to be sure.

"Jake…Stara…" Stockton had known that Tyler would be there, but the two had never expressly stated that, and he was relieved despite his expectation. He really wanted to see his friend one more time…at least.

"Tyler…I'm glad you could make it."

"Of course, Jake…you knew I would be here." He might have had a difficult time getting away so early…except that Andi was off even earlier. The two had been incredibly close for years…but now there was something coming between them, and the fact that both of them knew what it was didn't help at all. He didn't even ask where she was going, though of course his mind had been busier even than usual this morning. He didn't actually expect Stara to disagree with him on Jake's surgery, but he hadn't told her…and that alone was part of the problem. "Hello, Stara…" He knew Stockton's companion would be in a more difficult condition, but in truth, she was perhaps a bit better than he had hoped.

"Hello, Admiral…" Her expression was tiresome, perhaps, but as much as she would have cancelled Stockton's surgery if she'd been able, he realized she'd known that it was coming. Stockton had surprised her only with the haste of his actions…and as much as she'd wanted to argue against the procedure, she'd known it was coming. And, in her heart of hearts…she didn't really object to it.

"Hello, Tyler."

Barron turned toward Stockton. "I knew you'd be early…but I was even earlier. The doctors are almost ready."

Stockton nodded. He was sure about the surgery, but now as the time approached, he was becoming a little edgy. "It's time." He said the words, more for himself than for his two comrades.

"It is time…" Barron repeated his words. "Do you two want some moments together?"

"No…we've said everything, Admiral." The words were surprisingly from Stara Sinclair, and the lack of doubt shocked Barron. She recognized the surprise, and she said, "I don't want this…both of you know that. But it's not a surprise either, and I know how important this is to Jake." She looked across the room at both of her companions, her expression hard. It was clear to Jake, and to Tyler as well, that she *was* shaky, struggling to hold herself. But she *was* holding on.

Stockton turned toward her, and he extended his arms, taking hold of her hands. He looked at her for a minute, gripping her hands tightly, and then he leaned in, kissing her. Then he turned toward Barron and said, "I'm ready."

Barron moved forward, and he extended his hand, shaking Jake's. "Right through there," he said, pointing to a door.

Stockton stepped back, and for a few seconds, he looked like a child, as though his stamina was going to drain away. But then he recovered, enough to offer a final glance at

Tyler and Stara…and then to walk through the doorway, toward the waiting operation.

Chapter Ten

Highborn Flagship S'Argevon
Imperial System GH3-2307 (Beta Telvara System)
Year of the Firstborn 391 (329 AC)

"We are ready. If our timing goes off as planned, the attack deeper in enemy territory will occur shortly after our own. It is, of course, a secondary operation, with only positive results possible. The enemy just *might* manage to assemble enough forces to defend against the secondary attack—though that is very unlikely with the newest forces I have sent—but even a defeat would be a near run affair, which would leave the enemy far too little to invade the Union itself."

Still, it was clear Tesserax questioned whether it was worth launching the secondary assault at all. "Nevertheless, I believe I will send orders to the secondary force to stand down for the moment, while we launch the main assault here. While I don't feel there is much risk, neither do I feel there is a significant amount to gain. I also feel that Villieneuve has a large number of new Union ships under construction, all significantly superior to the previous vessels he had had."

Gaston Villieneuve and the Union had been, first and foremost, an ideal conquest, one accomplished with

astonishingly little force. If he'd known how well his forces
would have done there, Phazarax would have dispatched
more Collars with them. He knew he would catch up
eventually, but for the moment, most of the Union spacers
were not so equipped. Another reason to wait.

"I agree, Tesserax. While I do not think failure is likely, I
do not see the offensive at this time to be anything
approaching critical." Phazarax agreed with Tesserax, at
least in the most part.

He had no doubt that the Confeds were now in every
way the foremost of the powers standing against the Union,
a distinct change since the top position had been occupied
by the Hegemony. His data on how many ships the Confeds
had held back versus how many it had advanced to the
primary theater was less complete than he would have
liked...but it didn't really matter. Whatever happened in the
Union sector was secondary, and therefore, not really
essential.

The true result will be determined here, in the main sector.

"Still," Tesserax said softly, "I wonder if sending word to
the forces present in the Union to stand down makes sense.
They cannot harm us by acting, even if they cannot do so by
remaining in place either."

Tesserax spoke calmly. He was the leader of the entire
war, and it was his place to sound confident. Phazarax
reminded himself that he was confident as well. He feared
more trouble from the enemy, perhaps, more difficulty in
completing the conquest than his friend. But he didn't
exactly see any chance the humans would actually
prevail...just that the total conquest would prove more
difficult than expected. Which, of course, it already had.

Phazarax more or less discussed every major operation
with Tesserax, but he accepted that his primary purpose, the
appeasement of occupied populations, was paramount to
him. Part of his motivation for that, most of it, in fact, was
based on the realization that it was simply true. In point of

fact, Phazarax was behind on his own schedule, more so than anyone knew. He told himself that was because Tesserax hadn't delivered the systems quickly enough, and while there was *some* truth to that, he had to acknowledge, at least to himself, that the enemy was just difficult to contain.

He had suffered somewhat on his own, but he had still performed far better than Tesserax had. He didn't exactly wish ill prospects on his partner, not at all actually. But if one of them had to look bad, it didn't take long to figure out who it should be.

"I believe that it will be best to delay the secondary operation, Tesserax…" And mostly, he did. But he also suspected that without considerable success soon, his partner just might be replaced. He had hidden his own problems well enough that he *probably* wouldn't be switched out along with Tesserax, but he liked his associate, and despite a few concerns, he preferred things to remain the way they had been. And it was better for both of them to avoid any heavy glances from above. "…but I just want to state that this next assault—the main one, I mean—will have to show considerably more gain than the last one. The action in the Confederation is secondary, and it can be postponed."

The room was silent for a moment. Then Tesserax responded, on a totally different topic. "I believe the initial scans and readings on the humans were incorrect. They are a more difficult opponent than we expected, especially the Rim-dwellers." A pause, only a few seconds. "That said, I do believe we are finally able to launch a decisive attack. We will take the remnants of the enemy's station and drive them from the system. Our regular fleet is probably sufficient to accomplish this, but the four new ships definitely are. The offensive in enemy space can wait. I believe that if we send an order of that type now, it will arrive shortly after the latest reinforcements…and in time to take effect."

Phazarax nodded. Again, he agreed with most of what

his friend had said. Certainly, the four new ships, the most powerful on either side, would make a huge difference. The enemy's single vessel of comparable size and power had been blasted almost to a wreck...and even given the best possible repair efforts, it could only be very moderately returned to duty, if that. He also considered the fact that the enemy had put that ship up against the first of the copies...and they won the fight between the two vessels, if by the smallest margin. That was a reckoning, that the enemy possessed the edge, at least in combat between nearly identical forces. Worse, perhaps, the human version of the ship was old, more than three centuries. The Highborn version, on the other hand, was brand new...and yet it lost, if only by a small margin.

At least that ship would be out of the next fight...or it would move in, expecting to be the only monster of its kind...and it would be faced with four fully operational versions. Either way, it wouldn't be a major part of the battle, not really. And Phazarax knew that was good...because the humans were racing toward imperial-level technology, and they would reach it soon. Another reason to win the war as quickly as possible.

"I agree, Tesserax...with the caveat that we must win this fight soon." Again, although his own progress was also below initial expectations, it was better than Tesserax's. He might survive his companion's fall...but he didn't want to chance it. "We must at least take the base this time and drive the enemy from the rest of the Hegemony. At least." His voice became serious, and he looked across the open area, staring right at his friend.

Tesserax returned his gaze, and he said simply, "I know." A few seconds passed, and then Tesserax said again, "I know."

* * *

Percelax sat quietly, analyzing the approaches. He had three ways he could go to reach Grimaldi, three routes that all closed on the immense fortress. *The once immense fortress*, he thought. He knew that the enemy was rapidly repairing it, but he also realized that even a Herculean effort would fall short in less than several years. The enemy might get more done than he expected, but they would never complete more than a small part of the total job…not in the time he was going to give them.

That amount, the time, was fixed now. He'd had to estimate the arrival of the last convoy of warships sent from home, but now he knew exactly where the ships were…in the Union itself. They were still a dozen transits away, but that was nothing at all compared to the distance they had come. And it meant his assault could begin in less than a month…perhaps as little as three weeks. He could use the time to prep the rest of his fleet, though he'd pretty much kept his forces ready to attack the instant the new ships arrived.

"Commander…we have brought Villieneuve to see you."

Percelax nodded to the Highborn. He didn't have many of them in his force, less than an eighth as many as the main fleet. He'd decided to maintain good relations with all of them, even though he knew many of them hoped for casualties among them…and the requisite increase in rank. The Highborn commanded ships at least, or they filled roles in his command structure…and they advanced almost uniformly when one of them was killed. That worked, of course, for everyone but him, the commander of the theater.

And anyone already higher-ranked than the lost Highborn…

He was the only one whose death would allow every one of the Highborn in his command to advance, and he never forgot that. The forces assembled under him didn't exactly *hope* for heavy casualties among the Highborn…but it *was* a way to advance, and for most of his top personnel, probably the only way, in the short term at least.

"Bring in Mister Villieneuve."

"Yes, sir." A moment later, Villieneuve entered.

"Mister Villieneuve...greetings." The sound of the Highborn's voice was respectful, but it was only lip service. None of his people saw the humans as anything except tools, certainly not individually. He didn't either, but he demanded some level of responsiveness from his Highborn, and he decided to set the standard himself.

His attitude toward Villieneuve had changed somewhat in recent months. He still remembered the man's insolence before his Collar was installed, with some anger. But he had to admit, since the installation of the control device, the leader of the Union had gotten downright pliable...to him at least.

"Greetings, Commander Percelax." The tone was perfect. Villieneuve was as gruff as ever with his Union forces, perhaps even worse than he'd been before. But he was the perfect gentlemen with Highborn.

"I wanted to update you on the situation. We will be attacking Grimaldi again in approximately three weeks. I want you to use that time to assemble as much of your fleet as possible. Any ships that can be done and here in time— even if they're not one hundred percent complete—should be here." This was a change from Percelax's original planning, but he understood that the enemy was stronger than he might have anticipated...and he was going to bring all he could to bear.

"Very well, Commander Percelax. I believe that we have a number of ships close enough within a range of 90-95% completion. Three weeks including transit time will reduce the number of ships considerably, but with your permission, I believe I can assemble a fair quantity."

"Very well, Villieneuve...go now and assemble all you can. We will leave in approximately three weeks. We will hit the enemy hard, and we will prevail." He gestured for the human to leave, without any further communication and, after a bow, he did. Then, he exchanged glances with the Highborn still present. His intention was the same as with Villieneuve, but the Highborn didn't get it as well. Not until he said," Go now…I want some time alone."

He watched the Highborn leave, and he wondered about whether the superiorities his people felt above the humans were factual. But such a thought only lasted for a moment. Then he dove right into thinking about the offensive…and about the forces he was likely to have available. And how they were very likely superior to those he would meet.

* * *

"I appreciate your presence, Phazarax. You could have justified staying away, and I will remember that you did not." Tesserax spoke softly. It wasn't long after their last encounter, but he had noticed that his—friend, he guessed, though he still wasn't sure—had remained. He'd considered ways to handle Phazarax that still defended against any effort by his companion to challenge him, but he'd decided that he had to simply hope his counterpart remained genuine. He was the cockier of the two most of the time, and he did expect to prevail in the coming fight, by every measure he could calculate. But he'd begun to worry at least somewhat about what surprises the enemy might have left to unveil.

"This force is the greatest we have presented to the enemy, Tesserax…even without the four great ships. With them, I can't imagine that the enemy will stand. I will be honest, I am still worried about the campaign in its totality, especially if a large portion of the enemy fleet escapes, but I am not truly concerned about the battle." Phazarax was silent for a moment, then he added, "If I may suggest one thing, Tesserax…perhaps the new ships would be best deployed in the rear. Or at least back from the front lines at first. When the enemy realizes we have four ships of that type, I can't imagine that they won't pull back immediately...and I think the more we can draw them in, the better chance we have of wearing them down."

"Your opinion matches mine, Phazarax. The ships are well back. They will not even transit until the battle is joined...and if the enemy decides to pull back once they detect them, they will already be engaged. At best, they will suffer terribly. At worst—for them at least—they will be virtually destroyed."

"I agree completely with your thinking, Tesserax. Completely." He did. Phazarax knew he was the more conservative of the two commanders deployed to eliminate the human threat...but he genuinely did not see a way to lose the coming fight. He could envision the enemy perhaps pulling out in better shape than he expected...but there was no way his vision could encompass a human victory. Even with his realization of previous encounters, and the unforeseen enemy actions, he believed that this time, at least, the forces Tesserax had assembled, were more than sufficient. He was not ready to see victory in the war, at least not without some considerable amount of fighting, but he did believe that the coming fight would be a profound victory.

"I go out now to order the transit into enemy space. Would you care to come with me?"

Phazarax hesitated a moment. Tesserax was definitely different. He knew it was the time the campaign had already taken—far more than expected—and the uncertainty about the humans, and about just how much he would have to crush them to secure their total defeat. He knew his companion, perhaps better now than anyone else, and he was sure Tesserax would return somewhat to his old style once the battle was over, and hopefully the situation was noticeably better. But Tesserax wouldn't entirely forget the difficult fight the humans had put up...and that would be enough for Phazarax.

"I would be delighted, Tesserax. Let us go and take the enemy fortress. Whatever remains of the enemy after the fight, it will be a major victory."

Chapter Eleven

Forward Base Striker
Vasa Denaris System
Year 329 AC (After the Cataclysm)

Barron sat still, silent…waiting. He had a million things to do, but his mind was stuck on Stockton. He'd spent the first hour sitting in the room outside the surgery center, but then he'd realized the operation was going to take hours. *Hours.*

He finally broke free, came to his office and tried to work on the other things he had to do. Unfortunately, he could only work for a few minutes before his mind went back. Stockton was a close friend, very close. He had given in to Stockton's wishes because he'd known it was the only way…but now that it was underway, he second-guessed himself. He knew he couldn't blame anyone else if the surgery went poorly. He hadn't let anyone know about it, almost no one save the doctors and the rest of the medical staff. He told himself now that he should have convinced Stockton to wait a few more years, that the situation would have been better, but he realized he didn't know that. Not really. In fact, he honestly thought now was as good a time as ever, especially since he expected things would likely get worse, not better.

Most of all, he realized he had reacted to how well he

knew Stockton, which was enough to tell him his friend couldn't endure years longer. The right answer was varied for different people, but he was sure he'd made the right choice for Stockton.

Most of the time, at least.

He pushed through some of the paperwork on his desk, piles of manifests, reports on new production—and on the division now in place that sent him only about two-thirds of the production of the shipyards. He knew why that was. He'd even agreed with it, one hundred percent. At least when he thought of himself in terms of the joint command, which he did most of the time. But there were moments when his own position enveloped his overall point of view...and he realized that he could lose in both places, when he might have at least won on the primary front if he'd delivered all the new ships to his location.

That was not true of course. If he'd sent all of the ships to his current location, he would have left the backward path totally open...and the enemy would have scurried forward and taken out his source of all supplies. The overall situation was far worse even than he allowed himself to believe, but he realized the backward position was as important as the forward one, perhaps even more so, at least in some ways.

But mostly, his mind went back to Stockton, again and again. One instant he was glad for what he'd done, and ready to face off the pressure he knew would mount as soon as anyone else found out about it. The next, he was almost ready to call down, to see if it was too late to stop—which by then, of course, it was.

A soft buzz went through the air. For an instant, he was unmotivated, but then it repeated itself. He looked down at his desk and slapped down on the small control. "Yes?"

"Jake...it's Andi."

He was surprised. Once, he might have expected it was her, but the relationship between the two had grown quite—strange—in recent months. It was no secret they had become poster children for two sides of the same debate...and as much as they had remained together, they had also come apart.

He pressed the button, opening the door. "Andi," he said, trying to hide his surprise, but failing to do so, at least enough for someone who knew him so well.

"Tyler..." Her words were as forced as his. It was the most difficult meeting he could recall between them, and as much as he knew why that was the case, he felt the urge to find a way back.

"Andi...I..." As much as he wanted to get past what had troubled them, he found himself stuck. He didn't know who had more support, but he was sure it was moving in her direction. Perhaps she had the majority already...and honestly, if he lost any of the strength he had, he was dead. He was probably dead already.

"Tyler...I wanted to talk to you, to try to work this out. We both want the same thing. We both care about the Confederation, about the future. It's just how we get to it that differs."

"That's true, Andi." The words came out of him, almost without effort. But then he went silent for a moment, realizing that she had expressed a valid concern, but not any real proposal. "I'm just not sure how we can do that."

"I wasn't either. I'm still not, but honestly...I can't just ignore you, and our relationship. I know you feel like you have a *real* chance, and I understand why." There was a short gap, and then Andi continued. "But I wanted to say, it will be another month before I can do anything, anyway. There is no way of knowing whether that month will see an enemy attack, but we're both on the same vein until then. I will work with you any way I can for that month. I can't promise beyond that, but for now, I think a month is something worthwhile, at least."

Barron sat still for a few seconds, but then his head

began to nod. "You're right, Andi. For the next month, we're more or less on the same vein…and if the enemy doesn't attack, not in that month, you're probably going to gain support. I agree that taking the matter bit by bit is the way to go. I can't promise you that if the enemy does not come in that time, I will be on your side." He stopped. But I don't think you expect that."

"No…I don't. But right now, I'm willing to settle for a month of being together…and we'll see what happens after that. Okay?"

Barron shook his head, and the reached out for Andi. "It's a deal." He pulled her close to him and he hugged her hard. He knew they had only agreed on a month of peace, but that seemed a long time to him just then. And, despite the fact that he was against Andi's position—then at least—part of him knew he might get to it. If the enemy came in the next month, if they drove his fleet back from Striker…would he still be against striking back in *any* way?

He couldn't say…and he probably wouldn't know until that moment, if it came. But he was glad for a month of freedom, for 30 days of a united front.

He enjoyed it for about two minutes…then the buzzer on his desk went off, and he found out his 30 days had been cut down to one.

*   *   *

"Alright…we're almost ready to start removing the construct. Bear in mind that this is connected to him in fifty different ways…and if we miss even one of them, his life is in danger." The senior surgeon, Jordan, spoke as his hands moved all around Stockton. He was nervous, edgy…and despite his willingness to do the operation, he was now second-guessing himself. He'd done two of the previous attempts, and he was 0-2 so far. But he'd studied the procedure for years now since his last attempt, and he'd make definite progress. He was far from sure he could do it successfully, but he knew he could take the procedure farther than he had before. He might have turned down someone with a normal device, but Stockton's was at least deactivated…and the chance to work on the only such device had overcome his caution.

"I think we should go over every connection one more time…just to be sure. This thing looks simple, but in fact, it's the most complicated device I've ever seen, and I don't want to overlook anything." The second doctor, junior only to the chief surgeon, spoke, his voice carrying both legitimate warnings, and also some hesitancy. He sounded much like the chief surgeon, and the head of the operation thought for a moment about stopping. But that wasn't a possibility. They'd gone too far, and there was as much likelihood that Stockton would die if they stopped as there was if they continued.

"I agree." The head of surgery wasn't sure that his agreement was anything more than buying another hour before he had to lead the crew in actually removing the strange device. But he couldn't find anything else to say. "Let's start down at the bottom. The lower connections all seem to be separated…or deactivated. Do you agree?"

The second surgeon—subordinate in a procedure for the first time in at least ten years—reached down and took a moment longer, but then he replied simply, "Agreed."

"Okay…" The senior physician moved his hands slowly, feeling his way around. He worked his way slowly up. "Lower connective devices appear removed as well. There is still a connection…but as far as I can tell, it is just for blood flow."

His co-surgeon, number two, but also one of the few doctors that had worked on a patient, trying to remove a Collar—with no more success than the senior surgeon— was silent for a moment. Then he responded, "I can't see anything…but that doesn't mean there isn't something else running through the one connection. I mean besides blood."

The senior surgeon looked back at his cohort for a moment. "Look…we can say that there are unexpected aspects to all of this, which there are. But all we can do is the best we can."

The second doctor nodded after a moment. Then he said simply, "I can't see anything else."

"Very well…" The lead surgeon reached up a little higher. But the klaxon sounded before he was able to say anything else. He told himself it could be a hundred things, only one of which meant a major enemy attack. But he knew what it was…and it only increased the already crushing pressure on the whole team. "Alright," he said, "even if that is warning of an enemy attack, it is at least two systems away. We'll be finished with the surgery by the time anything can reach here…so just stay focused, and let's get this done.

* * *

Barron raced out of the room, followed closely by Andi Lafarge. They'd enjoyed a very short time together—very short—before the alert had pulled them out to the bridge.

"What is it?" He asked, but he knew what it was.

"We don't know for sure, sir. Some kind of enemy activity."

Barron ran across the open area toward his chair, gesturing for Andi to take the chair next to his as he passed it. His eyes were already fixed on the screen, as his hands moved across the controls, bringing the image up.

He'd known what it was before…but he'd fought against it, imagined other things. But the first glance at the screen told him all he needed to know. The enemy fleet was coming…and it was a large force. The month he had discussed with Atara, the time he had considered before, was gone. The main enemy fleet was two jumps away, possibly even one jump just then…and there wasn't any doubt about it. It was a major attack force.

He stared for a moment, and then he looked back at Andi. She was still…but just as sure as he was. It was the main enemy invasion…and it wasn't coming in a month, or two weeks even. It was coming *now*. And it would be through the jump gate and present in twenty-four to forty-eight hours, depending on the assortment of vessels the enemy placed in their vanguard.

"That's the main attack…there's no question."

Barron was still looking at Andi as he spoke, and her eyes told him she agreed with him completely. A second later, her voice re-emphasized it, saying one word. "Yes."

"I want all the data we can get before those scout ships have to depart. And I mean, I want the newest vessels to stay as long as they possibly can." Barron knew just what he was asking for, especially with the crews he'd picked out for the forward ships. Some of them would probably stay too long, even by design, deciding their survival was secondary to gathering the greatest intel possible.

Barron hated himself for it, but he was hoping the same thing. He'd come a long way into accepting death among the legions following him, and even if he wasn't ready to join Andi—and probably many of the others—on their route toward a true fight to the finish, he'd become far more bloodthirsty and violent than the man he'd been before. Casualty levels that once would have laid him out were now just the results of a mild skirmish, and the biggest battles were almost unimaginable nightmares.

"Yes, Admiral…they have been so ordered, but we will repeat, and add your request."

Barron was silent for a moment. He felt a momentary urge to tell the aide not to send the message…but in the end, he allowed it to go through, only speaking once it was done. "Send word to all officers…I want everybody here in two hours for a meeting." He knew the term "all officers" wasn't specific enough, but he also knew his aides knew who he meant.

"Yes, sir."

"And track those incoming forces…I want updates every hour, wherever I am." He got up, only a moment after sitting.

"Understood, sir. Every hour…wherever you are."

Barron nodded, and then he looked at Andi. He'd been at odds with her for months now, but he knew he could count on her…certainly in the current situation. "Will you join us in the meeting, Andi?" His voice had lowered, not enough to make his words indistinguishable to the others present, but sufficient to make it clear he was talking to Andi.

"Yes…of course." She sprang to her feet, even as he walked past her, heading toward his office again. She was right behind him, and she followed him back into his office.

Chapter Twelve

Forward Base Striker
Vasa Denaris System
Year 329 AC (After the Cataclysm)

Barron sat at the table, his mind still reeling, despite almost twelve hours since the enemy was first discovered. Or at least since word had reached the station…Barron knew that even at full speed, that took a number of hours.

He'd had a large meeting, nearly thirty people, but now he had retained just eight. The others had been sent back to their ships, to prepare for the fight they all knew would be the toughest yet. He had to let most of the others go soon, too. They were, for the most part, the highest rankers in the fleet…but he had one thing to discuss with them first.

He had excused himself three or four times to check on Stockton, and to his amazement, the surgery was still underway. That formed a record for survival, at least, as Stockton was still alive considerably longer than anyone else had lasted. But the doctors had projected a time of eight to nine hours, and they were well beyond that now. Barron had planned all along to tell the key people about Stockton's…situation…but he'd hoped to at least have a finished status, whatever it was. He didn't have anything like that, just the fact that Stockton was in surgery—which would be news to everyone there, including Andi—and he had no real idea how things were going.

"I wanted to keep you all here to discuss one other thing." He had intended to just blurt it out, but now he found himself having trouble. He sat still for perhaps twenty seconds, not very long in one sense, but it seemed like it. Then, he said it. "General Stockton…he wanted to try and have his implant removed. He came to me, and I approved it. I assembled the team, and they're working on it as we speak."

Barron didn't know how the officers surrounding him would react. He'd have bet that the Hegemony personnel, and the Alliance leader, would take a lesser view. But he had a number of other officers who might object.

"Now? You mean he is in surgery *now*?" Clint Winters spoke first, sounding surprised, but not exactly committal, either way.

"Yes…right now. I mean, it started before we got the word on the enemy, of course. I would have put it off if I'd known."

"We've known about the enemy for almost twelve hours…it's been going on longer than that?"

"Yes, Clint…about thirteen and a half hours so far. I probably shouldn't have done it on my own anyway, but I definitely wouldn't have had I known this was going to happen. I mean, six months of nothing, and the surgery starts a couple hours before the enemy is contacted. There are some things you can figure…and others that just happen."

The room was silent for a moment, but Barron took the lack of anyone erupting at him as a good sign.

"I understand why you did it, Tyler." The voice was different, and Barron recognized it instantly. "And I understand why you couldn't tell any of us." Andi sat a few seats down the table from Tyler, and she looked at him. "Aside from the question of what to do, generally, I realize that you consider yourself Stockton's mentor…rightfully so. And I expect it was his insistence that drove you to it."

Barron looked out, first at Andi, and then at the rest of those present. Chronos and Akella, along with the Imperator, looked on, but though they knew Stockton, they didn't really expect to be notified of anything, and they were more or less just there. The rest of those present, all Confederation people, had various levels of ability to get upset, but generally, they all looked like they at least understood Barron's intentions.

"Thank you—all of you. I was afraid there would be some…more trouble. I just believed, in the end, it was Stockton's decision…and I can assure you that it *was his*. I didn't really want to proceed with it, but I felt that he had the right to make it." A short pause. "Of course, if I'd known the enemy attack was coming…"

"There was no way to know that, Tyler." It was Clint Winters, who had beaten out Atara by the briefest amount. "But your timing was almost perfect. And the surgery *has* been going on a *long* time."

"Yes, it has." Barron looked down for a moment, and then he glanced back over the table. "I just wanted all of you to know about it. I assume the surgery will be done before the enemy attack arrives, and I will send Stockton out of here before the fight begins." Assuming he survives was not said, but everyone present heard it nevertheless.

"So, now that that's done, I suppose there is nothing left to do but send you back to your ships. I considered whether to position myself here or on *Dauntless*, but I decided to remain here. The station isn't as strong as it was, but I'd bet we're tougher than the enemy thinks." He turned toward Atara. "You're in command of *Dauntless* again of course, and the entire section of the fleet she leads. You did as good a job as anybody could have last time, and I am absolutely sure you will do it again."

Atara nodded her head. She looked like she wanted to

question Barron's decision, but she didn't.

"Okay, so thank you again for understanding my decision regarding Admiral Stockton...and I will see that any updates are immediately sent out. We don't need this to be generally known, of course...especially not to the pilots." He stared for a moment at Reg, who paused for a second, but then nodded her own approval. "Very well...return to your ships. With any luck, we will all be here in a few days." He said it, but he didn't believe it...and he didn't think anyone else did either.

He watched the leaders shuffle out, until only Andi remained. Then he looked over at her, suddenly devoid of whatever assurance he had possessed. "Andi...I hope I'm right. I hope that we can hold again, drive the enemy back." He paused for a moment. "But if we can't...well, I'm not ready to sign on to your deal yet." He paused. "But if we lose the fight, if we look like we're going to lose the fight...I want you to promise me something."

She looked across the room at him. "Of course, Tyler...what?"

"I want you to promise me, if I fall here, if the enemy is too strong...I want you to escape. I want you to try your way. I'm not ready to give up, but I have decided if it comes to a choice between being conquered or striking back any way we can...I'm with you."

Andi looked back, clearly troubled by Tyler's statement. But she just answered him, clearly feeling that it wasn't enough, but not knowing what else to do. "Yes, Tyler. I will do that." She was clearly unsettled at his tone...but she didn't say anything else.

*   *   *

"Alright, pull it now!" The lead surgeon on the team cried out, even as his hands were buried inside Stockton. He and his team, more than a dozen in all, had encountered one thing after another. To be honest, he was stunned that Stockton was still alive...and he knew that it wasn't by much. He'd progressed to removing what he believed were the last of the implant mostly because he couldn't imagine his patient would survive much longer...not because he was sure he had cleared away all of the obstacles.

"Alright...I'm pulling now." The second surgeon sounded just as concerned, and the two of them pulled as hard as they could. They both knew there were components of the device that they still didn't understand, but both of them in agreement, they had used all the time they had.

Maybe even gone beyond it.

"Remember...when we pull the thing out, he's gonna bleed...badly. We've got 20 units of blood ready, so the two of you on that, think of nothing else."

"We got it."

The two surgeons pulled as hard as they could...and slowly, the implant began to move. For an instant, the movement was slight, and then, almost as one, it came forth.

And it was out.

The blood poured, almost unstoppable at first, and the two attendants started pouring in replacements two at a time. Even with the insertables, they seemed to be losing ground at first. The two primary doctors put the implant down, and they immediately began working to seal off the damaged arteries. For a minute, it didn't look like they were accomplishing anything, but then, the blood flow diminished. It was a little at first, but the two professionals, as exhausted as they were, continued to work, and the blood loss gradually slowed. There were at least two dozen places pouring out blood at the start, but within a few minutes, fewer than half a dozen remained, and the flow of replacement blood pouring in exceeded that flowing out.

Still, the doctors worked, shutting more bleeding wounds until none were left...at least none that were still bleeding profusely. The first patch jobs were temporary, and now the doctors went back to them, working steadily on each one. By the time they had finished, they had pumped eight liters of blood into Stockton…but finally, they stopped.

Their patient had been through hell, that much was true, and it was far from sure he would survive. The surgery had been more difficult than either had expected, and they had encountered one problem after another. But their patient was still alive…and the implant was gone. Whether any bits remained, whether Stockton would survive the surgery, was still anyone's guess.

But they had come farther than anyone had yet…and their patient was still alive. Whether he was brain damaged, whether his survival would last more than a few minutes, they didn't know. But he was alive, longer than anyone else had survived…and that was something.

* * *

"Thank you, Doctor…there is no way to know what will happen, but your ability to bring him through is noteworthy. Congratulations." Barron was edgy, worried that Stockton would never regain consciousness. He regretted his decision to allow the surgery, at least in some ways, and he hoped, with all his heart that his friend pulled through. Stockton had become the first to survive the removal of the enemy pod, and even if he died later, he would remain that. But Barron only cared about speaking with his friend, seeing him up and around. He didn't have any odds on that happening, but he guessed they were less than fifty percent.

"Thank you, Admiral. I sent my companion, and most of those who participated in the operation to bed. I'm going to stay with him, though, at least until my partner has gotten some rest. That was a tough fight, but I was the senior one, so…" He let his voice trail off, but Barron understood completely.

"Again, doctor, whatever happens, your ability to save him…even if he doesn't make it the whole way…" Barron spoke the words, but he wasn't sure what he expected. One instant, he was sure Stockton would survive, while the next, he was just as certain his friend was lost. And the doctor didn't do anything to help with any of that. It was only Barron's guess, but he was pretty sure the man was about 50/50 on Stockton's survival. The fact that he had remained on duty, despite being profoundly exhausted, told Barron the surgeon figured the first day or two would be the most critical.

"What can I do for you, Doctor?"

"Nothing." Then the doctor said, "Just hope for the best. There was no traceable damage during the surgery, which means less than it would in a more familiar situation…but it is still good."

"Well, doctor, first, I've got to move you. I've got the enemy coming as you know—they have already transited into the adjacent system—and I've got to get you out of here."

The doctor looked back at Barron, and in an instant, the naval officer knew something was wrong. "What is it, Doctor?"

"We can't move him, Admiral…not for at least a day, maybe two."

"No…I understand that you might normally not want to…"

"Sir, it's impossible. If he is going to survive, it is going to take a lot. But if we move him in the first day, and more likely the first two, he's definitely going to die."

"Definitely?"

"I'm not sure what has kept him alive so far, sir. If we move him right away, he's going to die."

"But in a day, two days certainly, we'll be in the middle of the fight."

The doctor stood for a moment. Then he replied, "Then

we will be here during the battle...but I can't leave him. And I don't imagine any of the team will be willing to either."

"Doctor..." Barron felt uncomfortable. Most of the doctors and other professionals who'd conducted the surgery were not regulars...and the two senior participants were not military at all. They had come forward, worked alongside the spacers for more than two years now, but Barron understood that was different. "We may not win, Doctor. We may be driven off...we could even be wiped out. We don't know what is going to happen."

"Admiral...you have many fans, both back home and here. Me, for one. Some people may overestimate our chances, but I am not one of them. I will stay here, and I am sure my team will as well, though I will ask each of them. You have to focus on the fight that is coming, I know this. And I have to fight for my patient. If we are destroyed...well, odds are, it will just be a bit earlier than it would have been. There are people in the Confederation—and in the other places as well—that will likely choose life even with servitude...but I am not one of them."

Barron still felt the urge to argue with the doctor, to convince him to leave. But he knew the words about Stockton were true, and his loyalty went to his friend first. It was bad enough the pilot was stuck where he was, that he would have to go through the early part of the battle...but if he had to remain, Barron was okay with his doctor—with the whole damn team—remaining too.

"Thank you, Doctor...really." It was all he could think of to say. That, and one other thing. "I've got to go now, Doc...but thank you. And thank you from Jake." *Even if he never wakes up to give it...*

Chapter Thirteen

Highborn Flagship S'Argevon
Imperial System GH3-2318 (Telus Draconis System)
Year of the Firstborn 391 (329 AC)

"Launch the first wave." Tesserax sat still in the center of the flagship's main bridge. He was sending forth the largest number of ships he had ever commanded, though his first wave was less than half of the vessels at his disposal.

It was all the enemy could expect, all he had allowed to advance before each of the last three systems was fully secured. It left a break in his formation, of course, spreading his second wave out farther from his first...and his third out even more. The third was just four ships, but in some ways, it was the heart of his force. Certainly, his four largest and most powerful ships. He had almost removed the flag from *S'Argevon* and transferred it to one of the monsters...but he'd decided to hide the mammoth vessels until the battle was heavily engaged. He was still tempted to transfer to one, but in the end, he'd decided that he had to be farther upfront...even if he intended to stay back from the lines of engagement.

"The first wave acknowledges, sir."

Tesserax listened to the words, but he barely heard them. He knew what they would be, and that they would come, but despite his outward appearance, he was edgy. He knew he had the enemy, and he was sure that his forces, especially including the four mammoth warships to the rear, were more than strong enough to defeat the enemy. But he'd come to fear the humans as well, at least on one level. He knew that he had the power to crush them, he was sure of that…but they were stronger in every way than he had hoped.

Still, the time for that method of thought was behind him. Now it was time to crush the humans, to destroy their ability to resist his forces…and to begin the final stage of the conquest. That last bit could take years, perhaps, though he knew once the fleet was mostly destroyed, the end result would no longer be in doubt.

He sat back and watched his forward line move toward the jump gate, the route into enemy territory. He'd been in many battles, titanic conflagrations on the alternate front before he'd been sent to the human battle line. But the coming fight would be the largest he had ever endured.

He saw as his forces, as the hundreds of ships in his first line moved up to the gate, dropping in one after the other. He knew they were appearing in space in the enemy controlled system, several lightyears away. In less strict times, he'd wondered about the transit points, speculated on whether they were natural occurrences or the creations of some long-ago creatures. He'd never come to a conclusion, but he'd decided, through nothing more than speculation, that some ancient, long-dead species had created the network.

He watched for a few minutes, as more ships moved up to the point and vanished. The total transit would take a long time, hours. He'd watched it many times, so many that he'd stopped being amazed at the majesty of it all. But just then, he realized how many tons of ships were being moved, farther in just a second or less than they could have gone in fifty years through normal space.

Tesserax wondered about the universe, and for a few seconds he postulated about a reality where mankind—and its creations, as he realized the Highborn were, at least in that moment—lived in peace, alongside each other. It was a ludicrous assumption, of course, not just opposite the Highborns' notion of running everything, and practically against human history. For hundreds of years, thousands no doubt, mankind had fought with himself. Even the centuries of imperial rule had eventually become based more on the exhaustion and the fading advancement of the people. He wondered if there was any way, any methodology that could result in true peace...other than the conquest of the humans.

No! His Highborn training struck back against the thoughts, *his* training—and his core attitude—re-establishing their position. The Highborn were superior, they were made to rule mankind. It was natural, and the humans' ability to resist more effectively than expected meant nothing. His people didn't want to *destroy* mankind. They wanted to control them, to see to their future. The war made sense...it was the right course. Mankind had built the empire, yes, and it had endured for a very long time. But it had seen civil wars, too numerous almost to count. It had endured all kinds of conflicts, all sorts of struggles...at first to establish itself, against the other human cultures...and then against itself. It had lasted a long time, but even that period was superficial. When the Highborn had defeated the humans, and when it had won its other fight, it would impose a great domain on all, one based on its superiority...and all would live under it as long as civilization endured.

That was the idea, at least. Whether it would come to pass, whether the Highborn would continue to respect those developed earlier...remained to be seen. Tesserax wanted to believe the current hierarchy could remain, if only because of his position in it...but then he imagined being even higher, perhaps replacing Ellerax at the top. It was unthinkable, of course…but he thought about it anyway.

He shook his head, cleared the thoughts from it. First, he had to win the war here, and do it quickly. Victory would give him great appeal…as another defeat would bring him doom. He had to win, and he was sure this was his last chance.

Fortunately, he had a powerful force, stronger than any that had come before it. It was enough, he was sure of that.

As sure as he could be anymore.

*   *   *

Percelax sat quietly, watching as the ships transited into the system. It was the final shipment, the last vessels he could expect until the final battle on the main front was fought.

He considered that for a second. Certainly, Tesserax held a higher place that he did—something he had accepted, more or less—but was his position, so much farther out from the Confederation, really the primary one anymore?

The Hegemony had been considered the primary human establishment, but that had been before the humans out on the Rim had been identified. The Union had been easy enough to take over, through control of its single leader, Villieneuve…though he wondered how many of its people still supported the defeated opposition. But the Confederation, if only because of its position, back farther from the enemy, was now the most serious contender. More than half of the Hegemony was occupied, and the effect that had on trade and internal support had reduced production even more. Percelex didn't have specific data on the percentage of ship development that remained active in the sections of the Hegemony that were still possessed by the humans, but he would have been surprised if it was 25% of the prewar total.

And the Confederation's was at least 200%, of an already very high quantity. Something had been loosed in the

Confederation, some kind of raw power, and despite Percelax's derision for his lowly human opponents, he had to admit, it was a surprise.

The ships coming in were enough, he guessed, by almost any means to defeat the enemy, to destroy the remains of their fortress, and to push on farther. But it wasn't enough to *really* launch an attack on the inner systems, or at least it wouldn't be by the time the battle was over. Percelax wanted to take the best numbers, the most pleasant results…but he'd fought the humans before, and he knew that they were completely aware of the threat he posed. He would win the first fight, he was sure of that, and he would destroy everything the Confeds put up to fight. But they would hurt him, too, and probably badly.

He needed more ships to win the war…and he knew he wouldn't get more unless Tesserax broke through. Which made the success of his own effort largely dependent on that of his rival…or his ally, depending on how he broke it down. There was no way to overturn Tesserax, not if he won. He would do better as a loyal ally.

And a successful one.

If Tesserax was somehow pushed back, and if he lost his command…well then Percelax would really have a chance to take overall command. But only if he was successful, only if he took Grimaldi…and beat back the Confederation forces in their own space.

Either way, he had to make the attack…and he had to win. It was either his glory alongside Tesserax's…or separate and exclusive. He'd pondered a hundred times whether it made sense to launch the attack at all, or if the battle would be decided on the main front. It was possible that waiting made the most sense…but not to him. His own glory depended almost entirely on reaching out and fighting the battle. On winning it.

"As soon as the last ships are through, I want to set up a transmission to all personnel. We will be setting out for the enemy fortress almost immediately, and I want to speak to everyone before we do."

It was time...time for him, at least. He had to win his glory, before Tesserax grabbed it all.

* * *

"I am going forward with Tesserax. I believe he has correctly formulated an attack now, and especially with the four massive ships, he will drive the enemy back, and destroy their Striker Base. I am less certain than he at least appears to be that he will obliterate the enemy fleet. Even if they are lured into a close fight, I am inclined to believe that more of them will escape than he assumes. Still, I believe his assault will be successful, and will mark at least the beginning of the end in terms of this conflict. It is possible, likely even, that a devastating enough attack, even if it leaves some significant portion of their fleet intact, will result in a shattering of the enemy's power. The Hegemony and the Confederation will come to a point that may even drive them apart, and their civilian and military forces may diverge. There is no way to predict exactly what will happen, but I believe it was only the 'victory,' or at least the fact that they held the system after the last battle, that was critical last time. Had we waited, had we had sufficient forces to drive through the enemy, and take the fortress, I believe we may have already seen a more precipitous drop in enemy preparedness."

Phazarax spoke freely, more so than was wise perhaps. The only man present, however, was Dothorax, whom Phazarax trusted as much as he did anyone. His aide was far enough beneath him that he lacked the temptation to betray him, preferring to work with him on joint operations. He was ranked tenth overall on Phazarax's team detailed with operating the captured territories...but as far as Phazarax was concerned, the man was number two.

"So, you feel you should go…to be present when Tesserax concludes a victory?" Dothorax spoke softly, though the two were alone.

"Yes, basically. Understand that, while I do not wish to go down if Tesserax fails, I do believe he is actually the best choice for the military role. I believe the humans are more powerful than we expected, and that, while we can still defeat them, it will be more difficult than Tesserax originally thought." Phazarax stopped for a moment, but then he realized again it was just Dothorax with him. "More difficult than I anticipated as well."

"I understand…you want to be present when the victory is won. But what of your own efforts? They are running behind schedule, too…and several of your aides are not entirely trustworthy. Is it wise to separate yourself from them?"

Phazarax exhaled, a bit more loudly than he'd intended. "I understand there is a risk, but I have assumed that Tesserax would not be replaced prior to the coming fight, and I was right about that. And I feel my position is stronger than his. If the coming battle fails, if he is withdrawn, there is some doubt that I will remain…but I feel we have this fight. If it is won, and I fully expect it will be, then both of us will be secure, for at least another year, and very likely two. And if the battle *is* won, I believe it will be the primary moment of the conflict. While I expect certain aspects of the enemy forces will continue to fight, some for a long while, perhaps, I believe that the ultimate victory will be assured. And I am sure Ellerax will agree with that…and all realistic assessment of any problems for Tesserax or for me will be gone."

"I agree with your assessments, Phazarax." Dothorax spoke carefully. "So, where would you like me to go? I assume my presence here is not by chance."

"You assume correctly, Dothorax. I want you to leave the fleet immediately and return to the capital. I will not be away long, but I want you to keep an eye on things while I am. I want to take no chances, especially not if Tesserax is indeed about to prevail." He looked closely at his aide, by far the most reliable of his people. "Do you understand?"

"Yes, I understand."

Phazarax nodded. He had done everything he could do. The rest would be fate.

Chapter Fourteen

Forward Base Striker
Vasa Denaris System
Year 329 AC (After the Cataclysm)

Barron sat quietly on the station's bridge. He was second-guessing his own decision to remain on the station instead of *Dauntless*. The choice was easier the first time. Striker had been by far the most powerful entity in his fleet, and as much as he preferred the confines of *Dauntless*'s bridge, he'd recognized that his place was on the station.

Striker was still the most powerful component in his fleet, that much was fairly certain. But it was maybe twice as strong, and not ten times or more, as it was before. The bridge looked pretty good, as he'd had it cleaned up and repaired as much as possible...though there were still a number of signs that the fight before had been a near run thing.

Barron had been almost everywhere on the hull—and out in space once too, floating around, looking at breached sections, trying to decide which ones were the most crucial, and which ones could wait. He'd emphasized weapons wherever possible, but the station was at best at a third of its prior ability, and probably less than a quarter, if he considered all aspects.

Still, he'd decided to remain on the station. First, it was hard to leave after remaining the first time. That would only have enhanced the realization that the station, and the whole fleet, were very likely outgunned. Second, it would have emphasized that while he was fighting, when push came to shove, he was far from sure his forces could hang on...and he was more comfortable someplace that could run.

And, third, though this had not been part of his planning, Stockton's presence made his own all the more vital. That wasn't a real reason, or at least not one that he could state...but he couldn't leave while Stockton was still there. And at last check—about twenty minutes before, the officer was still out. Whether he'd wake up at all was an argument for doctors to have, perhaps, but Barron knew he couldn't leave until Stockton did, and the pilot's surgeons were still saying moving him was the equivalent of putting a gun to his forehead and pulling the trigger.

Still, Barron had a small ship maintaining its readiness, and he was prepared to order the doctors to leave with Stockton regardless of their opinions. He wasn't sure how far he would go, how deep into battle he would allow the station and its huge fleet to get before he issued the order. But he knew he would send Stockton on his way before the station was destroyed. Whether he actually survived it was up to him.

He fixed his eyes on the main screen. There were over 200 enemy ships already present, with another one coming in every few seconds. He knew the enemy fleet would be big, but in truth, he didn't have any real idea what to expect. That, at least, he would know soon enough. So far, it was an enemy force he could take...but he had no true expectation of what was coming in total. If it was as big as the last fleet, he had a chance, barely. If it was bigger, well, whatever prospects his fleet had sunk rapidly.

"Forward line...prepare to advance." He had been a bit timid before, held his forces back. But now he realized, he had to take advantage of any benefit he had, even if it wouldn't last. He had positioned his forces somewhat forward of their position during the last battle…and now he was going to send them in. He was well aware of the dangers of tying his fleet up so far, but he knew the battle about to commence was the last chance to stop the enemy. If he lost the battle, he was sure he would lose the fight to eradicate the enemy.

Losing the fight about to begin would be bad, but he didn't see any route to victory aside from it. Except for the last effort…and to be honest, he didn't think that would work. They might kill a large number of the enemy—if the serum worked and if the enemy had not cured it already—but not enough. And if effort made the enemy decide to destroy the humans instead of capturing them…well, they possessed almost two hundred billion Hegemony citizens just as a starting point.

"Line is ready, sir…they're awaiting your word."

Barron nodded. He knew what he had to do. He'd considered it a hundred different ways, and he'd discussed it with all his friends and co-workers. They had all agreed. But now that the time had come, he was not so sure. He would hit the enemy before they were all through, that much was true. But if there were more of the enemy, more than he could handle, his forces would be farther forward. He almost reversed course, ordering his people to stand back. But then, he realized that everyone had agreed…and even that his position as commander of the combined fleet was simply the result of an informal agreement. He couldn't change things, not now. There wasn't time to disturb all his colleagues with something that could be, almost certainly was, just his nerves.

"All ships…attack."

*   *   *

"You heard the command. Forward, all units. Let's hit the enemy hard. We don't know what's coming, but we know what is here. So, let's hit it and hit it hard."

Atara listened to Clint Winters's voice, as it was coming through on every Confederation ship in the formation. She was number three now, in the Confederation command, by nothing less than Tyler Barron's order. The man she was listening to was number two, and to her, far above her and not just one rung up. She knew her promotion was ahead of several other officers, but she also realized, she had been behind for a long time, and there was fairness in it, of a kind at least.

Assuming she wanted it, which she wasn't sure she did. The truth was, while she didn't have any thoughts that Barron lacked, she tended to believe their chances were small...and she was closer to coming around to the belief that the only real hope was to *truly* attack the enemy, to fight to the end. The real *end*.

"Alright, people...you heard Admiral Winters. All ships...forward." Whatever she believed, about the chance for victory, or about other alternatives, she knew where she was now. Whether or not she believed they had a good chance, she was already in the fight. And one thing Atara knew about herself...once she was in the battle, she was in.

"Yes, Admiral."

She heard the confirmation, and she just nodded her assent. She was focused, staring straight ahead. *Dauntless* was once a model of the best the Confederation navy had, but it had been eclipsed by the *Excalibur*-class...and a number of others. *Dauntless* was still a powerful ship, of course, but she would still have to endure enemy fire for at least 30,000 meters. Her side to side maneuvering gave her a decent chance of closing to enemy range, at least, but Atara knew she would lose ships before the enemy did. That was just a facet of facing so many enemy vessels with longer ranges.

So be it. We will face whatever.

She felt her doubts fading. They weren't gone, but she had the ability to focus on the fight at hand. Whether her forces could win could only be decided by the battle, and what they would have to do to get there was already decided. Now, there was just one thing left to do.

Fight.

She stared at the screen, watching the distance countdown. The enemy fleet would open fire soon, and no matter how well her ships evaded, she knew she'd lose some before they were able to fire. The first battles with the enemy were harsh, but the Highborn had learned from their experiences, just as her people had. The incoming fire was focused now, designed to accomplish the most possible before it became a true two-way fight. If her ships performed their evasion a bit better, fewer would die, at least before they could fire. But only three of the Confederation vessels, all under Winters' command, could actually shoot at close to the enemy ranges. It was one of the worst disadvantages her people had been forced to deal with, and even if the difference had declined somewhat, it was still probably the enemy's greatest superiority.

She watched as her ships moved into range of the enemy ships. She wasn't sure exactly what distance the enemy would open fire at—there wasn't so much an actual range as a point the enemy's targeting and the impact of the weapon would make sense. There was judgment there, whether to open fire at longer range, with lower effectiveness, or shorter distances, with more power. The enemy had done both before, but as she pressed onward, she realized they were waiting this time.

Longer even, than before, she realized, as her forces moved more than twenty thousand kilometers beyond the farthest the enemy had opened fire at.

Still, there was no fire. Thirty thousand kilometers…and the three superbattleships in Winter's command opened fire first. The vessels were enormously powerful, but there were only three of them. They were welcome…but they weren't decisive. Not alone.

Two of them scored hits on the first shot, an edge, she realized, especially at the length of the range. One enemy ship was badly damaged, and the other moderately so. It was relatively meaningless, she realized, nothing that made much of an impact on the overall fight. But she still found herself cheering, surprised that her side had scored the first hits.

Thirty-five thousand kilometers. She was below the lowest range the enemy had ever used to open fire. She was beginning to get unnerved. In another fifteen thousand kilometers, her fleet would open fire. She couldn't believe the enemy was waiting so long.

And she knew they wouldn't wait until she entered range.

They didn't. At forty thousand kilometers, the enemy's forward line opened fire…as one. The blasts came forward, hundreds of them…and they were aimed at only ten ships. Most of the shots missed…but the ten targets all received hits, and four of them were badly battered. One of them was knocked out completely, and Atara wondered if the ship's com was out…or if everyone on board was dead.

She didn't find out, at least not just then. A second wave of shots rang out. Again, more than ninety-five percent of them missed. But the ones that hit, struck hard. Two of the damaged ships were destroyed, and half a dozen others were hurt.

But it was almost time for her own ships to open up. She faced one more round of fire, with only the three superbattleships responding, and then her own battleships would be in range, too. That didn't mean her forces would gain the advantage, but they would definitely start shooting down enemy ships as well as losing them.

The timeclock advanced, and just before her ships opened fire, the enemy forces fired a controlled volley. Almost ten percent of the shots hit her forces, and four more ships were destroyed or at least taken out of the fight.

It was worse than she'd expected, worse than her lowest expectation. But now her ships could fire, too.

She looked straight ahead, and she mouthed one word. "Fire."

*   *   *

Chronos watched his ships open fire, and he saw the effect. His flagship was dead on, and it scored no less than fifty percent hits, but overall, it was a rather weak effort. He knew the morale of his forces, between seeing the Confederation rising in prominence, and just in dealing with a conflict that had cost more than half its worlds, was declining. In some cases, sinking rapidly. He understood, knew that he had forces that had families left behind, men and women who were dead, or who had probably been turned over to the enemy. Or even who'd received the Collar, a terrible result to any non-controlled person.

Chronos understood...but he knew the only way to overturn the enemy attack, to free those who had survived on occupied worlds, was to win the war. The only problem was, he didn't believe it any more than the rest of them did. He would fight, he would struggle onward, but he had begun to wonder when his people, still officially part of the Hegemony's old system, would begin to think more for themselves. He had met with relatively little trouble yet, though it was perhaps double what he'd seen before, but he was sure if the current battle was lost, he would see vastly more problems.

He would *be* more of a problem, too. He had held firmly to Tyler Barron's plan, and he had to admit, so far, he had endured more than he could have imagined. He'd steadily lost influence too, as his own production levels slid to virtual meaninglessness next to the almost unbelievable production of the Confederation. He needed the Confeds, like he'd never needed anything before...but he was sure if the current battle was lost, his vital ally would opt to retreat, well past the entire Hegemony, and into the Confederation itself.

Unless they decided to launch the last-ditch effort to destroy the Highborn. Chronos had tried to avoid it, tried to think of continuing the fight. But he knew, as well as he could, that not even Tyler Barron could prevent the retreat if the battle was lost...and his own allies, the Council, would never agree to yield up the last of the territory it controlled. They might support the decision to strike at the enemy with the final weapon...but short of that, they would try to fight, even if it was just them.

And they would lose. Badly.

Then, after they were defeated, some might actually retreat to Confederation space...but others would probably yield to the enemy, and they would help bring legitimacy to the occupation. Chronos liked to believe that no meaningful percentage of the established Kriegeri would agree to join the enemy, though he was far from sure of that. At their heart, the divisions of Hegemony culture were only guidelines. If the enemy came in and declared the Masters replaced, would those who had always served rise up?

He didn't know, and he tried not to allow himself to care. He had a battle raging, and if he was doubtful of his ability to win it, he was far from sure. His people were going in, and he had promised himself one hundred percent to it. If he lost—and survived—then he would decide what to do next.

But for right now, he would fight...he would fight like no one ever had.

Chapter Fifteen

Forward Base Striker
Vasa Denaris System
Year 329 AC (After the Cataclysm)

Barron watched the battle unfolding before him. The enemy ships were still coming through, and that was a point of endless concern. When would the enemy force finish its transit? When would the last ship come through?

There had been a hesitation, about an hour without any transit. He had been sure the enemy would have *some* more ships, but as the time continued to pass, he'd imagined that he was wrong, that the enemy actually didn't have more vessels. He told himself they were as backed up with damaged ships as he was, that his shipyards had actually superseded theirs.

Then, the progression resumed...and it had continued since.

The second enemy force, the ships that had transited after the delay, stood back for a moment, holding off their involvement for close to another hour...before the first batch headed forward. Then, he picked up the ship his records stated had been the enemy's flagship in the prior battle...and he believed the enemy commander was present.

The fighting was beyond the station, at least so far. He'd

sent his ships in, expecting the enemy to pour forward from the transit point the instant they were able to come through. But now, the second half of the enemy force had given his ships added time to hurt the forward vessels, and his people seemed to be winning. Whether they *were* winning enough to prevail against the enemy's second line depended on how large it was. And even while the first part of it was just beginning to advance, more was still coming through the point.

Still, the battle was going well...too well, perhaps. Everything Barron could see was better than he'd expected. It was what he'd hoped to see, how he'd felt in his wildest fantasies. But now, it was different. He found himself not believing it, assuming the enemy's second wave would be even larger than the first. Something was wrong, he was sure of that...suddenly.

"Send word to the top commanders...I want to speak to them all." The words were stark, unexpected, even by him. But he'd said them, nevertheless.

"Yes, sir...just a minute."

Barron nodded, and as he thought, he decided even more assuredly. He couldn't explain it...by every measure, his forces were getting the best of the fight so far. But he wanted them back...now. They would have a chance, for a little while. The enemy first line was disordered, battered. His forces could probably pull back before the first tranche of the second line reached them...if they moved now. That didn't make much sense, of course, not with the enemy approaching from behind. He might still lose, but he couldn't have hoped the battle would have gone better. Still, something told him to pull back. Now.

"Top commanders all assembled, sir. On your line."

Barron just nodded to the officer, and he tapped the comm. "I'm sorry to disturb you all now...I know you've got a lot going on." He paused a moment, trying to decide exactly how to put it. He'd sent his ships forward, and that had worked better than he'd hoped. Now, he was going to pull them all back. He wondered if any of his people would understand, if he even did. "I want all of you to disengage, to pull back."

He waited, just a couple seconds, while the signal traveled the distance to the ships of the fleet, and the first response came back. He'd hoped it would be from Atara or Clint. He was far from sure they would agree, of course, but they were the ones most likely to at least listen, if only because they were officially under him.

But the first response was from Vian Tulus. The Alliance Imperator was the commander of the fleet's third force, and the least advanced. And he almost always agreed with Barron. But this time, his blood was up. "That is not possible...not now! We have the enemy, and even if they continue to bring in more ships, we have the best chance possible!"

Tyler wasn't surprised at Tulus's remarks, especially since he didn't have anything but a feeling to back up his own. The officers would have to agree with him. His position as commander-in-chief was still informal, and they would all have to take his position, in spite of what appeared to be the best possible situation in the fight so far.

Barron knew all the officers would respond, and he didn't want to allow the time to pass. They would all say the same thing...they didn't know if they were going to win, but they thought the situation was as good as it could be. Barron knew that...because he had felt the same way. Until a few moments before.

"Look," he said, speaking over the others starting their own comments. "The enemy has never been this careless. Perhaps they didn't expect us to advance so quickly, I'll admit that's a possibility. But think, really *think*. The enemy we've faced, would they really advance in such a sloppy way? Would they leave over an hour before sending in their second group? Or are they exactly where they are supposed to be? The enemy has been a difficult fight, always. Are you willing to believe that after the last battle, they would enter this one with *less* planning? Are you prepared to bet your lives on it?"

Barron didn't know how he had done with the others, not yet, but he was surer than ever that sending his forces so far forward was foolish. He just *knew*.

"Tyler, you're asking us to give up the best chance of victory we've had, to pull back and allow the enemy to transit all of their forces in. Can you give us more...why?"

Tyler was glad to hear Atara next. She was the one most trained to following his orders, and he guessed she would be the most easily convinced. And he was actually the commander of the Confederation forces, which mean that she, and Clint Winters, would have to obey his orders ultimately...or take things to another level.

"Atara...I don't have anything more. I just think we're doing what the enemy wants us to do." He paused for a moment, and then he said, "What would you do if you were the enemy? If you had more ships, and if you wanted to finish us here?"

The comm was silent for a moment. Then, Chronos came on. Barron knew he was probably the most crucial one. His own subordinates would obey his orders in the end, he believed that. And Tulus would as well, though he would probably put up the biggest fight. But Chronos...

The top commander of the Hegemony forces would need to retreat, he told himself...he couldn't stand alone against the enemy if everyone else pulled back. But he wasn't sure. Not until an instant later, when his voice broke through.

"All right, Tyler. You've led us well. Let us fight for another twenty minutes...that will be the point at which the enemy's second group is closing. It will extend our period of advantage, and we will destroy more enemy ships. Then we will retreat...and see if the enemy really has the level of forces we're afraid they do."

Barron sat for a few seconds, his mind doing calculations. Twenty minutes was close, especially for damaged ships, which would have reduced velocities. He knew it would kill more of his people...but more were going to die anyway. Worse, if he was wrong, if he was giving up the best chance to win the fight...

"Okay...twenty minutes, and not an instant longer. Agreed?"

The responses came back after what seemed like a longer period than just the small delay imposed by the distance. "Yes," his officers replied, and so did Chronos. It took longer, but Tulus came out last, and he merely said, "Yes."

Barron leaned back, knowing his action had only saved the fleet from being caught up too far to retreat. If the enemy was going to be stronger, it was still going to be...and all he would add to his own mix was what was left of Striker, and possibly the even smaller remains of *Colossus*, which he had held back, away from the fight so far.

It wasn't much, but it was all that he had, and it would have to do.

* * *

"All ships...and vessels with damaged engines, begin to pull back now." It wasn't something discussed in the recent communication, but Winters knew it made sense. Any ships with badly damaged power systems were likely to be caught and destroyed by the enemy, but maybe some of the ships would make it. It was a hope at least.

"Yes, sir." The officer responded, and he immediately reissued the order to all human ships.

Winters thought for a moment about speaking to Chronos, and also Tulus, but he decided it was pointless. Chronos would see what he was doing, and if he hadn't thought of it himself, he would copy it. Tulus would be slower, and the damaged Alliance ships might suffer…but Winters didn't have the time to deal with the him now, anyway. He had less than fifteen minutes until the entire command would join the damaged ships and begin the retreat.

The repositioning, not the retreat…

He reminded himself, the fleet was not withdrawing from the fight, not yet. But he was starting to realize that Barron must be thinking already beyond the battle. If the enemy's second group was not large enough, his forces would have done better far to the front, where they were. There was a point in between, where the addition of Striker and *Colossus* would matter, but he realized it was relatively small.

And then there was perhaps the likeliest scenario, where the enemy had enough forces to win no matter what. Winters had done all he could to keep that thought from his head, though he realized it had always been the most likely. As he sat in his place, he came to a stunning conclusion, one that radiated out, against the resentment he had felt against Barron's orders. He realized the command met his expectations before the fight began, and suddenly, he agreed completely with Barron. He'd allowed his experiences in the early battle to color his view…and now he realized, he had done just what the enemy wanted.

It was the right thing to do…he was sure of it suddenly.

"All damaged ships are heading back, sir." A pause, and then: "At least four of them are moving at less than fifty percent speed though…"

Winters understood. The four ships—and possibly more—weren't going to make it. He'd known that all along, but there was nothing to be done about it. Far more ships would be destroyed in the fighting before the battle ended, whether that end was in victory or defeat.

"All remaining ships, maintain fire at full." He ignored the last bit of his subordinate's report. There was nothing he could do about who would make it and who wouldn't. All he could do was sustain his position, make sure everything was done the best it could be. He had suggested the twenty minute delay, but now he doubted it was worthwhile. Still, there wasn't really time to change it, not much anyway, so he was determined to get everything he could from it.

"And I mean *full*, Commander," he added.

*   *   *

Tulus sat calmly on his bridge, the ultimate Palatian leader, ignoring the damage, the absolute carnage affecting both sides. He had argued against the suggestion to retreat, but he knew that was mostly his Palatian side. He tried his best to show his people that he was entirely Palatian still, but the truth was, he had become half Alliance and half Confederation. Even his Palatian desire to carry on the fight, while it was strong, was not enough to cause more than the sole argument he had made. He was still Palatian in his expectations, mostly, but he knew enough to trust Barron's point of view.

Still, he believed most of his people were against pulling back, and he felt the need to maintain their urge to fight. They were only moving to a new location...and the battle had a long way to go.

"Alright, you heard the orders...prepare to pull back." A short pause, then: "And remember, we're just repositioning, not fleeing. Stay focused."

He knew his orders would be followed. The Alliance Imperator was the absolute boss, in peacetime yes, but especially during war...and Tulus was a candidate for the most revered Imperator in Alliance history. Even if most of his warriors disagreed with his decision, they would follow it.

"Yes, sir." The response only reiterated his point of view. The deliverer didn't agree with his orders—that was fairly clear—but he wasn't even close to speaking about it, much less disobeying. And that was fine with Tulus.

He turned his head, snapping out a reminder he suspected was unnecessary. "Maintain full fire."

"Yes, sir." A little more excited than the previous one, but Tulus was sure both of his orders would be obeyed.

He turned and he looked up at the screen. His ships were among the weakest ones in the combined force, stronger only than the small commands contributed by the tiny powers on the Far Rim…but somehow, they fought well, even though they were no real match for the enemy craft.

At the moment, his forces were even dominant, nearly 60 craft stationed against perhaps a dozen alien ships. It was a passing moment, he knew, and the result of his own force's position on the extreme right of the formation, but it made it extremely difficult to follow orders. Even for him.

"Increase rate of fire." His ships were already firing at full speed, but they could go a bit more. He knew it, and he was sure his people did as well. "All ships fire at maximum possible rates…in excess of posted maxes."

"Yes, sir!" That time, Tulus was certain his aide was on his side. He'd turned down two requests already by the ships of the fleet to switch to the absolute maximum rate of fire, but not knowing how long the fight would proceed, he'd declined both.

Now, he had issued the command himself…and he watched as his ships continued their engagement, seeing the vessels with no damage, and the ones with top crews, surging just a bit ahead of the previous rate of fire. It wasn't a large differential, but it was one that paid off almost immediately, as one of the enemy ships caught shots from three of his largest vessels…and after just a few seconds, it blew up. It was just one ship, and he'd lost more than he'd taken out so far, but it was well-timed, and he took it as a sign.

And he had about six minutes to go before his fleet had to depart. Six minutes to take down more enemy ships.

Chapter Sixteen

Forward Base Striker
Vasa Denaris System
Year 329 AC (After the Cataclysm)

Barron stared at the screen, watching as his fleet—and official or not, that's precisely how he saw it, as *his* fleet—prepared to withdraw. There were about two minutes left, and he was impressed by the effort his forces had put into making their last few moments before withdrawal into something truly special. The pullback, when it began, wasn't going to be all that far. It was just back to the position of the previous battle, just far enough that it brought the station—and an assortment of mostly damaged ships that had remained back—into the fight. Most importantly, it would give the enemy the chance to show what they had in their second wave. If it was small enough, Barron would confess that he had been wrong, that his caution had cost the fleet a real chance at an early victory.

But he didn't think he was wrong.

Barron had been considering the situation, from before he'd issued the still-controversial order, to beyond, and he was surer he was right, even than he'd been. The enemy made mistakes, certainly—the fact that the battle was still raging attested to that—but he couldn't believe they had invaded with too little. Besides, his forces were not at their strongest fighting up so close to the front. It was better to withdraw, to make a stand alongside the station, where they had fought before.

One minute to the withdrawal. The flow of incoming section two ships had slowed, and Barron knew if he'd been wrong, he'd just allowed the enemy to bring their forces together. But he was sure he wasn't wrong. He didn't know why, exactly, or how…but his worry was that the second enemy force was too large, not too small.

Despite the current slowdown…

He saw that the flow of enemy ships had declined sharply, though…and if most of the Highborn fleet was already present, he *was* making a mistake. But he didn't think he was seeing the whole enemy fleet, and despite the doubts, and the signs that the whole force was, in fact, already through, he expected more.

He counted down, slowly, to himself over the last thirty seconds. He had the assurance of every major officer that they would obey his orders, that they would pull back. But he still didn't entirely believe it. Not until a few seconds later, when almost as one, his entire force began to retreat.

Barron felt some joy at the unity, but he also had another wave of uncertainty. He was sure the enemy had more ships than those that had appeared already…but the transit rate had definitely slowed, almost stopped, and he couldn't help but imagine that he was wrong. If he *was* already facing the bulk of the enemy force, his people had the time to cancel the order, to reverse the command. He would look foolish if he did that, but that was the least of his concerns.

But he still believed there were more enemy forces, probably more that he could handle even at the station. He wanted to believe he had called the fleet back to fight in a new position, and on some level he had. But he had also called it back far enough that some of it, at least, could escape if necessary.

What good that would do if he lost the fight, he didn't really think about. He just looked quietly as the ships began to pull back, and he pushed aside concerns that he was wrong about the size of the enemy fleet.

He wasn't wrong, he was sure of that…somehow.

He looked forward, at the enemy forces, wondering what else was coming…and if he could hold it, or if his entire effort was just a waste of time.

*　*　*

Sonya Eaton sat quietly, on the bridge of *Colossus*, trying to maintain her calm. She was a visitor to the battle, at least so far, and she hadn't been authorized to advance. She knew that made sense. After all, six months of repair had just been a start to bringing her ship back, and *Colossus* was at *maybe* twenty percent of its total capability.

And maybe even less.

Still, the battle pulled on her, and watching the fleet fight…and then withdraw…was difficult. She understood what Barron was doing pulling the forces back, but she was uncertain if it was the right thing to do. Could the enemy have more forces waiting to come through? Absolutely. But was it certain? No, it wasn't.

She tried to imagine what she would have done, but all she could come up with was a realization that she was glad she didn't have to. She felt the urge to pull her own ship forward, certainly, but she couldn't really argue for that on any logical basis. *Colossus* wasn't ready to fight, not on any level, and she knew that.

But she still felt the pull to sally forward.

"Status?"

"All systems active, Commodore…as much as possible. We're as ready as we can be."

Sonya listened to the report. She could tell by the tone that the officer was ready to go forward, to launch *Colossus* into the mix, to fight with everything. But despite the clarity of his tone, his training affected his words, and there was hesitancy as well. She felt the same way. She *wanted* to plunge forward, to throw her ship into the mix…but she understood why she was being held back.

She just watched the screen, saw the fleet pulling back. She understood the situation, and she knew why Barron had issued the orders he had. But she wasn't sure what she wanted. She understood what Barron feared, and she knew he might be right. But she just didn't know what she wanted.

Except to lead her ship forward…which she knew she couldn't do. Not without Barron's okay, at least. And that hadn't come yet.

She watched the fleet breaking off, saw the whole line pulling back. The ships had an advantage, at least until the lead ships of the second enemy force arrived—then it would become more even—but they were sacrificing that now. They would gain the support of the station and a few damaged ships that were held back, but whether they were doing the right thing or not was beyond her. It was a guess, and she just didn't know what answer was correct. She realized what still mattered the most was, did the enemy have more ships…or was most of their available force now online?

She would find that out, fairly soon. If there were more enemy forces, they would have to advance shortly. Holding them back for a few hours made sense, perhaps, but any longer, and they wouldn't get into the fight.

She stared ahead for a moment, and then she turned quickly and said, "I want a full check done…all active systems." Eaton knew it was likely Barron had no intention of putting her battered ship into the mix, but she knew he might have to, and she was going to whatever she could to ensure the vessel was ready.

Ready for whatever.

* * *

Chronos looked at the enemy line, battered and ravaged. They were staying behind, holding their positions, waiting for the second wave. It's what he would have done, too, though he was still surprised the enemy hadn't pursued his forces with everything they had on the line. That would have just continued the fight, of course, and it would even been a disadvantage to the enemy, for a while...but he'd expected it, nevertheless. Perhaps the fact that the enemy was remaining behind, waiting for the rest of its forces, suggested that they truly *were* smaller than he'd expected, that the forces in the system were all or most of what they had.

But for some reason, something he couldn't express, Chronos didn't believe that. He'd been swept up in the fighting at the front, convinced pursuing the enemy as aggressively as possible was the way to prevail. But as soon as he had actually pulled back, he saw Barron's point of view, too. So much so that he'd begun to agree with the commander.

The enemy forces were sufficient, of course, but they didn't exactly measure up to the worst of his concerns. He'd spent no small amount of time pondering what the enemy would throw at the defenders, and he had to admit, the current forces were smaller than he'd expected. While he was on the line, fighting, he thanked the powers that be that the enemy force was less than he'd feared...but once he'd begun to retreat, his mind had freed up, and he'd seriously begun to consider the alternatives.

"I want constant scanning of the transit point...and I mean constant." In truth, he didn't know if more forces would come through, but he'd begun to believe they would. He knew he was probably still in the minority, but the more his ships pulled back from the first fight, the more he believed it.

The enemy is not foolish...they would know by now what we can do. They wouldn't have attacked with just the force we can see now...

"Yes, sir...we have six ships scanning the entire area."

Chronos could tell that his aide was convinced pulling back was the wrong choice. Hell, he figured that almost all his people did. But the more he stared at the transit point, the more he became convinced there were additional enemy ships that would come through. He didn't know how or when, and he had no idea how much additional force there was. But suddenly, he was sure it was there...and positive Barron had made the right call. He knew most of his people—and most of Barron's—were still upset at the pullback, but he was suddenly sure it was the right call.

He was just worried about how much there was still to come through...and whether the forces he and his allies had would be enough to put up a good fight, to have a chance at victory.

Or whether they would limp away with whatever could escape. He knew he was committed to the battle...but he was just as sure that if the fleet couldn't win this fight, he'd be one hundred percent behind the effort to destroy the enemy completely, to take whatever chance they had with the virus. He knew that was partly because it would be the only alternative to utter defeat.

But another defeat would leave him angry too, enraged. It would cost him the rest of his territory, and it would leave him with no other option.

None at all.

*   *   *

Barron watched the ships coming back...and the transit point, now utterly silent. He'd decided that the enemy had more ships, that they had held some back for a while, hoping to draw him in. But he'd pulled his fleet back, and the remnants of the first force had waited for the second group to join them. He rejoiced in the momentary break in the violence, but he felt a pain in his gut, too. He hadn't given up on more enemy forces, far from it, but he had begun to at least question the presence of them.

If the enemy didn't have more vessels, his forces would still have a chance. They'd have been better off dealing with the enemy in two waves, and the Highborn were definitely more powerful the way they were, but he still had a chance to defeat them.

"Fleet units are out of range of all enemy ordnance, sir. They will begin to arrive in approximately forty-five minutes. Any orders?"

Barron turned and looked at his aide. The officer probably disagreed with his actions, if only because it seemed to him almost everybody did, but he was unreadable. His question was the one he'd ask, whether he agreed or not, and Barron started to think about what to say.

"Tell them to form up in the same positions they occupied before…right alongside the station. We will be the left flank." Barron had thought a long time about pulling back his forces…but he hadn't really considered where to put them. So, he just ordered them to the same place they had occupied before.

It didn't really matter. The enemy would probably come straight ahead, and if they did something different, he would have enough time to react. It wasn't the tactics that troubled him, nor the enemy's method of approach. It was just what they had, how much force he had to deal with, and whether his fleet had a chance.

He knew that was important for a variety of reasons. But there was one that stood above the others. He knew this was the last chance to defeat the enemy…at least conventionally. He realized, on some level at least, that he would have to embrace the alternate plan, the proposal to destroy all the Highborn. His opposition to that plan came from deep within. It wasn't that he felt any kindlier toward the Highborn than those already prepared to launch the final blow. He despised them as much as any of his people did, and perhaps more in ways. But he hadn't seen them all, and he found it hard to believe that they were all as bad as those he had encountered. The plan to destroy them wouldn't necessarily destroy them all, of course, but it would be indiscriminate. It would take military operatives and civilian personnel just the same. It would destroy those who had done everything possible to bring the conquest to a conclusion, as well as any who might have argued for more temperate measures.

Worst of all, perhaps, if it worked, if the enemy had not found a cure for it, it would sweep from Highborn to Highborn, with no regard for the outlook or opinion of the victim. The data he had on it wasn't perfect, but it seemed specific about one thing. The virus was extremely transmissible, and it affected all of the Highborn.

And unless the battle currently raging turned out to be a success…it would be the only chance for Barron's people…and in such a situation, he realized, even he would go for it.

Chapter Seventeen

Highborn Flagship S'Argevon
Imperial System GH3-2327
Year of the Firstborn 391 (329 AC)

"Damn...I really thought they were going to fall for it."
Tesserax sat in his office, aboard the flagship of the
Highborn forces. He spoke half to himself, and half to
Phazarax, the only other person present.

The battle was displayed on both the small screen on the
desk, and the larger one on the wall. Both told the same
story. The enemy was pulling back, all across the field of
battle. For an instant, he'd been worried the entire force was
pulling out, a truly unexpected measure. But he quickly
realized the fleet was just repositioning, that it was returning
to a line extending from the station.

The remains of the station, at least.

"It looks like they're just pulling back. It's a bit smarter,
perhaps, but if you feed the rest of the forces in, you will
still carry the day." Phazarax spoke matter-of-factly.
Tesserax had trusted him to an extent, but he'd also stayed
aware of the fact that their destinies were not entirely
related. If the current battle turned into a defeat, he was
finished. He was almost sure of that. Phazarax might go
down with him, too, but he might not. Still, he was pretty

sure Phazarax preferred him to be successful.

"Yes…that's true. But we have to feed the rest of the forces through carefully. Too much, too fast, and the enemy might bolt. And we need to hurt them here…very badly." *At least I do…*

"I would suggest putting half of the rest through and holding the other half—and the four specials—until we are fully engaged with the enemy. That way, if they try to run then, we will be able to hurt them at least…and if they stay too long, well, then we can really end things here."

Tesserax knew everything Phazarax said was true, but he was more cautious than he'd been before. He didn't exactly credit the enemy as much as he should, perhaps, but he was well-aware that the foe had fought much better than he'd expected. He knew that if he'd told himself five years ago, he'd still be fighting, he would have laughed at the thought. Now, he expected as much as another five years before the enemy was completely wiped out…and that assumed he won here.

"I was thinking the same thing." Tesserax wasn't above claiming that, even if it wasn't true, but in this case it was. He turned toward the comm unit, and he tapped the controller.

"Yes, sir?"

"Bring through half of the remaining forces. The balance, and the four specials, are to remain in place until I call for them."

"Yes, sir. At once."

He turned off the connection and he looked at Phazarax. "Once the enemy is fully engaged, we will call in the balance of the forces. That will be enough to take out the enemy, and even if they flee as soon as they pick up the approaching reserves, they'll be so badly beaten up by the time they escape, we'll have accomplished our mission. It will almost certainly take several more years before the war is truly over, but it will be decided here and now."

"I agree, Tesserax, and I agree that I believe holding back the truly overwhelming portion of our forces for a time is indeed the best strategy. Half of the remaining forces, minus the four specials, is fine, and I wouldn't send in any more until the lines are truly engaged...even if this costs us more in losses."

Tesserax listened to his friend's—and occasionally his rival's, too—voice. He'd been almost certain that Phazarax was entirely on his side, but now he was truly convinced. He knew his ally would part with him if the battle was lost, as he himself would do if their roles were reversed. But the two were allies, at least through the fight...and that was all he needed for the moment.

Tesserax sat in his place for a few seconds. Then, he stepped up and reached out, extending his hand to Phazarax. "This will be the last fight where there is any question as to the final result.

* * *

Percelax walked across the bridge and sat on the deck of his flagship, a battleship, one of the four he had received along with the mostly lighter ships that formed up his fleet. It was a new vessel, and he hadn't hesitated to transfer his flag. He was heading toward the enemy forces, determined to blast the fort to oblivion, and to destroy as many ships as possible, while driving any survivors deeper toward the center of the Confederation. He knew, on most levels at least, that he didn't have enough force to sweep the enemy away *and* close on the main worlds of the Confederation, not without considerable reinforcements. But he had enough to clear out the targeted system and maintain supremacy anywhere between the border and the inner planets, and he intended to do just that, at the very least.

He knew the main fleet was moving on the human forces deeper in the galaxy, and he was sure they would get there before he could reach Grimaldi and the human fleet stationed alongside. But he was determined to reach his destination as quickly as possible, before word reached him to stand down and wait…a definite possibility, especially if the other great fortress, Striker, fell.

He assumed the force would win the fight out on the main front. The forces present there were more than sufficient, especially with the four great new ships. He'd tried to get one of those himself, though he had failed. He knew his own position was somewhat less superior, though he felt he had more than enough to prevail. As long as he reached the enemy without any orders to stand down.

"Status of the force?" He mostly knew, though he was a little uncertain how much ordnance Villieneuve would manage to put together. The formerly difficult head of the Union was much easier to get along with now that he was properly controlled…and Percelax had almost forgotten how difficult Villieneuve had been before.

"We have…" The officer droned on, starting with a review of the Highborn section of the fleet, but Percelax knew that entirely…and he was sure it was all he was going to get, at least until the fight out at Striker was over. His mind wandered, listening only for the word that the report had turned to Villieneuve's force. Then he listened more carefully.

Villieneuve was a strange ally, much more like his usual self with other humans, but controlled and compliant when addressed by Highborn. The implants had worked on every human they'd ever been tried on, but the results varied from person to person. There was always obedience to the Highborn, of course, but the amount that remained of the subject in the presence of other humans, even those loyal to the Highborn, varied considerably.

And Villieneuve, while he obeyed any Highborn without question, was far less likely to work with his human colleagues, at least if 'work' meant anything but exerting full command. It wasn't exactly an odd effect, but the degree of it was far more than any Percelax had seen before. It wasn't a huge problem, but he had to remind himself to always have a Highborn dealing closely with Villieneuve…especially when so many of the Union crews were still not controlled by the Collar.

Percelax was surprised at the forces Villieneuve had assembled for the battle. He wasn't sure how much of it was from obedience, and how much from the latent desire of the Union leader to strike against the Confederation, but he had assembled far more than even Percelax's wildest views.

"Very well…" Percelax tried to hide his surprise, and he suspected he had managed fairly well. "Onward…we should be at the next jump point in just over four hours…" *And through the next four jumps in just over a week…and to the battle…*

That is far quicker than anyone expects. We will take the system, and we will at least threaten the rest of the Confederation…and we will do it before new orders can arrive from the main fleet. Orders telling us to hold.

* * *

The last of the forces had passed through the transit point, at least all of those that had been called. Half of the remaining ships had appeared, satisfying the perceived notion that the enemy had expected some more forces…while still holding back a large contingent for the final advance.

Tesserax watched, and his assurance of victory grew, though he realized that his hopes of enticing the enemy forward had been dashed, and along with them, the chance of ending the war in one fight. The enemy had formed a long line, extending out from the fortress, and it was clear they wouldn't be coming forward. They had enough strength to have a chance against the forces he had already sent in, though the visible reinforcements made things a lot worse.

But Tesserax had no intention of pulling back. He had sufficient reinforcements…and the enemy had none at all. He considered every option, every possibility, trying with all his ability to see what he hadn't before. There was nothing missing, no chance the enemy could prevail. They might do well, better than he expected…but in the end, it would be the same. They would be destroyed, or in the worst case, a battered and wrecked group of ships would flee…a problem perhaps, but nothing he couldn't handle easily. The fight about to begin was the final huge battle, he was sure of that.

He'd done everything he could to maintain the assessment that the ships that had just transported were his last vessels, that now he had nothing to do except watch the fighting.

The enemy would battle harder, he assumed, trying to take out as much as possible before the arrival of the new ships. That made sense, but it also wore them down, and that served Tesserax's purposes well. When the still-hidden forces drove forward, the enemy would have a choice…fight to the death, or flee, and leave themselves open to taking more damage as they fled.

Either way, it led to victory, and the most the enemy could hope for was to break off when the still-hidden forces surged forward. That might add a few years to the whole thing, but it wouldn't accomplish any more than that.

He tried to consider every possible alternative, every action the enemy might take…but there was nothing. The humans were finally cornered. They would fight, almost to the end, he knew, but they were finished. All he had to do was see to the fight now underway and destroy as many enemy ships as possible.

Chapter Eighteen

Forward Base Striker
Vasa Denaris System
Year 329 AC (After the Cataclysm)

Fortress Striker was alive now with the fighting, the battle raging all around. Barron watched, and he was sure now he could have won, if only the enemy hadn't sent another hundred plus ships through the jump point. He'd been sure the enemy had more forces, or at least he'd been fairly certain, and now, he realized the added ships took his chance of victory from perhaps sixty percent to thirty percent. Maybe even less.

Still, thirty percent was good, at least by the standards he had. He'd gone into the battle hoping for the best chance, and he had to admit that thirty percent was at the high end of what he'd given himself before. Part of him had placed the odds at ten percent or less, so even with the new enemy forces, the reason he had pulled his forces back, he was still ahead.

But something was still bothering him. He'd imagined that the enemy had more forces, but now he realized that, as much as he'd expected, there had been no new transits for hours. He'd imagined overwhelming numbers, and for all that the enemy forces had wretched away the advantage, he

137

realized he was still surprised at the relatively small number of ships the enemy had.

Did his forces really still have a chance…or were there more enemy forces ready to come, waiting for some word? He knew he'd be close to alone in that assumption. The enemy had always been more or less straightforward in their efforts, and a third major force seemed an odd conclusion. Especially one that allowed the battle to progress, and dozens of their ships to be destroyed, whether they won or not. It didn't make much sense…but he couldn't completely purge the thought from his mind.

"The battle is completely engaged, sir. Our ships are fighting well, perhaps a bit better than the enemy's."

Barron heard the report, and he acknowledged it. It was true. So far, his forces were fighting very well…perhaps they had better than a thirty percent chance of victory. That all depended on the amount of abuse the enemy was willing to take. He still imagined they'd had a chance in the last fight, too. He had won because they had yielded, but his forces were badly battered, too. If the enemy had been willing to fight to the end…he just didn't know what would have happened.

And the enemy didn't know either…but they knew, at least, that there had been a chance. Would they fight harder this time? Would they battle to the end?

Barron looked around the control room. He was surprised, for about the thousandth time, how little there was to do in the middle of most fights. It was important for him to be there, of course, crucial at a few key moments. But his ships knew what they were doing, and his subordinates were the best he'd ever seen.

He could see that the station was fully engaged, its weapons firing at full speed. His fleet was also engaged, every sub-command fighting at full, each group of ships battling with its own abilities. His forces had come together, the newest ships at least, but there was still a difference between his various nations. The Alliance ships were the least powerful, save only for the tiny contingents from the Far Rim, and they were on the far side, angled forward, closer to the enemy than the other forces. There were fewer Highborn ships opposing them as well, as the enemy too, realized now that there was difference in the ships' abilities.

The best ships in his fleet had been those of the Hegemony, but his own newest vessels were just as strong, and in some ways, even more powerful. He hadn't spoken about it to any of his comrades, but he knew the Confederation had become far and away the most powerful element of the force. Even he had been surprised at the production that had spawned forth from the Iron Gate worlds, and the other locations where shipyards, both old and new, had been put into their best working order...and now spawned new ships at a rate the exceeded even Barron's most unimaginable hopes. He wasn't sure it would be enough, but he was certain that it was the main reason why the war still continued. And he was sure Akella and Chronos understood too.

Still, his mind scrambled, part of it watching the battle taking place all around him...and part of it fishing for whatever he had missed. There was something more...he knew it. Whether it was more enemy ships, or something else, he couldn't say. But he was certain there was something he was missing...even as he knew there was nothing he could do but fight.

Fight to win...and the sooner the better.

* * *

"Forward, all ships, move up at thirty percent power." Atara was focused, one hundred percent on the battle raging all around her. She knew moving her forces forward was risky, but she had lower ranges than the enemy, and she knew she had to adjust. The Highborn vessels had awaited their reinforcements, and then the entire force had advanced. But they had stopped outside much of Travis's ideal ranges.

And she was going to fix that, right away.

"Yes, Admiral." The officer almost immediately repeated her command to all the ships in her force.

Travis expected Winters would do the same—the Alliance had even shorter ranges, and they had already done it—but she knew he had more of the newer ships, including the three superbattleships. The Hegemony still had the longest-ranged vessels, on average at least, and they hadn't advanced at all, not yet at least.

Atara's eyes darted around the bridge, checking on the status of *Dauntless*, and then on the other ships in her command. Her flagship hadn't been completely restored before the battle, but she'd come close, and she'd only taken a few smaller hits so far. The same couldn't be said of many of her other ships, some of which had been outright destroyed, while others had been battered in varying degrees. But the enemy had been hurt as well, and they would take it even harder as the fleet moved up to its own optimum range.

She knew her ship could be battered at any minute, and she was aware that it would be eventually. The battle was to the death, she knew that, even more because Tyler Barron knew the only option that would remain after a defeat was the one he had tried to avoid. She believed he would support a fight to the finish, if it was truly the only way to go, and she was even more ready. She had been left out of the meetings she knew had taken place, mostly because she was deemed to be utterly loyal to Barron, which she was mostly. But she would have been ready to consider any other plan, save defending at Striker again. She couldn't say she preferred that option, not exactly, and she was perfectly willing to fight it out, to try to win conventionally. But she would have listened to alternatives, at least.

If they failed, however, if the battle was lost, she was

completely ready to support what would remain of the only real option, and while she imagined Barron would be then, too, she was willing to separate from him if he remained fixed against it. It would be the most painful thing she ever did, but she would do it.

"Entering primary range, sir."

"Cut thrust...in one minute, begin negative thrusters." The minute was an extra little bit, something that she imagined would take her people by surprise. She had already closed the distance, brought all of her weapons into primary range.

But the extra minute would bring her into *close* range. Pointblank. And that increased whatever chances her people had. She knew what she would do if the battle was lost and she survived. But first, she was going to do everything possible to win the fight.

"Increase rate of fire to 110 percent. Up reload rates correspondingly." She knew she was pushing her ships, harder than she should. She would lose ships, almost certainly...but she needed everything she could get. She would worry later about next steps. First, she had to do everything she could to win the battle.

Everything.

* * *

"Bring us forward...align us with the Confederation ships." Chronos spoke softly, his demeanor almost immune to the incredible stress surrounding the fight. He was fairly sure he was controlling himself well, but actually, inside he was on the verge of losing it. He could have held his ships back...their average range was farther than any of his allies, but the Confederation forces on the one side had advanced, and the Alliance ships on the other had gone even farther ahead, though against a lesser grouping of the enemy. Chronos had almost remained in place, but then he'd realized that the battle line would be at its strongest maintaining a fixed position...and he ordered his ships forward as well.

He watched as his fleet fired, as *all* the ships on his side did, and he felt a gasp of hope with each enemy ship hit, each one destroyed. His own fleet suffered as well, losing ships, with others being battered to near wreckage. He tried to keep count, to judge which side was winning...but all he could see was despair and destruction, on both sides.

He couldn't tell who had the edge, who would win the fight. That was good, he knew, since his forces were outmatched. He couldn't quite decide if his people, and their allies, could hold out, but he was sure, if the enemy was completely dedicated, the battle could progress to almost mutual eradication. He wasn't sure if Barron was *that* dedicated, or if he himself was, but he didn't think about that much now. There would be time...time to consider just how much of his force he was ready to throw away to attain victory.

And if 'almost all' was really his choice.

He watched as the fleet moved forward, as they came into line with the Confederation ships alongside. Then, suddenly, he felt the reverse, the thrust in the opposite direction, bringing his ships to a halt. A few seconds later, he heard the report. "Ships adjacent to Confederation vessels, sir."

"Very well...all vessels, continue fighting." It was probably the least crucial order he had ever given, but it had come out anyway.

"Yes, sir," his aide replied. Then the assistant repeated the order, commanding ships already firing at full, which had maintained such since the fight had begun...to fire at full.

Chronos sat back and watched, seeing two of his ships lost in just a moment, along with one of the enemy vessels. He twisted his face, tried to run the calculations in his mind.

If both sides decided to fight to the end, he knew he'd likely be dead, along with most of the other leaders. The only question in his mind was, would he die in victory, or in defeat?

*   *   *

Sonya Eaton sat and watched the battle unfolding, becoming more upset with each passing moment. Her orders were clear, to remain stationary, outside of range of the enemy. She understood the command. She knew the reasons, the purposes behind them. She realized she was still badly hurt, and she knew the enemy would almost certainly target her ship if she brought it into range, seeking revenge for *Ellerax*, her match in the last fight.

But she didn't care. She wanted to push *Colossus* forward, engage the enemy. She'd done the mental gymnastics a hundred times, and she knew there was a good chance her forces would lose—even with *Colossus*. But she also knew her ship, however battered it was, along with the rest of the savaged and barely repaired vessels, could make a difference. Especially *Colossus*. She might have accepted that the other ships held back, about forty total assembled up alongside her, were too badly damaged, too poorly repaired yet to rejoin the battle. But even at fifteen or twenty percent of full power, her ship was stronger than most battleships...considerably. It was too much to leave out of the fight.

Yet, out of the battle was where she remained.

She pondered a variety of tactics, including just pulling up without orders. There was nothing Barron could do about it—except relieve her—and she wasn't sure who her people would obey if it came to that. She bet that Barron wouldn't push it, though. He might argue with her, order her to remain...but if she brought *Colossus* forward, he would allow it.

At least she thought he would.

But she wasn't sure…and she wasn't ready to take such a step anyway, not yet at least. All she would do was think about it, all the while sitting, watching…dying inside.

Sonya had been at the center of every battle for a long while, and it was more difficult sitting, watching, as ships were destroyed. Would Barron fight to the finish? She didn't know…but her gut told her he might come close. She—as every other commander had in one way or another—looked out and tried to calculate what would happen in a true fight to the death. She'd done it three times, and she'd come out with one victory for her side, one for the other…and one that essentially destroyed almost every ship present.

She knew if Barron remained, if the fleet fought to the end, at some point, she would get the orders to engage. She fought back against her urge to advance now, redoubled her belief in Barron's abilities. She had followed him a long time, and she was going to continue to do so, until she was taken in one of the battles, this one or another one later. She'd used to assess that slightly differently, adding in a possibility that she would survive, that she would live to retire.

But she didn't believe that anymore, not really. She knew she would die, that all of them would die, at least all of the senior officers. She just hoped they left behind a victory in their wake, that they somehow managed to face off against the Highborn…and win.

Before they were all killed.

Chapter Nineteen

Forward Base Striker
Vasa Denaris System
Year 329 AC (After the Cataclysm)

Striker shook—hard—the third large explosion to rock the facility in as many minutes. Barron knew his station was tough, even with much of it still in wreckage, but he was also aware that the enemy was focusing on it more than last time. They weren't going to leave it standing this time, he was sure of that.

"Divert power from tertiary guns…keep all operable main and secondary turrets firing at full." *Whatever that is now.* He knew his people were mostly veterans, but they were human too. He'd told himself, he at least, was ready to lay down his life, and he was mostly. But he suspected that even he would think differently when it came down to time to make that final choice.

"Yes, Admiral…diverting power now." There was a period of silence, and then, "We've got just over one hundred percent power for the primaries and the secondaries." He didn't add, "Until we get hit again," but Barron knew his subordinate thought it.

He thought it as well.

Barron's mind was racing, trying to decide what to do.

Other than directing the station, which was rapidly being reduced in effectiveness, he didn't really have anything much he *could* do. The fleet was under his subcommanders, and every one of them was among the best. They would fight as well—better perhaps—than they would under his direct command, and as much as he felt the urge to interfere, he didn't. He trusted all his subordinates, at least with respect to their abilities, and he knew, wherever each of them fell on the choice that lay before the fleet, he was sure he didn't have one who would back out of battle once joined, even if he or she felt that fight was pointless.

He wondered for an instant what would happen if he was killed. The alliance between the allied powers was detailed in various documents between the nations...but none of them set forth an overall commander. Tyler Barron had served in that role in recent years, but it had been a purely voluntary response of the others to follow him. Clint Winters was number two in the Confederation, certainly, but the Hegemony and the Alliance both would both complain if Barron was lost. He wondered then, what would happen if he was killed. What would the others do? Would they continue the fight until the end? Or would they pull back and resort to the other option?

Suddenly, he felt a strange feeling. Even if he lived, how long would he remain in charge, at least if he maintained his view? How much damage could he watch his fleet take...before he, too, came to the conclusion there was only one way to go?

He didn't know, and the long stretches of time he had, between hits on Striker and orders to the fleet, made it even worse. His mind raced, and he wondered, how much of the fleet's presence in this cataclysmic battle, was his fault? Would his companions have fought here...or would they have pulled back, and launched the other attack on the enemy?

No, he told himself. They didn't have the final word yet.

They didn't know the virus worked, or that the enemy hadn't discovered a treatment for it. He was certain they had all thought about it, but he was sure no one, not even Andi, would move that way, not until they knew for sure the agent worked.

That was something, at least, a break from the relentless barrage he'd given himself. He would still have to decide when to pull back—*whether* to pull back—but until then, his people were united. That was a help, at least. He led one last battle where everyone was on the same side.

But as much as his eyes told him he had a chance, there was something eating away at him, telling him he didn't. He'd wondered if the enemy had even more forces hidden behind the warp gate, but it had been almost eight hours now since the last forces had come through. Even the enemy command group, while out of his reach, had moved forward from the gate. Everything seemed to point to the fact that the enemy had thrown its greatest force forward, that there wasn't anything else left.

But Barron still wondered. No, he did worse than that. He began to believe there *were* enemy forces back behind the transit point. But even he couldn't act on that, pull his forces out. They were heavily engaged, and any kind of withdrawal would be extremely difficult. Especially on nothing more than a feeling.

And that was all he had.

*   *   *

"Maintain position, all units with fire potential remaining. Units with no active weaponry are to retire." Admiral Winters spoke, his voice hard. Inside, he was unsettled, as anyone would be in such a situation, but outside, he was as cold as ice. It was his reputation, and he was clinging to it, through the worst battle humankind had ever seen.

Still, despite the grievous losses, despite the terrible

casualties, Winters had to admit, he thought the situation had changed slightly...to his side. He wasn't sure the odds had actually crested, that his people had taken the advantage, more than one chance in two to win. But he was fairly certain the chances had changed from thirty percent to close to fifty. And that was good news by any measure.

"Yes, sir...all ships staying in place unless completely damaged." The aide's voice was good—not as cold as Winters', but solid nevertheless. Still, Winters saw at least ten ships pulling back, and he'd only guessed that six or seven would. For an instant, he felt angry, as though some of his people were taking advantage of his command. But a quick review of the recent tapes showed him that all ten ships had been utterly silent before his command.

"Very well," he replied, perhaps a moment later than expected. "All ships...continue to withdraw as soon as all weapons are knocked out." He knew that would be fewer than he might have expected. Most vessels were destroyed *before* they lost all of their guns. The ten he'd had was more than he'd expected, and he began to realize that the enemy was targeting his ships in a new way. They blasted his ships hard with their main guns...but before the vessels were totally destroyed, they focused on new targets, and left the damaged units to the fleet's smaller ships.

"Get me Admiral Barron." He knew there was nothing to do, not really. But he figured the admiral should know...if he hadn't figured it out already.

"Admiral Barron, sir."

"Admiral...the enemy has changed their approach somewhat." Even as he spoke, he checked Atara's ships, and Chronos's too. Both commands had more damaged vessels with eighty percent or more of their power knocked out. "They've changed their targeting, switching before a ship is destroyed, turning their heavy guns onto another vessel while their smaller ships finish off the battered units. We've got at least twice as many shot up units as we would have." Winters realized there was a good aspect to that, more surviving ships, assuming the battle was actually won. But it also meant faster damage to his existing battleline.

And we're still gaining…a little…

There was a moment of silence, and then Barron responded, "You're right, Clint." A pause, no more than eight or ten seconds, but seeming much longer. "Still, I don't know what we can do about it."

Winters realized he had expected Barron to have some plan, some special mechanism to stop the enemy from doing what they were. But he realized, that was foolish. Tyler Barron had proven himself to be an extraordinary leader, and he'd taken the fleet farther than anyone could have. But he realized, Barron was almost out of fuel. He'd done everything he could do, brought the fleet farther than anyone could have. But Winters realized at that moment that Barron was spent…and he knew where *he* would land if the current fight ended in defeat, or even in a victory that left the fleet wrecked.

He hoped Barron would be in the same place…but he was sure *he* would be. He would fight like hell, do everything possible to win the struggle they were in. But if they lost, if the enemy drove them away from Striker…he knew where he would be. And he hoped Barron would be there with him.

But if he wasn't, he still would be.

* * *

Akella sat quietly, down in her section of Striker. She'd spent the other battles out on the main control center, or in one of the Hegemony's ships, but this time she'd stayed in her quarters. She wasn't sure why…it was no safer. If the station was blown away, she'd be dead, too…even though her quarters were in a relatively safe spot.

She realized she had remained in her quarters partially

because she wasn't sure whether her forces should have taken the fight or not. Part of her was in favor of it, perhaps the largest component. But there were doubts as well, and they were growing. If the enemy had allowed enough time for the virus test, if she had absolute proof that the pathogen worked, she might have changed her point of view.

But it didn't...the enemy invaded, and we were forced to defend.

She knew she had been in favor of the fight, as much as she had been of any of the other battles that had occurred. She was still in support of it, mostly at least, but she had concerns, too.

She sat for a moment longer, but then, suddenly, she felt a burst of energy. She'd allowed herself to sit out the fight, to remain in the relative sanctity of Striker, but now she realized she couldn't remain. She had to go. She felt the urge to join Chronos, but she knew that wasn't possible. Her companion was out on the battle line, leading the Hegemony's fleet. Or at least what remained of it.

But she could join Barron. She could sit on the bridge and watch the battle. She couldn't fight, couldn't really contribute in any real way...but she could be there. If the bridge was destroyed, so be it. It was as resolute as her chambers were. But at least she would be in the center of things.

She stayed where she was sitting for a few more minutes, and then, suddenly, she leapt up. She made her way out into the halls, and toward the lift unit. Her place was on the bridge, she had decided that, and she made her way quickly. She wasn't that far, and she reached the bank of lifts in just a minute. A few seconds later, she was on her way up to the bridge. She felt some relief that the lifts were still working, but that was all she had time for. Then, the door opened, and she saw the bridge. It was massive, even if part of it was still damaged, and she scanned the hundred or more people present, looking for Barron.

He was right where he should be, in the center of the bridge, looking out over his small legion of officers. She stood where she was for a few seconds…then she began to walk toward him. She got about halfway there when he saw her.

He paused for an instant and looked at her. He stared for an instant, and then the vaguest dropping of his head signified his recognition.

Akella had been following the battle, even in her quarters, and she had been somewhat positive. Nothing overt on Barron's face caused her to feel otherwise…but something did, nevertheless. She didn't think any of the other officers present had caught it, but she knew. Somehow.

Barron was fighting…and he would battle to the end, she knew. But he didn't expect to win. He didn't even think he had a chance.

* * *

Barron sat on the deck, appearing busy, but mostly just watching…and waiting. The battle was going as well as he could expect, but the more time that went by, the more he grew certain his forces couldn't win. He'd scanned the Highborn's production, considered their abilities…and it just didn't add up. The enemy should have more forces. Maybe he was wrong, maybe his adversaries had more trouble than he imagined, building production centers, or managing impressed labor forces.

But he didn't believe it.

He could only go with his own opinions, and they told him, despite the length of the encounter so far, that there were more enemy forces out there. He'd have brought them in if he'd been in the enemy's position, and he was sure all of his officers would have as well. But the enemy was more tolerant of casualties, as long as they won the fight.

Still, it had been a long time, and he knew the lengthier a period that went by, the less chance the enemy had forces hidden. It had been a considerable period now, even for them. Barron figured most of the officers who had held similar beliefs, had lost them.

But he held firm. He was considering withdrawing the force, yet, giving up the battle entirely. But only two things kept him where he was. First, there was the fear that he wouldn't be obeyed, or at least that there would be a huge argument in the middle of the fight. Second, he knew that if he lost at Striker, he was out of ideas. There were no systems just behind that provided the same blockage. He would have to fortify at least three systems to provide the same defensive ability, and the enemy would only have to hit one.

And that assumed he had the time to build more fortifications, which he wouldn't.

He looked across the bridge, at his people. They were actually feeling pretty good. The fight going on, and while it still was uncertain, it was better than any had expected.

Akella…

He saw her as his head moved across the bridge. Her presence wasn't exactly unexpected. He knew she had remained on the station…but she had stayed in her quarters for a long time. Now, she was on the bridge.

He normally wouldn't mind her presence. She was Number One of the Hegemony, and a friend. But it was taking all his will to maintain a brave front for his junior officers, and he was worried that Akella would see what he could hide from the others.

He glanced her way, pausing for just an instant, and trying his best to send her a greeting that didn't share his own negative view. He did a good job, good enough to fool almost anyone.

But not her…he was almost sure she'd read through his effort. He didn't know if she had divined his true thoughts—or for that matter, what his thoughts actually were. But he was sure she had figured something, at least. Whether it was the full total, or just that he was worried about something, he didn't know.

He watched as she approached his position, and he turned to her again and said, "Welcome, Akella...please, have a seat." He gestured toward one of the unoccupied seats across from his, trying again to look as confident as he could.

And failing again, at least enough for her to see.

This time, he was sure Akella saw through his words.

Chapter Twenty

Highborn Flagship S'Argevon
Imperial System GH3-2327
Year of the Firstborn 391 (329 AC)

"You have waited very long, Tesserax. I understand a delay, but if you do not launch the final reserves soon, it will be…too late." Phazarax would have sent in the reserves, at least three hours before. He'd kept his concerns to himself, tried to keep his nerves a secret, but now they burst out. The battle was fierce, raging with all abandon…and he was afraid the enemy would actually prevail against the forces so far committed.

"Very soon, Phazarax…very soon. But not yet. The enemy unquestionably realizes they have a chance at victory, and they no doubt believe that we have sent in everything we have. Surely, they would have anticipated—even if we had more forces, that we would have released them by now. When they detect the reserves coming, they will realize the battle is over, and they will try to retreat. I would have as few as possible of their ships escape…even at the cost of several more of ours. I did everything possible to reduce the importance of the upfront forces. Indeed, I have quietly reduced the Highborn present in the forward ships. We will suffer losses, of course, but most of that will be ships…and humans. The Highborn will suffer losses, of course, but they will be far below any rationale estimates from the number of ships involved."

Phazarax stared at the screen for a short time, and then at his comrade, again. He was amazed, at the icy determination of Tesserax, and the cold realization that had gone into his planning. Even reducing the complement of Highborn in the forward vessels…it was amazing. By far, his friend's greatest effort.

He was still speechless when his companion continued. "I know I should have told you, Phazarax…but old habits die hard. I understand that you are with me, but yet, I still hold certain things close. I am sorry."

Phazarax looked back at his friend, wondering whether Tesserax was being straight with him, or telling him what he wanted him to hear. He decided it was a bit of both.

"I understand, Tesserax, I truly do. Your holding back of the forces so long was correct—" …Phazarax had to admit, holding the reserves for longer than he would have might have been the right call… "—but surely, now is the time to launch them into the battle."

Tesserax smiled. "Soon, Phazarax, very soon…but not yet. The enemy is deep in battle, and the possibility of victory will take them. Then, we will send in the reserves…at 110% of normal speed. The enemy's detection will be slowed by the fighting…and they will have the choice between running and exposing themselves to the fire of the forward ships…or standing and fighting everything."

Phazarax stared back at Tesserax, stunned at the detail his partner had put into the fight, the removal of many of the Highborn from the lead ranks, the grim patience with which he'd watched the battle proceeding. He was shocked, a little bit at least, at his companion's lack of caring for how many ships he lost…as long as he prevailed in the end. He didn't disagree, not entirely at least…but he realized that Tesserax was going all in, doing everything possible to win with enough power to cast aside his prior problems.

Phazarax also realized that he had fallen into Tesserax's orbit, more even that he'd thought. The plan was brilliant, although cold, but most of all, it told him if it didn't work, if Tesserax's forces didn't win, he was doomed.

And Phazarax realized, in that case, he was doomed, too.

* * *

Percelax sat calmly on the bridge. He knew he wasn't supposed to be able to bring his fleet into action so quickly, that all his senior commanders expected him to still be waiting when he received word of the victory on the other end. And what else but victory could come? Tesserax had the strongest force he had ever possessed, and he was bound to win.

Percelax knew the importance of winning the second battle for Grimaldi, especially after the first fight had failed. And winning it *before* news reached his forces of the victory at Striker.

He hadn't lost his command...partly because he led on a secondary and hard to reach front, and partially because he'd reported the enemy forces completely, even exaggerating the amount of ships that were present. But now, he'd acted flawlessly, even recklessly, to bring his units into action. He couldn't get into battle before Tesserax could...but he was going to go into his fight little more than a week later, and that was amazing. He knew he was supposed to be far enough back that he could receive orders, *would* receive them, he had decided, to stand and wait for the main force to advance, before he had a chance to fight the battle.

He wasn't going to take any chances on that. He'd raced his ships up to the front, as quickly as he possibly could, and soon he would hit the enemy. He would destroy their fleet, and their base at Grimaldi. He knew he probably wasn't going to do much better than that, that any effort to advance and take more territory immediately would probably be impossible. But destroying Grimaldi, and taking the system that it held, the one that controlled much of the path of access into the Confederation from the Union, would be enough. He would be heralded, by Tesserax's supporters in the event that the main battle was also a success…or by those of his replacement, if that was to be the case. Either way, he would remain…as long as he took Grimaldi. And that was all that mattered to him.

He looked down at the screen on his desk, at the estimates. He was solid on his forces, though less so of the enemy's. He knew the foe was producing a lot of ships, but he was equally aware that a large percentage of them were still being sent out to the main front. Nevertheless, he'd used the highest estimate, the greatest concentration he could imagine. He was sure he could still prevail, that his forces were sufficient to take out the enemy…and Grimaldi. He would lose a lot of his ships, perhaps, but that was okay. As long as he took the system.

And *that* he was going to do…whatever the cost.

* * *

"Now." Tesserax sat, almost unmoving, knowing he was taking Phazarax by surprise. He leaned forward slightly, over the microphone, and he spoke softly. "Order the remaining vessels forward."

Phazarax looked surprised, despite Tesserax's assurance the word would come soon, that he would call for the rest of the fleet. It was about an hour past their previous discussion, and most of that time had been given to silent watching of the battle going on. The enemy forces continued to make progress, but it was slow, and they were suffering terrific losses themselves, even as they were harming the enemy more.

But the enemy had reserves, forces that had been silent in the adjoining system for long enough that none of the enemy probably believed they were there. The ships would begin coming through in just a few minutes, at a rate that exceeded normal levels, and they would move right to the scene of the battle. Their courses into the transit point were fixed, and they would exit it already moving at a decent speed. Then, they would accelerate, right toward the enemy.

The humans could withdraw, though that action would turn the tide on the engaged front, from a slight edge to the humans to a rather more decisive advantage for the invaders. Tesserax hoped that the enemy remained long enough for his new ships to engage, but even if they didn't, he would have what he needed. The enemy would be sent on the run, their battered but still-functional station taken...or destroyed. They might pull a reasonable amount of their forces out, though Tesserax intended to give them every bit of hell he could manage before that. But they were beaten. They would lose as many as half of their total ships.

And if they were still there when the rest of the forces arrived, they would be destroyed. Utterly.

"Yes, sir...sending dispatch now."

Tesserax was alone with Phazarax, as he'd been for most of the battle. He avoided his companion's gaze, at least until he heard the response. Then he looked across. "It is time, time to end the fighting." He spoke calmly, quietly, almost as though he was talking about something routine. That was his intention, at least, but inside, he was on edge, even as he expected victory. He did believe that he had done everything correctly, that he would prevail...but he was still worried, at least a little. But he kept that to himself, sounding completely confident, even to his number one companion.

"I believe we have won the fight, Tesserax. I do not see how the enemy can stand against the rest of the forces, especially the four superbattleships."

I can't either, my friend…

But Tesserax only nodded, and he said simply, "We are in good shape, I believe. Now, it is time for the final stages of the battle."

Chapter Twenty-One

Forward Base Striker
Vasa Denaris System
Year 329 AC (After the Cataclysm)

Barron was tense, and it was only getting worse. Left to himself, and not to Akella and Chronos and the others, he would have withdrawn already. At least he believed he would have. If was difficult to be honest about that, much because he felt like the only person in the fleet who believed things were going badly.

At least badly by comparison to the enemy. His force had lost almost 20% of its hulls already, and perhaps 35% more were badly battered. Some of those hulls might survive the fight, if they got lucky enough to avoid future hits. But almost all of them would be lost if he abandoned his position right now. It was becoming even more difficult to decide what to do, fight to the finish, assume the enemy was down to its last bits of strength, and that he could defeat them in the long run...or decide the enemy actually had more ships, that they were waiting to dispatch. That last option would reduce his options to a single one—issue orders to flee, and then prepare to flee himself...or to die inside Striker station.

He looked back, at Akella. She was silent. Save for a few sentences when she'd arrived, she was just watching the battle. He really liked her…and in truth, he didn't know many people well outside the service. She was one of the few…and in fact, she was just about the only non-military type he would call a friend.

She'd been his enemy once, though he hadn't known her then, and then for a long time, a difficult sort of friend. But he realized that the years of allied fighting had almost set aside the prior battle between the Hegemony and the Confederation. Like it or not, Akella *was* an actual friend, as was Chronos. He didn't know the other members of the Hegemonic Council, and he was sure he wouldn't like some of them…but the warriors were not terribly different from his own.

He turned toward the display, and he watched the battle continuing. The two forces were right in front of each other, which meant that if either side broke and tried to run, the other would lash out and destroy a large number of ships. That only made the idea of running off more unthinkable.

But it still pressed at him from inside. He just knew something was wrong…though he did not know what.

"Admiral…"

His eyes caught it, even as the officer was calling to point it out. His scanners were only picking up emanations from the transit point, and he thought for an instant, it was most likely just a scout ship, or something similar.

But then his stomach went cold. Part of him knew what it was, almost immediately.

Worse, he couldn't react, couldn't issue orders based on what he was sure was happening. Not until it actually took place.

His eyes were fixed on the display, watching for the ship he knew was coming through. Or the ships…perhaps even a large fleet. His mind wrestled with itself, trying to accept that it was just a messenger ship, or something similar. But he knew what it was.

He turned and looked at Akella. He wasn't sure what she thought, whether she was aware of what was happening. But he made eye contact with her, and he saw in her eyes that whatever effort he'd made to hide his concern had failed. She looked almost as bad as he was, as though she was thinking about enemy forces coming through the point, herself, closing…and forcing the fleet, whatever could escape from it at least, to flee.

Barron turned toward the front, noticing a strange silence on the bridge. Everyone present was aware, and while some were more convinced it was nothing but a transport or two, others were becoming edgy, worried.

Barron turned back. *He* was sure what it was, but he realized he couldn't move on that alone. In a few seconds, he would *know* what was coming…and he would know what to do.

He just wasn't sure it would do any good.

*   *   *

"Oh God…" Atara spoke softly, but she hadn't intended to speak at all. The rumblings at the transit point had been difficult enough, but she'd told herself it could be communications ships, or something else…not necessarily military-grade vessels.

Now the first ship was through…and it was a battleship.

One heavy unit wouldn't make a noticeable difference, of course…but what where the chances it was only a single ship? She couldn't tell, and while she could examine the transit point, and try to figure out what else was coming, she knew the only way to be sure was to wait. And watch.

Her mind was split now, part of it still watching the battle raging all around *Dauntless*…and the rest of it focused on the point. She tried to wrest her thoughts away, to keep her focus for as long as possible undivided on the enemy ships actually around her forces. But once she had seen the first enemy vessel coming through, that had become impossible.

That didn't stop her from trying to maintain her crew's focus. If she'd been able to hide the arrival of the enemy reinforcements, she would have...but she had multiple screens on every ship that could scan the transit point. Hiding it wasn't possible.

"Alright everybody...stay focused. *Dauntless* is still in pretty good shape, and we've got a job to do." It was all true, and pointless, too. Her people would continue the fight, of course, but now they were distracted...and that alone could lead to their destruction. "It's probably just a couple of ships..." A second vessel had just appeared, much like the first one. Two battleships wasn't really a meaningful force, but if more continued to come...

"Yes, Admiral..." Her lead aide responded, trying—but mostly failing—to divert his attention from the new arrivals. "...everybody, keep your attention on the fight we've got now."

Atara leaned back in her chair, as the third enemy vessel slipped through the transit point. She tried to tell herself that it was just a few renegades, but she didn't believe it. She didn't believe it at all. She had seen Barron's actions, and she knew he'd been concerned about more enemy forces. She had too, though she had to admit, the amount of time that had passed had relieved her somewhat.

Now she realized that Barron had been right all along. And she wondered, assuming there were more enemy vessels coming, how much of the force could escape before the enemy reserves made it up to the front.

She had no idea of the answer to that question, but as she was looking, the fourth enemy ship came through.

* * *

The room was fuzzy, hazy. He wasn't sure who he was, or why he was there. No, that wasn't entirely true. He knew his name. Jake Stockton. The more he thought, the more came back to him.

He wriggled, trying to move…but he was mostly bolted down, held in place almost everywhere he could move. He could jerk his head forward, a bit, and he could wiggle his toes. Nothing more.

He tried to speak. The words came out, in his head, but there was no real volume. He wasn't sure whether there had been the slightest speech or none at all, but he was sure whatever had come out, no one could hear it.

His mind was lost, various thoughts moving in and out. He'd had surgery…he remembered that suddenly. Of course…the implant!

He remembered suddenly. He'd gone into surgery to have the implant removed. He tried to move his hand around, to feel the back of his neck, but he couldn't even come close.

"Admiral Stockton…"

He heard the voice, the sound of his chief surgeon, he remembered. He looked up, seeing the man, and two female assistants, standing behind him.

"You may not be able to respond…but we're thrilled to have you back. We have removed the implant, Admiral. It is gone."

The words made sense, sort of. He remembered the implant, but it was still fuzzy to him. He tried to respond, but again, he made no sound.

"Admiral…you are still hyper-critical. I urge you to remain calm."

He heard the words, simultaneously reassuring and difficult.

"We are thrilled that you have come through the surgery…but…"

Stockton knew there was something wrong, something beyond his own situation. But he couldn't really understand.

"There is a battle going on now, Jake…a large battle. And we are in the middle of it." The doctor was checking him as he spoke, reading various components. "I'm sorry to have to discuss this with you now, Admiral, but I have no choice. Now that you're awake, I'm going to see about moving you to a ship, getting you out of here."

Stockton was growing tired, starting to lose some of whatever awareness he had. But he could tell the doctor was upset, and he knew, at least in a way, that moving him was dangerous. But he still didn't understand, not entirely.

He tried to speak one more time, without success, and then he slipped back into unconsciousness.

* * *

"Admiral Barron…I'm sorry to bother you in the middle of the battle…"

Barron turned, surprised by the voice of Dr. Jordan. He'd been deep into Jake Stockton's surgery, but since the battle had begun, and especially since it had turned critical, Barron had only given the doctor a few passing thoughts. It was totally rational, but he felt bad, nevertheless. And his feeling was dark, that the doctor was going to tell him Jake Stockton was dead. That would still represent a major step forward in medicine, he knew, as no one had even previously survived the surgery, but it was still bad as far as he was concerned.

Fortunately, it wasn't true either.

"Jake Stockton woke up, for a few minutes. I can't say he is going to survive, but the signs are very good. He is still weak, and he isn't able to speak, not audibly…but as much as I can tell from the instruments, he is in…as good a shape as we could have hoped."

Barron felt surprise, and a welcome relief from the

coarseness of the battle. He was still focused on the six
battleships that had thus far appeared at the transit point,
praying with each transfer that it be the last, but the good
news—and whatever happened, it *was* good news—pulled
him from the edge.

"That is wonderful, Doctor...but..." Barron was already
thinking about withdrawing the fleet, and everyone who
could be taken from Striker as well. He knew his own value
to the cause...but he wasn't sure what he would do. There
was a good chance he would die here...but Stockton, at
least would have a chance. For a while longer, at least. "...I
want to withdraw him from the fight. I know it's far too
early, but put your whole crew on one of the transports and
get the hell out of here as quickly as you can." Barron was
silent for just a few seconds, and then he added, "Thank you
for all your work on Jake, Doctor. Stay with him, pull him
through...and you will have my thanks for all time."

The doctor responded, but Barron only heard part of it.
His attention had shifted back to the situation at hand.
There were eight battleships in the area of the transit point,
and his gut told him, there would be more. He'd anticipated
the situation, almost expected it...but now he was tied up,
unsure what to do. Did he order the fleet to withdraw, to
scramble to escape...and almost certainly lose a cataclysmic
number of ships? Or what? What else could he do? Sit and
hope—without cause or likelihood of success—that the
eight ships, no nine now, was all that was coming? Nine
ships was a decent force, enough, at least, to start changing
the odds. But was it nine? Or the beginning of ninety?

Or nine hundred?

He looked at the screen, trying to convince himself of
anything but the worst scenario, but then the tenth ship
appeared, and it destroyed Barron's efforts.

The enemy had a large force coming in, he was sure of it.
And as much as he wanted to give up, to surrender, he just

couldn't. He had to fight to the finish…it was how he was made.

"Get me the contingent commanders now…"

Chapter Twenty-Two

Forward Base Striker
Vasa Denaris System
Year 329 AC (After the Cataclysm)

"Move him carefully..." Jordan followed just behind the corpsmen moving the mobile stretcher. The surgeon's mind was in a hundred places, part of it focused on how he'd come so close to the enemy. He wondered if he'd been careless agreeing to conduct the operation on the front line...but he just decided he'd been unlucky, that if he'd done the surgery even a week earlier, that he'd have been fine.

Perhaps more surprisingly, while he was certainly scared, he realized he would have done the surgery no matter what. He'd performed the first successful removal of an alien implant, and while there were a lot of specifics—Stockton's amazing endurance, the partially deactivated status of his unit—it was still incredible progress. Stockton might not live, he knew that himself, at least deep inside, but he was completely dedicated to preventing that. He was one of the most celebrated specialists in the entire Confederation, but just then, he had only one patient, and he would continue to serve that one man...until it wasn't necessary anymore.

He looked up ahead, at the rear entry hatch of the

transport. "Okay, take him inside, and get this hatch closed. We need to get the engines started." *And get the hell out of here.*

He hadn't really had cause to judge his courage before, not in any real way. Sure, he was brave in a sense, but for all the confidence and effort his career sometimes required, it was his patients, and not himself, really in trouble. His own life, outside the stress brought on by his profession, had been extremely tolerable. He was rich, well-respected, considered one of the best in his field. But now, he understood true courage. He had conducted surgery just before an enemy attack, and he had sat with his patient, pretending he wasn't feeling every hit on the facility. He had been terrified…but he wouldn't have been anywhere else.

His prior patients, the ones he'd tried to free from the implants, had died. He had been sorry, as he always was when he lost a patient, but somehow, Stockton was different. He hadn't thought about the man's life, about his years of almost mind-numbing sacrifice…until the surgery was complete. But sitting in the waiting area, focusing on his patient's post-operative coma, he'd begun to consider just who he'd operated on. He'd performed surgery on a few people of note over the years, but he realized that Stockton was by far the greatest. He'd considered his own grandeur, and he'd compared it to his patient's. For the first time, he felt outclassed, overwhelmed. Virtually every citizen of the Confederation knew who Stockton was…and many of those in neighboring cultures as well. And he was determined to save Stockton's life…whatever it took.

He watched as the corpsmen moved the stretcher onto the ship. Stockton was asleep, and he was tranquilized too, so he would stay out through whatever happened in the next few hours. But his readings, while still hyper-critical, were stable. He was in danger from a hundred causes, but he was strong, too. He would survive, Jordan was sure of that.

As long as you get him out of here…

"Okay…I want that stretcher tightly placed, and I want Stockton affixed to it every way possible." He knew the ship was fast, that it would flee the fight as quickly as possible, and he was determined that Stockton would be as safe as he could be. He knew the patient was still in multiple forms of danger, but there was nothing he could do about that. He had realized the danger before, but now there were more enemy units streaming through the portal leading into the system. Jordan's military knowledge was no more than any other citizen's, but he was sure Barron would have to withdraw…and soon. That meant that Striker would be captured…or destroyed…if he remained. Either way, he had to be off…now. However much he didn't like the idea of moving his patient—and he didn't like it at all—the idea of staying was just out of the question.

He watched as the crew placed the stretcher on the ship, and the numerous personnel he had assembled as Stockton's staff loaded onboard. Then, he climbed aboard himself, sitting in one of the launch chairs…and he signaled to close the doors.

The ship would launch in a minute…and he thought, at least, it was far too small to attract attention. It would make its run with a full effort to avoid any targeted shots, of course, but he didn't imagine any of the forward enemy units would be targeting his ship, even if they could.

He would make it, out of the system, at least. But what would happen if the fleet was destroyed? What could he do if the Confederation, if all the powers he knew of, where captured by the Highborn?

He put those thoughts out of his mind, not because he didn't believe them, but because he didn't have any answers. He had to worry about Stockton, and he didn't have time for anything else.

* * *

"We've got to get out of here." Barron knew everyone considered him the senior commander, but he also realized that was informal, that if all his people disagreed with him, it could be a problem. There were fourteen enemy ships through now, and if that was all, it was a problem…but perhaps not an unbeatable one. But he didn't believe the array would stop anytime soon, and his gut was that none of his people did either.

"Agreed. The enemy has more ships…and if we wait to see exactly how many, it may be too late to escape." Clint Winters spoke calmly, though Barron understood that the officer, his number two, at least over Confederation forces, was almost panic-stricken. He felt the urge to try to help his comrade, but he felt the same way.

Worse, even.

Barron considered Winters' words, and he was still trying to put his next bit together when Chronos spoke. "I agree. You were right all along, Admiral Barron. Our effort to hold here was a fool's errand. We should have known that the enemy wouldn't attack again without a large enough force to overwhelm us." Barron listened, and even as he did, he found himself wanting to argue that there were only fourteen—now, sixteen, actually—enemy ships, that maybe the enemy wouldn't exactly overwhelm them. But he didn't believe that, not at all. He'd expected the enemy to launch a great enough attack to drive his ships away, and when the actual assault had proven more of a matchup to his own force, he'd assumed there was more to come. He knew there was nothing he could have done, that he couldn't have ordered the fleet withdrawn, Striker abandoned or destroyed, without at least making an effort to hold on. But he still felt self-hatred for not doing something.

"We can't all pull back at once. My forces will go last…we will hold back the enemy." The voice was surprising. If anyone had been expected to put up a fight, to take the position that maybe there wasn't a huge force, maybe the enemy had just kept—seventeen ships, now—a force in reserve, it was Vian Tulus. But Tulus instead was volunteering to stay back...and that meant he was likely to die.

Barron paused a minute. Everyone on the comm did, until Chronos spoke.

"I agree with Tulus...except that he can't be the one. The Alliance forces are just not numerous enough." That was also a nice way of saying that they weren't strong enough either. "I will stay."

Barron listened, and he knew leaving Chronos was the best possible option. The Hegemony forces had been the most powerful in the force, but now they were number two, and by a distant—and growing—margin. They were also the ones least likely to agree to pulling back to Confederation space.

But he knew he couldn't allow Chronos to command the holding force. Not when there were two Confederation commands.

"No," he said, his words leaping ahead of his thoughts. "I appreciate your willingness, Chronos, but it has to be a Confederation command. With the death of Ilius..." He didn't mention the lack of new reinforcements. "...you command the entire Hegemony force. And we have two commanders of the Confederation fleet." He already knew who he had to order to remain...he just hadn't accepted it yet. And he never had to...she did it for him.

"I will stay, Admiral." He heard the sound, the voice he'd listened to more times than he could remember. He wanted to say no, to tell her she had to leave...but he knew she was the right one to stay.

The comm was silent for a moment, and then Clint Winters came on. "No, Atara...I will stay. You go with the others."

Barron sat stone still for a moment. Then he said, "No, Clint. Atara is correct. She is the right one to stay...and I will remain at Striker until the last moment."

There was nothing but silence on the line. Everyone felt an urge to be the one to stay, but they all knew Barron's plan was the best…except him staying.

"Tyler…I can do this. You have to withdraw at once." Atara sounded as pert as usual, but Barron knew she understood the odds. Some of her ships might escape, but her own chances weren't good.

They weren't good at all.

"No." His response came without thinking, without any view toward rationality or anything else. He was simply not going to leave, not until the last of his forces did. If that meant he died there, instead of somewhere else, so be it.

The truth, the knowledge that Barron kept to himself, was that he didn't think there was any chance anymore. His escapees would continue to fight, he knew that, but they wouldn't win. And while he knew if he lived, he would support the other plan, unlike his wife, he didn't really believe it would work.

Tyler Barron was beaten, in many ways, and he almost craved a death in battle. It would be an escape really, a way out. He heard his people objecting, especially to his remaining to the end, and he just said, "That is the way it is going to be. Now, do what I say, please." He stopped for a moment, and there was nothing but silence on the line. His eyes darted to the image of the transit point, now with twenty-two enemy ships assembled. Then he began to issue orders…to retreat.

* * *

"Please, Andi…go." Barron had issued the withdrawal orders…and he had ordered all the non-essential personnel to abandon Striker as well. Atara's force and the station would be the only units still present, and however well they did at holding back the enemy would make a huge difference in how many of the ships fleeing actually made it. But now, he was in his office, right off the bridge, talking to Andi. He'd already dealt with Akella. She'd given him a hard time, insisted she was going to stay on Striker along with him…but she'd been relatively easy to persuade. It wasn't a lack of courage, Barron knew that well enough, but Akella was the head of the Hegemony, and she would have work to do. Whatever followed, whether he lived to see it or not, Akella would have her hands full.

Andi was a different story…but he had one secret weapon to use there.

"No, Tyler…I will leave when you do." That was unacceptable, mostly because Tyler didn't expect to leave. He wasn't outright suicidal, but he didn't see any way to escape either.

"Cassie…" Barron said the word, the one he knew his wife had already had in her mind. Their daughter, loved by both of them, perhaps the one thing more important to the two of them than each other. "This is my job, Andi…not yours. One of us has to get out of here, at least." Barron realized he wasn't ready to give up himself either, though he knew there was a great chance he wouldn't survive.

Andi looked at Barron, a combination of anger and love in her expression. "Please, Tyler…come with me. You can't do anything here…you know that."

Barron realized he had scored, that Andi was going to leave. But she was going to do everything she could to get him to go as well. He knew that, understood it perfectly…and part of him wanted to give in. But he couldn't.

"I can't go, Andi…not while the battle is still raging. And you *have* to go." He paused for just a second, and then he added, "And I've got to get back out on the bridge." He felt himself tearing apart, and he believed there was an excellent chance this was the last time he would see Andi. He'd been standing about a meter from her, but now he reached out and grabbed her. "Please...just go. Take care of Cassie." He knew his tactics were unfair, but he was sure that Andi's escape was only good for a short while. He didn't believe there was any way to defeat the enemy. Still, he hoped he would survive, escape to fight again.

He just didn't believe he would.

"Go," he said again...and he put everything he had into pulling himself away. "I'll be right behind you," he said, but he knew she didn't believe him anymore than he believed himself. He stopped and looked at her, for perhaps ten seconds. Then, he turned and raced out of the room, and back to the bridge.

*   *   *

Atara shook one time, a bit of normalcy amid her otherwise calm and cool attitude. She knew she was the center of attention on *Dauntless*'s bridge, and she wasn't sure who had seen her moment of weakness, or if it had even been visible for what it was. But her control slammed down into place once again, and she directed her entire force, seeming like the battle taking place all around was just some kind of exercise.

"Stretch out the forces...extend the distance between all ships by three times." She hadn't been given specific orders, but she knew that extending her forces, covering much of the original front, was what she'd been expected to do. She knew it was the best way to occupy the enemy forces. She wasn't thinking of her escape yet, not because that wasn't important, but because she understood just how crucial her first job was. The enemy was battered, too, at least beyond the forty plus ships moving in from the transit point, but she was aware they would try and pursue the retreating ships.

And the only thing to stop them was her.

That made sense, but if she was successful, she would be

facing four times what she had been before, if only for a short while. She would lose ships, she knew that for sure. What she didn't know was whether she'd get any of her vessels out.

Regardless of whether she and *Dauntless* were destroyed.

"Forces stretching out, Admiral...approximately two minutes until the order is completed."

She just nodded, unsure of whether the officer saw her or not. She was immensely calm, by normal standards, but deep down, she was barely holding on.

She turned her head, looking at Striker on the screen. The station was no match for what it had been in the previous battle. It hadn't been even at the start of the fight. But as she watched the enemy forces begin to understand what was happening, she saw that the station was being left mostly alone.

Of course...the new ships will obliterate it...

She felt the urge to do something, to try and convince Barron to abandon the station, to leave with the earlier deportees, and not, as he likely would, with the last to go. But she knew what a waste of time that would be. She was sure Andi had at least tried...and failed. Barron *might* make it out, but Atara figured his chances were no better than hers...and maybe worse.

She forced her attention back to the screen in front of her. The ships had started to pursue the retreating units, but her expansion of the line was interfering. The vessels chasing the retreating ships could continue after the fleeing units...but they would expose themselves badly to Atara's ships. It made more sense to defeat her first, and then chase after the others.

But she was determined that wouldn't happen. She didn't know how many—if any—of her ships would make it out. But she was sure, if the enemy stayed back, she would fight them long enough to allow the others to escape.

And if they didn't, if the enemy pursued the fleeing

ships, she would follow them, and tear them apart from behind.

Chapter Twenty-Three

Forward Base Striker
Vasa Denaris System
Year 329 AC (After the Cataclysm)

Barron watched the screen as another ship blasted out from the station. It was just another vessel, at least to most of those watching...but he knew *Pegasus* everywhere he saw her. Andi's ship was definitely female, that was something he had decided on years ago, even though it didn't make much sense.

He watched it for a few seconds, maybe half a minute, but then he forced his attention back to the screen, to the battle taking place all around the station. The enemy had mostly ignored Striker, at least since the fleet had begun its retreat. They had expected to pursue the fleeing forces, but Barron sat and watched as Atara spread her force, covering most of the battle line. Where ships ignored her, and sallied through to try and pursue the escaping vessels, her forces went after them...with such severity, the enemy in most places gave up their efforts to chase down the fleeing ships and turned to face hers.

Atara had always been one of the best officers Barron had ever known, even back to her time as his executive officer, on the old *Dauntless*. But he'd never seen her perform better than she was doing now. There were bits and pieces of the enemy fleet still chasing down the fleeing units…but eighty-five percent or more were fighting her ships. Barron knew that meant her force would probably be almost destroyed, and for a brief moment, he pondered how likely she was to die in the battle.

She'd had an advantage, surprise, at least for a few minutes, but now the numbers were coming to bear. And the casualties were beginning to mount. Barron watched, and he ached to be on *Dauntless* with his old XO, one more time. Despite his best efforts, he couldn't see it as anything but the last chance. In all probability, one of them would die here…but the chance that they would both survive, along with *Dauntless*, seemed almost impossible.

Still, he thought about it, about *Dauntless* slipping away, with both of them aboard. It seemed impossible, but he just couldn't push it completely aside.

He wasn't surprised that the enemy was ignoring Striker for the ships, though. The station had some movement capability, of course, but nothing that allowed it to escape. The enemy was going to gain the system, that was certain, and destroying the station could wait until the hostile ships were all gone.

Maybe they intend to try and take it, rather than destroy it…if that's the case, good luck…

He had no intention of seeing Striker taken…and he had multiple backups on destruction systems. He wasn't overly likely to escape, but he wasn't going to end up a prisoner either. No way.

He glanced at the scanner again, watching as six ships departed. He had ordered Striker to be reduced, even beyond the few levels that had been there before. Only the most necessary people were to be left aboard. He had a fight with Akella, who had argued to remain. He had finally won that one, and she had departed on *Pegasus*, with Andi. Neither of them wanted to go, but he had used different techniques to trap each of them.

He smiled, a strange act considering the situation, but one he understood. He had gotten both Andi and Akella to leave, and that was something. Even if he died here, he knew those two, along with many others who escaped, would carry on the fight.

He knew what they would do, realized how different it was from his own plan…and while he wasn't sure it would work, he knew there was still a chance. Whether he made it out or not.

He turned back, toward the main screen, watching as the station fired at maximum power—110% of maximum, actually—and gutted two different enemy ships. The Highborn fleet was putting as much distance between itself and the station as possible, but Atara's expanded front came close to Striker…and that kept at least some enemy ships in range.

He felt some joy at the series of hits, and he pushed back against his negative feelings. He was in command…and whether he survived or not, he was going to fight.

He was going to fight to the finish.

* * *

Chronos struggled with his operations. Fleeing the battle was difficult enough, though Atara's almost perfect actions had vastly reduced the forces in pursuit. He still had some enemy ships chasing his fleeing forces, but at most a quarter, and probably much less, than he would have normally expected. And it was Atara's work that he had to thank for it, almost entirely. Most of his forces would escape…except for the battered vessels lagging behind, with less power to feed to their engines. Many of those had been turned over to Atara…because they weren't going to escape anyway. That had been a difficult effort, since both he and the captains knew their vessels were being sacrificed.

He felt a strange sequence of feelings. Sorrow at the losses, even assuming he made it out. Worry about the future, about how the only remaining option with any promise of victory actually went. And sorrow for Atara Travis and her forces. He knew some would probably escape, possibly at least, but he was sure most of her forces would be eliminated. He didn't know Travis all that well, but he took her closeness with Admiral Barron as all he needed...and he was sorrowful about leaving so much of the battle to her.

But he knew his duty, and what he had to do. "All ships, switch to 110% power...as soon as you're out of close range from pursuers, go down to full speed. We've got to get out of here, and quickly."

"Yes, sir."

Chronos looked at his staff, at all the officers on the bridge. There was no question they were doing their duty, but they were also glad to be leaving. He wasn't sure his flagship would make it out, but it was looking pretty good. He knew he should feel the same way, and to an extent he did. But he also ached for all those lost, and those still to be sacrificed. Those were mostly going to be Confederation personnel, he realized, but he had come to see less and less in the distinctions between his people and their allies.

He ached as much for Atara Travis's forces as he would his own...or damned close to it. But all he could do was get as many of his ships out as possible.

Even though he knew that was not going to be enough.

He turned and looked at the display. He was thankful for one thing, at least. He'd expected somewhat of a fight from Akella about retreating...but Barron had handled that. His—he wasn't sure what to call her, even he wasn't ready to say 'mate'—was in *Pegasus*...and even closer to jumping out than his ship. He was grateful for that...something else he realized he owed Barron for.

Tyler Barron...the head of the military, even if it was

informally. Chronos thought of Barron, and all the other leaders. He realized Tyler was the only one with a real chance to hold the force together. He knew how difficult that would become, and he dreaded dealing with his own comrades on the Council...but he knew they needed Barron.

But would they have him? He didn't know...but his gut told him, there was definitely a good chance that Barron would die in the current fight. And if he did, he suspected a good chance the entire alliance would fall apart.

Chronos stared at the screen, at the extreme edge, where Striker sat. He wondered if Barron would pull out...and he decided he wasn't even intending to try.

"Bring us around." He spoke, almost without thinking it through. "Just this ship...toward Striker. The rest of the force is to continue out of the system."

He felt his stomach tighten at the thought of going back, perhaps into the fight. The enemy was mostly laying off Striker, though, and one battleship just might make it through...and offer Barron an escape.

He knew it was a difficult proposition, that Barron might fight him on it. But he also knew he had to try...and he figured he just might have the best chance of all to pull him out.

Which still wasn't great, he realized, but it was a whole lot better than nothing.

* * *

Atara leaned forward, shouting out one order after another. She wasn't leading a suicide force, not exactly at least. Some of her ships would escape...though she realized that might only be a few. But she was going to do her best to hold back as much of the enemy force as possible...for as long as she could.

"Extend the right flank...We need another thirty

thousand kilometers." Her eyes were on the edge of the display, watching the enemy ships pouring forward. It was a small percentage of the enemy force, perhaps, mostly those ships that had been deployed against Tulus. But the Imperator's ships were trying to escape now—probably with the barest intentions of the Alliance leader—and she had to find a way to hold back some of the pursuing vessels.

The Alliance forces were generally smaller, and less technologically advanced, than the rest of the force…but they were the third largest grouping the fleet had, and some of them at least had to get away. With the Imperator, if at all possible. Vian Tulus was half-Alliance for sure, but he was also half Confederation, and anyone who replaced him would be lesser, almost for sure.

"Yes, Admiral…" She heard the words from her aide, and she could tell he was near the edge. All her people were, she told herself. But they would do their duty…she was sure of that.

She spun around, checking the entire frontage of her force—the range that had until recently been that of the entire fleet. The enemy had been somewhat surprised by her actions. Some of the ships had advanced, chasing the other contingents, and some remained. But even those that remained were somewhat shocked. That gave her few moments of, if not an outright advantage, at least a parity.

It only lasted a few moments, however.

Now, there were enemy ships coming in from all sides, in front, and behind. She had massive forces before her, and now she had some of the ships that had pushed past her coming back. That was good, at least in the sense that anything coming back toward her was no longer pursuing the escaping ships. But it also meant she had more vessels to deal with herself.

Even as she watched, the mix went against her, the short period of at least some advantage she'd gained from surprise fading, and the sheer number of enemies starting to mount.

The assembled fleet had been almost exactly as strong as the Highborn force, minus the new arrivals, of course—now over 100 ships and still transiting. But against only her forces, it was close to four to one...and now that edge was beginning to add up.

"All ships...go to maximum overages on weapons output. All ship commanders are to fire the most they can." She snapped out the orders, knowing as she did that at least some of her commanders were closer to outright crazy than others. Some of them would damage their ships, going too far into overload territory.

Some would possibly destroy their vessels.

But those ships were likely to go anyway, sooner or later, and her only advantage was that the enemy knew they had reinforcements coming...and she was the last of her side. She believed some of her forces would escape, some number of her ships...at least probably. But she suspected it would be a small number, ten percent, maybe twenty. And that meant, as many as ninety percent of her vessels were fighting their last battle.

And if it was going to be her last fight, she was more determined than ever to make it a memorable one. She would fight...like nothing she'd ever seen before. She probably wasn't going to make it out with the ten percent or twenty percent—in fact, she had already committed herself to dying. But she was determined to get anyone else out that she could.

Her eyes moved over toward the station, and she thought of Tyler Barron. He was the closest person to her, and she knew he had to survive. But as she looked at the station, as her mind fixed on him...she realized he wasn't going to escape. Not unless she went to take him off the station.

But that meant surviving the fight now underway...and going to Striker. It seemed impossible, but Atara Travis suddenly swore to herself, under her breath, that she would do it. Somehow.

She didn't know how she would make it happen, but if she was going to survive, there was only one thing important enough to make that a reality.

Tyler Barron.

It seemed unlikely, perhaps impossible...but she found herself almost believing it was possible.

Chapter Twenty-Four

Forward Base Striker
Vasa Denaris System
Year 329 AC (After the Cataclysm)

Barron sat on the edge of his chair, tense and irritable in some ways...but strangely calm in another. Striker was firing it's remaining main guns, but there were no other ships near enough for anything smaller to hit. He was not even using all the energy his remaining reactors produced...though he knew he might get the chance before the fight was over.

He speculated that the enemy intended to at least make an effort to take the station, if they got close enough to land any kind of force. But if they did that, he'd sworn they would be sorry.

He had barely a hundred people left on the station, not even a fraction of the usual. It was enough to fire some of the remaining secondaries when the enemy came into range, but that was all. The sickbays were empty, the hanger decks...everything. Except the bridge and the gunnery stations. There weren't even any engineers left onboard, no damage control at all. But that didn't mean Barron wasn't going to give the enemy one hell of a fight. He was.

And he wasn't going to allow the enemy to take the station. He had three different sets of explosives ready to go, any one of which would blast Striker to bits. He had them all lined up, one of them even set to explode on the hour...unless one of his people cancelled it.

He was sure most of his crew members knew they might be fighting their last battle. He'd selected those willing to fight to the end, even as he had issued withdrawal orders to the others. It occurred to him that he was keeping his best people to fight to the finish, if need be, and it ached at him. But he did it anyway.

He hadn't been entirely honest with himself until Atara had been assigned to hold back the enemy. Then it had come to him that he'd always intended to die in the fight...unless he won it, of course. That was something he knew he'd never really believed was possible. He wanted to pick at himself for not withdrawing at once...though he realized there was no better place to fight than Striker. The chance the fleet had had at victory, whether one had considered it seventy percent or one percent, had been stronger there than anywhere else.

Now, the fleet that escaped was badly damaged...and the chance of finding someplace else to stop and reorganize was nil. He knew many of his people would fight on—though he expected some would give up at some point—but the chances of actually winning the war were gone. If he'd had any doubts of that, the force still transiting into the system took it away. The enemy had more than enough strength now to wipe out what remained of the defensive force, and they could follow it anywhere. He knew there remained one chance, Andi's plan, and he was ready to support it...he just didn't believe it would work.

Still, despite his realism, he felt a motivation to escape. Now that he'd sent the last ships aboard Striker away with most of the crew, he second-guessed his decision to die there. It was almost as though there were two of him, switching back and forth as in command. One was determined to die, to escape from the balance of the fight…but now that it was too late to change that strategy, the other side manifested itself, telling him he had to live, for Andi and Cassie, if not for himself.

He regretted his not holding back the last ship, being so cavalier, not only with his own life, but with those of his last people. He was sure they felt as he did, a combination of ready to die…and prepared to live. But they wouldn't get the choice. He had made it for all of them. He regretted it, but not enough to call a ship back.

All he could do now was fight…and he'd always intended his last battle to be his most fearsome. If the enemy really wanted to take his fortress, he would have a chance at least.

A chance to fight as hard as possible…to die as he had lived.

* * *

"All units…begin pulling back. One quarter thrust…or whatever they've got." Atara Travis issued the command to her units, more ships than she'd expected to survive, though her casualties had still been great. She'd lost almost half her ships so far, and she was going to lose a lot more on the retreat…but she felt some satisfaction at the job she had managed to do. So far, at least.

"Yes, Admiral." Her senior aide repeated her orders. She knew they would be received with great joy, but she also knew a lot of those ships wouldn't make it out. She had done well…so far. But there was a lot left to do.

Including what she did next. "*Dauntless* is not to go with the fleet. Engage at full thrust…right toward Striker." She knew most of her people would know why she was heading there…or at least they would quickly figure it out. She was also sure many of them, most perhaps on *Dauntless*, would be with her. But she didn't really care. Her ship was battered, but it had escaped much of the damage it could have suffered...and she took that fact almost as a supernatural enhancement of what she intended to do. It was no guarantee she would make it, of course...but she was going to try.

There was a slight delay, but then the answer came back from her top aide. "Yes, Admiral!" She knew immediately, at least one of her people knew exactly what she was going to do...and was completely onboard with it.

She felt her ship move a little seconds later. The vessel had all the new and effective countermeasures against thrust, but she could still feel it to an extent. *Dauntless* had just fought an enemy ship—and destroyed it—and there was a moment when none of the Highborn were within range. The new force—over 140 ships, and still coming, including many battleships—was on the way. But even with her detour, she wouldn't have to face them. Just. And her forces, *all* the forces engaged in the fight, had done well against the enemy.

She looked ahead, along the route to Striker. The station had been mostly abandoned by the enemy fleet, especially as it came together on her ships. It was mostly stuck in place, and it would be there when the enemy force had the time to finish it...or take it. She figured the enemy had at least some thought about seizing the station, about taking some prisoners...but she knew Barron would never go along with that. He wasn't planning on escaping, she was pretty sure of that...but he wasn't going to give up either.

Neither was she. She was going to Striker...and she was pulling the admiral and his skeletal crew out of there.

She wondered if he would fight her...if he had already resolved to meet his end. She didn't know, but she was going to give him all she had, and she was sure that would be a lot. She knew herself well enough to be certain of that.

She just wasn't sure it would be sufficient. She knew Barron well, too.

* * *

Chronos sat, snapping out orders one after the other. He was heading to Striker, and he was well ahead of the fleet, at least all the units save for Atara's battered forces. Even they were beginning their withdrawal. He knew his effort was crazy, that it would make his ship the farthest from the transit point...but the enemy had mostly ignored Striker, at least for now. One ship wouldn't attract a lot of attention...at least he hoped it wouldn't. He was going in around the outside of the battlezone, making a run at Striker from the opposite side.

He gazed at the screen, at the approaching station in the center of it. He was maybe fifteen minutes away. No, he told himself, that's too optimistic. Twenty.

He had the cover of Atara's ships on the way in, but by the time he was heading back, those vessels, any that survived, would be ahead of him. His race to the point would be a tight one. If Barron agreed to come with him quickly, he would stay ahead of the enemy's fresh reserves...but whether a portion of their advanced forces would attempt to close on him, or whether they would write him off as one ship, pointless, was still a mystery.

"Increase speed to 115%." The order came out, almost by itself. He'd already been at 110%, which was high for a Hegemony ship. He'd seen Barron go to 115%, and once or twice, to 120%, but he hadn't dared to go that high.

Until now.

He knew a malfunction—almost anyone—took whatever chance he had of completing his mission away. But his gut told him to advance, to push on to the end.

"Yes, sir." The officer who answered had served a long time. He was a veteran of many wars, and while he definitely seemed to be in agreement with Chronos's orders...he was concerned, too.

Chronos stared at the screen, watching as his ship

increased its speed to 115%. The difference in arrival time
didn't vary that much at all, less than a minute coming off.
But Chronos knew that minute could be the one, the
separation between destruction and escape.

He looked at his crew, wondering how many truly
understood what they were doing. He was chasing after
Barron, with no orders to do so, no guarantee that the man
he had come to save wanted saving. He told himself that it
was a noble mission, that he would survive it…but he knew
he wasn't sure about any of that.

He looked down at the comm station, wondering how
soon he should call Barron. He would have contacted him
long ago…except he didn't want his comrade to tell him not
to come. Because he didn't care what Barron had to say, or
what his crew thought. He was coming…and he was going
to extract Barron and the last few survivors on Striker,
whatever they thought.

* * *

Barron was somber, mostly silent as he sat aboard Striker,
waiting for the enemy to arrive. His long-range guns were
still firing, lancing out at the three or four ships still in range.
Those vessels were moving away, chasing after the now-
fleeing reserves of Atara's force. He hoped she'd get
away…and then he realized *Dauntless* wasn't retreating. The
ship was heading almost directly toward Striker.

For an instant, he thought it was just a coincidence…and
then he remembered what Atara was like, and he realized
she was coming in for him. He paused, for just a moment,
looking at the screen, and at *Dauntless* heading right for
Striker. He wondered, for just an instant, if she could
actually make it. But then he decided it wasn't worth the
risk.

His hands moved down to his comm unit, and he
punched in the codes for his direct link to Atara. He hadn't

expected to talk to her again, and despite the situation, he was glad for the chance.

"Atara...this is Tyler." The terminology was all wrong, but Barron figured it would be the last time they spoke.

"Tyler...this is Atara." Barron heard her voice. She was tired, and terrified, but he knew he was the only one who could tell. To her people listening on her bridge, she was a rock of Gibraltar. He felt an urgency, a realism about telling her to leave. A realization that she wasn't going to listen.

"Atara...you've got to go. Back. You can pull *Dauntless* out of here, and you can make it out." That wasn't entirely true, but she did have a chance, which was more than he'd expected when she had been ordered to remain and hold back as much of the enemy as possible.

And coming in to rescue Striker's last inhabitants reduced that chance...considerably.

"That's not true, and you know it, Tyler. We're coming toward a barren part of space. The risk of picking you up is not that great. Get ready—get all your people ready—and we'll have as much chance as we would going right back."

Barron suspected she knew that wasn't true, that *Dauntless* had more of a chance making a dead run for it. But he also saw what she spoke of, and he wondered how much less chance the ship had of pulling his people out.

He found that he really wanted to go...that the thought of surviving was still powerful in him. He couldn't decide what to do, and as he was still thinking, his aide spoke.

"Sir, we've got another ship approaching the station...it's a Hegemony battleship."

Barron turned and looked across the bridge. He was surprised, no shocked. Finally, he said, "Get it on the comm now." Then he went back to Atara. "Atara, please hold."

He waited, no more than ten seconds, though it seemed like an hour. Then the aide turned back to him. "Commander Chronos, sir." He spoke the words fairly evenly, but Barron figured one more truly senior officer was about all the man could take.

"Chronos…get out of here. Now."

"No way, Tyler. We're both going…or neither of us is."

"Don't be ridiculous, Chronos. Just go."

"I'm not going, Tyler. I'm coming in, and you're coming aboard…you and everybody onboard. The battle is over. It's lost…but I'll be damned if I'm going to leave you behind."

Barron was lost for a moment, unsure what to do. He looked around the bridge, at the small crew remaining. For an instant, he resolved not to go, to tell both Chronos and Atara off, to challenge them both about sacrificing their crews for nothing.

But that only lasted a few seconds. Suddenly, he realized he had to pull out, that remaining in the station wouldn't contribute anything of note to the defensive effort. He paused a few seconds more, and then he looked at both ships, at their positions. His instinct was to ride with Atara, to return to *Dauntless*…but he realized that Chronos was closer, and his ship was farther back. He was the clear choice.

"Atara…I need you to go, to get out now."

She started to object again, but he spoke more loudly, "I'm coming, Atara…but Chronos has come for me, too. You can confirm it on your own screen. He's closer, and he's coming from behind. It just makes sense. Your best chance is to run, right back…right now. I'll follow with Chronos." He paused a moment, and then he added, "You know I wouldn't lie to you about this. I'm coming…and honestly, I've got a better chance on the Hegemony flagship."

There was a moment of silence, a bit of time Barron could never decide was enough for Atara to check her scans, to confirm that Chronos was, in fact, there. Then she said, "Okay, Tyler…good luck."

"And to you, Atara." *And to you.*

He looked down at his controls, pausing for just a

second before he flipped the switch back to Chronos. "Alright, my friend…come and get us. We'll be in…" He paused, thinking about the locations of the survivors, and the likeliest spot for them all to meet. "…docking station G-1."

Chronos didn't reply at first. Barron knew his position had dramatically changed in just a moment, and he was about to speak again, to try to explain, when Chronos's voice erupted. "Okay," he answered. "We'll be in place in twelve minutes…don't make us wait long."

Chapter Twenty-Five

Hegemony Flagship Basilarus
Vasa Denaris System
Year 329 AC (After the Cataclysm)

Chronos was silent. He had given orders, many orders, far more than he would usually have. He was the top military commander of the Hegemony, and if that was a smaller role than it had once been, it was still large. But now, he wanted to make sure everything went right, that his flagship docked properly. The portal was in decent shape, but only that. Virtually nothing on Striker was in top condition anymore.

Chronos knew Barron wouldn't have told him to dock with the station if he hadn't intended to evacuate. He realized the crew, most of them at least, would be there, soon if not immediately after he docked. He was somewhat less certain about Barron himself, though he was operating on the assumption that the leader was being honest with him. He'd always been that way, at least since they'd been allies, and he was fairly sure about it now.

"Twenty kilometers, sir." The words were routine, mouthed by his top aide. Normally he wouldn't have responded, but this time he did."

"Very well...maintain approach."

It was weird to be conducting such an operation himself.

It had been a long time since he had served in such a capacity, and it felt strange...and kind of good. He was accustomed to thinking about whole fleets and focusing on a single ship was a pleasant alternative.

Of course, the man he was trying to rescue—and while he was glad to save all the people on the station, he was there for one alone—was his leader. He knew that Barron was officially the same as him, and as Vian Tulus was. But he knew that was nonsense, too. He'd come to think of Barron as the overall commander, and while there was still some angst in the ranks, many of his people had more or less come to the same conclusion. He knew there would be more trouble, soon perhaps. Barron would probably agree with the final solution...but what would he do with the rest of the fleet? If he stood anywhere near the current system, he would almost certainly be destroyed. But if he pulled back to the Confederation border, the safer bet, at least for the short term, the Hegemony Council would almost certainly object.

Chronos would have complained about that, too, at one point. But he'd come to view the situation in real terms. He knew there were all kinds of possibilities that the desperate plan that Andi supported wouldn't work. In three centuries, it was possible, probable even, that the Highborn had found a way to block the formerly deadly virus. That was one possibility the whole side had barely discussed. There was no way to combat it, nothing to do but continue to work on the formula...and hope it worked.

Of course, it was also possible that the version the alliance had created wasn't exactly correct, that it wouldn't work at all, even if the enemy had not developed any treatment. There were other possibilities, too, which is why he had remained with Barron himself, right up until the current moment. But now, he knew, whatever chance the virus offered, it was the only one his people—all of the people—had. Any other effort, regardless of what the

Hegemony, or any of those involved in the alliance, thought, was pointless. He knew that, as surely as he knew why he was chasing after Barron.

He had fought against Barron, engaged him in war for more than six years. He had hated him at one time, and even after the two had come together to face the greater enemy, he'd viewed him as a necessary ally. But that was long ago—at least it seemed so—and he realized he thought of Barron now, almost as his superior, not just informally, in keeping with the general policy of the alliance. No, he was thinking of Barron as his commander, at least in certain ways…and he was determined to rescue him, whatever the cost.

"Five hundred meters, sir…"

Chronos looked ahead. He could see the indentation of the landing module, though not yet the details. The station was battered, badly damaged, and most of its docks were at least wounded. But the designated station, the one to which he'd been directed, was still in good shape.

Reasonably good.

That didn't mean the approaches, or the area inside the station from which the survivors were streaming, was in good condition. It didn't mean Barron, or the gunners and others present would be able to make it to the docking area.

But Chronos didn't think about any of that, at least no more than he had to. He was coming in, and that was all he could do. The rest was up to Barron and the last hundred or so occupants of the station.

* * *

Barron had ordered his gunners to depart immediately, and a moment later, he'd muttered out a similar command to the few officers gathered on the bridge. Within two minutes, he had everybody ready to leave. Except himself.

He considered the situation, and he knew he would go.

He knew his bridge personnel wouldn't leave without him. But he remained seated for just a moment, the last vestiges of his suicidal urges.

"Sir, we have to go."

He knew his senior aide would prompt him, and he was sure that he would go. But still, he remained in his chair, silent, for perhaps another fifteen or twenty seconds. Then he just looked up and nodded...and a few seconds later, he stood up and followed the officers off of the command deck. He paused again at the elevator bank, turning and looking at the bridge for a few seconds. Then he spun around and slipped inside.

The other occupants had already punched in the destination. The deck was a long way from the bridge, and the journey would take five minutes or more...assuming the route was clear. It was open, at least as far as Barron's instruments had depicted, but he knew there was at best a fifty percent chance that was right. The scanners and detectors had been badly damaged in the previous fight, and the replacements had been partial and far thinner than the standard.

But there was no other way. Chronos would wait, he knew, as long as he could. But Barron also knew that the enemy ships would start closing on the system fairly soon...and Chronos would have to leave sooner or later. All he could do was hope that he was there in time.

He felt the direction of movement change. The elevator had been going up, and now it was moving to the side. Every second that past was another bit of the journey done. It brought him that much closer to escape...and that was what he wanted now. His past thoughts of death were gone, save only his remembrance, and the fact that not one, but two friends had come for him had refilled his will to endure. He knew he would have to allow the effort with the virus now, that there was no other realistic choice. If he continued to oppose it, he would probably be the only one.

But he wasn't against it either, not anymore. It still troubled him, killing millions of the enemy, perhaps billions, if that many existed. But it was the only way…the only option save surrender. And that was utterly unthinkable to him.

The elevator car continued on its way, reaching 80-85% of the way…and then stopping.

He came out of his deep thought, and he punched at the control, twice, three times. Nothing.

"I think the way is blocked, sir."

He turned, realizing his aide was right. He thought for a few seconds, and he was almost ready to order everyone out. But the way was still fairly long, and there were blocked passages and other problems along the way. He almost gave the order anyway, and he went so far as to think of how far back he would have to bring the car to get his people out.

But that's not what he said. "Okay, Jerry, Clark…help me open up the forward side. Chances are, it's just a small patch in the way. Maybe we can get it out, and go the rest of the way." He sounded confident, but inside, he was far less. It could very well be a small blockage holding them up, but he had no way of knowing. It could be a massive impediment as well, or even the tunnel crushed. He just didn't know.

He extended his fingers under the panel's edge, pulling, even as his two companions did the same. The car was built to allow for the side to open, but it was battered, beaten up in two battles, and Barron knew it might be subtly misshapen. That possibility only progressed in his mind as it didn't move at all when he first reached under and started to pull.

Then his friends grabbed on as well, one above and one below where his hands were…and the panel started to shift. It moved slowly for a few seconds, and then it popped off.

Barron fell backwards with his two companions, and it took him a few seconds to get back up, to look out into the panel. He feared seeing nothing but collapsed decks and other garbage filling the entire area…but when he managed to actually take a look, he saw that there was only a small pile, mostly easy to move, with one large piece of a girder in the way. If he was alone, he doubted he could move it, but there was no question that three or four of his people could. That left many questions, among them, whether the large chunk of steel would move…or whether it would trigger a further collapse. But he knew he didn't have time to think about it. Chronos would stay as long as possible…but he only had a limited time until the enemy ships—both the new ones and the ones that had stopped pursuing the fleeing fleet—reached the station.

"Clark, Jerry…come on. Let's get all of this out of here and see if we can get the car started again. Let's get the small stuff first." He heard the grunting acceptance of his two drafted counterparts, and in just a minute or two, they had everything removed. Except the piece of girder. They were standing around that, looking at Barron…waiting for the word to proceed.

Barron looked at the chunk of metal, and he figured he had a good chance of moving it to the side without bringing down more. At least a decent possibility.

"Alright," he said, "let's grab it and move it here." He gestured to what he perceived as the obvious location…but he wasn't taking any chances. "On three…one."

He reached out, grabbing the chunk of metal. It was sharp underneath where he reached first, and he moved his hands over, to a smoother part.

"Two."

He sucked in a deep breath, and he exhaled hard.

"Three."

He pulled, and for an instant, the chunk of steel didn't move. He'd considered it, run his mind through it. The three of them should be able to move it. But it stayed where it was.

For a few seconds. Then it began to move…and Barron

realized it was connected to part of the metal below. "Hard...as hard as you can..." He muttered the thought, at least he thought he did, but when it came out, it was almost a shout.

He turned and looked at his two companions. They were pulling with all they had...and the chunk of metal was moving...slowly. He had four more people in the car, but he realized he couldn't fit anymore in the section of the elevator tunnel. He pulled again, with all he had left...and the chunk of steel pulled a little. Then it broke free, and it moved much more quickly. Suddenly, it was over, almost far enough, just a single corner extending in the way.

"We've almost got it...one more push, and we're there." He had no idea if the elevator would work. There were a hundred other things that could be wrong. But something told him, if he could just clear the way, the doomed car would get him and his seven companions where they were going.

He shoved, pushed hard on the chunk of metal, and as his two companions again joined him, it gave way, and fell out of the way. The track was clear, more or less at least, and it was time to get back in the car, and to see if it moved.

One of his companions regripped the panel to the side—now the front—of the elevator, but Barron shook his head. "No," he said, "we don't have time." That was one thing that had been growing on him all the while he and his people had moved the barricade. He knew Chronos well, and he was sure the Hegemony leader would wait...as long as he could.

But he wouldn't wait too long. And Barron didn't have any more access to the data, to potentially approaching enemy ships. All he had was his gut...and it told him to hurry.

"Alright...everybody, stay away from the front of the car. If there's something else in the way, it might come in here." He closed his eyes, just for an instant, and he pressed the button.

The car started moving!

Barron hadn't really expected it to work, though he only realized that after he knew it was working. There were still a dozen things that could go wrong, but he was on the way.

* * *

Chronos waited, his eyes bouncing back and forth, one instant on the hallway to his front, the next on the small screen he had set up on a stand nearby. He was committed to stay, to wait for Barron...though he knew he had to leave. Soon.

With or without the Confederation commander.

He was going to wait, as long as possible...but the approaching Highborn fleet units made that a short while. By some standards, he should have pulled out already...but he was working on the tightest figures he could manage. And he was running out of time, even then.

He had all the personnel from the station aboard already, all but Barron and his reduced bridge crew. His mind bounced around, wondering if Barron hadn't misled him, if he hadn't intended to leave at all. But he pushed those thoughts aside. Barron was tired, worn...but he wasn't a liar. If he'd been determined to stay, he would have just said so. Besides, without his gunners in place, he couldn't do anything anyway. The guns were still firing, but their targeting was entirely automated, and that meant they weren't hitting as well. And Barron's bridge crew was among the best in the fleet. He wouldn't leave them to die for no reason, and Chronos was sure they wouldn't go without him.

Still, he knew the time would come when even he had to give up, to pull away knowing he was leaving Barron to certain death. He tried his best not to think about it, to consider almost anything else. But with each passing minute, it became more and more difficult.

He turned to face his number two, at least at the current location. It was a Master, a man named Barrister, and Chronos was pretty damned sure his aide recognized his attachment to Barron, even if he didn't share it. That last part wasn't clear, not even to Chronos, but he was at least fairly sure Barrister was at least sympathetic.

"Sir...we can wait five more minutes. Maybe. Then we've *got* to get going. Even that could be too long. I'm sorry, but..." He paused for an instant. He'd gotten the basic part of his feelings out, but he was too troubled to finish. Chronos suspected Barrister *did* feel the way he did, if not as passionately.

"I know, Barrister...I know." He felt the urge to clear away his colleague, to give him something to do. "Go inside...and get the ship ready to go." The vessel was more or less ready for a maximum speed lift off, but it was the best reason Chronos could think of to clear the man, and most of the others as well. "All of you...go inside and get ready to leave. I'll remain here for...four more minutes. Then we'll leave."

He watched as the small group around him hesitated, and he gestured with his head toward the door. He was about to follow up with another shout, when they began to move—slowly.

His attention was diverted, and it took close to two minutes for all of them to pack up and get aboard. He missed the sound of the approaching car...at least for the first few seconds. Then he spun around and listened...and he realized he did hear the car coming. He felt his heart beating, and his hands began to sweat. He knew Barron would come by the vehicle, but he still couldn't believe it.

He *didn't* believe it, not for another moment. Then the car stopped, and the door opened. Barron climbed out, followed by seven of his people...the last live occupants of

Fortress Striker. Barron looked worn, as Chronos knew they all were. He was tired and battered. But his eyes shone brightly, and as he saw Chronos, he smiled, for just a second. Then he stepped forward and hugged the Master.

Chronos found himself returning the gesture, and the two men stood, for perhaps twenty seconds, and embraced. Then Barron pulled back and said, "My guess is, we don't have long to get the hell out of here."

Chronos nodded, and he said, "No…we're down to the last couple minutes." He kept silent that he might have waited too long. "But we're ready to blast off, so let's go." His eyes widened to the others, and he said, "All of you…onboard now. We're ready to lift off."

Chapter Twenty-Six

CWS Dauntless
Vasa Denaris System
Year 329 AC (After the Cataclysm)

Atara watched as Chronos's ship blasted hard from Striker. She had plenty to worry about around her, the status of the surprisingly undaunted *Dauntless* chief among them, but she found her thoughts drifting again and again to Tyler Barron. Chronos's ship had indeed separated from the station and headed away at full power...but it hadn't sent any messages. For the first minute or two, she figured the commander was focusing on accelerating away, but then she started to get nervous. She knew Chronos, not nearly as well as Barron did, but well enough to tell her the Hegemony Master would have announced he had succeeded in his efforts.

She almost turned *Dauntless* around, determined to bring the ship back to Striker, to find Barron if Chronos hadn't...but she knew her chances were exactly zero. She checked half a dozen approaches to the station, but none got her there before the new enemy force.

She felt her eyes moisten, something that had never happened in front of her crew before. She was on the verge of realizing Barron was lost...but then, just a few seconds later, the comm unit engaged, and Tyler Barron announced his presence on the Hegemony flagship.

"Tyler...I'm thrilled that you made it!" Atara was one of the coldest, most to the point officers in the fleet, but for that moment, she let it all slide away.

"Atara, I'm glad to hear from you. But neither of us is away, not yet. So, let's focus on getting there, and then we can talk."

"You're right, of course, Admiral." Her voice, and her exterior tone, were back to normal. But inside, she was still happy, still cheering. Barron was right, of course, her ship—and his—were not out of the system yet. Not only that, but she didn't know what they were going to do, even if they did escape. They had lost the battle, and the force they would have was barely half what they had started with, at least taking the most damaged ships out of the mix. She knew there would be discussions, debates...and she knew what would win. The last chance at victory, and it wasn't another conventional fight. That was over, the chance of winning the war with normal weapons. She knew that...and she knew that Barron would as well.

The last chance was to strike at the very existence of the enemy, to try to kill them all. She knew Barron thought that was outside the realm of war, that striking at the very existence of an enemy was above and beyond what was called for. But she was also sure he would give in, that he would realize there was no other choice, no way to prevail save for the desperate attempt. He would hate and despise himself...but he would go along with it.

Atara had already decided on her position. She would go along with Barron, and she would act like she felt the same way. But the truth was different, and far harsher.

Atara had lost too many people, seen too much death. She was more than willing to launch the desperate attack against the enemy. She was excited, anxious. She wanted to destroy the Highborn, every last one of them that existed...and she didn't care about anything else.

* * *

"I don't know what to say, Chronos...except thank you."
Barron stood inside the Hegemony dreadnought, looking
tired, but still glaring with defiance in his eyes. He'd thanked
Chronos already, twice actually, and he'd told Atara that he
was aboard. But he knew what lay ahead of him. And he
found it terrifying.

"You're welcome, Tyler...again. You would have done
the same thing for me, I am sure of that."

Barron sat for a few seconds, considering what he would
have done. He wanted to object, to argue that he would
have allowed Chronos to die...but he knew it was nonsense.
Somewhere along the line, he'd come to view the
Hegemony as staunch allies, and he'd almost forgotten that
just a few years before, they were the enemy. He knew that
was an imperfect thought, that his opinion of his allies was
based on his impression of Akella and Chronos, that the
two of them, and many of their military subordinates, were
the standard. He knew that wasn't true, that the Hegemony
was a large and complex organism, just as the
Confederation, with different viewpoints and positions. But
for the moment, he saw the entire thing as though Akella
and Chronos ruled unquestioned. He knew it wasn't true,
that he would encounter the complexities and problems of
the actual situation rapidly...but for the moment, he just
decided to just believe his allies and he were completely
bound.

He'd realized something else, too. He had been against
using the virus on moral grounds, that was true...but it had
been even more about the fact that he didn't expect it to
work. He'd just realized that, truly realized it, and he hadn't
shared it with anyone. He could tell Andi about it, usually at
least, but in this case she was so determined to carry out the
operation, he couldn't see informing her that he didn't think
it would work, all the more because it was only his point of

view, and not any kind of real insight. For all he really knew, it would work, even well. His negative view wasn't the result of real consideration. He didn't even know what it was about. But the lack of any hope on the conventional military front didn't leave any choice, none that he could accept.

He had to support the new operation...and he had to believe it would work. There was no other choice.

None.

"Chronos...I just wanted to tell you, I'm supporting the operation with the virus. I did my best, we all did, but we don't have any chance of winning...any other chance." Barron hadn't chosen Chronos as the first one he would tell about his change of heart, but he figured the order didn't matter much. The Hegemony grand commander had been on his side, right through the just-concluded battle, but he was fairly certain Chronos had come to the same conclusion he had. There was no other choice.

"I'm glad to hear that, Tyler. As you know, I have been in favor of a conventional military response, much as you. But that is gone now. There is no other option...save surrender. And that, I will never do. Never."

Barron stared back, and even as he did, he felt surer, more confident. "Neither will I, Chronos...neither will I."

Barron's eyes diverted, to the screen, to Striker. What had been the image of the base, at least. Now, it was just a massive plasma, expanding even as he watched. He had left the charges in place, and he knew it was going to happen, counted on it, even. But it still took him by surprise, and he looked, seeing his massive fortress reduced...to nothing at all. And with it went any doubt that had lingered about what he had to do.

*   *   *

"I want to thank you all for coming. I know we've all had different opinions on how to proceed, but I feel we are in the same place now. The enemy forces are too large, too powerful for us to defeat, even with the Confederation's increased production rates. The Hegemony is half occupied, and whatever we decide to do regarding the other half, it will fall. We just don't have the power to mount a defense. Striker was located well, in a section where the two halves of the Hegemony met at a single point...but there are no other such alternatives, no other areas where there is only one course of advance. If we do not engage in the plan to use the virus, and do so immediately, we will fall...without question." Barron felt strange, urging his comrades to support the plan he had been so against...indeed, he realized, he had been perhaps one of the most opposed. But he was a realist, at heart at least, and he understood there was no other way.

And Tyler Barron would do anything except surrender.

The gathered assembly remained silent for a moment, but no one objected. There were men and women who'd already been in favor of the current plan, and there were others who'd been as opposed as Barron himself. But no one questioned him.

Finally, Clint Winters spoke. "Tyler, I agree with you." He paused for few seconds, looking around the enormous table. Then he continued, "I think we all agree with you. It is the only route to success, whether that chance of that is five percent or ninety-five. But what of the others? We are all military men and women..." His eyes caught Akella's. She wasn't military, at least not in her background...but he'd come to rely on her decisions. He almost excepted her from his statement, but she'd earned a place with the military, at least as far as he was concerned. "We will fight, whether our civilian masters argue to yield, whether some of our junior members would choose to discuss terms. We will fight...and I, for one, will not survive final defeat. So, let us proceed, with the only way the enemy has left to us."

Tyler Barron was glad to hear Winter's words. He was

one of those Barron wasn't sure about, and he was glad to have him aboard.

Or more accurately, probably, for Barron to be aboard.

"I agree, with you, Clint...as I suspect everyone here does." Barron turned toward Andi, surprised to hear her speak up. Things were going exactly as she wanted, and he wasn't sure what she had to gain by talking. "Look, most of you knew where I stand on this. It's not a secret. But I agreed to wait out the battle, to see if there was any chance we could win that way. For a short while, I even thought we might...but in the end we didn't. Now, Tyler is aboard, as I suspect all of you are, whether it is because you really want it, or you just believe there is no option. Either way, I propose that I lead a small force out to the test planet...that I grab a few of the Highborn there. The infections should be making themselves apparent soon, and if we have some of them, we can see at once. If the formula works, if the Masters become sick, we will know at least that it works...and I'd wager we can next determine if there is some kind of medicine or other treatment that can alleviate it."

Andi paused, for a moment, and then she continued. "If the virus doesn't work, or if the enemy has come up with some kind of vaccine or other treatment...we are lost. We will all have to decide whether to yield—assuming the enemy even takes prisoners among the military—or to find our own deaths." She left no doubt where her own choice lay. "But if it does work, and if the enemy doesn't have a treatment, then we're back in this...at least with a chance of success. Whether we can truly achieve complete victory, eliminate the entire enemy population or not, we will have a deadly weapon, one that will change the fight forever."

Barron listened to Andi, knowing she was trying to hide her hatred for the Highborn. He hated them too, everyone present did, but he knew that Andi's was on a different level. But despite her strong feelings, she had agreed to wait until his effort had failed. Now he had to support hers. Whether he thought it would work or not, it was the only possibility that remained.

He sat silently for a while, as did everyone else, but he looked around, and he saw that everyone agreed with Andi. He even did. He had tried with all his might and skill to avoid this, to find another way. But there wasn't one…and he realized his people were fortunate to have even the chance. Without the virus, he would be facing a hopeless defense…and an ultimate total defeat.

Finally, Barron spoke. "I agree, Andi. It doesn't matter whether anyone thought this was the best way to go before or not. And it doesn't make any difference what the others think, the Senators and Council members and the like. This is a military decision." Barron thought about that last part, about whether it was in fact just the choice of the military. He didn't know how the enemy would respond, but he at least surmised that they might strike back, change their target from the conquest of humanity to its destruction. It's utter destruction.

But he didn't care. From his point of view, there was no other choice, no option, and while he knew billions back home would have a different opinion, it didn't rate with him. "This is the only option we can take now, the only way to give us a chance at victory. I say we do it, we do it and hope for the best, for success. But I don't think we have the time to go just for the test planet. I think we have to assume the virus works…and we have to strike with it. Now."

Chapter Twenty-Seven

Highborn Flagship S'Argevon
Imperial System GH3-2327
Year of the Firstborn 391 (329 AC)

"Brilliant, Tesserax, simply brilliant." The words weren't exactly true. Phazarax thought Tesserax had held back the reserves for longer than was necessary, that he'd lost more ships than he might have, and suffered greater damage to many units. But the result was the same. A decent amount of the enemy force had managed to escape, more perhaps than he would have liked to see, but it wasn't enough to mount a real defense. Phazarax was sure the enemy was beaten, even if it took a few more years of fighting to prevail against all the remaining units and planets. He'd been of the opinion that the force had been strong enough to defeat the enemy, to drive them away from their great station...and he'd been correct. And despite the greater than expected losses the forces had suffered, Tesserax hadn't even had to deploy the four special units. They were still a surprise, and an even deadlier one than they had been.

"Thank you, Phazarax...your thoughts are greatly appreciated." Tesserax had been easier to get along with in the months before the assault. He'd known that his forces were probably sufficient to knock out the enemy, but

Phazarax suspected the doubts were still present. Now, Tesserax had accomplished enough to secure his position, probably through the remaining several years of battle. Phazarax was glad, he had a reasonable relationship with Tesserax, and he'd chosen to keep that if possible. But he was a bit concerned as well, a bit afraid that his 'friend' bore failure better than success.

"Part of me wants to chase them now…but a quick look at the fleet tells me we've got to do some repairs first." He paused a few seconds, then added, "Though not long enough to allow the enemy to complete any meaningful reinforcement. Do you agree?"

"I have considered just those thoughts. I believe the decision is close…but I am inclined to agree. If we were only discussing the phase three ships, it would be easier, but we have the four greater vessels too, most likely still unknown to the enemy. In the end, it was a very close decision…but I agree, we have to conduct some repairs first. Four months…six at an absolute maximum. Then we will proceed forward…and we will engage whatever enemy forces remain." He was silent, for just a few seconds. Then he added, "Then we will begin the final part of the effort, the complete destruction of the human empires, and the establishment of Highborn rule over humanity everywhere."

Phazarax nodded. He was a bit concerned about his partner's apparent return to self-assurance, but Tesserax still seemed to be guided mostly by solid reasoning. "I am pleased that we agree, Tesserax, truly pleased."

"I am, as well, Phazarax. I will tell you, and you alone, I was beginning to fear that the enemy would find a way to hold out, and the Supreme Leader would have acted…aggressively. I am grateful that I was able to win…in time."

Phazarax understood what Tesserax was saying, and he understood. He knew it was a weakness of sorts, admitting to his concerns…but it also told him that his associate had

not lost sight of the enemy's skills, their capabilities. They
were dangerous...Phazarax knew that, and he was glad to
find that Tesserax did as well.

"We have entered the final phase of the confrontation,
Tesserax. The enemy is beaten, and though some portion of
their forces will fight on, likely to the end, there is no more
hope...if indeed there ever was. You have succeeded in
your endeavor, Tesserax...and you will see it through to the
end, to an illustrious victory." His words were chosen,
carefully constructed based on the situation. But they were
true as well, for the most part. He would have handled
things differently than Tesserax if he'd been in command,
but he had learned enough from the humans to realize that
they would have fought bravely against him as well. He'd
learned a lesson, from his own experiences with the humans
as well as Tesserax's, and he realized they were more capable
than he had imagined at first. They would lose the fight,
certainly, but Phazarax would save as many as possible of
the best of the enemy. They were worth it, worth the extra
effort to bring into line.

He wondered how Tesserax felt, whether he wanted to
save the enemy leaders, at least as many as possible...or
whether he wanted them all dead.

* * *

Percelax sat quietly, smiling to himself as his forces prepared
to jump. His actions were all guesses really, but he had a
good notion that Tesserax would attack soon—if he had not
already done so. That was good, and he was sure Tesserax's
forces would prevail, and probably by a considerable
margin. He was equally certain the overall commander
would send orders for him to hold, to await further action.
That made perfect sense, at least to most points of view.
Why risk an operation against the enemy so much deeper in,

when their fleet had been destroyed…or at least badly damaged.

But that wasn't what he wanted.

He knew he would benefit anyway, just being part of the command structure of Tesserax's victory. But he realized he would gain more esteem, far more, if he was successful on his own. His record was currently 0-1, and that total looked bad, far worse than it really was. He wanted to at least equal that total, and do it with the second fight, the larger and more important one. He knew the victory would reflect well on him, even as Tesserax took the bulk of the glory. He was fine with that, with just part of the credit, but he knew his commander wanted it all, or as much as he could claim.

"Begin the attack…the first ships are to advance." That was why he had pushed his forces, done everything possible to prepare for the attack, pushing them forward at an almost impossible rate. He had the authority, even if that was only because no one back in the main headquarters thought it was possible for him to strike so soon. He was sure his orders to remain in place would come as soon as Tesserax's battle was over, but it would take weeks and weeks for it to reach him. The trail back to the main fleet was long, stretching over a distant arc…and with his speed, he had managed to get into position. Far more quickly than he guessed Tesserax had imagined possible.

He had managed to organize the fleet for the assault as well, the one that would secure for him his share of the glory. He had put his ships through hell, even as they were moving at maximum speed toward the battle. He had done everything he could think of, taken every precaution, every measure he could think of. His mind made up a million excuses for the previous defeat, and while many of them were self-serving and pointless, his realization that he had almost prevailed last time—that if he'd been willing to really push, he might have *actually* won—was perfectly valid.

"The attack has begun, Commander. The forward force

has started to advance."

Percelax nodded, but he didn't say anything. He'd given the orders, and his fleet was lined up, ready to advance. It was time to prevail, and he told himself retreat wasn't an option this time. He simply *had* to take the system, and damn the consequences.

Damn them to hell.

* * *

"I want scouts sent after the enemy fleet. I want to know where they are, every minute. If they separate, I want to know. Is that understood? Take as many small ships as you need, Barterax, and engage as required. But don't lose any major force. Understood?" Tesserax was being far tighter than he had been, and despite his own—and apparently everyone else's—opinion that he had prevailed, he was still operating at a strange level of urgency. Part of him had expected the enemy fleet to fight on, regardless of what he poured into the battle. There was no better chance out there, for retreating, not really, no other way he could imagine the enemy prevailing. But they'd pulled out the instant his reserves began to appear.

And they'd executed their withdrawal brilliantly, better than he'd imagined.

It wasn't good enough, though, and he'd intercepted dozens of enemy ships that were damaged, vessels that were racing for escape. Some ships made it away, but many didn't. He had ordered his pursuing vessels to go full speed toward the enemy's escape point...but no farther. Chasing even a defeated enemy was difficult, and Tesserax had decided to stop...for the moment.

The enemy was battered, and while he didn't know where they would retreat, he knew their options were poor. There was no place in the Hegemony that was even a close match to the system he'd just taken, no position he couldn't just slip around. He even hoped the foolish enemy would begin building a new base in a poorly located system…though he didn't believe that would happen. He'd come to respect the foe, in spite of his earlier feelings, and he was fairly sure they would retreat back to the Confederation border. That was good, in the sense that it would leave the rest of the Hegemony to him, and provide more systems he could take and advise HQ back home about, but it was bad in the context that it was probably the strongest plan, especially if the Hegemony forces remained with them.

But it wouldn't be enough. He had decided he would keep his fleet together, every unit he could assemble, and he would pursue the enemy. He would stay in touch with them as they pulled back, and he would launch his full force at them in four months, six at the outside. That wasn't enough time to fix his entire fleet, not even close, but assuming he could pull up sufficient portable units, to match the fleet bases he'd established around, he could do *enough* repairs.

The enemy would bring in new ships as well, and pushing them back on their lines only drove them closer to the booming Confederation production lines. He was mystified at the number of Confederation hulls he had engaged, and he still couldn't quite figure out where all of them had come from. Especially since the enemy had assembled another force at Fortress Grimaldi, to counter the battered Union, and the relatively small forces he had sent there.

He knew Percelex well, understood the way the commander of the force's mind worked. He even respected it, in a sense. Percelax wanted to open a second engagement. He wanted to erase any disgrace that remained from his defeat in the same place. And he would have the chance to do just that. But as part of the final move against the Confederation, in six months and not now. Tesserax had already sent the orders, to continue to assemble the force, both additional Highborn ships and the growing Union contingent...but not to attack without specific orders from him to do so.

He wondered for a moment, if Percelax had managed to move his forces more quickly than he'd assumed, if he'd positioned himself to attack...before the word came not to attack. He didn't think so, but he didn't really care either. If Percelax was aggressive, if he managed to launch his assault before he got the orders not to...it was fine. He would likely prevail, and take Fortress Grimaldi, leaving the enemy in even worse shape than they were, possibly with a final battle line not along the frontier, but in the Iron Belt itself.

And if he failed...well if he failed, he would do incredible damage to the Confederation forces, and to what was left of Grimaldi...and Tesserax would be free of one more officer who was useful, but in the end, just a hanger on.

Chapter Twenty-Eight

Fleet Base Grimaldi
Krakus System
Year 329 AC (After the Cataclysm)

"Sam...you've got a huge part of the fleet...remember that. I've got Grimaldi, and the shorter ranged units surrounding it, but most of the rest is yours." Colin Simpson sat, as close to bolt upright as he could bring himself. He had sent out a bunch of messages to fleet units, all through Larson James. He'd taken James onto his staff reluctantly, as a last choice, but despite his doubts, the man had performed brilliantly, something all the more important since he longstanding aide, Isaac Johnson, had been loaned out to Taggart, and bumped up to command two dozen ships.

Still, Taggart he communicated with directly. It was only fitting, as she was his second in command, but it was also necessary. Taggart was a perfect officer, aside from her tendency to swear. She was clearly trying to cut back on it, with some success, but Simpson was well trained to get her on a direct line whenever possible.

"Colin, I just want to address the breakdowns again. You've given me too much. I was just a captain a few months ago. It was enough of a bolt upward last time to give me *Constellation*...much less a big chunk of the fleet.

Now, I've got more than twice as much as last time."

"Sam, you can handle it...and to be honest, even if you couldn't, you're the best we've got, so you're going to have to do your best." He held back some of what he truly believed, that she was the best officer present, himself included. There was no point. They had their positions already, and while he had the authority to relieve her, he supposed, he didn't have the ability to make her number one and himself number two.

But he could give her a large portion of the fleet...perhaps too large. And he had done just that.

"Colin...I mean..." She was silent for a moment, and Simpson knew he was being spared a litany of curses. "Thank you," she finally said.

"Your welcome. Now, why don't you..."

Simpson froze, his own eyes catching the image as quickly as Jaymes's. Though the aide's warning came through while he was still staring at the screen. "Enemy ship..." And possibly the appearance of the entire enemy fleet. Though Jaymes didn't say that last part, Simpson heard it, nevertheless.

"Sam, we've got at least one enemy—no two now—coming in. I don't know if it's the attack we've been expecting, but we'd better be ready, just in case it is."

"I hear you, Colin. Good luck Admiral." There was clearly no doubt in her voice that the two enemy ships—three now—was the main attack they'd been waiting for.

"And good luck to you, too, Commodore." He flipped off the comm unit, and he turned toward Jaymes. "Five ships so far...we've got to assume this is the attack we've been waiting for. Message to the entire fleet."

"Communique ready, sir." The speed of Jaymes response told Simpson that he had been preparing the transmission since the first sighting.

Simpson paused, just for a minute. Then he reached down and touched the mike, causing a rippling sound. A second later, he was talking.

"Alright, everybody...we've got seven ships so far, and they don't look like they're going to stop anytime soon. It looks like this is the attack we've been waiting for. You all knew it was coming...so just do your best."

He nodded over to Jaymes, who cut the line. His message had been short, very short, but he knew he'd told his people what to do at least fifty times before. They all knew what was coming...and from the look of things, ten enemy ships now, and still coming, it had arrived.

Simpson realized something that he'd considered at least a hundred times over the past month. The enemy was almost certainly too big for his force to hold back again. Holding the position was still the stated purpose, but Simpson knew his job was something else.

To damage the enemy before he was driven away—or destroyed outright. To buy the Confederation at least a few more months, maybe half a year, before it was attacked at the core...and likely destroyed. His survival, or that of any of his people, any of his ships, would be a positive.

But it wasn't essential.

*   *   *

Sam Taggart sat in her chair and watched. She hadn't doubted the attack was the final one she'd been waiting for, not when it was only two enemy ships. But now, there were more than sixty, and the number kept increasing. Whatever minor questions she'd had, any hope that what she was watching was anything but the attack she'd expected for six months, was completely gone.

She harbored some vestigial hope that the force they'd managed to assemble could hold out against the enemy attack, but in her heart of hearts, she'd never really believed that. She considered the 'victory' won six months before as pure luck. She'd known that Simpson was close to calling it, to ordering what remained of the defending forces to withdraw…but the enemy had retreated first. There were ways to call that legitimate, to applaud her side's stamina, just a bit better than the other side's, but to her it was just luck.

"*Gravamere*, *Hermes*, and *Scintilla*…one-quarter thrust. Back up, and form with the line." She understood the pull some of her people felt, the urge to advance and force the conclusion that much more quickly, but it didn't make any sense for her ships to be spread out. Whatever happened—and she saw it as more or less as a loss, no matter what took place—she needed to get the most out of her force. And that meant everything in line, and not a bit farther forward. Her line would hit together, as quickly as possible, and the fight would be on.

"All three ships have responded, Commodore."

She heard the sound of Lieutenant-Commander Johnson. He'd been with her for a long time, and he'd followed her escalation in rank. He was a terribly efficient officer, and a great aide too, she had discovered, but she could hear that part of him agreed with her…and part of him didn't. He knew the fight was probably a mismatch, that the enemy wouldn't have attacked without enough force to push her people out of the system. But he was charged up for battle now, and at least part of him had forgotten that the fight was hopeless. He understood her orders to the ships to pull back…but it was clear he harbored some thoughts about outright victory.

"Very well, Lieutenant-Commander…we want to hit the enemy together." She hadn't intended to answer at all, but she found herself trying to justify her actions to her subordinate. She knew it was pointless. Whether he completely understood or not, he would execute her commands flawlessly. But she needed *someone* to understand. Most of her people had worked themselves up, convinced that they had a real chance. She was jealous, in part…and also sorry. But she didn't see any way to win.

She just wanted to damage the enemy, hurt them badly enough that their advance stopped where it was, that they didn't push on, through whatever wreckage was left of her fleet toward the Core and beyond. That would buy some more months at least, and as long as time stretched on, so did hope.

Whether or not she survived.

"Alright, everybody…the enemy has a longer range than us, so be ready. We'll be taking fire for two and a half minutes, maybe three…so jazz up your engines and do your best not to get hit. Starting now." She turned toward her assistant, and she issued the orders for *Constellation*. The massive ship was the biggest on either side, and while she hadn't been able to repair it totally from the last battle, it was in surprisingly good shape.

For another few minutes at least…

She knew the enemy would target her vessel. It was by far the largest on her side, and size wasn't something that could be easily hidden. In another battle, she might have kept her flagship out of range, but *Constellation* was a massive part of her force. It *had* to be right in the center…and that was exactly where she had it.

"Commander, engage engines…plan alpha-3." She was *Constellation*'s commander as well as that of much of the fleet, and she remembered her duties.

"Yes, Commodore…engaging now."

A few seconds later, she felt a strange sensation, the engine running ahead of the dampeners. It only lasted a second, but it told her she was in battle once again.

About twenty seconds later, the enemy barrage opened up…and she really knew.

* * *

"It's alright…just stay on the enemy fleet. Fire all weapons in range, and be ready to open up with the shorter ranged guns the instant the enemy is close enough." Colin Simpson sat on Grimaldi's bridge, directing the base's defenders. Vast sections of the base were still in ruins, left over from the past battle just over six months before. Simpson was amazed at the weaponry—and it was mostly weapons that had been restored—that was operational, but as the battle commenced, he had quickly realized just how much hadn't even been touched. The enemy's third hit in as many minutes had only dimmed his hopes. He didn't expect to win the battle, not really. But he was hopeful his forces would badly damage the enemy. Damage them enough to halt them at Grimaldi, at least for a while.

At what will be the remnants of Grimaldi that is. One thing he was *sure* about was, the enemy would gain control of no station, nothing worth anything at least. He intended to fight until Grimaldi was nothing but a hollowed out wreck...but even if he left the station earlier, he would destroy it, or at least any of its functionality.

It wasn't going to happen unless his luck got better though...at least destroying the station wouldn't be his problem. The drives were vastly smaller than those in his ships, but they had been repaired, and the enemy's sequence of early hits was just luck. A bit more of it, however, and he would have a real problem, much earlier than he'd expected.

"We're fixed, sir. All guns in range firing at full speed." Larson Jaymes sounded remarkably calm, and despite the fact that Simpson knew it was bullshit, he found himself feeding off of it. Just another surprise in Jaymes, who had come very far from the man Simpson had met out along the border.

"Very well." Simpson knew he was drawing conclusions from a few lucky early shots, but he was still upset...until another few minutes went by with no hits coming in at all...and his own heavy guns began to find their mark. The base station secured three hits of its own—no, he realized as another struck one of the enemy ships hard, four. And Commodore Taggart's force was doing even better. He began to realize that, in spite of the damage to the station, his force was actually doing well.

He sat in his place, watching, waiting. There was often little else to do at this stage of a fight. His people had their orders, and most of them were surprisingly optimistic. He knew that, at least, would fade, that he would be forced to bolster his people's morale before the day was over. But for the moment, there wasn't much to do except watch his forces fight…and hope for the best.

He sat back in his chair, and he looked. There was nothing else he could do, not at the moment, nothing except wait and see how well his people did…and whether they could at least take the strength out of the enemy fleet before they were pushed back.

Or destroyed utterly.

* * *

Samantha Taggert looked out over the force, her eyes moving from the guide that told her of her fleet's condition to the one that told her of *Constellation*'s. The super-battleship was doing fairly well, the result of both its size, and its luck. Most of the rest of the fleet was doing substantially worse.

She took the losses in stride, especially since her ships were causing even more harm to the enemy. The fight had a long way to go, but she was hopeful, at least, that her ships, and the Admiral's, would manage to at least pause the enemy. She didn't see any way to win long term, but she'd learned to shift her focus downward, to the matter at hand. She'd settle for any signs her force could seriously damage the enemy…before the survivors, whatever was left, retreated.

So far, she didn't have any clear signs that was

happening…but she had some fuzzy ones, and just then, that was enough to keep her fighting at her best.

She thought about the battle, about her ships and weapons. The enemy had advanced for a time, but now they had stopped. And they had ceased their advance outside the range of her smaller guns. She wondered for a moment, debated whether it made sense to advance—and whether she needed permission from the admiral.

She realized that she probably *should* check with him, at least, that she should ask him if advancing was reasonable. She looked down at her comm unit.

Then she just decided.

"All ships…minor thrust. Let's move forward thirty thousand klicks, and bring all guns into range."

"Yes, Commodore." She could tell Jaymes, at least, was on her side. Actually, she figured most of her people were. They were not quite as excited as they were at the start of the battle, but they were still in the fight, and most of them were passionately so. She knew that wouldn't last, that she would end up doing everything in her power to hold them to their posts by the time the battle was over. But this, at least, she would do now, while her people were still with her.

While they were still in the fight.

Chapter Twenty-Nine

CWS Dauntless
Beta Draconis System
Year 329 AC (After the Cataclysm)

Andi walked slowly through the familiar corridors of *Dauntless*. She hadn't spent a lot of time lately in the great ship, but she'd done her time before that, just as she had in the old *Dauntless*. She knew her husband still thought more of the older vessel as the real *Dauntless*, but she realized she had come to consider the new vessel the real thing. She understood that. She had spent some time on the older ship, of course, but that vessel had been the first large command for Tyler Barron, and he'd served aboard her until the last battle of the old Union War, when she was sacrificed to win victory. If she'd been in Barron's shoes, she probably would have felt the same way.

But she wasn't.

She loved Barron, more that she'd loved anyone, save only for her daughter. But she saw things differently than he did. At least some things.

She'd known for a long time the plan was what she wanted, more or less at least. She also knew things had gotten there only because the other option had been tried and had failed. For herself, she was ready to undertake the operation before the last fight, to allow the fleet to pull back away from the enemy. If she'd been able to do it, she would have saved hundreds of thousands of lives in the battle. That thought had pressed against her, at least until she'd realized that the entire civilian populations of the Confederation, the Hegemony, and the Alliance, were all on the line. The losses in the recent fight—in all the battles of the war—were almost incalculably small compared to the numbers at risk. She knew the Highborn didn't want to destroy humanity…they just wanted them passive and docile. To her, at least, and to most of those she knew, that was too much to ask.

But what would the enemy do when they realized what mankind was up to now? If the plan worked, if they started dying, would they lash out at humankind? They already possessed half of the Hegemony, and the other half was there for the taking too. Would they change their opinions? Would they unleash massive death on the humans under their control?

Andi thought about that, and it came as close as anything to derailing her. But there was no way she wanted to live, if the only way to do it was as a slave to the Highborn. She knew other people would disagree with her on that, but she didn't care. She was right, at least as far as she was concerned…and she was going to do her best to carry out the mission.

To infect as many of the Highborn as possible…all of them, if it was doable somehow…and if not, as many as possible, in the likely event that she couldn't get them all.

She waved her hand in front of the door, and it opened. Tyler's quarters on *Dauntless* hadn't been altered since the day he'd first taken command. They weren't enormous, but they were large by military standards. Atara could have taken them, of course, *should* have in fact, but Andi knew Travis wouldn't seize Barron's quarters in ten years or a hundred, at least not while he was still alive. The two had an odd relationship, one she had come to understand, at least partially. She'd had a tiny bit of jealousy, early on, but then she'd realized the two didn't have any kind of attraction between them. They were comrades, and friends, nothing more.

And nothing less.

"Andi?"

She heard Barron's voice, and she was as attracted to it as ever. She might disagree with Barron at times, she might even be forced to fight him, as she had almost been over the method to fight the enemy. But she loved him, regardless of whether they agreed or not.

"Yes, Tyler...it's me." A stupid statement, of course. Who the hell else would it be?

"Are you getting ready to go?" Barron walked out from the room next door, and he continued toward her.

"Yes...we're leaving in about an hour. I just wanted to stop and see you first." She didn't feel it was necessary to say, 'in case we don't meet again,' despite the fact that either of them could easily be killed, almost at any time. Tyler was drawing together the remnants of the fleet...and pulling back. He didn't know what he was going to do, not really. Except retreat...and try to keep the enemy's attention while Andi and Clint Winters led the effort to impregnate as many occupied Hegemony worlds as possible with the still unproven virus. Andi had been in favor of the plan for a long while, so much so that she'd overlooked the difficulty of it, the numerous chances that it wouldn't work. Now that she had the approval to go, however, she found her doubts growing. It wouldn't stop her—nothing would—but she realized that she was far from certain the plan would work.

But she knew it was their last chance at survival.

"Andi...I just wanted to say, good luck. You know I was against your plan, but my effort has failed. Your alternative is the only chance we've got. And on that basis, I'm completely aboard. Go...go with the best wishes of everyone in the fleet."

Andi was stout, and she rarely lost control. But now she was wavering. "Thank you, Tyler…really." She managed to keep her tears in, but she knew he understood how difficult things had become.

He leaned forward, taking her in his arms…and he hugged her. She lost track of the time, of everything, for just a few moments. Then he pulled back slightly, and he told her, "Go now. Get this done…and then we can go and just live." He didn't believe it, and she knew it, but she tried to think the best.

She knew he might have come to the conclusion that the effort was the only one with a chance of success, but that didn't mean he really believed it would work. But whatever he believed, whatever she believed, the only thing that mattered was it was the only option with a plan for success. And that meant they had to do it.

"Goodbye, Tyler…I will see you soon." She truly meant the first part of the statement. The second bit was hopeful, but she wasn't sure she really believed it. She thought for a moment that this might be her last moment with Tyler…and she came close to losing it. Very close.

"Goodbye, Andi…and I will see you soon, too." Somehow, she knew that Tyler felt exactly the same, that the chance they would meet again seemed somehow small, that the two of them would both be engaging in desperately dangerous proceedings. The odds were against them both surviving and returning to each other…and Cassiopeia. But she fought against that, told herself that both she and Tyler would survive, that the three of them would live years together, quiet and free of danger.

She knew she didn't really believe that…but she managed to push herself enough that she imagined it was true.

*   *   *

"Andi...I just wanted to contact you, and make sure you're okay." Clint Winters spoke softly, as cool and calm as she had ever heard him. She knew part of it was his effort to retain his composure in front of her...and part was because, while he was convinced the effort was the only way to go, he was also almost sure it would fail. That last part didn't make sense to most people, but she understood...and she was glad that her own hopes for success, while weak, seemed better than his.

"Yes, Clint...I'm fine. How about you?" Andi *was* in better shape than he was, at least since the force had pulled back from the fleet...and from Tyler. She'd always had a way of pushing aside her personal thoughts and focusing on what she had to do. She suspected that had come from her upbringing, from the terrible experiences of her early life, and despite the fact that it had ebbed somewhat in recent years, she was still able to focus on the matter at hand...most of the time.

The mission was clear enough, even if it seemed more difficult now that it was in process than it did before. They had 340 ships, divided into four groups. Every ship was loaded with the virus...and they would hit four planets at a time. They would cover all the easiest worlds first, all the locations decided to have few if any defenses. It would take many weeks to cover only half of the Hegemony—half of the half the enemy occupied—and by then, the first subjects, the planet she had bombarded over a month before, would probably start to show symptoms.

Or they wouldn't...and the whole effort, the last chance, would be over almost as soon as it had started. Andi knew it was possible that the virus wouldn't work, or that the enemy would have a serum or other treatment for it...but she wasn't sure why those doubts weren't stronger. She wasn't sure why, but her concerns were more about getting enough of the enemy population infected that it would make a major difference.

"I'm fine, Andi." A lie, but a decent one, at least told to someone less perceptive than Andi. "The fleet splits in this system…I just wanted to say, goodbye to you, and good luck."

"Goodbye, Clint…and the best of luck to you." She paused a moment, and she cut the line. She commanded only one of the four forces, but she knew she was the most aggressive of the leaders, and the one tasked with gathering the Highborn from the first planet infected…as soon as she infected ten other worlds. She had hoped for movement to her side, but she was surprised at the gravity of it all after the last battle. She'd expected to retrieve Masters from the initial world first, but things had zoomed almost out of control…and she was going to be part of the first strike, of the effort to seriously hurt the enemy.

She looked across the bridge of the cruiser, feeling far stranger than she had the last time. That was an experiment, one she would gather the results on soon. But now, the situation had progressed much farther, and she was about to issue orders for her fleet to leave, to head toward one of the six transit points in the sector…and then on its way, to infect a dozen Highborn occupied planets…and then to come back the way she had gone first, and pick up the Highborn present on the world she had already attacked. Some of them, at least.

She knew her mission, larger than she'd imagined before, and despite the fact that she was edgy, more worried than she had been, about whether it would work and whether she would survive, she knew she would comply with her orders…flawlessly.

She would see the fleet through its mission, and she would pick up the infected—hopefully—Highborn on the first planet. She would live at least to see the plan come together, to view evidence that the project had worked…or she would see that it was all a waste of time, that her people, at least as far as she saw them, were doomed.

* * *

Clint Winters sat calmly, watching the third force transit. He had completed his last efforts as joint commander, seen three forces blast off to two different systems. Now, he was just the commander of one force, smaller than he'd led in years...yet more vital perhaps. The forces he led, the quarter of the total that were still under his command, represented the great effort, the last real push his side had to win the fight. He knew that, almost without a doubt.

He had no idea how many planets he would infect, whether his forces would reach the end of their lists...or run into an unexpected force early on and be blown away. He had no conception of how many additional worlds would be infected through the movement of Highborn traveling from infected worlds before the symptoms erupted. The effort could infect most of the enemy, including its fleet, or it could just cover some of the worlds occupied. His people could run more operations, he realized, struggle to spread the disease farther, but once the enemy realized what was happening...all hell was likely to break loose.

"Alright...that's force three. Let's set a course for the next transit point, and jump." His targets were the farthest away, something he'd argued with Lafarge about...but only for a moment. He'd normally have expected such a fight to go on for a while, but he'd had an ace up his sleeve. The first system.

It hadn't been clear who would pick up the Highborn at the first planet, the one already infected, who would get the subjects that would determine whether or not there actually *was* a chance. Lafarge had expected Winters would want to do it, and he did. But he knew there was only one person in the fleet with the true right to go there. The same woman who had led the force that had infected it.

After he'd given her the added task of taking the

Highborn—*not* an easy job, by any measure—she hadn't really been able to argue against getting the easiest group of planets to attack first. The two jobs went together.

"We're ready, sir...prepared to embark as soon as you give the word."

Winters looked around, at the bridge, at the personnel seated there. His ships were mostly smaller, but his crews were among the best remaining in the fleet. Everyone in any position of power agreed, this was the last chance they had. Whether his junior officers and spacers understood that as much, whether they looked out on the current situation so starkly, or they just considered it part of the overall operation, he didn't know. He suspected that some knew, and others didn't...and that was fine. If the desperate ploy worked, if his people managed to infect a sufficient number of the enemy, maybe they had a chance.

And if they didn't, he wasn't sure what was better...if the enemy simply wasn't infected, or if they struck back aggressively, and destroyed his ship early.

Chapter Thirty

Fleet Base Grimaldi
Krakus System
Year 329 AC (After the Cataclysm)

Admiral Simpson watched as Samantha Taggart's ships moved out, as they closed with the enemy. For the briefest of instants, he thought she should have at least asked him, but then he decided it was her show. For better or worse, he had taken command of the station, and the smaller ships positioned around it. He wasn't sure if it had been a decision based on the actual situation, or just a realization that he was a good officer...but Taggart was a great one. Despite his outranking her, he knew that was the case.

The station was very large, even though much of it was still in ruins, and its immensity gave him the option to take command there. But he realized that the main fleet was the most powerful force that he had...and he had placed most of it under Taggart's command. He wasn't sure whether that rated congratulations or disparagement, and he finally decided perhaps some of each. But he was firm in his assignment, as firm as he'd been when he had made it. Taggart had at least as important a role to play as he did, and probably more so, whether she knew it or not.

He turned toward the great screen, checking on his ships,

and on their enemies. He knew he didn't have much to do himself, that he was free to watch the fight going on, for the moment, at least. The fact of command was simply this—there were instants that cried out for the leader to take charge, but once the formation was set and the battle joined, there was often little to do, not until the situation called for withdrawal...or to urge the remaining spacers to remain in the fight.

And very possibly, to die.

Simpson watched the bulk of Taggart's ships move forward, and a moment later, he ordered his own vessels to do the same. "The fleet is to advance 30,000 kilometers at half speed." Grimaldi had powerful guns, and it could still stay in the fight, even at the advanced range...but the mostly smaller ships under his command had to be closer. Taggart had moved forward, and it made sense to push his own ships up to match those at their side.

"All ships are moving in accordance with your orders, Admiral." Jaymes's voice was solid, and Simpson knew he, at least, agreed with the decision. He suspected most of his people did...at least for now. But he was determined to fight it out, to ensure that the enemy fleet was battered, that even if it gained control over the system, it couldn't go any farther, not for a long while, at least. He had people willing to go that far, but he had others too, who were newer, fresh recruits manning some of the newest ships he had. He realized they were good, as good as they could be, but he wondered if they were prepared to go as far as he was.

"Very well." It was all he could do. When the battle went further, if his spacers started to break, he would need more. And he would see if he had it.

Until then, he had to watch...and hope for the best.

*　*　*

Sam Taggart watched, her eyes moving across the display,

her attention apparently simultaneously focused on every ship under her command. That was becoming marginally easier as more of her ships were destroyed, or wounded so badly she ordered them to fall back to the transit point. The enemy had made some effort to follow the first couple of ships she'd ordered back, but now they were happy to see anybody go.

The battle was getting even more intense, and the ships were now all within close range. *Constellation* was still in better than expected shape, though not as good as before. The rest of her fleet was a different story though, with many ships badly damaged, and a decent number destroyed outright. Her forces had inflicted similar losses on the enemy, more even, but she was surer than ever that she was fighting only to ensure the enemy lacked the resources to continue on, at least not without reinforcements or a long period of maintenance and repairs.

And she was surer—but not sure—that she could achieve that. It wouldn't be pretty, and she was far from certain she'd have anything left at all, save for the badly damaged ships she was sending home now. *Constellation* would almost certainly draw all kinds of attention from the enemy. Her ship was by far the largest and most powerful one present, but she knew its condition had more to do with good fortune than anything else.

And she knew how quickly that could leave her.

Her attention turned suddenly to *Revellus*, unquestionably her second most powerful ship. And one that hadn't been nearly as fortunate as *Constellation*. The vessel was bracketed by three enemy ships, and it was close to the end of its considerable endurance. The battleship had been fighting well, but it looked like all its main guns were out. There were three secondary weapons still firing, but that wasn't enough to justify keeping the vessel in the line.

But Taggart was far from sure it *could* withdraw.

She opened her mouth, but before she could say

anything, *Revellus* took another hit. It was still there, though barely she thought, but now it was down to a single gun. There was no point in keeping the battleship in the line...but she was far from sure it could escape.

Still, there was no choice.

"*Revellus*...withdraw at once!" She said the words into the comm.

She watched as the ship began to pull back almost immediately. She'd expected some bullshit from the battleship's commander, but her tone had left no room for it. None at all.

Still, she was far from sure the battleship would make it. It was badly damaged, though its engines were still functional enough to give it a chance. The biggest question was, would the enemy ships that had been attacking it pursue...or would they transfer their fire to another ship.

Taggart's eyes were fixed on the drama, watching the battleship's plight almost hypnotically. She was rooting for the ship, for what remained of its crew, even as her eyes fixed on the closest enemy ships, trying to decide if they would continue hammering the withdrawing vessel, if they would seek to destroy the ship...or if they would focus on something in better shape. For an instant, Taggart believed the enemy *would* follow up, that it would destroy the fleeing battleship. Her eyes danced around, searching for any friendly ships that could intervene, but there were none...not close enough.

She drew in a breath, holding it for a few seconds, as the pursuing Highborn ships opened fire. But all the incoming shots missed, and the ships turned away, directing their future fire at other vessels.

They had given up.

Taggart stared for a moment, watching the scene...and realizing that *Revellus* was going to escape, as long as its remaining engines held out. That was a good thing, in the sense that her damaged battleship was likely to get away.

But it was bad, too. The enemy was focusing on her ships that were still in the fight. All that mattered now was how the battle went, and whether her ships were able to inflict enough damage on the enemy to prevent them from following up. She figured she had a good chance of doing that, but no real chance of holding on, of actually winning the fight. There were just too many enemy ships, both Hegemony and Union forces, for outright victory to be an option.

But she was determined to at least hold back the enemy, to damage enough of their ships to stop them at Grimaldi, and not to allow them to advance further. She told herself she would stay, at least as long as that took, but she knew she didn't have total control over that. Her force, whatever was left of it, with whatever reserves could be rushed to it from the shipyards producing new craft as quickly as possible, would be all that remained between the enemy and the heart of the Confederation. She had to buy some time, at least…whether she made it out or not.

*   *   *

Simpson watched his ships, and Taggart's too. The vessels were fighting hard, as was the station, but he couldn't tell if it was good enough, or just shy of it. There were more enemy ships than he'd expected, by a good measure, but his fleet was performing above expectations, too. The question of whether Grimaldi could hold was already answered, at least as far as his thoughts went. No…there was no chance. But he could still hurt the enemy enough, pause them at the station for a matter of months at least.

That wasn't likely to make an enormous difference, he realized. He knew the vast nature of the shipyards, both new and old, built around the center of the Confederation…but he also realized that almost every ship that was done enough to launch, even if not completely finished, was already up there…or with the main fleet. His fleet would gather *some* ships, he assumed, given six months before the enemy was able to push forward…but he realized he would be adding that to his badly battered fleet. If he fought to the finish at Grimaldi, he realized how few ships might survive…and there was still only a chance that the enemy would be stalled. He understood that he had a good chance of blunting the enemy's advance…but it was only that, a chance. And if the enemy came through with enough strength to push on, he would have nothing left to face it, not now.

If he was even alive, which in that case, he doubted.

He turned and looked down the whole line. He'd been troubled about some reserves the enemy had kept, too far back for his ships to engage. But now they were forward, into the fight. He didn't know for sure that the enemy had nothing else, but something told him he saw everything they possessed. It was more than he'd expected, but not irrationally more. He still had a chance to hurt them, to blunt their ability to move forward.

And he was going to do everything possible to achieve it.

"Get me Commodore Taggart," he said abruptly. He hadn't planned on communicating with his subordinate, but something was suddenly in his mind.

"Yes, sir…" A moment later, "Commodore Taggart, sir."

"Sam, I need you to alter your targeting scheme. You're—we're—trying to destroy enemy ships before moving on to the next. But we've got to hold the fleet here, at least while they conduct some repairs. We've got to batter the ships…to a point…and then move on to the next one. You understand?" He'd just blurted out his realization, without even a hello to his number two. He felt concern, wondered if the move he was ordering was smart…or whether it was foolish. Or some of each. He didn't know, but Sam responded in just a few seconds.

"I understand, sir...and I agree totally."

Simpson breathed hard, feeling relief that his subordinate agreed with him. It was difficult, no question, to decide when a ship was badly battered enough, how much damage it took to force it into the repair line, instead of the fleet. But it was the only way to go, and even as his mind rattled back and forth with countermeasures, he knew it. Somehow.

If his fleet was to have any chance, any chance to achieve the level of success it could, it simply had to reduce the invading force...and at least force it to stop for repairs.

Whatever it did to his fleet.

Whatever.

* * *

"*Carstairs*...pull back!" Taggart was cold, almost as though she was supervising a drill, and not leading a force in one of the most decisive battles of her day. She knew she couldn't win, and Simpson did as well. But stopping the enemy at Grimaldi, buying six or eight months, was enough for her just then.

Still, she was late on *Carstairs*, and she knew it. She knew it even better when the ship exploded a few seconds later.

It wasn't her job to track each ship, and she knew that. But she was new to the level of command, and she found it difficult to focus, to stay within the bounds she had.

"*Carstairs* destroyed, Commodore." Lieutenant Commander Johnson spoke the words, despite the fact that he knew it was obvious to her.

"Yes, Lieutenant Commander...I see that." There wasn't any animosity in either of their statements, just routine duty.

Taggart sighed, fighting to remain focused, to put all her abilities into the battle. She knew the fight would be over eventually, but she had no idea yet, what would be the result. It was that close.

She watched the fight unfold, saw another three of her

ships, and four of the enemy vessels, destroyed in a matter of minutes. She was thrilled on one level at the destruction of the enemy forces, but she knew that was not what her people had been ordered to do.

"Put me on the wide broadcast, Johnson." Her words were touched with the first emotion she had shown. Anger. It wasn't that she didn't understand the desire to destroy enemy ships, but she agreed with the admiral. The only chance her side had was to damage as many as possible of the enemy…and to switch targets before actually destroying them.

"You're on."

"Attention all ships…this is the last time I'm going to say this." She understood the desire of her people to destroy the enemy ships, but she'd told them that was impossible. And she expected to be listened to. "You are to damage the enemy ships, knock out most or all of their premium weaponry…and then you are to direct your fire against another ship. Is that understood?" It was a question, but not really…and she didn't think any of her people would interpret it as anything but what it truly was. "Do NOT destroy the damned enemy craft, not unless they are taken out while they still have significant weaponry. I trust this is understood." She shut the comm line at once, before anyone could have answered. Assuming anyone was going to, which she doubted seriously.

She could feel most of the eyes on her bridge looking at her. She understood, but she didn't let it get to her. She knew what her people had to do to win…or at least to forestall immediate enemy advances, and they were going to do it, whether they liked it or not.

She just didn't know if she could push them through, if they could damage enough of the enemy forces. That she wouldn't know until the battle was almost over.

If she lived that long.

Chapter Thirty-One

CWS Donallus
Coranus Tylus System
Year 329 AC (After the Cataclysm)

Andi watched silently as her ships approached the planet. She knew her list of worlds was the easiest, and she would have argued against it...except its last entry was the original planet, and the attempt to actually take prisoners.

She wondered whether the enemy would figure out what her people were up to. Almost certainly, she realized, but it would take more time to get the word out to other systems. That gave her an edge, at least at first, and she intended to use it as much as she could. She doubted it would last through all the systems she and the other three fleets were targeting, but then the enemy *was* forward deployed, and it would probably take considerable time to realize what was happening, and to respond.

Assuming, of course, the attack was really dangerous, that they had developed the correct formula in their virus, and that the enemy hadn't managed to find a vaccine or treatment. She knew there were lots of ifs and buts, but she found herself convinced that it would work...at least if they could get it done.

"We're in position, Andi...ready to begin

bombardment." Tarren spoke calmly, coolly, but she knew he was as edgy as any of her people. She had more ships than she'd had in the earlier operation, more than she'd ever directly commanded, and she was worried too, and despite her grave pronouncement that the scheme was sure to work, she had plenty of doubts floating around.

"Begin bombardment." She spoke calmly, and despite her assurance that the current system was toast—there had been only three small ships stationed there, and her fleet had managed to destroy them without any losses—she was worried about the whole operation.

"Yes, as you command."

She listened to Tarren relay the orders, and perhaps twenty seconds later, her display began to show the preliminaries to the bombardment. Thirty ships were targeting the planet, and the rest were in position around it. The bombardment would take about half an hour to complete, and then her forces would begin their trip to the next world. She didn't have any real information, but she realized that time was crucial. She'd been worried that her attack on the preliminary world more than a month earlier would generate some kind of action by the enemy, but perhaps it had been too close to the assault. She'd been concerned at first, but now, she assumed that the enemy fleet command had simply been notified that a force of ships had stumbled onto the planet and had fought a battle with the local forces before departing. Perhaps they were just lost, or something similar.

But whatever had covered her on that first mission, it wouldn't apply to the dozens of reports that would stream in from the current attacks. She knew the enemy would understand, she just wasn't sure how long it would take, or how much time would be required to warn—and protect— their systems. Perhaps the forces could complete all their missions before the enemy could mount a real defense. That was the intent, the reason each system had ten target worlds and no more. But to be painfully honest, she had no idea exactly what would happen.

But she knew her duty, and she struggled with every fiber of her being to consider only that, not to think of Tyler or Cassie, or anything else. Maybe she would be successful and live to rejoin her loved ones…but that had no place right now.

She watched the bombardment continue, the ships moving according to very specific routines, dropping an almost undetectable sequence of viral infestation. It was more than enough, she knew, if it worked, but she was adhering completely to the sequence. Perhaps later, if she ran into any significant defensive forces, she would lose enough ships that she had to start doing partial runs, but this was the first planet, and she had a full force. Whatever happened tomorrow or next week or the following month, this system would be fully and completely bombed.

She watched for almost half an hour, and she knew just when she'd get the report.

"Bombardment complete, Andi…ships are reconfiguring for transit out."

She took a deep breath, and she let it out. Then she said, "The fleet will move directly toward transit point two as soon as all ships are in position." She leaned back and looked forward, but her vision was obscured, by images of Tyler and Cassie. No matter how hard she tried, how much effort she put in, she couldn't forget about them, not even for a few moments.

She figured she was stronger because of it…but she realized that was a convenient analysis, too. It was as easy to say she was weaker, that her images of strength were mostly the result of the vastly larger forces she commanded than she had in her days before she'd met Tyler. Or any of a dozen other impressions.

But as much as she loved him, as despondent as she'd been since her daughter had departed for Megara…she knew she would carry out her duty, however many times her loved ones appeared to her. She *had* to complete the mission before she could return, and just maybe, it would be successful...and she would prevail.

And her family could settle down to a normal life.

* * *

"Begin bombardment." Clint Winters sat in his chair, struggling not to rise, not to jump up and join the fight. The first system he'd attacked had been almost too easy, but this one had fourteen enemy ships, more than he'd expected. His own fleet was considerably larger, of course, and it had eliminated the entire Highborn force, but it had lost nine ships of its own. That was too many, far too many for one mission, or even two, counting the first one as well. He hoped it was an exception, that it wasn't a sign of things to come.

But in truth, he just didn't know. He had guessed that the force the enemy had deployed to win the recent battle had at least compelled them to strip their forces...but in truth, he just didn't know. The enemy could have many times as many ships as they'd used to win at Striker. He didn't believe that, of course, not when the enemy had been defeated in the previous battle, but he realized he had nothing but meaningless conjecture about what they had, and what they could do.

"Yes, sir."

Winters sat still, barely, as his forces bombarded the surface of the planet. His scanning results were poor, as always when studying Hegemony-held worlds, but they suggested a larger than necessary bombardment. That was intentional, and though he knew that if he continued to lose ships, he would get to the point where he would have to have lesser bombardments, he was determined to do whatever damage he could.

His eyes were fixed on the display, watching as his ships moved back and forth, spraying the virus all around. He knew the attack would take about thirty-five minutes in total, which wasn't a long time, certainly not against the context of traveling from system to system. Still, it seemed long, even as he watched, each second passing slowly, and moving into the next one.

He kept his view, for what seemed like a long time, but when he checked the timer, her realized that less than five minutes had elapsed. He returned his eyes to the display, watching his ships moving about the planet, dropping the hopefully deadly virus everywhere. He'd known all along that the operation was still a guess, that not enough time had passed for the virus to take hold where it had been tested. He'd been leaning toward supporting the operation anyway, once it had proven to be effective...but the enemy had attacked too soon, and that had left no option except to launch the full attack, based on hope only. He knew, if the virus proved ineffective for any reason, the war was as good as over, that it was still the best hope for victory. The only hope.

His eyes remained fixed on the screen, but his thoughts drifted. He imagined Barron, with what was left of the fleet, pulling back, slowly or quickly, depending on what the enemy did. He wondered about Chronos and Akella, and their efforts with the Council. They were doing what the Council wanted, but would that be enough? If the enemy pushed forward, the fleet would have to withdraw, and if the advance came on quickly, Tyler would have to fall back to the border of the Confederation...leaving the rest of the Hegemony defenseless. Would the Council agree to that? Or would they fight? And if Chronos, Akella, and most of the other senior officers stayed true to their stated positions, would their forces rally to them...or would they rebel against them?

Vian Tulus was with Tyler to the end, at least. Winters

couldn't see any other alternative to that. Tulus was at Barron's side, in almost any scenario, but even if he'd been willing to consider any turn of affairs, his forces were too small, and too backward to have any chance on their own.

Winters knew the only real hope was with him, and with the three other groups...but he wondered how much chance there really was, and how much was just his own invention, and that of his comrades. Maybe the universe wasn't as it appeared, subject to all sorts of interference. Maybe there was an ordained way things always worked out. That was as much a hopeful burst of thought as it was a negative one, though he saw mostly the downside.

"Sir...the attack is complete."

He heard the sound. He was lost, his thoughts had disappeared into his head, but now he forced them back.

"Very well, Commander. All ships are to form up...and head to the next system."

* * *

"All ships have reported back, sir. The attack is complete."

Vian Tulus sat perfectly erect in his seat, looking neither desperate nor worried. He was both, of course, and the part of him that had learned from Tyler Barron knew that the expedition then underway was the most desperate effort imaginable. Apart from the prospect that the virus was simply wrong, or the potential that the enemy simply had an easy to take medication to stop what had been a deadly assault three centuries before, he knew there were numerous other things that could go wrong. Even if the virus was correct, even if it was still deadly, he knew it was more likely to kill a lot of the enemy...but not all of them. The fleet certainly needed to be hit, and he was hopeful enemy personnel would travel back and forth, including to the ships.

But that was the purest speculation.

Even if all of the ships present managed to hit all of their target worlds, and hit them completely, that was still less than half of the occupied worlds...and none of the fleet. Without movement back and forth, the attack would be much like the other operations had been in the war, good...but not good enough.

"Very well...order all forces to line up. We've got another world to hit, so there's no point wasting time."

"Yes, sir!" Tulus commanded all the Alliance ships, and some Confederation ones as well, but the staff on his flagship was all Alliance. He'd come a long way toward seeing things how a Confed would, at least at times, but he was still, in his heart of hearts, an Alliance commander.

He turned and looked out, watching his people. At one time, he'd considered his Alliance spacers, at least the first order of them, to be unbreakable. They weren't invincible, though, and he realized that now. He'd come to understand that his people were good, very good...but perhaps not better than the warriors of other nations. And he was sure even the best of his people felt fear, though they might compartmentalize it, and keep it hidden. They were good men and women, of that he was sure. But they *were* men and women, too.

"The fleet is assembled, your Supremacy. Prepared to depart for the next system."

Tulus sat for a moment, no more than ten or fifteen seconds, contemplating. The situation had brought him to a strange place, one he couldn't understand completely. Did he prefer the idea of fighting conventionally...or of using the virus? He knew there was no real choice now, that there was no way to continue the fighting conventionally, not with the hope of victory. Still, he knew if they had done that, or even if he had stayed with Barron, he might have come to believe there was a way. It was the Alliance part of him, screaming that the ship production, the tactics and strategy would all work out. But he'd not only chosen to support the virus plan, he'd decided to lead one of the forces, and he'd requested that most of the Alliance's smaller ships be assigned to him. He wasn't sure which side of him had done more, though he suspected it was the Confederation component more than the Alliance.

He sighed, softly and mostly unknown to those around him. He'd put the thoughts aside, pushed back against the unknowns. He had a job to do, and that he understood perfectly...whether it worked or not. Then he said, simply, "Full speed ahead...and then jump."

Chapter Thirty-Two

Fleet Base Grimaldi
Krakus System
Year 329 AC (After the Cataclysm)

Admiral Simpson sat in his chair, amid the chaos and wreckage of the station. In the early stages of the battle, the enemy had focused mostly on the fleet, but now an entire unit had moved on the station as well. Grimaldi fired all its weapons, its biggest guns, down to the smallest batteries it possessed. Anything that could fire was firing, but Simpson knew his station would not endure forever. It had survived so far through the brilliant maneuvering of its tiny drives, combined with the fact that the enemy had not focused heavily on it until recently, but now, even with well under one percent of enemy attacks striking, the station had been hit a dozen times in the last twenty minutes. It was starting to lose command of many of its stations, and barely half its weapons—those that had been reconfigured for the current fight, not the original total—were still functional.

They would all be out in an hour, two at most...assuming the station could endure that long. Which it couldn't. If the enemy attackers weren't reinforced, if his fortune—and the engines that supported his limited drive system—held out, he would endure perhaps forty-five minutes. Maybe even less.

"Withdrawal number 2," he said, trying hard not to sound depressed. He knew the fight was almost over, but he still wasn't sure if his people had done enough to render the enemy fleet incapable of further immediate action. It was going to be close, and he knew most of the Confederation's inner systems had strong fixed defenses, that they required any attacker to possess considerable strength…but he didn't know if the enemy fleet was going to be battered enough to prevent any further actions.

"Withdrawal number 2 in action, sir." He heard Jaymes, and he felt pride in the officer's inherent strength. He couldn't tell whether he knew how likely it was he had entered the last hour of his life, though he'd come to respect Jaymes's intellect far more than he'd ever expected to. He decided that the officer was perfectly aware of the situation…though he wasn't sure whether Simpson would choose to die there, or whether he would order the withdrawal 3 actions at some point.

He looked around at the bridge, watching as more than two thirds of the crew got up and moved toward the elevator. Number one withdrawal had been held before the enemy had even reached the station. It was the removal of all non-military personnel. The number two withdrawal was far more severe, and it left only the most vital personnel on the station. Number three, if it came, would be the total abandonment of the facility, though whether that would come, and if it did, whether it would include *him*, were still questions to be answered.

His head turned toward the great display. Once, it had been the wonder of Grimaldi, but time had come a considerable way to wear down much of the station's newness, it's effect. Still, it was impressive, and it was new, the old one destroyed during the first fight, and replaced almost immediately. It was even bigger than the one it had replaced, and the graphics on it were tighter, sharper.

He knew the withdrawal order was an admission that he would lose the battle. That was something he had been resigned to do from the beginning, though he shared those thoughts with none of his cohorts. His real goal was to damage the enemy, significantly enough to halt their advance...and he *thought* he still had time to do that.

"Maintain full fire...we're still in this fight, even if we've got fewer people." He sounded good, almost confident, though he knew his order for most of the station's personnel to evacuate told another story.

"Yes, sir...all stations remain effective." Jaymes sounded better than he did, but even in his aide's voice, he heard something. It wasn't despair, not exactly, but it was realization. The next hour would tell whether his fleet had damaged the enemy badly enough to prevent an immediate advance...and the odds of it happening seemed just about even.

Just about even...Simpson remembered the words, and he repeated them to himself five or six times. *Just about even...*

No, that's not good enough...we have to hurt them enough, take them out of the fight...

"Larson...we have to pick up our rate of fire. Go to one hundred twenty percent." He said the words, but he almost immediately took them back. Almost.

"Yes, sir..." Jaymes was nervous before, he was sure of that, but now he was clearly so. "...one hundred twenty percent."

The man paused, waiting a few seconds. Then he leaned over his station and said, "All weapons...go to one hundred twenty percent power. Repeat...one hundred twenty."

Simpson leaned back in his chair and closed his eyes for just a moment. He knew the risk, the great danger, of going to one hundred twenty. One oh five, even one ten...they imposed an additional level of risk on firers, but it was worth it, usually. One fifteen was a deadly level, far more dangerous, and used only when there was no option.

One hundred twenty was almost unheard of...and he knew he would lose guns and crews. But he would also gain, devastate the enemy crews. Which would be more effective, he didn't know, but he figured he didn't have a choice.

Not really.

* * *

"You heard the command, Isaac. The entire force is to obey at once." Taggart spoke, softly, almost sounding as though she was leading in an exercise, and not fighting one of the deadliest battles in history. Even her tendency for swearing was mostly gone. She suspected Isaac Johnson wouldn't know exactly what to expect next from her...but then, that would only place him in line behind her. Because she had no idea what she would do next either.

Except obey Admiral Simpson's order...even though they had only been issued to his station, and perhaps also to the ships he led. She knew she needed to take them though as well, though, as insane as they sounded. It was the only way to be sure her fleet did enough damage to the enemy...assuming it didn't just blow up her ships.

"Yes, Commodore...at once." Johnson managed a reasonable response, but he was clearly terrified at the order. Her ships had already been firing at one hundred ten percent, in fact, that had become almost the norm, more or less, for difficult battles. One hundred fifteen was a marked increase in risk...but one hundred twenty had not been done enough to provide sufficient data to know whether the increased damage of the firers overcame the devastation they inflicted. "All ships...go to one hundred twenty on all weapons."

Taggart sat upright, looking out over the bridge. Anyone staring at her would hardly know whether she was fully in control...or whether she was facing certain death. That was good, she realized...because she wasn't sure either.

She watched the battle, saw her superbattleship ripping into enemy craft. *Constellation* was the strongest ship present on either side, one of the four superbattleships produced so far by the Confederation. She knew the vessel's status as strongest was only the result of the relatively light enemy forces present. On one hand, she saw what she had to fight as damning, almost overwhelming…but she realized that her force was facing a fraction of the power that Admiral Barron had to deal with. Barron had more strength, too, including the other three supers, but he was, if anything, in even worse shape than she was.

But her opposition was *her* problem…and *Constellation* was being hammered by the enemy. She realized the ship might be gone already, save for its incredible evasion percentage. She had worked on the enemy's attack routines, tried to keep her evasions new…and that was, perhaps, the main reason that she had endured, that and the level of repairs that had been completed on Grimaldi. The station hadn't been the focus of the enemy's assault yet, and it had dealt out a lot of damage, probably more than the enemy had expected. But what would happen in the next ten minutes, half an hour? She had no idea.

She looked at the display, watching as her ships upped their firepower, at least the vessels that still had full strength left for their guns. She knew she would have ships damaged, that some might even be destroyed by the massive increase in throughput power…but in her gut, she believed it would be worth it.

She watched her ships battling, firing everything they had. Three enemy ships vanished in just a few seconds, but they were followed by three of her own. She began to fear that the fight underway would deteriorate to a battle to the absolute finish, that none of her ships would escape. But then she realized that might actually be acceptable…as long as the enemy was battered into submission as well.

Besides, she knew that couldn't be the case, that some

ships, at least, would survive the fight…if only because she'd already sent back almost twenty hulls that were completely or mostly shut down, but still could move. Those vessels would need massive repairs, and none of them were moving at full speed, so if the enemy really broke through, they just might catch them. But Taggart realized that the enemy was badly hurt, too, and as she studied the screen, she realized that they wouldn't be following up immediately, no matter what she—or they—had left.

The question was, would they require a long period of rest, or would a short repair session put enough of them in condition to follow up. She just didn't know the answer to that…not yet at least. But she realized her purpose was to gain months now, as many as possible.

She saw her ships ripping into the enemy formations…but the Highborn were striking back just as effectively. Every few minutes, she'd see one of the enemy vessels destroyed, and she would begin to feel that her people were going to prevail. Then, a moment later, one of her ships would go, and she would shift the other way.

She continued to watch the battle unfolding, and gradually, she began to gain some hope. Her force would be almost obliterated, she was sure of that, but she was beginning to expect the enemy fleet would be badly battered, too. *No, they will be badly battered no matter what…what you're hoping is that they will be damaged enough. Enough to stop them here.*

She realized her hope to accomplish just that level would take almost everything her fleet had…possibly including *Excalibur.* She was prepared for that, on one level at least. But she realized one could only be ready for death so much, that some portion of her would always want to survive.

But to live for what? We fight to the end, it's what we do, some of us, at least. But there is no victory in this war. You are struggling for six months, maybe eight…and that assumes that Barron somehow manages to hold the enemy off, that he, too, buys another six months.

She fought off the negative feelings, struggled to maintain at least the appearance of true hope. But the truth was, she was fighting maybe to gain six months, and it started to descend on her.

She saw more ships, on both sides, destroyed, and she realized her fleet's performance *was* likely to be good enough, at least to gain six months. She didn't have a chance of holding Grimaldi, she knew that, but she would badly damage the enemy fleet. Her ships would be battered, her force almost wrecked, and Admiral Simpson's even worse...but they would also stop the enemy. She'd realized all along that Grimaldi would be lost, but suddenly, it occurred to her that the admiral didn't expect to retreat. He didn't even plan to.

She was ready to die as well...but her recent reaction had told her she would live if she could. But Simpson had given up, she was suddenly sure of that...and she had to stop him.

"Get me the admiral," she said.

"Admiral Simpson, Commodore." The connection took a few seconds, the unavoidable result of distance, but it didn't take any longer.

"Commodore...how are you?" Simpson's voice was strangely calm, and it only enhanced her fears that he had already decided on his fate.

"Admiral...I think you have to be ready for a phase three withdrawal. The enemy is focusing more on the station, and you don't have much time."

"No worries, Admiral. The withdrawal is already underway. I've split the sequence, ordered everyone but the firing crews to leave. The remaining personnel are under orders to depart as soon as their guns are no longer effective."

Taggart felt a certainty now that Simpson wasn't planning to come himself. "Sir, you should pull out...now. There's nothing left for you to do there." She knew that was mostly true, but she also understood just how much chance there was that *she* would leave her still-fighting ship. Or the station, if she'd commanded there.

"I can't leave, Sam…" He left a long pause, long enough to purge any doubts she had about Simpson's intentions. The he added, "Not yet, at least."

"So, you're planning to depart when? When the last gunnery crew goes? What's the point of you remaining there? Sir, you've got to go now. You've got to."

There was silence for a moment. Then he said only, "Focus on your ships, Sam…and try to get some of them out of here."

"Sir…you've got to go now. Sir! Sir?" She realized the comm line was dead, that Admiral Simpson had terminated it.

She looked at Grimaldi on the screen, watched as more ships began to pull away. Most of the base's scant remaining crew was leaving…but not its commander. Not the leader of the entire fleet.

"Admiral Simpson?" She tried to reach the station. "Admiral Simpson!"

But there was no reply, nothing but the sound of her own voice…and the soft crackle of the line.

Chapter Thirty-Three

CWS Dauntless
Beta Draconis System
Year 329 AC (After the Cataclysm)

Tyler looked at the hulk on the screen in front of him, amazed that after more than six months of constant repair, it still looked so bad. He knew *Colossus* was better than she looked, much better in fact than she had been…but the damage was obvious *everywhere*.

"Commodore Eaton, thank you for coming here. I'm afraid we haven't really decided where the fleet should be yet. We're back three jumps from the battle, and so far it doesn't appear the enemy has advanced more than one jump in every direction…but that's a game that has an end to it. They might do some repairs—we damaged their fleet pretty badly, except for the last segment, of course. That might be enough…but they have a pretty good chunk of unengaged ships, too, so who knows? At least, that's my best guess two weeks after the fight."

"I'm inclined to agree, Admiral. If they really wanted to push immediately, they'd have stayed right on you…and you'd have had to decide what to do already." Eaton didn't express any thoughts on that, but Barron knew her opinions, what almost all the Confeds thought. But he knew that would be a difficult proposition for Akella and Chronos…and he wasn't sure whether they'd have universal support among their military. Chronos would certainly have a lot of units that simply followed him everywhere, but if other members of the council raised the flag of defending the Hegemony, it was entirely possible they could split the forces.

Of course, attacking the enemy with half of the Hegemony force alone was the epitome of foolishness. But Barron had seen his own side make idiotic decisions too, and he didn't write it off. Akella was off with the council now, arguing for a temporary removal of the forces from Hegemony space…with emphasis on the temporary. He knew she'd have arguments, but he hoped the council, a majority of it at least, sided with her. He figured the odds were about fifty-fifty, but he also knew her own expectations were somewhat worse.

"We can hope at least." Barron looked again at her ship, the largest by far in the Confederation navy, in any force engaged in the current war. It was really bad…but he'd called Eaton there to certify it for combat. It wasn't ready by any means, but it was still the strongest ship in the fleet…and with the damaged vessels and all the ships destroyed in the fighting, he didn't have any choice.

"Anyway, Commodore, I can guess you have a good idea why I called you here. Honestly, *Colossus* isn't ready for action by any measure, and keeping her out of the last fight turned out to be the right call, as she wouldn't have made a serious difference. But we need everything we've got right now…and as badly damaged as your ship still is, it's still the strongest in the fleet." His mind went through the other ships he had. Taking out the badly damaged vessels, some of which had to travel for months just to reach open birthing facilities, was bad enough. The last thing he'd needed, at least from a purely combat point of view, was to strip away almost half of the smaller ships, and send them away, deep into enemy space, to take a shot, a desperate shot, at really damaging the enemy. He'd overcome his earlier doubts about executing the strategy—he just wanted the war to end, and any way that was possible, outside of defeat, was acceptable to him. Even so, he didn't really believe it would work. His people hadn't yet extracted the Masters from the first attacked planet. They didn't even know the virus worked…and if he had to bet, he'd have bet against it. Still, he recognized it as the best chance his people had, and he supported it.

"So," Barron paused for an instant, still troubled by certifying the ship for action, "…*Colossus* is fully active again. I know she's not ready, not by any measure, and I realize I am asking you to work miracles. But I'm afraid we're all in that position right now."

He could see from her expression that she was happy, that he had fulfilled what she had anticipated. That was nothing less than he'd expected from her…but he felt only sorrow. He wasn't capable of ordering any of his people to give in to the enemy, it was something he knew he would never do himself, but he imagined a vessel like *Colossus* perhaps pushing out into deep space, finding a new home. It was pointless, he knew, just the kind of nonsense he felt just then…but was it really better to fight a hopeless battle, to die in the field?

"Thank you, sir. I know that *Colossus* is not up to full power yet…" An understatement if he'd ever heard one. "…but I am sure she will perform. She's in better shape that it looks like, sir."

Barron doubted that. He'd checked every report, every bit of information he had on the massive ship. It was remarkably workable, considering, but it was at twenty-five percent, *maybe* thirty percent, of its maximum power. It looked worse even than that, but he understood the focus had been on the vital systems almost entirely.

"Well, whatever shape she's in, we're going to have to

make it work. With so many of our dreadnoughts badly damaged—not to mention the number destroyed—we're going to need everything we've got."

"Yes, sir...I can promise you *Colossus* will serve you well. There's going to be a moment, I know it, when she stands up and makes you proud, Admiral. I am sure of it."

Barron just nodded. He had been sure of such things as well at one time. The destruction of the original *Dauntless* was still told in the classrooms of the Academy, one of the great stories of Confederation arms. He had enjoyed aspects of that moment himself, even as he had suffered greatly from it. But he'd come to realize that few of the truly phenomenal moments in history were more than small bits of excitement. Perhaps *Colossus* would get her moment...but it wouldn't match what it was supposed to be.

Only the plan had the chance of really making a difference, whether he thought it had a one percent or ninety-nine percent chance of success. He would fight, of course, to the finish, but he really didn't think his side had any chance at all in conventional encounters.

But there was enough of him left to pay attention to Eaton, to serve her, even if it was through dishonesty. "I am sure you will, Commodore...I'm sure you will."

* * *

"Please...I need you, at least." Akella spoke softly, but her voice showed her tension. She'd come back, to the planet where the Council set itself up, the fourth location in the past five years...and she'd run into nothing but a nightmare. She didn't have the votes to support a move to Confederation territory, and she had resorted to dealing one on one with her Council members, trying somehow to put together a sequence of deals, some kind of setup that would allow her to at least keep the alliance together.

Keep the Hegemony forces together. She'd spoken to at

least six leaders in the fleet before she'd left, and she was pretty sure about four of them. But the other two were question marks. It wasn't that they were disloyal, but they were problematic. If the choice came down to obeying her and Chronos, or the Council, she didn't know where they would go.

"Akella, I want to support you, you know that. But we have been pushed, farther than ever before in our history. I understand why the Confeds want to pull back, I truly do. But if we stand, if we insist that another spot be chosen to try and hold onto at least something of the Hegemony...maybe they will agree."

Akella understood the words, she knew her comrade's position. And she knew it was wrong. She understood the Council members, all but Chronos somewhat protected from the realities of the moment. That wasn't entirely true, of course...they had been driven across half of known space, and they knew the fight had to be won. But they couldn't accept their power's position as number two. They believed they were more powerful than the Confeds, at least they had been, and it was difficult to make the point that they weren't anymore. That the enemy had occupied half their space for almost five years, that their production was greatly cut, while the Confederation built ships at an almost alarming pace. She *knew*, and it had been hard for her to accept, that the Confederation was now the number one power in the race, and she realized her effort would largely depend on convincing the others of this.

That should have been easy, she knew that...but she realized why it would be difficult. "Pulcheria, please, listen to me. The Hegemony is not the senior power anymore. We don't have the most ships, either in the field or under construction. We don't have the most troops, nor the ability to transport most of what we do have. We are beaten in this war, and whatever chance we have—and I don't think we have all that much of one even I convince a majority of the

Council to vote with me—rests with the Confederation. I know this—and I assure you, Admiral Barron does as well—and it is time for you to accept it as well. The Confederation is our only chance, either in normal military efforts, or in the deployment of the virus, which was jointly developed, but on which they carried most of the burden. And without your support, I have no chance. If I can't persuade you, I will fail utterly…and the Hegemony forces will split. One portion will go with me, back to the Confederation, and the rest will form up here somewhere. They will speak boldly of defending you…and they will be destroyed, utterly and completely, and you will be lost, all of you."

Akella wasn't crying, but she was close. She'd contemplated her meetings on the journey she'd taken, and she knew, if she didn't get the vote to go her way, she would, at best, return to Chronos, beaten, to see how much of the fleet sided with him, and with the plan to leave the Hegemony.

And how many sided with the Council…and remained to be destroyed.

That was the best she could hope for if the vote went against her. The worst was her own death, and she knew that was a possibility, that or her confinement, which she considered the same thing. She knew the enemy was coming no matter what, and that the Hegemony would be fully occupied. Maybe she couldn't persuade her people to accept their fate, to fall back with the Confederation and Alliance fleets…but if she couldn't all that would mean was there were even fewer ships with the last force.

For an instant, she even hesitated, wondered if it would be better to die there, in defense of the Hegemony, with no chance whatsoever. She knew her people were going to lose anyway…did it really matter if it was a year later.

Yes, it did matter, if only because of the desperate mission even then underway. She knew there was no hope of victory, not conventionally, not anymore if there ever was. But perhaps the virus would work, perhaps it would kill many of the Highborn. That still seemed almost unreal to her, but she knew it was a possibility, and one reason to strive on, to fight until she was completely beaten.

Pulcheria looked doubtful during the entire conversation, and her frown remained on her face. But she said, "Akella, I have never seen you quite this way. I doubt your plan...but I will listen. Show me the true state of the fleet, prove to me that the Confeds are demonstrably the most powerful component...and I will consider my position."

Akella felt a hope, at least part of one, and it filled her with some kind of excitement. She didn't know she would gain Pulcheria's support, and even if she did, she wasn't sure it would result in her victory. But it was a place to start, and she was going to give it everything she had.

"Okay, Pulcheria...here are the fleet breakdowns. I want you to pay close attention..."

* * *

"What are his chances...really?" Barron stood outside the room, looking in on Stockton, even as the man slept. Stockton *had* awakened, three times since the surgery, but mostly, he'd been unconscious, and it was starting to worry Barron.

"Are you asking me what his chances of survival are? I don't really know, but assuming we got everything out—and although we believe we did, there's still at least a chance we missed something—I think pretty good. I would have been much lower right after the surgery, but in truth, his body *is* recovering, if slowly. I'd say seventy percent, at least if we got everything."

Barron listened, though he realized he had been asking two questions at the same time. The first one was the obvious one, the one Dr. Jordan had answered. But he also wanted to know what chance, if any, Stockton had of returning to him. Of really returning.

Of ending up back in a fighter.

"That is good news, Doctor...but I also need to know what chance there is of his returning...to service." Barron felt terrible, even as he asked the question. But he needed to know...and he didn't really believe Stockton had any other thoughts either, at least to whatever extent the man had focused thoughts.

The doctor didn't respond right away, and when he did, he was slow. "I just don't know, Admiral. In theory, there should be no reason he doesn't...at least nothing medical. At least if he fully recovers. But there are a hundred things that could have gone wrong...and any percentage I gave you would be little more than a guess. I think we should just continue with his treatment, here on *Dauntless*, if that works for you. In a few weeks, I will be able to give you better information. Probably."

Barron didn't especially like the final word of the answer, but he realized it had been honest. The doctor knew better than he did, and he knew better than someone farther away from the whole thing, but no one actually knew. All he could do was wait...and see.

Chapter Thirty-Four

CWS Donallus
Coranus Tylus System
Year 329 AC (After the Cataclysm)

Andi watched closely, but she didn't say a word. She had been quiet, through four planetary operations, and the battles that had preceded each, and she intended to be through the fifth one as well. She'd uttered the orders to attack, but she had been silent since then, even returning two subsequent reports from Tarren with nothing more than a pair of nods.

She was pleased, at least as much as that was possible. She knew she had by far the easiest sequence of targets, an intentional compensation for her last stop, which was back to the first target. She wondered if she would run into a major fleet there, and if the Highborn would be showing signs of the disease yet. If they weren't, she knew there was still time, but she would be disappointed too.

She looked as her ships completed their bombardment, destroying nothing, not even doing any visible damage. The only thing they were dropping was microscopic, but if everything worked as it was supposed to, it would kill all the Highborn present on the planet, wherever they went. And all the Highborn they came into contact with if they left the planet before the disease actually started.

Atara had been confident, sure for some reason that the formula was right, and that the enemy hadn't come up with any method to resist…but now, doubts were beginning to develop. She wasn't exactly of a mind that the plan *wouldn't* work, but now that she was closer to finding out, she was less certain.

"Bombardment complete, Atara…the last ships will be in position in four minutes."

She turned and looked at her aide, and she even managed to smile a bit. "Very well, Ross…as soon as the last ships are in position, we take off. Planet six awaits."

"Yes. Understood."

She turned and faced forward, her eyes focusing on the main display, on the planet she'd just bombarded. She looked at it, completely aware that it would disappear soon enough, that the last of her ships would move far away.

She looked, wondering what would happen there in the next several months. Would the Highborn all die, even spread the virus to other worlds? Would they be at least concerned, forced to rely on some old treatment they'd developed? It was possible that, even if the enemy *had* defeated the virus, they would be badly surprised. Perhaps some of their people would die anyway, before the cure was distributed…enough even to make a difference?

No, she realized. If the enemy had a cure, the best she could hope for was to kill some of the Highborn…but actual victory would require an enemy endlessly open to the attack, not just a few early fatalities. That might be the worst of all possibilities, at least for those who might accept life after defeat. Would the enemy respond with its own change of directive, would they destroy all the worlds they controlled, and all the ones they were going to take?

But maybe it would work as she'd expected. Perhaps it would sweep away the Highborn, kill them in the hundreds, in the thousands, at a time. She just didn't know, and she realized her uncertainty was the only way to review the situation. She'd done everything possible to make it function…now it just had to *work*. And there was nothing she could do in the interim, nothing except wait and see.

"All ships in position. Ready to initiate thrust."

Andi saw that the main screen had gone dark, that its image of the planet had given way to one of the space around it. There hadn't been any significant enemy forces present, much as there hadn't been on the past several planets. She knew she had the easiest grouping, and she wondered just how much worse of a time the rest of the force was having. Were they even still operational? She knew the forces had taken as many ships as possible from the main fleet, as many as they thought the primary force could do without, at least in terms of the enemy knowing that they had detached forces. Every functional vessel in the combined navies wasn't enough to face the enemy, however…no more.

She wondered what Tyler had done, or more accurately, what he had been forced to do. Had he pulled back to the Confederation, to the final stage of the battle. Or was he still in the Hegemony, holding on, more the result of an enemy pause than anything else?

Or had he been caught already? Was he dead? Her intellect told her she didn't know, but her gut believed he was still alive. She just wasn't sure if it was a genuine belief or just what she needed.

"All ships…forward at one half thrust. Target, right for transit point two." She didn't know what was happening, anywhere but around her fleet. And she barely knew what her force would face. The enemy was focused on its main assault, she was sure of that. But that didn't mean there couldn't be forces deployed in the occupied worlds that could give her a fight, even defeat her. Ideally, forty-one planets would be infected when the effort was over…but she knew that depended on a lot, on everything going exactly right. If the enemy caught wind of what they were doing—and the odds of that increased with every planet bombarded—they would likely radically alter their plans.

And then they would come for the attacking ships...in force.

She knew they would figure it out...she just had no idea how long that would take, and how much time would be required to shift their plans around, to find the attacking fleets and launch devastating assaults. Maybe, just maybe, it would be after the fleets had all finished, too late to interfere. That had been her assumption earlier, and while it had faded somewhat, it was still there.

She wasn't sure whether it was just her belief, or if she was just kidding herself, but she saw no reason to change now.

* * *

Tulus looked out, at the world, the fifth one his fleet had attacked. Like all the others, it appeared exactly as it had before his fleet had descended, save only for its defending force of ships. That had been more than he'd encountered before, and if they were all smaller vessels, there were still twenty of them. The fight had been fast, and it had been furious, and while his force had won, it had lost eighteen ships, and many more were damaged. He told himself it was just a coincidence, that if the enemy had truly discovered what he was doing there, they would have sent many more vessels. He knew he was right, that in all probability, the enemy had not pieced together the fleet's actions—at least not enough that the main fleet had been alerted and responded. Still, perhaps the main fleet hadn't yet been contacted, but maybe the neighboring systems had been. Perhaps the force he had faced had been reinforced from the adjacent worlds.

That was possible—likely even—though it didn't change

a thing, certainly not for him, and for his mostly-Alliance force. He was capable of pulling back, barely, but only when his force was too battered to continue...and it wasn't, not yet.

"Status?" He basically knew, but he was curious about the details. Part of him didn't really care, but the part that had been most effected by Tyler Barron was edgy.

"We'll be ready to leave in three minutes, sir. All ships have completed bombardment, and they are returning now."

He nodded, but he didn't reply. There was no need for it. The Alliance lord that he was would lead the force, from planet to planet, even if it was battered down so much that it could only partially bombard them. The Confederation part of him, so often in the lead, would fall to second place in this circumstance. It would remain silent. He knew that...even as he also knew his chance of completing his entire mission was virtually zero. He had just about the minimum number of ships he needed to bomb the next planet...which meant, if he lost more than a couple in the next fight, he would already be down to partial bombardments.

Or, worse, he could run into an enemy force that could take out his entire force. He was heading back now, toward the center of the Hegemony. That didn't mean he would run into increasingly difficult forces...but it meant that was a dangerous possibility.

He looked down at his timer. Three minutes had passed since he'd checked, and he didn't feel the need to do it again. He just turned his head slightly and said, "Let's head to the next planet. Initial thrust at 60% of capacity."

"60% thrust, sir. Engaging."

He felt the small push of the thrust. His Alliance ships weren't the equals of either Confederation or Hegemony craft, and he'd come to know very well. Both of those engaged better systems, and they rarely even showed any signs of acceleration, at least when they were operating at full power. His own ships were shielded now too, though that was as much because of technology provided by the Confederation as anything else. Twelve or fifteen years ago, his ships were mostly unshielded, and they traveled at speeds barely half of those they were capable of now. He thought for an instant about the advances his fleet had seen, the fifty or a hundred years forward they had moved in fifteen years...and how they were still behind their allies.

At least they *were* allies. Going back another five years, his Alliance thought itself the best, without match. That was foolish, certainly, and also the result of its relative place, on the Far Rim, adjacent only to small entities on the rim of occupied space.

Still, he promised himself, if the war was won—somehow—he would see that his people reached parity with their neighbors. He turned and looked out at the display, at the whole fleet, and he knew one thing, even if it was mostly the Confederation side of him that truly understood it.

The mission he was on was the true hope, not that pursued by the remnants of the main fleet with Barron. That was why he had argued for a role in the operation, why he had led one of the forces. Now, he wondered if he would make it back, if he would complete the list of worlds and return...or if he would die out here.

He just didn't know.

* * *

Stantia looked out at her people, watching as her force completed the fifth assault. She knew she was fortunate to command the fleet, that Ilius would have, almost certainly, had he lived. Stantia was a Master, of course, but she was fairly far down the line, at least among those near the top. Her ranking was in excess of ten thousand, which was not bad in a civilization of nearly three hundred billion, but it wasn't high enough to justify her position either. But she knew she was Chronos's most trusted aide now that Ilius was gone, and even if there were ten or twelve others at the same rank, she'd suspected she would be the senior commander's pick to replace him.

And she had been.

That was amazing enough for anyone ranked one thousand, but for someone over ten thousand, it was almost unimaginable. She knew she'd have trouble occupying the role as Chronos's replacement, that much higher-ranked individuals would argue to push her aside. There had even been some complaining about her assignment to the current mission, but with Chronos insisting, and the realization of just how dangerous it was, she had managed to take the job without too much hassle.

She looked out at her forces, the only group out of four to consist of Hegemony craft. She'd been a top officer during the war against the Confederation, when the enemy had been clearly outgunned. Even early in the war against the Highborn, the Hegemony had been the superior partner. Put the combination of severe losses, and the staggering construction rate of the Confederation had turned things around. Many of her people argued against it, claiming it was just a temporary situation in the war. They outright refused to accept the Confed's role as the superior partner. She herself had endured some hassles of her own making the change, but she couldn't argue with the cold hard numbers…and she wondered how anyone else could.

"Commander, the fleet has completed the bombardment. We will be ready to push on in five minutes."

"Very well, Sebastino…carry on and prepare the fleet to depart."

She had led her force through half its targets now, without suffering any terrible damage. She'd lost six ships, and she'd fought against some enemy vessels at each of the five planets she'd attacked. But she knew the last five would be—could be, at the very least—the toughest. The enemy hadn't seemed to guess what she was doing...though she doubted it would be long before they did. She didn't think she had any chance at all of finishing the five worlds she had left, not without the enemy realizing what was happening. She just wondered if they would be able to do anything significant before she was done. If they had time, they could mount a defensive force that would obliterate her entire fleet in one battle. But to do that, they had to realize what was going on, and where she would hit next.

She'd spent a lot of time figuring the answers, and she'd come up with around fifty-fifty. Fifty that she made it back, with losses, but with ten enemy-occupied worlds hit, and fifty that she ran into a large enemy force, that her ships were destroyed...or at least driven off.

She paid secondary attention to her aide, and to his carrying out of her orders. She trusted Sebastino completely, and she didn't feel she had to do more than just be there, in case something unexpected happened. Still, she realized she *was* listening, making sure that everything was going as planned.

You finished half of the total already...if the rest of the forces have done the same, we're at the halfway point. If the formula works, and if the enemy doesn't have a cure...just maybe it won't matter if you finish. Maybe half is enough.

She thought about that, wondered if it was right, if half *was* actually enough...or if the whole thing, all forty-one planets, would be too little. She had no way of knowing, not really. She acknowledged that it would depend on how many Highborn traveled...before realization sprung its own deadly trap.

Assuming, of course, the enemy didn't laugh at the effort, and just issue a treatment to everyone infected. The one thing Stantia knew about the virus they were spreading was that it was not quick. It took a period of months before symptoms even appeared...and months more before those infected actually died. Still, it was one hundred percent fatal to any Highborn touched by it, and completely harmless to normal human beings.

Assuming, again, that the enemy had not invented a treatment…and that the formula had been redeveloped correctly. There were a number of things that could go wrong, but she knew it was her people's only hope too, so she went with it, even convinced herself to believe it would work.

It was the only choice that remained…certainly for her people, for the Hegemony.

Chapter Thirty-Five

Fleet Base Grimaldi
Krakus System
Year 329 AC (After the Cataclysm)

Admiral Simpson looked around the bridge, or what was left of it. He'd given everything he had to the fight, everything he was made of...and he was fairly sure the enemy was going to suffer enough damage to delay their continued advance. He even smiled, for a moment, and nodded his head at the thought of success, or at least what passed for it in the current situation.

"Go...all of you. Now." There were only five people left on the bridge. He had held them back from the phase three evacuation, but now he knew, he had to let them go. If he was ever going to. "I said go!"

He looked around at the four others present. None had moved at first, but now, three of them began to shift slowly. They knew they'd be leaving their commander behind, though he hadn't said as much, and they were clearly troubled by it. They all appeared ready to speak, but one of them got to it first.

"Admiral...you should come too." It was Commander Tellium who spoke, the other two individuals standing right behind him. "Please..."

"Go, Commander...all of you." He paused, and then he added a not very credible, "I will come soon."

The commander didn't buy it, but he looked at the admiral, and at the one other man who hadn't moved. He looked like he was going to say something, but he didn't. He just stood in place for a moment...and then he turned and walked away, clearly struggling as he did.

Simpson watched them leave, and as he did, he turned toward the sole remaining occupant on the bridge. "You too, Larson...go. Go now."

"Not without you, sir."

The words were soft, but they were firm, too. Simpson looked at him and repeated his demand, but he knew the words were pointless. He was ready to sacrifice himself, to leave the command of whatever remained in the capable hands of Sam Taggart. But to do it, he would have to take Jaymes with him.

"Larson...please...go..."

"No, sir...not without you."

"It's an order." It was a last effort, but even as he said it, he knew Larson Jaymes was resilient.

"Then I'm afraid I have to ignore it, sir. You can hold me up on charges, assuming we get out of here."

Simpson looked down. He had decided to die here...but alone. Taking Jaymes with him wasn't part of the plan. He resolved that his associate could choose to die if he wanted to...but that only lasted maybe half a minute. As much as he tried to tell himself that Jaymes was making his own choice, he knew the only reason the man was doing it was to counter his own resolve.

He couldn't allow the man to kill himself...but how could he stop it? If he committed suicide, he assumed Jaymes would then retreat...but could he do that? Fighting to the finish was one thing, an end with a bit of heroism, but killing himself? That was cowardice, at least to his point of view.

His hand moved slightly, toward the pistol at his side. He stopped suddenly, realizing that he had to move quickly, that if Jaymes realized what he intended to do, he would try to stop him. He had to do it fast, almost without pause...and he decided he would.

But he just stayed the way he was, his hand unmoving, his head a mess. He wanted to die in the fight, at least part of him did. Whether that was the realization that Taggart was the better candidate to hold the top command, or simply an acceptance that the fight was functionally over, that even his goal of delaying any enemy advance would only buy a period of months. Simpson realized his intentions weren't entirely pure. Yes, he did think Taggart was a better officer than him...but he didn't believe she had any more chance than he would. The war was over—unless Barron had managed to win some kind of great victory— and buying six months before the enemy advanced was both all he could gain from the battle, and at the same time, totally pointless.

But he couldn't let his friend die. He knew Jaymes would fight to the end if he survived, and he was sure he would never surrender. But, the rationale that worked so well for him didn't extend to his officer.

"Alright, Larson...let's go. Let's get the hell out of here."

He jumped up, suddenly realizing how close he'd come to meeting his end...and wanting to live.

* * *

"Keep the settings at 120%...and fire as rapidly as possible!" Samantha Taggart spoke, her voice hoarse, but her tone strong. She had decided to fight the battle until it was clear to her that the enemy was battered, that they wouldn't have the strength remaining to push on forward for some time. She was close, very close, but she had to keep her line in the fight, at least a little longer.

The station was out of the battle, at least. It had been blasted down to only a few beams left, and Admiral Simpson had ordered the remaining crew to escape. It wasn't an unexpected move, but Taggart had dreaded it nevertheless, especially because she'd had a strong impression Simpson wasn't going to leave. But she'd heard that he was with the withdrawing personnel, at least it seemed so from the transmissions she had received. She still wasn't sure he would pull back, despite what she'd been told, but even uncertainty was a lot better than she'd been before.

"Yes, Commodore…" Isaac Johnson was worn, tired…and afraid. But he held his position as Taggart's aide, and he held it well. Taggart knew the command was unimportant, that it merely repeated the standing orders…but she knew her people needed everything they could get. She had barely a third of her ships left in the line, and if another third had pulled back, near to death's door, she had still lost one ship in three, outright. Even if every vessel that had escaped was fully recovered, and every vessel still in the fight, too—a virtual impossibility—she would still have lost a third of her ships.

And it was going to be more than that, she knew.

She watched the line, and if the enemy force was as badly battered, or nearly so, as her own, it was only a passing joy. The enemy ships were a tiny part of a vast force, a lesser component of a fleet that was fighting another— unknown—enemy as well as her side's main fleet. She hadn't gotten herself out of the Confederation herself in years, and she only knew of the Highborn, and their history, from scattered bits and pieces that had come back. It seemed impossible to her that the enemy had its own foe, besides her people, that the Highborn had even attacked the humans in the hope that, once defeated, they could aid against this completely unknown force.

She scoffed at that, imagined that the Highborn would

eventually win the war...but that everyone truly useful against the unknown enemy would be dead. She knew that wasn't expressly true, but she told herself that, at least, that all those already in the service, those worthwhile at least, would be gone...slain fighting off the Highborn for as long as possible.

The ship shook, hard, and she knew it had been hit. Badly. *Constellation* had escaped heavy damage for a long while, but now it had been hit three times in the past few minutes.

Her eyes moved to her private display, showing the interior of the ship. The hit had come in at an angle, and it had taken out one engine...maybe two. The second one, if it was down, might be repairable, but the first one was almost gone. That meant an extra two months, at least, on the line to conduct repairs. Assuming the ship made it out of the battle...which was starting to look very dicey.

She scanned the main display, looking at the battle line. Her fleet was gutted, almost destroyed...but she finally decided it had done enough. The enemy fleet was battered, too, and she doubted its masters would order it forward before major repairs were completed.

She was sure enough to make the decision, finally, to give her survivors a chance to escape. To give herself a chance.

"Isaac...we're going to withdraw. Let's start with the half of the ships most damaged. The others will stay in the line and try to hold back the enemy." It was a difficult scenario for any force to face, but she knew the enemy had been badly chopped up as well. With some luck, a good portion of her last line would escape.

Maybe even Constellation...if we're lucky.

She knew she should run the idea past Simpson, but he was in the middle of his escape from Grimaldi. She wasn't even sure could reach him...and she was sure it would take too long, even if she could.

"Yes, Commodore…at once." There was a touch a joy in Johnson's voice. It was tempered by the realization that *Constellation* might not be one of the ships to make it out—in fact, it seemed likelier than not that it wouldn't—but there was also a realization that the fleet had managed to complete its goal, that even though they were battered and driven away, even though Grimaldi was going to be lost, and possibly *Constellation*, too, they had done the minimum they had to do. They had bought another six months, maybe closer to a year.

And that was a reason to be excited…at least the best reason they had.

* * *

Simpson sat, quietly, simultaneously ashamed at the suicidal streak that had almost taken him, and still depressed over the situation. He knew all his thoughts had been correct, and he was sure Taggart was a better officer than he was. But he knew there would be a place for both of them, even if it was only in an eventual defeat.

Assuming Taggart made it out, of course. That was what he realized now, the fatal flaw to his suicidal urge. What if Taggart was killed in the battle? He'd decided she was better than he was, but knew he was a good officer, too…and losing them both would only hurry the disaster that seemed to be coming no matter what.

He looked up, catching Jaymes's concerned glance for a moment. He owed the officer a thanks, and a fairly long explanation, but that would wait until they were alone. For the moment, they were on the last shuttle from Grimaldi, traveling back toward the point. Given any luck at all, they would make it, and he would continue to serve the Confederation. But now he became worried about Taggart, about the very officer he'd come so close to suicide to protect. Was it possible that *he* would escape, and *she* wouldn't?

He leaped to his feet, fumbling with the seatbelt for a moment. He saw Jaymes move, unsure at first what he was doing. But he waved the subordinate off. He was just heading for the small screen in the shuttle. He turned it on, and brought it about, to focus on *Constellation*.

He would regret the loss of Grimaldi, he was sure, and the defeat in the battle, but at least inflicting enough damage was something. In the context of the situation, it was everything.

But now he had to get Taggart out...and the instant he saw her ship, he knew that was going to be difficult. *Constellation* was one of the few ships remaining, and the enemy was closing all around. The battle was entering the end stages, and while he didn't expect Taggart to lose her will to survive as he had, he didn't think she would be anything but the last ship out either.

"Larson...help me here. I've got to get a message to *Constellation* before we jump." His voice was strained, and his subordinate leapt up and raced across the cabin to his side.

"What is it, sir?"

"It's Taggart...we've got to get her out." He said the words, as though he had the power to do anything except send her a message, and hope both that it got to her, and that she didn't ignore it.

"Right...okay, let's try to send a signal." Jaymes spoke softly, but it was obvious he was worried about the amount of time he had...and the strength of the unit on the small escape vehicle. He moved forward, taking control, using all his skill to focus on the target ship.

He failed. The distance was just too great, and *Constellation* was almost surrounded by enemy ships, putting out all kinds of interference.

Simpson watched, knowing he would hinder rather than

help if he got involved. Jaymes was still trying...but there was nothing. He managed to extend the range of the communicator, but he just couldn't penetrate the enemy interference. Still, he tried again.

Simpson looked at the distance to the jump point. He had a few minutes, but then, if he ordered the ship to bypass it, the next possible jump would be in more than twenty minutes. Twenty-one point eight, actually.

He looked around the point, tried to decide whether he had more than twenty minutes. His vessel wasn't a warship, it was just a small escape ship. It wouldn't take much from the enemy to destroy it. He felt a bit of the old force coming back, but he pushed it away this time. If Taggart might not make it out, he *had to survive*...one of them had to. He wasn't ready to give up...but he wasn't going to throw his ship back into the mess, not for so long. He didn't think so, at least.

He was looking at the link to the control room, considering whether it was worth it to risk the extra time. But he didn't have to decide. He heard the sound on the comm unit...the sound of Sam Taggart's voice.

Larson Jaymes had done it, he'd managed to get a signal through. That was only the first part, Simpson knew, and perhaps the easiest...but it was the first.

He grabbed the single comm unit, and he strapped it onto his head. "Sam, are you there? Listen to me, you've got to escape...and you've got to do it now!"

Chapter Thirty-Six

CFS Constellation
Krakus System
Year 329 AC (After the Cataclysm)

Commodore Taggart waved her arm, sending a message to her subordinate. She wasn't sure if the meaning would get through, but she was trying to do about six things at once and speaking to the admiral was only one of them.

"Sir, we're pretty cut off...but I think we can hold a decent size chunk of the line, for a short while, at least while some of my people pull out."

"Forget it, Commodore. The battle's over, and now it's just about escaping. The enemy is hurt enough that they'll have to wait for significant repairs or reserves...and that's the best we could have hoped for." *And if the enemy is careless, if they move on the remains of Grimaldi too carelessly, they will catch one more nasty surprise.* "It's time to get out of here. And that means you! You've got by far our greatest ship, so figure out a way to escape! Now!"

Taggart felt a wave of excitement, but only for a few seconds. It was all well and good for Simpson to urge her to escape, to order her too...but that could only do so much. She was trapped, or damned close to it, and even as she realized Simpson was correct about the enemy fleet, she doubted she could escape.

But she'd try.

"Blast the engines at...whatever we've got left!" She wasn't even sure what her engines had, but whatever it was, she was putting all of it into escaping. "And tell all other ships to break off and escape."

"Yes, Commodore."

She turned back to the comm. "I'm doing everything I can to get away, sir, but in case we don't make it...you've got to transit as soon as you reach the point. You're in a tiny ship, and one decent shot could take you out. I'll make it if I can. I promise." She didn't believe she would escape, but her words were honest...she was going to try.

The other end of the comm unit was silent.

"Commodore...I will try every way possible to get out of here, but you have to go first. You have to!"

The silence continued for another moment, but then Simpson answered. "Alright, Commodore...I'll go through as soon as we reach the point. But you'd better be right behind me, or I'm going to..." He didn't say anything further, but his point was clear, nevertheless.

"I promise, sir. I will do everything possible to escape. Now, you...go!" She cut the line, almost immediately, and she turned toward her bridge crew. "Alright everybody...let's kick it up to evasion routine, alpha-5...and let's get out of here!"

"Yes, Commodore...evasion routine alpha-5 engaged. We're moving off at sixty-three percent power, but the engineer tells me he thinks he can get it over seventy in a minute."

Seventy percent...good, much better than she'd expected. But still, maybe not enough.

"How much power do we have left after the engines?" She had a basic calculation of her own, but she wanted to make sure she was right.

"That's somewhat variable, Commodore. It looks like 10

gigawatts, maybe closer to 11."

That was a bit more than she'd hoped for, but it didn't matter. Her orders were the same. "Fire the main guns, at least as many as the power can." Her guess was, maybe half of the remaining guns could shoot, but she knew her ship would cut them off before it would overtax the power.

"Yes, Commodore."

The orders actually cut the fire down more than in half, at least from what it had been moments ago, when her plans had been different. She didn't want to die, but she was willing to if need be...and if she wasted power on her engines and didn't escape...

Her vessel was clearly the strongest one on her side, on either side, and the enemy would want to take it out. She was also just about the farthest from the point...but even if forcing the enemy to focus on her ship got a few of the others out, it was a good thing.

She stared at the screen, at the enemy ships around her. She'd surprised them with her sudden move, gotten a bit of a jump on them. It wasn't going to be enough, probably not through to the jump at least, but it was going to help.

And every extra second was worthwhile.

* * *

"Captain...*Constellation* is pulling out."

The words echoed all around Captain Antonio Graves. He was closer to the point than Taggart was, but he was still farther back than most of the force. He commanded four ships, down from seven, and he'd been wrestling with the fact that Taggart was going to stay and hold the line...and probably die doing it.

Now the flagship was pulling out, abandoning its position, and surprising the enemy. That last part was good to gain somewhat of an edge, but it didn't take him long to realize that *Constellation* wasn't likely to make it.

At least not without some help.

"Bring us around." The words came out of his mouth before he'd even decided. They weren't technically a violation of orders, at least not until Taggart realized what he was doing, and commanded him to return to his previous vector. But he wasn't thinking that far ahead. He was hardly thinking at all. "All four ships…back to *Constellation*, now. As quickly as possible." He knew he was gambling his life, and the lives of his crew, though he also realized they were far enough back that those were already at least somewhat in the mix anyway.

And more now…

"Yes, sir…" His senior commander responded, sounding like a combination of excited and terrified. But he was strong, and Graves knew he'd be okay. He knew all of his people would be, that they understood the importance of the mission, and the critical nature of saving both the commodore and *Constellation* from destruction.

Even if it cost him his own ships.

He watched as all four remaining vessels turned around, blasting their engines at full power in almost the opposite direction. He tried to imagine what was going on aboard Simpson's great vessel, and he told himself she wouldn't even notice what his ships were doing, not until they were deep into it.

But she noticed almost at once.

"Sir…I have Commodore Taggart on the line for you."

It was earlier even than he'd imagined, and he cursed her for the capabilities he had so often praised. She was in the middle of a nightmarish fight, but she was still keeping watch on her ships. He wondered what he would say, how he would respond. He honestly didn't know.

He pulled the comm unit onto his head. "Commodore…" It was all he was going to say, at least until she told him why she was calling. He knew, of course, but he didn't plan to make it any easier on her.

"Antonio…I need you to resume your previous course. Do not attempt to return and interfere with *Constellation*'s escape. We will make it alone."

Her tone was good, but he realized the last part of what she had said was a lie. She didn't expect to make it, he knew that. She had *maybe* a ten percent chance of escaping. Maybe.

"Commodore…you need help. And my ships are the closest to yours. It's clear cut…and to be honest, it would be better to lose my four ships than yours." He regretted saying the last bit. It was completely true, but it was better to assume all the ships would make it.

Even if it wasn't true.

"Captain, this is an order. Withdraw immediately."

He cringed under the onslaught…but he didn't give into it. Not quite. "Sir, you *need* the help, and you know it is the right thing to do. My four ships have less crew total than yours, and far less value." That was true in both real and imagined terms, though he realized some of them were perhaps not as valid as they once were. It would take at least a year to repair the superbattleship, and more likely, closer to two. And he didn't think his people had anywhere near that amount of time. His smaller ships were easier to fix.

But he was decided. And if it came to it, he was prepared to fight it out, to go against orders…and to see if his crews would follow his commands.

"Antonio, I appreciate your loyalty, but I have to insist that you withdraw." A short pause. "Please."

The last word struck him like a cannonball, and he struggled to endure the hit. He almost gave in, ordered his ships to reverse their thrust again. But he held. "I'm sorry, Commodore, but we're coming in…and we'll all get out." He cut the line immediately, as much because he didn't expect he could endure much more. He'd kept the line private, and only he had heard Taggart. But she could call back, anytime, speak to any of the others, or all of them. Then he would see if his people would ignore their senior commander's order to follow those of the man who'd led them for a few days.

But so far, the comm was silent, and his ships were decelerating, preparing to reaccelerate toward the approaching *Constellation*, and the array of enemy ships beginning to pursue the flagship.

He expected the comm to go off any second…but there was nothing, only silence on the line, and in fact, on the entire bridge. He wasn't sure it would last, but as the time went from seconds to minutes, he told himself it would…and he continued on his course.

* * *

"The enemy is withdrawing, everywhere." The bridge of the Highborn flagship was in good condition, courtesy mostly to Percelax's presence. He wasn't a coward by any measure, but he did view his own survival as crucial to the mission, and he'd kept the flagship back from the closest range fighting.

Percelax nodded, and then he said, "That is good. Order the fleet to follow up, and to inflict as much damage as possible on the enemy." He was going to let them leave, what little they still had. He'd let himself imagine winning a decisive victory, one that allowed him to follow up immediately, but he knew that was out of the question now. Still, he *was going to win*, and with many of his ships still there, if damaged. Six months, eight outside, and he would be ready to move forward. But for the moment, he would take the victory he'd won and celebrate.

"Send ships to Grimaldi…perhaps the enemy failed to set up a self-destruct." He knew that was unlikely, but he imagined how much more glory he would gain if he managed to capture the fortress. "Only four ships, though." That was all he was willing to risk.

"Yes, sir."

He turned and looked up at the screen, at the situation on the battlefield. Things were going well, even if he had lost more than he'd intended. Now, if his forces could just take out the enemy flagship—and capture Grimaldi—he would be truly happy. He'd seen enough battles to realize the end position meant far more than the losses suffered to get there.

He watched Grimaldi, which had been unoccupied for two hours now. He'd expected it to explode once the last of its people had escaped, but it hadn't. He'd ordered his ships to stop firing at it, and he'd even sent two of them close, very close...but nothing had happened. He didn't really have any choices. He could destroy the thing, or he could try to take it. And he decided to try to take it.

He watched as the ships closed, as they docked with the station. There was no explosion. Nothing. Perhaps his forces had compelled the enemy to withdraw quickly enough that they had failed to set up a self-destruct. He hadn't imagined taking the station when the battle began, not really at least. But now, he wondered.

He watched as the ships all docked...and as they entered the station. He'd held his breath for a few seconds, but then he got the message. The ships all had personnel aboard. He took a deep breath, and he realized that he just might take the station.

That lasted about two minutes. Then: "Sir, we've triggered something." For an instant, he didn't know what it was. Then, he realized.

"Get out...now!" But even as he uttered the words, he realized they were too late.

He heard the sound the boarders were transmitting. "Four...three...two...one..."

He closed his eyes, realizing what was happening without seeing it. The comm line vanished immediately, and a few seconds later, his aide put the profoundly evident fact into words. "Enemy station has destroyed itself…and all four ships."

Percelax shook his head, the thought he'd had of taking the station seeming just then to be crazy. *Of course, the enemy would self-destruct…*

He was deep in his mind, when his aide spoke again. "Sir, the enemy flagship is pulling out."

His thoughts flooded back to the battlefield, to the victory he had definitely won, but which was not yet complete. "All ships, forward. That flagship is not to escape." But even as he looked at the situation, he noticed the four other enemy ships moving forward…and he realized it was essentially a coin toss, a fifty percent chance the enemy would be destroyed…and a fifty percent chance they would make it out.

*   *   *

"Yes…do it!" Taggart responded to her chief engineer. The man had asked her if she wanted him to try to increase the thrust even farther…at great risk. She almost laughed. What risk could be more profound than that of being caught, of taking a few hits from the enemy and losing whatever chance she had at escape?

She grabbed the sides of her seat as the engines poured out thrust. Normally, *Constellation* would be immune to any effects from its engines, but she knew the systems that protected against that were damaged. She didn't know what effect they would have, but she was ready for whatever happened.

As it went, there was a little pressure, but the system mostly worked. She grabbed hold for a while, but then she realized she didn't have to, so she released it. The ship was moving, but it was two remaining engines blasting at over 80% thrust, which was 120% of what should have been possible. Still, many of the pursuers were damaged as well, so while she didn't give herself a good chance at escaping, she did feel it was possible. That was a considerable improvement over her opinion just ten minutes before…and though she didn't want to admit it, it was Graves and his four ships that were making the difference. The force would still be outnumbered and outgunned, massively so, but if the ships rushing to her aid could actually reach her…they *just might* make a difference.

She looked at the screen. The ships were three minutes away. That wasn't far, but she knew it was far enough. Her ship was badly damaged, but it was still partially functional. Still, one or two hits, in the right place, could end her escape, and leave her vessel helpless.

She had gone a long while without taking a serious hit, more than fifteen minutes, now. Part of that was the sophistication of her evasion routine, and part was the damage the closest enemy ships had suffered.

And a big part of it is luck, don't forget that.

She watched the four approaching ships, now less than two minutes out, and she took a deep breath. She knew her ship could be stopped at any moment, that the enemy could take out her engines or cause other terrible damage any time. But the closer the reserve ships came, the more her spirits began to rise. She had no right to be happy about the battle, even if she survived it, she told herself. Yes, her people had done well enough, had bought a period of time, delayed the enemy's forward advance…but she had lost a ton of ships, and almost everything that escaped was barely functional.

She'd smiled when the station had blown itself apart, taking four enemy ships with it, but part of her had also realized how much her thoughts had changed. Losing Grimaldi, the great station on the Union border for eighty years, was *not* good…however much things could have been worse. The only thing keeping such thoughts *mostly* from her at the moment was the excitement of battle. She knew whatever celebration she managed to mount from her actions, assuming she managed to escape—would be short-lived…and she would think of the darkness, of the enemy positioned in the Confederation, right astride the main route deeper in.

Her eyes moved back to the screen, just as Graves' four vessels streamed into range. The ships, all cruisers, were much smaller than *Constellation*, but they were in decent shape. And they tore right into the pursuing enemy ships.

The Highborn vessels had been firing at *Constellation*, trying to take her out before she managed to reach the point, but now they had multiple targets. Some maintained their attention on *Constellation*, but half of them diverted to Graves and his ships.

Taggart realized the lower intensity of fire immediately, and she knew it increased the chances of her escape. But she also realized that one hit, perhaps two, just right, would end her escape.

And she also recognized that Graves's ships, four smaller vessels that would almost certainly have escaped had they not come back, were at severe risk now. That fact particularly struck home when one of the ships took a direct hit. Watching the vessels, knowing they were putting themselves at risk to save *Constellation*, tore at her. She felt the urge to order them back…and the only thing that stopped her was the certainty that Graves would refuse. She could understand sending the ships home, accepting a much higher chance of destruction for *Constellation*, but she couldn't make Graves's actions those of a traitor, not for no reason. So, she remained silent and watched.

The enemy ships poured forward, save for one hit by one of *Constellation*'s main guns. The shot had been dead on, almost perfect, but the ship remained. Its engines appeared almost entirely out, though, and it was already falling behind. In a few minutes, it would be out of range, if it retained anything that could fire, which, an instant later,

Taggart decided it didn't.

She turned and looked at the other side of the screen. The transit point was getting closer. If her ship didn't lose any more power, if its abused and overused engines carried onward, she would make it out in about ten minutes. That was a long time, but it was also a lot less than she'd expected to see. Despite her thoughts, and her negative views, she began to feel some hope.

But Graves...

She had realized he was accelerating in the opposite direction that she was, that his vessels would now be behind her. Now, she calculated just how much more time he would need.

Almost fifteen minutes.

It was a long time, incalculably so in the current situation. He would have to face not only the ships who'd been able to catch her, but also at least half a dozen followers, too far behind to reach *Constellation*, but with a chance to catch the four cruisers.

She felt a burst of excitement, and for an instant, she decided to pull back, to stand and fight the enemy. But it didn't work. Her ship was moving fast, very fast, and the best she could do was stop accelerating, and avoid making the jump. If she cut off her thrust, reversed it, that would help, buying maybe two minutes, even three...but missing the jump would place her ship in a terrible position. She would add...and she did the calculation three different times because she couldn't accept the result...almost half an hour to her flight. That much time was unthinkable. Worse, it was outright suicide. Half the enemy fleet would reach her, and her chances at surviving such an onslaught were too miniscule to figure out.

She had to escape, and leave her rescuers behind, to make it or not. The thought pressed down on her, and it took a few minutes for her to accept it. She almost called Graves, but she decided he needed to focus. He knew the situation, better than she did probably, and he'd known it since before he'd advanced to her aid.

Still, it ate at her, and the more she imagined the four cruisers, flying back toward the point after she had escaped, taking fire from all directions, the more it tore at her. She would have sacrificed herself, remained to fight it out...but she couldn't do that to the men and women aboard the ship. She wouldn't really increase the chances of the cruisers escaping, anyway, and if she bypassed the point, she would basically be sentencing her ship to death.

She looked up, realizing that seven or eight minutes had elapsed...and that her ship was still running, only three minutes from the final jump. She'd been almost certain she was going to die for a while, and now, though every shot taken was potentially the one that would take her ship down, she realized the odds had turned, that she was probably going to make it.

She looked again at Graves's ships, at their position, now fairly far back. They had managed to cut their velocities down to nothing, and even managed to build some level of acceleration back toward the point...but they had a lot of enemy ships to get past, both between them and the point, and also catching up on them from behind.

She didn't know Graves all that well. Until just a few days ago, he was Simpson's aide. She'd met him, of course, numerous times, but she had never really become close.

Now, she was sorry. He was clearly a good man.

She knew his ships were less important than hers was, at least in a general sense. And, she was the second-in-command of the fleet, while he was ranked lower. She knew, though she tried not to recognize it, that Simpson considered her the strongest officer present. She didn't agree with that, at least not in any way she could accept, but yet she knew it was true. Now, she had another officer, putting twelve hundred of his people at risk to save her. She knew it made sense from his perspective, but from hers, it was more complicated.

The ship shook, suddenly taking a hit from the enemy. It was fairly bad, but she was close to the transit point now—and the hit hadn't affected her positioning. It had taken out two more of her main guns, and probably killed some gunners, but it hadn't damaged either remaining engine. The ship was still blasting toward the transit point...and a few seconds later, she felt the strange feelings of making a jump. It lasted perhaps two seconds, though she knew it often felt longer or shorter. Then, she flashed back, into the space beyond, the friendly system both next door and four lightyears away.

She exhaled sharply, realizing she would have to wait a moment for her instruments to return, for her scanners to refocus and pinpoint the transit point...and the rest of the fleet.

And to begin watching, waiting to see if Graves' ships made it back.

She knew it was possible that the enemy would come through as well, but considering the condition of their forces, she doubted it severely. She just hoped she would count to four, as the last of her ships in the system that had held Grimaldi transited.

She waited, what seemed like a long time. Her ship rebooted, and she watched, both the battered ships of her command taking position around her...and the transit point. She was watching to make sure no enemy ships came through, of course...but mostly, she was waiting for Graves.

Ten minutes passed...and nothing had come through. But she remained in place, watching, waiting. She could feel her people giving up...but she didn't.

And then, a ship appeared, one of Graves. It was badly shot up, but it was alive. Then, a moment later, a second one came through.

Taggart was joyful at any ship, but what she really wanted was for Graves's vessel to come through. She hurriedly checked both of the transited ships, but neither one was Graves's. Her eyes moved back to the display, watching, almost trying to pull the desired ship through. And a moment later, a third ship emerged. She checked it again...and it wasn't Graves's vessel. But his was the only one left...and she was sure she would see it in a minute.

Until the first vessel through cleared its system and communicated with her.

"Commodore Taggart...this is Captain Clarke." There was a pause, and part of Taggart knew why. But another section of her maintained a tenuous hope.

For another few seconds at least.

"The last ship has transited, Commodore." She recognized the resentment in the man's tone, not really directed at her, but there, nevertheless. "Captain Graves's ship was destroyed four minutes from the transit point."

Chapter Thirty-Seven

Highborn Flagship S'Argevon
Imperial System GH3-2496
Year of the Firstborn 391 (329 AC)

"I want to know when we will have the first third of our ships back in the line, and I mean exactly." Tesserax knew he was being unreasonable in asking such pointed questions so early, but he did it anyway. He'd come close, very close, to launching the renewed assault at once. He knew his force, especially with the four new—and still unknown to the humans—copies of the *Ellerax*, was powerful enough to prevail against anything the enemy had left.

But the losses suffered in the just concluded battle were worse than even his most dire predictions, and he was edgy about chasing down the humans and finishing them off. If he knew they would cluster together, offer one final battle, he might have gone for it, but the thought of them splitting up, of a dozen or more small battles, was just too much for him…at least until his forces were somewhat repaired.

Still, he'd just about been ready to overlook all of that and proceed forward immediately, when he'd received a communique from Ellerax himself. Tesserax had been sure his proclamation of victory would be received well, and it was. But he'd heard something in Ellerax's voice, something he'd never heard before. It wasn't fear, not exactly, but it was something close, and the Supreme Commander had asked him what forces he might have ready to deploy to the other front.

That was upsetting, even if it *was* mostly conjecture. He knew the war had been going as it had for nearly two centuries, but now he found himself wondering if things had taken a bad turn, if the enemy's fleet had won a decisive victory. That had, at first, pushed him once again toward advancing immediately, crushing the humans as quickly as possible. But as he thought about it, and the position a victory over the humans, followed by bringing badly needed reserves to the main front, would create for him, he had decided to wait, just a couple months. Until a third of his fleet was at least moderately repaired. That would give him more than enough power to quickly crush anything the humans had, and it would reduce the losses his forces would suffer.

All at a cost of several months…perhaps four or five.

He stared at the subordinate. "Well?"

"Sir…I just don't know yet. Six months?" The subordinate clearly saw that he wasn't going to get six months. "Four?"

"I asked you to tell me." Tesserax knew he wasn't being fair, that the aide hadn't yet had the time to review the fleet's status. But he didn't care. He would be reasonable, at least he told himself he would, but he was impatient, too.

"Four months, then. Honestly, sir, I don't think we can do it any quicker…not with the time to move damaged ships to available stations and the like." The officer sounded uncertain enough that he could complete the mandate in the stated four months. Tesserax wasn't willing to allow more time, not yet at least, but he put the thoughts of two months out of his mind.

"Very well…you have four months. Four months to have the ships back here, and ready to move out again." He glared at the poor officer, one of considerable rank, but wholly subordinate to Tesserax. "Understood?"

The officer was silent, just for a moment. Then he said, "Understood."

Tesserax nodded, and he realized that regardless of what his comrade had said, it was no better than a fifty percent chance that one third of the damaged ships would be ready in time. But he was sure of what he had said, and he planted his mind on resuming the offensive in four months...with whatever he had. However many of the damaged ships were ready in time, that is how many he would lead. The final offensive would begin in four months, and not a day later...and after the humans were defeated, his forces would then return to the primary front, and with any luck, save the day there as well.

Tesserax thought about the situation, and he imagined that he would achieve great success, against the humans, and maybe against the old and hated enemy as well. That was a long way from the failure he'd almost gone home in, and he imagined what his place might be after it all worked out. He would advance, from his already high position to one even higher. Perhaps even to number two, to the second in the entire Highborn, the conqueror of one enemy, and the salvation of the fight against another.

He stood where he was, trying not to let anything in his head out, anything except four months. He glared at the officer, and he said, "Very well...you've got a lot of work to do, and I don't want to keep you here." He flipped off a salute, responding to the one that had followed the acknowledgement of the four months, and then he turned and walked toward the door, his pace quickening with each step.

*   *   *

"Send the word...we have won. We have taken fleet base

Grimaldi...or at least its position." Percelax was annoyed with himself, at least over the four ships he'd lost to Grimaldi. He'd feared it would be rigged to self-destruct, but when it didn't, he allowed himself to believe the enemy had forgotten.

He wouldn't make that mistake again.

His forces had won, there was no question about that. Even if the largest enemy ship *had* escaped. That had been unfortunate, but not terribly important. It had been badly damaged, as had most of the surviving fleet, and he had taken the system, and the position, at least, of the great fortress. It was a victory, and if he was somewhat surprised at the cost, he didn't think that would make a difference in the end. The enemy was even worse off than he was, and that was all that mattered.

"Yes, sir." A moment, then: "Sir, we have received word from the main fleet. We are to hold our position and not attack."

Percelax smiled, his mixed temperament giving way to joy. "Advise them that we have invaded and taken the enemy station, and that we control the transit points leading deeper into the enemy systems." He paused for a moment before continuing, "Ask them if they want us to give it back?" He smiled as he said the words. He had expected the very orders that had just arrived...and whether or not he had lost a few more ships than he should have, he was in a good position. It would take some time to bring forward repair structures and send ships back to the Union for repairs...but the enemy was in worse shape, he was sure of that.

The main enemy fleet could chase him away, he was sure of that...but he was also sure that it would be defeated by Tesserax's forces, that in all likelihood, it already had. That meant it would be followed, closely, by the primary fleet...and whatever remained after the battle would be destroyed. Perhaps it would make it back, even compel him to retreat for a short while…but as far as he could see, the humans faced total defeat. His perception of them was that they were mixed, that some of their people would fight to the finish…but he also believed there were billions ready to give up, to yield. And his people controlled at least half of the Hegemony as well as the entire Union. That was at least half of the population of the entire area, of all humans living outside of the areas previously controlled by the Highborn. The war was almost over, at least in that sense, and despite the fact that he expected serious fighting to continue, he decided the war was as good as won.

He had achieved what he had set out to do, attained a victory, one Tesserax couldn't claim credit for. The overall commander would accrue most of the gain from the conquest, something even Percelex couldn't argue with…but *he* would also get credit, serious credit. And he patted himself on the back and drew in a deep breath. He'd known his forces were sufficient to defeat the humans, but only then, he realized just how much he had also doubted success. Now, he had won, and despite the condition of his fleet, he knew the enemy wouldn't have anything ready before he did.

He smiled again, and then he returned to the mountain of work he had, the effort to restore his fleet to something resembling combat condition.

* * *

"We've received a communique from the fleet positioned with the forces in the Union. It seems…" Gelliax was normally very fast when reading messages, but now he paused, almost unwilling to proceed.

Tesserax knew the message was a difficult one. He'd been both easy and difficult to get along with in his days commanding the forces fighting the humans, but he'd always been fairly kind to Gelliax. The man was a Highborn, much like himself, though he wasn't from the initial group like Tesserax. Still, Tesserax had always believed he needed a few truly loyal types around him, and he'd been sure to treat Gelliax well.

So, he was surprised at the subordinate's...hesitancy.

"What is it, Gelliax?" Tesserax was already worried, mostly about his recent communique from Ellerax, and the last thing he needed was something else that was wrong.

"He moved far more quickly than we had anticipated, sir. Before the recent orders arrived—and that is confirmed, by the way. He attacked Fortress Grimaldi..."

Tesserax tensed up, prepared for more bad news. But what he got was something else, something he wasn't sure was too bad.

"...and won, sir. The station was destroyed, and he controls the system." There was a short pause, and then Gelliax continued. "He suffered terrible losses, sir, but he prevailed. He isn't in a position to follow up, yet...but from all reports, the enemy is in even worse shape."

Tesserax paused for a moment, not sure whether he should be happy or sad. His orders had been clear, but he realized Percelax had actually done him a favor, and perhaps more, he had increased the pressure on the enemy. He decided that there would be enough credit to spare a bit for Percelax. He realized his subordinate had struggled to get his fleet in position soon enough to attack before the orders he had to know were coming arrived. If he had failed, Tesserax would have been cold, and he would have removed him from command at once. But he had succeeded, and Tesserax couldn't help but feel some joy at the victory.

Besides, it *really* put the pressure on the enemy. Barron would have to pull back now. He would have to abandon the rest of the Hegemony, whether his forces came or not. He couldn't allow any of the truly crucial worlds of the Confederation to fall, not without a fight at least.

But he didn't have enough ships to mount a proper defense, not nearly enough to stop the Highborn's main fleet. He almost changed his mind again, ordered whatever forces were ready to move forward immediately. But he held back, waited. He knew the next few months would do him more good than it would the enemy, and he could wait.

He smiled, and then he sat for a few minutes, enjoying the situation. Then he got up and nodded to Gelliax. "Take command, Gelliax...I'll be in my office."

He walked toward his room—actually, it was a suite of rooms—and he stepped inside, allowing the door to close behind him. He walked over to his desk, and he sat down, laughing as he did. The enemy was defeated...he was sure of it, even more certain than he had been before. That thought fed the smile on his face, and the laughter that burst out of him. For about twenty minutes, he felt great, almost invincible.

Then, the door buzzed.

He turned, surprised at the interference. "Yes?" he said softly.

"It's Gelliax, sir...I'm sorry, but I just received word of something...well, something strange."

Tesserax felt his stomach tense. His smile was gone, too. He didn't know what was happening, but he knew Gelliax well enough to decide that if the officer had come to his door, it was important.

He reached around and pressed the button on his desk, opening the door. "What is it, Gelliax?"

The officer stepped inside, allowing the door to close before he answered. "It may be nothing of any importance, sir, but..." He paused again.

"Come on, Gelliax...just tell me."

"We just got word from one of our planets, one of the occupied Hegemony worlds. The enemy attacked, and they conducted some kind of operation. The inhabitants were expecting—something—but the ships just ran some kind of strange route…and then they left."

"Maybe it was a lost force, like the one a couple months ago."

"I might have thought that, too, sir, but…" Gelliax was silent, but just for a few seconds. Then he said what he'd come to say. "Sir, the leader of the colonial force, Zabbliax is his name…he ran a test procedure, and he discovered something…disturbing. He found Virus X, sir, alive and active. The enemy has Virus X, and they are bombarding at least some of our worlds with it."

Tesserax stared back, almost disbelieving. A full minute passed before he even spoke, and when he did, his tone had changed. "Virus X, you say? That is impossible…"

But even as he said it, he knew it wasn't…and he knew it was right.

Chapter Thirty-Eight

CWS Donallus
Beta Telara System
Year 329 AC (After the Cataclysm)

Andi looked at the display, at the planet situated on her screen. There were a lot of places she wanted to go, and this wasn't one of them...yet there was no place she'd rather be, not at the current moment. She stared at the planet, and at the twenty-four enemy ships lined up in front of it. It wasn't the worst enemy force she'd expected to find, but it was bad enough.

She could win the coming fight, she was sure of that, almost at least...but it would cost. It would cost a lot. Perhaps even too much to leave her enough vessels to bombard the planet. But the planet had already been attacked, several months ago. All she had to do was capture a few Highborn, and one or two ships could do that.

Maybe.

"Bring the fleet to battlestations...prepare to attack the enemy."

"Yes, Andi." Tarren's voice was a bit parched. The past five systems had possessed fewer ships in total than the current one. But Andi's old companion was still there, ready to do whatever had to be done.

She just looked forward. She could think of a hundred things to do better than sending a force directly here, taking the Highborn where she'd first struck...but each of those things had negatives, too. And, despite the fact that she was going to lose ships and personnel, she was almost sure she would win.

The naval fight, at least. The ground assault that would follow was something entirely different.

She looked past the enemy ships, to the planet. She was glad, at least, that the Highborn had destroyed all of the orbital facilities, and the ground installations...the Highborn had, or the defenders had. If the planet had all the defenses it had during its years as a Highborn world, she would likely lose the fight. But the enemy hadn't spent any time rebuilding such defenses. They had poured all their efforts into constructing ships, enough to crush the combined Confederation—Alliance—Hegemony fleets.

But not enough to defend your conquered planets...

Andi stared, her eyed fixed on the planet. Her fleet would probably win the fight, and as long as a few ships survived, she would complete her mission. Assuming the enemy still didn't know what was going on, which she knew was somewhat of a risk.

She wasn't sure where Barron was, but she had a pretty good idea where he would jump to if he had to retreat from the position she still believed was his current one. She was one of the few who knew it, of course, and she realized that Barron had made a decision. He would fall back to the border of the Confederation if the enemy appeared to be moving on him.

Whether or not Chronos and Akella went with him was another matter. Even if they did go with Barron, there was no guarantee the Hegemony fleet wouldn't split up. And that would only make things worse than they already were.

But her thoughts were mostly focused on the planet and fleet right in front of her.

The enemy ships opened fire first, as expected. And two of her ships were destroyed almost immediately. That wasn't good, even though she knew it was just the effect of poor randomization, but she stood where she was, looking at the battle, but not saying a word. The enemy didn't have any battleships present, but neither did she...so even though the distance was lower than the range of Confederation heavies, the enemy still held the advantage.

For three minutes more...

Atara had never considered herself a naval strategist, though that was silly. She had commanded *Pegasus* for years, and she had led all sorts of fleets on desperate missions over the past fifteen years. She'd thought of *Pegasus* as something else, a single ship, and a small one. And the various missions she'd led, all successfully, were still exceptions to her. It didn't make much sense, and she certainly rated the commodore's rank Barron had given her. Except in her own mind.

Two minutes...

After the initial barrage, the enemy slowed down. The initial accuracy of their munitions fell, closer to norms, and she lost only another ship. She noted that the enemy was focusing on individual vessels, trying to take them out before targeting another. That was a good strategy, mostly...but she realized that it just meant she would be left with mostly lightly damaged survivors, instead of a whole fleet that was battered. That was particularly good, since she was heading home with whatever was in top condition...and leaving everything badly damaged behind. She would hate herself for it, she knew—she despised abandoning ships, even those badly battered—but she had to get at least some of the Masters back. If the first attack had worked, they would all be infected, and she was confident that she could get out of them, whether or not there was an effective antidote. Those were the two main barriers to her thought of the enemy's defeat...whether the virus actually worked, and whether the enemy had developed an antidote. She knew that even if the virus was effective, it wasn't a guarantee that her side would win. How the enemy would react was a serious question.

But it would put her side back in the race, of that she was sure.

If the first two items held. If it worked, and if the enemy didn't have a cure.

One minute…

She watched, waited, each second passing like an hour. The enemy was firing at full, and another of her ships blinked out of existence. But in just a few seconds, she would get to open fire. Then, it would be a truly two-sided battle.

She felt odd, strange. For once, her ship was back from the fight, her ship, and three others, out of range. It bit at her, cut her to the quick to watch her people fighting the battle without her…but she had survived this long, and she was going to lead the strike on the planet. She *had* to find some Masters, preferably a number of them, but at least one…and despite the fact that the enemy lacked any defensive mechanisms to counter her fleet, besides of course their own force of ships, they very likely had some infantry on the ground. Getting in, grabbing a few Masters, and pulling out…it had seemed like the quickest and easiest part of her plan…until now.

But she was determined to do it, however much it cost her, however much difficulty it entailed. It was even enough to justify her staying out of the fight in space.

She watched as her fleet opened fire, almost all her ships at the exact same time. The enemy fleet took a number of hits…but no ships were destroyed. That wasn't unexpected, especially since her force was targeting all the vessels, and not just a few at a time. But it dug at her nevertheless, and especially more when yet another of her ships exploded.

She kept looking, and even as the battle began to turn,

and as the enemy began losing ships, she found her thoughts focused on the mission ahead. Part of her considered her entire fleet expendable, save for the few ships needed to grab a couple of the Highborn...and another section of her felt every hit, every ship destroyed. But she stayed where she was, not moving at all. Nothing was more important to her than the destruction of the enemy...but it was the destruction of them all she really sought.

The battle began to go her way, as she had expected from the start. Half the enemy ships were gone, and the other half were badly damaged. Her fleet continued to close, and they continued to fire. Then, the last four ships attempted to escape. But she was ready for that.

Her ships had been warned, and they pursued immediately. They caught three of the four ships, and blasted them to bits...but the last one escaped.

Andi knew that had been a possibility, and she shifted in her position, a soft curse escaping from her lips. She knew that ship had a long road back to get help, and that she would be gone by the time it returned with any help. But it still pissed her off to watch it go.

Still, she had another job to do, and that's where most of her focus went. "All ships, except the four...do damage checks, and make some honest calculations. Anything that can get to 80% engine power or higher in an hour is a go. Everything else, set to self-destruct and get aboard the other ships." She figured half her surviving vessels would make the rating...and half would be destroyed. That meant a lot of spacers loading onto her surviving ships...but that wasn't her problem, not just then.

Her problem was getting down, finding one or more Masters, and capturing them. She had known about this part of the operation for a long while. She had known it would be difficult, but now it seemed almost impossible.

It's not vital, she told herself. If the enemy is infected, they are, regardless of whether we know it or not. But she realized she *had* to know, that the only way she was going to leave the system was with one or more Masters.

"The four ships...let's move forward. It's time to grab some Masters...and get the hell out of here."

*   *   *

Andi walked slowly, looking all around. She'd almost landed in the jungle just outside the city, but at the last minute, she'd changed her course and come down close to the center of the capital.

It was the best place to find enemy specimens, she knew, and she didn't have a lot of time. She didn't know for certain how many soldiers the enemy had on the planet, but she was sure it was enough to take out her entire force many times over. She had to strike quickly, as quickly as possible, and she figured the center of the capital was the best place.

"Andi...we've got one hundred twelve men and women ready. That leaves forty-six on the ship." Tarren spoke softly. "That's the minimum to fly it out of here."

"That's good...let's set out."

Andi knew that her ship was landable—obviously—but also that it had been in space since its construction, and that her landing effort was its first one. She hadn't figured out the minimal crew to conduct a liftoff, and though she was willing to wager that it could be done with fewer than 46, and far fewer perhaps, she was willing to accept those amounts. That gave her seventy percent of the crew for her expedition, and if that wasn't enough, well, there were three other ships. As a minimum, they only needed one of the enemy, though she would prefer four or five if they were available. Any more than that would just be extras. She suspected others in the high command anticipated interrogations and other efforts with captives, but she only wanted one thing. She wanted to see them start to show symptoms…and then she wanted to watch them die. She realized the possibility of getting useful information from some of them…she just didn't care.

She stood for about two minutes, allowing her aide to form up the group, and then she set out. The ship had come down in an unimproved area, just outside the main city's core, and she headed directly toward the center.

She knew many of the residents would be equipped with the spinal mounts, and be slaves to the enemy, but she suspected that millions of them would be held only by pressure, by whatever measures the enemy had taken to control them. She didn't look past that, however, and after much consideration, she'd decided to try an avoid as much contact as possible, to get in and out quickly…and not rely on any of the people present.

She just needed a few of the aliens. She knew the Highborn weren't technically aliens, but she'd come to think of them that way. She was trying her best to eliminate them all, and considering them aliens was useful.

She walked for about half an hour, coming into the center of town. The whole city seemed abandoned, though she knew that was just because of her incursion. The people were probably just inside the buildings, and she realized at any point, fighters could open up. She hoped the enemy didn't know why she was there…but she was sure they knew, at least, that she *was* there.

And they pulled everyone in…

She looked at the buildings all around her, wondering if there were Arbeiter and Kriegeri inside, or even Masters. She could imagine that the highest rated individuals had been killed, but also that they had been absorbed…or enslaved by the implants. She realized that although she had accepted the Hegemony forces as allies, and that she considered some of their senior officers truly reliable, she still held most of them in some kind of middle ground. She wouldn't say she viewed them as she had seven years before, when *they* were the enemy…but she hadn't come completely around either, and she doubted she ever would. For most of them at least.

She looked all around as she walked forward, checking everything. It was spookily quiet, which she took as both good and bad. It suggested that the enemy didn't have large forces present, but it also implied that there weren't many Masters there either. She realized that despite the effort behind the current push, and its massive reliance on the presence of Masters, it was uncertain how many of the alien overlords were actually present. She had done some calculations herself, come up with estimates that some hundreds were on Beta Telara III…but she didn't know, not for sure. Certainly, from the little she'd seen of the alien Collars, regular humans so equipped were nearly as reliable to the enemy as Highborn. Perhaps there were fewer of the aliens than she had expected. She even considered the possibility that there were none at all on the planet. That didn't seem likely, but it wasn't impossible. How would she proceed if she couldn't find a few enemies to bring back?

Well, you'll probably be dead if you can't find any Masters…

She didn't really consider the possibility that there were none at all on the planet, but a world was huge, with plenty of places to hide. It was definitely possible that she wouldn't find any…and she realized that while she could sacrifice herself, perhaps, and even all the people with her, she couldn't guarantee success. She would search, like crazy. She was almost certain none of her ships would *leave* without any enemy, but that was far from a guarantee of success.

None of her thoughts would change the outcome, of course, not really. But she *had* to know, and she had to know soon…whatever it took.

If there was any chance…any chance at all…

Chapter Thirty-Nine

CWS Dauntless
Vela Tracasys System
Year 329 AC (After the Cataclysm)

Tyler sat and watched the activity on *Dauntless*'s bridge for a while. The fleet had fallen back, three systems now, seeking to avoid any enemy vessels. The Highborn had pushed forward slightly, but they hadn't really attacked. He'd been worried they would, at least for a while, though he realized they were doing exactly what he would be doing in their shoes. An extra six months would get him some ships from home, of course, but not that many, and his own repair jobs would be grossly inferior to the ones the enemy could probably get done, at least unless he sent his damaged ships all the way back to the Core and the Iron Belt...and that trip alone might take two months of more...each way.

He looked across the bridge at Atara. The ship was her command vessel, and it had been for years now. He knew he'd overstepped his positions at times when he'd been present before, but now he tried to remain silent, to allow Atara to command her forces. He couldn't tell for sure that she'd noticed, but he decided she had.

He stood up, seeming sudden in his motions. He had decided what his plans were, at least for the short term. He would maintain his position, try to face the enemy close to their position, at least while they were more or less dormant. But when they moved, in force, which he knew was coming, he had decided to withdraw to the Confederation. It was a long way back, but it was really the only choice. The Hegemony didn't offer any other choke points, places where a multiple systems' jump gates converged. With the loss of Striker, he'd also sacrificed the rest of the Hegemony. He knew that, and he guessed that Chronos did as well. Whether that meant he would follow Barron, abandon the rest of his homeland, was still unresolved. Barron had spoken with Tulus, as well as the other Confederation senior officers, right before several of them left for the desperate effort that represented the only true hope for the Confederation and its allies. They had all agreed. It was okay to remain in Highborn space for a while...but the instant the enemy advanced, he had to withdraw...even if he left the viral teams, and Chronos, behind.

He suspected Chronos knew that, too. In fact, he was sure he did. But he didn't know if his former enemy, and now his true friend, would be strong enough to rise up, to lead his forces away, even if his government ordered differently. He'd come to view Chronos as an independent of sorts, but he wasn't *sure* he could ignore the orders if they came from his own masters, either.

Fortunately, he didn't have any leaders at the moment, at least none willing to try and order him around. Gary Holsten seemed to have managed to attain something of a parity of power with the newly elected Senate, with each of them controlling roughly half of the business. And neither had tried to interfere in military decisions. He knew that was permanent as far as Holsten was concerned, but probably only temporary as far as the Senate went. Sooner or later, they would try to interfere, in some way.

Barron was fairly sure there wouldn't be that much time, however. After the enemy advanced on the Confederation, in force, all of them, and not just the looming threat of the forces that had taken Grimaldi, things would start to happen quickly. There would be a battle, likely, but it would be quicker, and sharper, than the ones that had already occurred. Barron didn't kid himself, didn't try and argue that he had a chance. He would fight, because there was no other option, and he would retreat again, before his entire force was destroyed. Then, he would fight again, falling back, to the Iron Belt, and then to the Core. He fancied the final battle would take place around Megara, but he didn't know if he'd live that long.

Unless the virus actually works...

He knew there was a possibility, a chance that it *would* work, perhaps even that it would be enough to defeat the enemy, at least in a way. But he couldn't get over the doubt, the realization that any number of things could interfere with the success of the plan.

But it's still the only thing we've got that has a real chance of success...

He told himself that, he even believed it...but he still couldn't wrap his mind around the far-fetched plan actually working.

He'd been mostly silent on the bridge, leaving the command duties to Atara Travis. But he suddenly realized that he had bolted to his feet and then remained where he was. *Dauntless*'s crew was among the best, but he could feel the eyes of a number of those trying not to scan his actions. He felt suddenly exposed, and he rushed off, back toward the office where he could be alone for a while.

He realized, as he approached the room, that Atara had not taken it, that two years of him in the fortress, and her commanding from *Dauntless*, hadn't moved her to change from the second-largest room to the first, despite the fact that she had been promoted several times in the interim.

And it didn't surprise him at all. Travis had known he would return to *Dauntless*, he was sure of that, and she hadn't moved a thing. She hadn't taken his chair out on the bridge either. It was typical for her...and so atypical for most officers, and it enhanced his feelings for her, even more than before.

He slipped through the door, and he let it close behind him. He stood for a moment, and then he turned and walked around the desk, sitting and staring straight ahead...and wondering if he would ever see Andi again.

* * *

"I am thrilled to be talking to you again, Jake..." Barron had come at once when he'd gotten word. Jake Stockton was awake, and more so, reasonably alert. It was starting to look like the surgery had actually been a success.

"It is...good to be...talking to you...sir..." Stockton was awake and alert, but he was still weak. "I woke up...three or four times...before, I think, but...this is the...first time I...was really alert..."

Barron didn't know if he would go with "really alert" part himself, but he understood what Stockton meant. And the preliminary data the doctor had given him was good, too. Stockton could still die, he supposed, but he realized he didn't believe that anymore, not at all. He wasn't quite all the way to buying that Stockton had returned, that he was on his way back to one hundred percent, but it was definitely good.

"That is wonderful, Jake. You were famous already...and now you're the first one survive having an implant removed." Barron realized he might be the only one, too, for a long time. The doctors had made amazing progress on the operation, no doubt...but Stockton's situation was different from everyone else's too. Even if things continued to go well, and he survived, the next subject of the surgery could still easily die. He or she would likely be unwilling, and completely under the control of the enemy, of the

Collar...unlike Stockton. But Barron didn't think about that, not much at least. He had about fifty other things occupying his worries more than expanding the surgical roster for transforming people back.

Or more like five hundred other things.

"I...want to...fly again...sir..."

The words surprised Barron...for about three seconds. Then he remembered who he was talking to. "Jake, I know why you had the surgery done, and I won't stand in your way when the time comes...but you've got a lot of recovery to do before you're ready to fly." He paused a moment, and then he added, "A lot."

Stockton seemed like he was ready to leap up and climb behind a fighter's controls immediately...but he also looked ridiculous. He could hardly move, and he was already getting tired. Finally, he said, "I...know I'm not...ready yet...but soon..." He looked up at Barron, and the vulnerability in him was clear. He had been the best pilot, probably in known human history, but he had given himself to it entirely to achieve that. Barron had known that all along, but only then, he really got it. He knew why Stockton had been willing to have the operation, why he hadn't been prepared to wait.

"Jake, I'll make a deal with you. You get into shape, and I mean *really* into shape, and I'll hold open the door of your fighter for you. Just don't push it, don't try to get in before you're ready. Because that I won't allow." He knew as he uttered the words that Stockton would take them as a partial victory. But he was serious...he wasn't going to allow the pilot near a fighter, not until his doctors gave the go ahead.

But he thought to himself, even as he stood there, that he might not have the chance to wait long enough. Stockton wasn't in any kind of shape to fly yet...but Barron wondered if he would have the time to fully recover. He hadn't envisioned any scenario where he surrendered to the enemy, but he realized, Stockton had even more reason to avoid capture. If it came down to the final fight, could he really force Stockton to wait, to die as a traitor to the enemy?

It wasn't a difficult analysis just then, and Barron already knew what he would do…if it came to the very end. If Stockton could fly, even partially, there would come a time when he would allow it. It would be a combination, two near-opposites coming toward each other, Stockton's abilities vs. the situation with the enemy.

"Okay…sir…"

Barron could tell two things from Stockton's tone. First, he was tired, *really* tired…and he was going back to sleep.

And second, that he would raise the issue again…probably every time Barron saw him.

*   *   *

Atara sat quietly on the bridge. It had been over two months since the battle, and the enemy had not pushed farther ahead than one system past Striker.

What had been Striker. Atara knew the station was gone, that even if through some miracle, her forces managed to take the system back, the facility was destroyed.

She was on the bridge, as she had been almost as much as during the battle. She counted a couple times, but the numbers she came up with, and the smallest was more than seventeen hours, were too depressing, so she stopped. Seventeen hours was the least time she'd spent on duty in at least a week.

She didn't know why she put so much time in, especially when she had ships out in the system ahead. She didn't doubt the enemy would come…but she would have more than enough notice to get out of bed, shower, have a nice breakfast. Still, she was posted on the ship's bridge, almost like part of the equipment…waiting.

Tyler was the same, though he spent much of his time in

his office. Alone. Atara was spent, frazzled, she knew there wasn't much of a chance...but she couldn't imagine what Tyler was like. He didn't believe in the alternative measures, even though he'd allowed the second phase to begin. Atara knew he'd done that because he'd agreed to if the last battle was a defeat, because he felt he owed it to Andi, to all those who did believe in it. But she knew he still didn't buy it, that he didn't expect it to succeed.

She knew why he spent so much time alone, and despite his protestations and maneuvers, and the many things that he did with his time, it was simply that he didn't know what to do. He would fall back on the Confederation, she knew, with or without Chronos and Akella and the rest of the Highborn...but he knew there was no real hope. Atara wasn't a huge believer in the alternative measures either, but she did think there was more hope than she knew Barron did.

And Andi. She knew Barron and his wife had come together, more because he couldn't find any reason to oppose the plan, than he really thought it would succeed. But he probably didn't expect to see her again, or at least he thought her chances were poor. That was true of Vian Tulus, Clint Winters...a lot of Barron's closest friends were out on the desperate mission. But Andi was going back to the first planet they had assaulted, and she was landing. And both Atara and Tyler knew Andi well enough to realize she was going to be on the planet herself, and at the head of her team.

Then there was Cassiopeia. Atara knew Tyler and Andi ached for their daughter, that not a day went by, hardly an hour, in either of their existences, without thoughts of the young girl. Andi felt the pain, too, for herself, but mostly for the two parents, stuck deep in the fight while their daughter resided back home.

She pulled herself together, focused on what she knew was the only true hope her people had left. Perhaps Tyler couldn't believe in it, but she could. She struggled to accept that the attack would work, that her side would regain its momentum…and she mostly succeeded, at least for the moment.

That would likely pass, she knew…but then she would engage in the same thought process, the same effort she'd just gone through. She didn't know if she actually believed in the plan, or if she had just convinced herself it would work. And she wasn't sure she cared anymore.

Chapter Forty

Beta Telara III
Year 329 AC (After the Cataclysm)

Andi was soaked with sweat, pressed down behind a small pile of stones...and firing. Her entire force was shooting, except of course, the ten she had who were dead. They were spread out over about a hundred meters, and they were facing in multiple directions. The enemy was coming from almost three sides, and while they weren't overwhelmingly strong, they were making some headway.

"Jones, extend the right flank...at least another twenty meters!" She shouted out, hoping to cover the distance to her subordinate. She wasn't sure she'd managed it, not for perhaps a second or two, until the man's response came.

"Yes, Andi...right away!"

Andi didn't say anything else, not for the next couple of minutes. The fight was happening in the center of town, very close to her objective. She hadn't known what to expect from the enemy, or even whether Hegemony residents had been sufficiently broken to serve, to fight against their previous allies. She *was* battling regular humans, but everyone she'd run into on the mission so far had been possessed by one of the Collars. That didn't mean the invaders had no support at all among the unmodified population, but it did suggest that most, if not all, of the people were not trusted by the Highborn.

That, as vague as it was, bolstered her, at least a bit. She hadn't really expected that the Highborn had turned the population against her forces…but she didn't know all that much about the junior ranks of the Hegemony's population. She realized now that she had imagined large numbers of them at least listening to the enemy pitch…but so far, the only ones who'd attacked her people, at least all the ones that she'd realized, were those under wearing Collars.

She jerked her head to the side, checking on her orders to Jones. She had expected them to be obeyed, but even she was surprised how well he had relocated, himself and seven others. They were already out close to twenty meters, and they were holding their own.

She had tried to get an idea of the strength attacking her, of whether she was doomed, or if she had a chance. She was attacking an entire world, she knew, and that fact diminished her opinion, at least at first. But she wasn't trying to take the planet, she just wanted to capture a few of the Highborn…and as soon as she did, she would leave. Her people had come through eleven fights, the last one bloody and damaging, and now all she had to do was find a Master or two and she could go home.

Wherever that was. She wasn't even sure where Tyler was, and Cassiopeia was far away, back on Megara. She realized she had no home, at least nothing save a ship or two. She'd believed, at times at least, that she would eventually have a real place, and she knew her prisoners, the ones she was fighting to take, were the true route there.

She seemed so close to that goal, and yet so far. But she told herself that the enemy, at least the force currently engaging her, was fairly small. It wasn't hard to imagine overwhelming forces on the planet as a whole, but her people were at least holding their own. She wasn't sure if there were any Highborn with the force opposing her…but she figured there was probably at least one.

One thing she was sure about, though, was that the situation wasn't going to get any better. Time was definitely on her opponents' side, and she knew more forces would show up sooner or later. She had to increase the intensity now. She had to launch her troops forward, take on the enemy full bore…and maybe capture an enemy Highborn.

Or die trying.

She looked to the left, and then to the right, monitoring the fire, both coming in and going out from her forces. Her people had the edge, she was sure of it, at least a little…but that wouldn't last long.

"Ross, we're going to push forward. We're going to hit them hard, and we're going to do it now. There's a Highborn with them, at least one, there has to be…and letting more time go by isn't going to help us at all."

She could feel the tension from her comrade, but she was sure he agreed with her. She was convinced everyone would agree, at least that the longer her people were on the planet, the worse things would get.

"Yes, Andi…" Tarren looked both ways, too, scanning the line. She knew he was with her…but he was nervous, too.

"Alright, everybody…" She shouted, as loudly as she could. "Get ready…we're going forward in twenty seconds." Andi had learned a lot over her years of action, but nothing perhaps so effective as the use of time. Perhaps if her mission had been complex, if there had been much to learn, it would have made sense to delay. But it was simple…advance and fight, to the end. Either her people would prevail, or they would be wiped out.

And there was nothing to be gained by delaying either.

"Forward," she screamed, as she lurched ahead, driving on toward the enemy. "Forward!" she repeated, even more loudly, as she raced ahead, firing as she did.

* * *

Andi fought, perhaps harder than ever before. She had a rifle in one hand and a pistol in the other, and somehow, she was firing them both. She'd had the rifle exclusively before, but now she was so close to the enemy, it made sense to deploy them both.

They're not the enemy…they're allies, enslaved to fight…

She knew that was true, but it didn't really matter to her. The people she was fighting against were Hegemony Kriegeri, just like the ones that had fought at her side for more than seven years. But they had been surgically altered, enslaved by the Collars. They were victims, completely controlled, she knew that…but she didn't care. They were enemies, at least as far as she saw it…and she gunned them down like crazy. If she paid for it, it would be later, after her mission was done. And she could live with that.

Her attack had seemed insane, at least to anyone who hadn't been carefully watching. Indeed, her entire move against the planet seemed bizarre, at least to anyone who forgot that their purpose was simply to remove one or more of the Highborn.

She wondered if the enemy would know why she had come, and when she'd been attacked, she'd been close to assuming they did. But, she quickly realized that the enemy force was far from what she'd have expected if they had really been on to her.

She fired, again and again, taking down at least a dozen enemies. She'd taken one hit herself, but it was a light wound, a grazing of her back, and while she knew it was bleeding, she basically ignored it. She would do the same if she was hit again, even if it was worse. She had two speeds now…full and dead.

Her head snapped around, looking all over for any sign of one or more Highborn. The enemy force was big enough, she assumed, and she couldn't imagine that they were out on their own, without any of the Highborn leading them. But she hadn't seen any, not yet at least.

Then, suddenly, her eyes focused...and she realized she had spotted one. He was far back, but it was definitely a Highborn. That was clear just from his height, eight feet tall.

Andi realized that he would have the best weaponry and armor, better than hers, and she suddenly felt a few seconds of hesitancy.

But just a few.

Then, she moved forward, shouting out to the people around her. She knew leading them forward, exposing herself—and them—more, would cost lives. But the very purpose of the mission was in front of her. Everyone lost in the battle, and all those killed on the ground, died so she could get a chance at capturing one of the enemy.

Now, she had the chance. And if one of her people, any one of them, managed to escape with the captured Highborn, it would be worth it.

She redirected her fire, targeting all the personnel around her target. She carefully avoided the Highborn himself, aware that she needed him alive. He wouldn't be easy to capture, she realized, and she wasn't going to take any chances. And she wasn't going to allow anyone else too either.

"Do not fire at the Highborn...take everyone around him out, but don't shoot him."

Even as she spoke the words, though, she realized she was going to have to target him after all. The Highborn were larger, and faster, than her people, and when he realized what was happening, he would take off...and unless she was willing to shoot him, he would get away.

She felt her rifle angling, just seconds after she'd issued the order *not* to shoot him. And she still meant it, at least for her people. But she was going to aim at the Highborn, and she was going to wound him, and take him down. Whatever it took.

He was still far away, too far for precisely accurate fire, but she knew if she waited too long, he would pull even farther back. She had to stop him, and stop him soon, so she aimed.

She fired…and then again. It was only her firing at the Highborn, which reduced the chances of scoring a hit…but it also left him under fewer shots, perhaps too few to notice right away. He just might stay in place a while longer.

She shot, a third time, a fourth…and then a fifth. And the fifth shot scored a hit. The Highborn fell backwards, stumbling, and she could barely see the blood flowing from his leg. The shot had been almost perfect. It was a serious wound, but not an immediately life threatening one. The Highborn would have a difficult time escaping now…unless his Kriegeri could hold out long enough.

Andi was far enough back that she couldn't hear the Highborn's commands, but it was obvious what he had said. The Kriegeri had been retreating, but now they stopped. They scrambled to find rocks and logs—anything to hide behind—and they maintained their fire, even as their commander began to withdraw.

The Highborn was wounded, but he managed to get up, one arm over the shoulder of one Kriegeri and the other over a different one. It took a few seconds before Andi could see what he was doing…and she knew what she had to do.

She fired, slowly, carefully. She was aiming at the two Kriegeri, trying as hard as possible to avoid hitting the Highborn again. She snapped out her commands, reminded all the others not to shoot at the Highborn, or the two men helping him off the field.

They were hers.

She thought for an instant about the two Hegemony soldiers, about how they were controlled by the Collars, about how they likely despised what they were doing. How they were allies, save for the Collars controlling them. She knew that was probably true, but she pushed it aside. Millions had died in the war, perhaps billions would perish before it was done. She didn't have time to consider two Kriegeri…men who were helping the enemy she was targeting, whether purposefully or not.

And she wondered if it would matter if they were two Confederation soldiers? She couldn't be sure, but she didn't think so. Only success mattered now, and the cost was irrelevant.

She fired again…and one of the men went down. The Highborn stumbled…but he managed to continue with only one helper.

Andi raced forward, almost oblivious to the fire still sporadically ripping into her position. The enemy was beaten, at least until more came, but that wasn't the same thing as wiped out. And anything less than total destruction was insufficient against the enemy. The Collars kept the men and women fighting…until they were taken down.

She continued forward, firing all the way as she did…but she couldn't take down the last soldier. She was running now, almost oblivious to the remaining fire. She knew she could take a hit at any second, that she could end up out of the fight…even dead…any time. But she pressed on, even as her body began to rebel.

She was out of breath, and she knew it was affecting her shooting. But she was just as aware that the soldier had to be as well. She knew enough about the Collars to realize that the Kriegeri would keep going until he couldn't any longer…but the Highborn was also exerting some of the effort.

She fired again…and again…

And she hit the last soldier.

She was well beyond her troops, though she knew at least some of them had come after her. She saw the Kriegeri stumble…and then fall right to the ground.

The Highborn tumbled as well…and then he got up,

partially at least, and he was trying to get away. But alone, he didn't have the strength. Andi was tired, but she was far less injured than the Highborn. It took less than a minute to catch him. She was cautious at first, uncertain whether he had maintained some form of arms. But when she got to him, he just rolled over onto his back, and he looked at her.

There were a number of impressions she got from the expression on his face. But most of all, she got one…and exhausted, still worried about any enemy approaching, she smiled widely.

It was fear.

Chapter Forty-One

CWS Donallus
Vela Tracasys System
Year 329 AC (After the Cataclysm)

Andi sat on the bridge, tired—exhausted actually—but glad that she'd found *Dauntless* so quickly. She'd imagined Tyler had retreated all the way to the Confederation, even that the enemy had closely pursued, perhaps even that he was dead. But she'd found him just three jumps back from Fortress Striker's location…waiting.

He was waiting until the enemy advanced, until something happened. He hadn't heard from Akella yet, though Chronos and Vian Tulus had both survived their excursions. Actually, with her return, all four of the forces had come back, and if that meant they had completed all their missions—and to Andi it meant nothing else—at least 41 worlds had been infected. That was far from everywhere, every planet, the enemy fleet…but it was a lot, and Andi drew some satisfaction from that.

And she had brought back three of the Highborn, the wounded one she had captured, and two others taken by her other groups. Her four ships had lost a lot of people— thirty-one percent was the lowest, and the highest was over seventy—but two of her other teams had also succeeded.

She was glad about that, triumphant about the success…especially as what remained of her fleet set out.

But none of the enemy showed any signs of infection.

She knew that there would be no indication, not until the disease struck, and the information on the time that would take was spotty at best. She realized it could still work, that it could strike at any time. But she was beginning to lose hope.

Now, at least, she would see Barron again. She realized she'd been more than ready not to encounter him again…she'd actually expected it, on one level at least. But he'd already called out, the instant her ship was in range. Both of them had survived, so far at least. Andi was grateful for the chance to see him again. She thought about her daughter, too, who was far away, who had seen nothing more than a few videotaped messages in well over a year…but then she forced those considerations away. It was too painful, and she knew Cassie was as well off as she could be.

"We're about to dock with *Dauntless*, Commodore."

Andi looked over at Tarren, and she realized how glad she was that her subordinate—her friend—had survived. He had taken a hit as well, worse than hers, but the two of them were both on the bridge. Neither of them should be, Andi supposed…but she wasn't going to yield her position, and she wasn't going to make her friend do it either.

"That's good, Ross. Bring us in." Her voice was as cheery as she could imagine, at least with her growing sensation that the entire effort to infect the enemy had failed. She knew the virus, if not exact, was close to the one the First Imperium had used, that her people would get it eventually.

But she was just as sure there was no time for that. Her last shreds of hope were that the infection *did* work, that it just took longer than she had expected. But every day that went by drained that a little bit more…and she was certain there was no other chance.

"Yes, Commodore…as you command." Tarren spoke in as upbeat a manner as he could manage, but Andi saw through it. If her subordinate had really believed, maybe she could have drawn from him, extended her own period of belief. But she could tell that Tarren saw things exactly as she did.

She sighed, softly, trying to focus on seeing Tyler…and for a moment, getting away from the cold realities she—and everyone else—faced. However bad things were, however much they were drawn steadily closer to the end…there were *some* good things as well. Tyler was alive, and the fleet was a lot closer than she'd expected. That was good…certainly, even if only for a little while.

She tried to smile, but she only managed about half-way…and that was going to have to do.

* * *

Barron sat at the head of the table, looking out at the assortment of warriors assembled. He realized how many that he knew, how many great soldiers, both alive, like those present, and dead already, killed in the more than twenty years that he'd been fighting.

Almost four months had gone by since the battle at Fortress Striker, and Barron was amazed that the enemy hadn't even pushed out, experimented with driving him off. He knew that Andi had been surprised to find the fleet still so far forward, too, though she hadn't said anything about it. He suspected every warrior who had returned—and despite the considerable losses all four forces had suffered, the commanders had all survived—was surprised.

But the three Highborn that Andi had brought back from Beta Telara III showed no signs of infection. Two of the three had been seriously injured, and one had almost died, in the fighting, but there was no indication that the infection had set in.

It was only what Barron had expected, and yet he realized that he had harbored considerable hopes that it would work, more than he'd allowed his conscious mind to absorb.

"Well, it is good to have all of you back…" He had seen everyone already, but this was the first large meeting they'd held since right after the battle. Barron was low, depressed, and beaten…but he tried to press on, to move forward with everything he had, or could pretend to have. "It is good to see you all again." That was nothing but the hard truth. He wouldn't have given a five percent chance that everyone assembled would be there again, and he was truly glad to see it.

"Thank you, Tyler…I think we're all glad about that." The answer could have come from anyone present, but Clint Winters spoke first. "Am I correct in assuming that the Highborn remain unaffected by the virus?"

Barron had expected the question, but perhaps not so soon. He realized it was the only thing on everyone's mind, but his lack of any kind of positive response only wore him down farther. "No, I'm afraid not. They are almost healed of their conventional wounds, but there is no sign of any…effect." He thought about saying a lot of other things, 'there's still time' and 'I told you it wouldn't work' among them. But he just remained quiet.

"So, what do we do now?" Vian Tulus spoke, second rather than first as Barron had expected. The question could have been harsh, cold…but it wasn't at all. Tulus was Tyler's brother, at least in Alliance terms, and there was kindness in the words, even as close as a Palatian could come to softness.

"I honestly don't know…" That wasn't entirely true. Barron had been waiting to hear from Andi, but now that she was back, he was running out of time. He didn't believe he could win no matter what he did, but he knew he was going to try. And the delayed action by the enemy could end at any time. "…but I think we have to withdraw. We discussed a phase three operation, spreading more of the virus among the enemy, but we don't have enough of it yet anyway, and, well…" He didn't want to say 'it didn't work,' even though that was what he believed. "…and I don't think we have the time to wait."

Tyler paused, just for a couple seconds, and then he continued, "But Akella is still with the Council…and that leaves you here in command of the Hegemony, Chronos. What will you do if the rest of us withdraw? You have to realize you have no chance, none at all, alone."

Chronos looked as though he knew the question was coming…but also like he still didn't know the answer. "I would retreat with you, Tyler…regardless of the orders from the Council…but without Akella…" He paused. Everyone knew why that would be difficult for Chronos, but Tyler knew the whole truth, the fact that the two had been carrying on an illegal—at least by Hegemony terms—relationship for years now. Asking Chronos to leave—to abandon Akella—was much more difficult than most of those present realized. And if he did leave her behind, he would only hurt her ability to negotiate, perhaps even allow her opponents to utterly prevail…assuming she had any chance of success.

He would get less of the fleet to follow him, too. Half, Tyler guessed, but if Akella was there, he was sure they would get close to three-quarters. It would be a combination of both of their abilities…as well as the fact that two Council members, instead of one, carried a lot more weight.

Chronos still looked uncertain…but also that he knew he had to answer. He waited another few seconds, and then he said, "I will go with you, Tyler, with whatever portion of the fleet will follow me…in two weeks."

Tyler looked at his Hegemony associate. He knew the two weeks had been a random effort, a prayer basically, that

Akella succeeded in that amount of time…but it was more than Chronos had anticipated. Still, it wasn't really long, and Barron knew it wasn't. But anymore was asking the enemy to move forward, to engage his fleet where it was.

"Two weeks?" He looked around the table, mostly searching for any expressions that told him someone had a major problem. He saw a few people with somewhat doubtful looks on their faces…but no one who looked like they had a major problem. "Very well, Chronos…we will prepare to depart, but we will remain in place for two weeks longer. If Akella returns…that is great. But if she doesn't…" He didn't say anything further. He didn't have to.

* * *

Akella sat at the end of the table. She'd been arguing for weeks now, discussing options with every Council member she thought might vote with her. She'd made some progress, but not enough, and she believed she was still going to lose.

But she was out of time now. The fleet had decided to withdraw, in two weeks. She only knew about it courtesy of Chronos—and Tyler, she guessed—sending one of the experimental, high speed craft to tell her. Still, the trip took five days, and the return would take as long. That left her four days if she was going to withdraw, a bit less if she was going to have time to argue with fleet commanders about a split.

Assuming the Council let her go if she lost, which was at best a 50/50 chance.

"I have been here for two months now, and we have discussed this matter endlessly. But I have just received word that Admiral Barron had decided to pull back to Confederation space…immediately. That makes a decision crucial. Now."

She hadn't been sure exactly what she was going to say, but even as the words emerged, she realized it was the only choice. She didn't have time left to discuss individually with people, to work Council members. She had to have a decision now, and if it went against her, even if it resulted in her removal from the Council, so be it.

For that matter, even if the Council imprisoned her…she was glad that Chronos would, at least, get away. For now.

She noticed shock among most of the members of the Council, as though they had thought about the current problem, but only in vague terms. It struck her, in more precise ways than it had before, just how removed from reality her people were, the leaders at least.

She heard several of those present beginning to talk, but she didn't listen. She just spoke up again, her voice loud and driving. "Just so you know what that means, the Confederation, which constitutes fifty-nine percent of our combined forces at present, will pull all its ships back. The Alliance, thirteen percent of our total hulls, will also withdraw. The various smaller groupings, approximately two percent of our total, will also withdraw. That leaves us…and whatever you may think of our position in the hierarchy, we constitute roughly twenty-six percent of the hulls currently in the total force. That's barely a quarter. Of that portion, I intend to take any ships that will come with me. If you hold me here, try to pressure me in any way, Chronos will do what I would have done…and he will draw off at the very least, half the forces. That leaves you all, at best, thirteen percent of the current combined strength we have—*all* of which is insufficient, much less thirteen percent. I understand the pride surging up from you, but you have to accept—you *have* to—that this is no longer the case. Half our nation is occupied, our capital included, and our allies, the Confederation, have exceeded even our most fervent expectations on the production of new ships." There was real venom in her words, and she realized, even as she spoke, that she was angry, enraged. "They are, in every way, the primary part of our force now, and pretending anything else—or imagining that they will not turn back without us—is stupid and foolish. If you are distraught at the situation, beaten back by how battered we have become, I am with you. But if you refuse to accept this, if you continue to pretend that you still control the total forces on our side…well, then I am done with you. Let me go, and I will try to take as many ships as I can. Hold me, and Chronos will do the same thing. Now is the time, to make a decision, a real decision."

Akella stared at the people clustered around the table, and she saw the shock on their faces at her words, delivered more harshly than she'd ever spoken to them before. She was energized, if that was the right word, because she didn't really care…whether they agreed or not, whether they let her go or held her behind. None of it mattered, not really. All she was risking, probably, was another year or two…a time that would see all the forces slowly destroyed…unless the desperate plan actually worked. But she was done with all of that, finished with hoping against hope. She'd thrown everything she had into the mix, and now it was time to see if that had been enough…or if the Council was against her.

"So, let's vote," she said. "Let's vote now."

Chapter Forty-Two

CWS Donallus
Vela Tracasys System
Year 329 AC (After the Cataclysm)

Andi stood, stone still, watching the three Highborn prisoners. At one time, capturing three of the enemy would have been a tremendous success, all on its own. But right now, she wanted only one thing from the prisoners...some sign that they were infected, that they would die. And there was nothing.

She stared, looking for anything that told her, even suggested, that her efforts had been for something. But she saw nothing.

She had forced herself to believe in the serum, if only because she'd been utterly convinced there was no other way. But day by day, she saw nothing. The two injured prisoners recuperated, far more quickly than a normal human would have, but there was no sign at all of the disease, the hope she had that the prisoners had been infected.

She knew there were a number of possibilities. Perhaps the calculations were wrong. She thought they had infected all targeted worlds completely, but maybe they had miscalculated. Perhaps they hadn't used enough of the virus, at least not enough to infect the three prisoners she had.

She told herself that, tried to come up with ways the plan could have worked—at least partially—without infecting the three prisoners. But she was gradually running out of hope.

"Andi…"

She heard Tyler Barron. He had slipped into the room, without her notice. She was glad to hear his voice, happy he was there. At least as close to happy as she could become. She turned to face him. "Tyler…" She had intended to say more, but nothing else came. She moved toward him, put her face against his shoulder. But she didn't say anything else.

"Andi…I know you've been down here, almost every waking hour. You've got to stop. You know I've never been a big believer in the virus scheme…but you have been. And I'm telling you now, there is still time. But you can't spend every minute watching these three…especially since they are being observed around the clock. Even if you spot the first change in them, you'll only find out a few minutes ahead of when you will anyway. Come…with me. We'll be moving out in three days, but right now, I've got some time."

Andi smiled, for a few seconds. She knew Tyler didn't *really* have the time. But she was also aware that any moment together could be their last. He had put together a plan, devised a retreat order, created a way to hit the enemy at the former location of Fortress Grimaldi. It was a way, a plan to sneak away from the enemy present three systems from him, and to descend on the smaller force, before the enemy could respond with their main fleet.

It wouldn't change anything, she knew that…other than maybe extending the time they had left six months or a year. But she knew, just then, that they were working for weeks and months at a time. Maybe someone would come up with a plan, perhaps even hers would work, albeit a bit later than she'd expected. Hell, the enemy was fighting someone else, some power she didn't even know about. Perhaps that war would flare up, interfere in the one she was fighting. She knew she was grasping at straws, but she wondered what the status was on that fight, if the enemy's foe would be hers as well…or an ally.

She looked at Tyler, thinking about Cassie, as she always did when Barron was around—and most of the time when he wasn't. She even smiled, though just for a couple seconds. "Okay, Tyler…you're right. Let's go, let's…pass the time."

She reached out an took his hand, and the two of them walked slowly away, both of them overburdened with concerns, but for the moment, reaching out, grabbing ahold of some kind of hope.

*   *   *

Sonya Eaton leaned over the precipice, looking down at her legion of engineers. The work on *Colossus* went on, whether the ship was static or moving. There were hundreds of service personnel beyond the large force of permanent crew, and they were working around the clock. *Colossus* was the largest ship on either side, and Eaton knew how important it was to get her vessel as up and running as possible…quickly.

She was tired, no question, having spent at least eighteen hours a day on duty for…almost as long as she could remember. She knew there wasn't much hope, and what she did have was based on the alternate plan and not on a straight up fight. She hadn't given up on that, not completely at least, but she knew whatever happened, her ship was going to be needed. If the scheme actually turned out to work, and if it spread the disease to some of the enemy's ships, she knew it wouldn't do the job completely. She only hoped that it would bring the enemy down, reduce their force to something small enough to defeat.

Mostly, she was just on autopilot, though, working on

her ship, trying to get it ready for…whatever. If that was something that offered a chance of success, that much the better…but even if it was a hopeless fight, she intended to take down as many enemy ships as possible before they destroyed her.

Her eyes moved to the small display, and she saw *Dauntless* on the screen, along with several hundred other ships. She knew her future—the future of all of them—rested on what was on that ship. She had to fight off her growing doubts, but she still had *some* hope that the virus would work, that it would give her side at least a chance. Whether that was realistic, or just the only way she could imagine success, she didn't know…and it didn't matter. One thing she was sure of, *Colossus* would do its part, whether there was a chance of ultimate victory or not.

That she would make sure of.

She turned and looked back down at the crew, and she yelled out. "No…not there. Pick that up, and bring it over there." She gestured for a few seconds, but then she decided she needed to go down, to show them exactly what she was talking about.

Colossus would probably be destroyed in the coming fight, whether her side won or lost. She had more or less made peace with that…but she was going to do everything she possibly could to make sure her ship was as ready as possible.

Ready for whatever.

* * *

Vian Tulus sat on the bridge of his flagship, deep in his own thoughts. He'd been away from the ship for a while, with one of the cruisers in his force. He'd brought back fewer than forty percent of his ships, the lowest of the four commands, save only Andi's…and she had lost more than half of what she had on the final stop. He knew part of that

was just bad luck—and part was the inferior quality of his
ships—but now he was just glad his vessels had succeeded,
that they had completed their mission.

Even if it had been pointless.

Tulus had actually come to believe in the plan, to feel it
could work. When Andi had returned with three captives, he
was disappointed none of them were showing any
infection…but he'd told himself it just took longer. Now,
Andi had been back three weeks, and the time since
infection was rapidly approaching the longest projected
period for success. He still believed it would work, at least in
a way, but his doubts were growing, too.

Tulus looked at the fleet on the main display. It appeared
powerful, if too small to beat the enemy force bearing down
on it, but he knew most of the ships were badly damaged.
What work could be done was in progress, every second,
but he knew it would be at least a year, and probably two,
before the force was back to anything approaching its
prebattle power.

And he seriously doubted they had that long.

In fact, he knew the only delay, the only break the fleet
would get was the time until it reached Fortress Grimaldi.
What had been Grimaldi, at least. Tyler Barron had ordered
the plan, and he'd given barely enough time to carry it out.
It wasn't a route to military success, at least not beyond a
short time, but it did offer the chance of some success, even
if it only lasted a few weeks.

Tulus knew the main enemy fleet would pursue the
force, probably right after it departed. It wasn't even sure
that Barron could escape, that his ships could stay enough
ahead of the pursuing enemy to arrive with time to at least
take Grimaldi's location back.

But it was a hope, and short of the virus, the best hope
his side had.

Tulus knew Barron's plan was the best that was available,
but he was also aware that any success would be very short-

lived. The only chance at a real victory, at a chance of one even, was for the virus to work. But Tulus had checked every day and sometimes twice.

There was nothing. Nothing at all, and with each report that came in, the same as the last one, his mood sank deeper.

*   *   *

"I bet we make it back, and we take out every ship there." Jerry Collins spoke, his levity artificial, at least in part. He *did* hope that the fleet would reach Grimaldi's location in time, that he would experience one more victory…before the almost guaranteed defeat that awaited them all.

"Absolutely, Jerry…we will get there and crush what is waiting. Then we'll turn about and hit the enemy's main fleet…and this time, we'll beat it." The words came from Collins's partner, Tom Gareth.

Collins knew they were both full of it, though. He was sure the force faced certain defeat, that as much effort as Tyler Barron and the other senior generals had put into it, there was really no chance. Lieutenant Collins was far too lowly ranked to have any real say in things, but for whatever it was worth, he didn't believe in the chance that the enemy had been infected. He understood why the effort had been made, but he'd never given it much hope, and whatever he had put into it at first had left him, a little bit at a time. He had done the twice daily checks on the prisoners, looked for any sign that the disease was real, that it had taken hold. But there had been nothing, nothing except the steady improvement on the subjects' injuries.

Collins had given up whatever hope he'd had.

He sat down in his chair, startled by the absence of anyone. It wasn't the first time he and Gareth had been alone—save for the pair of guards down outside the prisoners' chamber—but it was damned close. Not even

Andi Lafarge was present, and she'd been there almost every time.

Everyone's given up on this. Over a hundred ships lost, a huge effort...and nothing.

He reached out, turned on the instruments. He punched in a series of codes...and he froze.

"Subject one has a fever...three point one degrees over normal." He felt some excitement, but he controlled it. One alien with a fever was hardly conclusive evidence.

"How about number two?" Gareth sounded the same as Collins...excited, but also cautious.

Collins hands moved over the controls, more quickly than before. He was excited...but the results of the test drew away some of his enthusiasm. "Number two is normal." He redid the procedure, just to be sure. "Totally normal."

He told himself it didn't matter, that subject two was just a bit behind...but it drained him anyway. Still, his hands continued to move. He had a third subject.

He stared and waited, no more than four or five seconds, but it seemed like forever. Then he saw the numbers.

Patient three was even worse than number one, almost four percent above normal. He felt strange, and he reminded himself that it was no guarantee, that it could be a number of things, that the enemy could still have a cure. But his excitement grew, nevertheless.

One thing was sure...he had to report this. He had to report it to Admiral Barron. Right now.

His hands moved to the communications, grid...as quickly as possible.

"This is Lieutenant Collins...I need Admiral Barron. Right now!"

Blood on the Stars Will Conclude with

Empire Reborn

Book 18

Appendix

CFS Excalibur-Class Superbattleship

The *Excalibur* is the first Confederation ship class to fully employ a combination of its own newest technology with that of the Hegemony, provided per the terms of the Pact. It was designed at a rapid pace in response to the dire situation on the front, and the *Excalibur* itself, the first, and to date only, vessel of the class to launch, was constructed at the Kirovsky Shipyards, orbiting the Iron Belt planet Belgravia.

The *Excalibur* is more than twice the size of Repulse-class battleships such as *Dauntless*, and the vessel carries a massive arsenal of weaponry and defensive system, much of them representing major leaps forward in Confederation technology.

Offensive Array

1 – Spinal mount antimatter-powered hyper-velocity railgun, launching 120kg projectiles.
4 – Quad 10 gigawatt Confederation "primary beam" particle accelerators (16 guns in total).
40 – Omega fourth generation 2 gigawatt laser cannons.
20 – Ground bombardment pulse cannons.
10 – Plasma mine launchers (1,000 mines held in magazine).

Defensive Array

60 – 200 megawatt point defense lasers in double turret mounts.

20 – Blast gun anti-fighter pellet launchers (developed from railgun technology).

4 – Deflector screen projection systems (designed to warp and distort incoming energy weapons fire.

Small Craft Contingents

180 – Lightning III ("Black Lightning") assault fighter-bombers (12 squadrons, 2 assault wings).

30 – Attack Wave ("Ironfist") heavy bombers (crew of 6).

20 – Heavy assault shuttles (capacity 20 Marines).

20 – Standard Fleet shuttles.

2 – Admiralty-3A class fleet command cutters.

Power Generation

Dual "Confed-1.0) antimatter reactor system.

12 – 15 gigawatt fusion reactors.

Complement

Primary ship crew – 1,620
Fighter-bomber pilot and flight crews – 960
Marine contingent – 840
Admiral's command staff – 40

Total – 3460

Initial Ships of Class: *Excalibur*, *Constellation*, *Starfire*, *Argo*

The Pact

The Pact is the document forming an Alliance between the Hegemony, the Confederation, the Palatian Alliance, and nine separate Far Rim nation states. The ratification of the agreement faced significant opposition by both the Confederation Senate and the Hegemonic Council. The Senate was wary of the economic burdens it would impose and the requirements it held for the Confederation to commit he vast bulk of its armed forces to the Hegemony front. The Hegemonic Council objected to the provisions requiring full sharing of all science and technical data, an obligation that flowed almost entirely in one direction as a result of the Hegemony's generally greater tech levels.

The name came to refer to the alliance itself, though such usage was not specified in the document and was entirely colloquial.

Blood on the Stars Will Conclude with

Empire Reborn

Book 18

Made in the USA
Coppell, TX
18 August 2020